Praise for

Same As It Never Was

By Claire LaZebnik

"LaZebnik has written a poignant . . . novel that's funny and touching . . . an engaging read."

—*Library Journal*

"An amazing, assured first novel full of dry wit, an observant eye. and a lot of heart. This is a romance with bite, and I enjoyed every morsel."

—*Jane Heller, author of* Female Intelligence

"Claire LaZebnik has written an amazingly sure-footed, witty, and delicious novel, romantic and smart. A pure pleasure."

—*Beth Gutcheon, author of* More Than You Know

"This book is a ride down Sunset Boulevard in a convertible: breezy, breathtaking, and hugely satisfying. While reading it, you won't want to be anywhere else."

—*Karen Karbo, author of* Generation Ex: Tales of the Second Wives Club

"LaZebnik's entertaining and poignant tale . . . is written in a bullet-sleek, knife-sharp prose that is a delight to read."

—*Jenny McPhee, author of* The Center of Things

"The first great beach read of the summer."

—*King Features*

Knitting under the influence

Claire LaZebnik

NEW YORK BOSTON

5 Spot
Hachette Book Group USA
1271 Avenue of the Americas, New York, NY 10020
Visit our Web site at www.5-spot.com.

5 Spot is an imprint of Warner Books, Inc.
5 Spot and the 5 Spot logo are trademarks of Warner Books, Inc.

Printed in the United States of America

First Edition: September 2006
10 9 8 7 6 5 4 3 2 1

Library of Congress Cataloging-in-Publication Data

LaZebnik, Claire Scovell.
Knitting under the influence / Claire LaZebnik.—1st ed.
p. cm.
Summary: "Three twentysomething women in Los Angeles deal with relationships and family, with their weekly Sunday knitting circle as the only thing holding them together"—Provided by publisher.
ISBN-13: 978-0-446-69795-8
ISBN-10: 0-446-69795-8
1. Young women—California—Los Angeles—Fiction. 2. Knitters (Persons)—California—Los Angeles—Fiction. I. Title.

PS3612.A98K65 2006
813'.6—dc22

2006003747

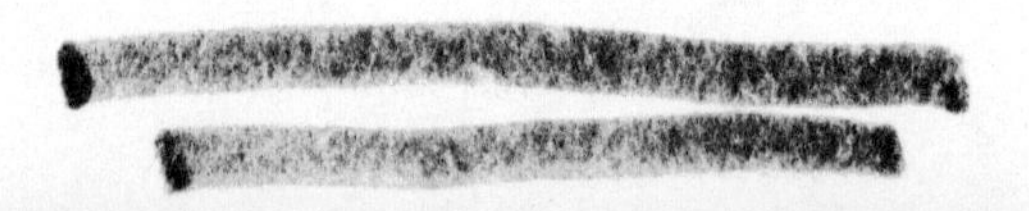

For my mother, Cynthia Scovell.

The oncologist, a soft-spoken Canadian prone to understatement, described the cancer as "not indolent." An appropriate disease for her then, since my mother was the least indolent person I knew. She was always moving—straightening up the place, puttering around the kitchen, making and returning phone calls, running errand after errand, soaring briskly along supermarket aisles, planning the meals she'd make when her five kids and twelve grandchildren came to visit, watering her plants and pulling their dead leaves off with a quick snap . . .

She wasn't a fan of sentiment and she never gushed. I miss her.

Acknowledgments

My thanks first and foremost to Emily Griffin for being one of those editors a writer dreams about, whose notes are always smart and whose enthusiasm never seems to waiver, and to Alexis Hurley and Kim Witherspoon for their support and top-notch agenting.

Two absurdly brilliant scientists were consulted in the course of writing this book, so anything scientifically accurate is thanks to Adam Summers and Alice Flaherty. Sadly, I twisted and manipulated their good science to make it work for my plot, so anything inaccurate is completely my responsibility.

I spent a fun evening mixing and sampling cocktails with Michael Broderick (former bartender and current actor) and Dana Commandatore (former New Yorker and current Angeleno) and couldn't have come up with all those drink recipes without their help.

If Aubry Dennehy hadn't been willing to brave L.A. rush-hour traffic to do basketball practice pickup and the like and to spend hours playing board games and getting the kids to go outside (not to mention the dogs), I probably would never have had the time or the energy to finish this book. The same goes for Rob, who, in addition to being the father of my children, is also my rock, my sanity, and my chauffeur.

I better thank my brother, Ted, because he likes me to do that in my books and he can still beat me up. And it wouldn't be fun for me to publish a book if I weren't able to get the names Will, Annie, Johnny, and Max in print and to embarrass them by publicly stating that I love them a lot.

Although the autism clinic and staff in this book are completely fictional, their methods were inspired by the Pivotal Response Training approach researched and developed at the Koegel Autism Center at the University of California, Santa Barbara. If you're interested in learning more about their clinic, their Web site is http://www.education.ucsb.edu/autism/index.html.

1

Casting On

1

It was ten o'clock on Sunday morning and the regular time for the girls to meet for their knitting circle, but when Kathleen opened the door to greet the others, she was still wearing her pajama bottoms and a stained "The Best Girls Are from Los Angeles" T-shirt. Her long brown hair was escaping in fly-away strands from her ponytail elastic, and around her eyes were traces of mascara and eyeshadow that clearly hadn't been completely washed off the night before.

Sari said, "You didn't have to dress up just for us."

"Or clean up," Lucy said. The huge foyer was strewn with glasses, bottles, crumpled napkins, and small plastic plates with food still on them.

"Give me a break," Kathleen said. "The party went late and I only just got up. Come to the kitchen so I can make some coffee."

They followed her toward the back of the house, their knitting bags slung over their shoulders. Sari caught a glimpse of the living room as they went by. It was easily four times the size of her entire apartment, but today it was as trashed as the rest of the house. She said, "I wouldn't want to be the one to have to get the stains out of the carpet."

"Cleaning help comes tomorrow," Kathleen said.

"You could at least pick up the trash," Lucy said with a backward look of disgust at a Coke can that was lying on an antique side table in a sticky brown puddle.

"Cleaning help comes tomorrow," Kathleen said again, irritably this time. They entered the kitchen. "You guys bring something to eat?"

"Bagels. Sorry, I know it's boring, but it was on the way." Sari dropped the bag of fresh bagels onto the island, and then tossed her knitting bag and purse next to it. She hoisted herself onto one of the high leather-upholstered stools. When she sat, her feet dangled inches above the floor. "Why is the kitchen so much cleaner than the rest of the house?"

"Caterers. They cleaned up in here before they left. You both want coffee?"

"Of course we want coffee," Sari said.

"You had caterers?" Lucy mounted the stool next to Sari. "Sounds fancy. What was the occasion?"

"The twins' twenty-fifth birthday."

"Wait a second," Lucy said. "That doesn't make any sense. If it was their birthday, wouldn't it be your birthday, too?"

"You'd think," Kathleen said. She was one of triplets. The other two were identical twins, which had made her, from birth, the odd man out.

"So what you're saying is, *you* had a birthday party and didn't invite us," Sari said. "Should we be hurt?"

Kathleen was staring at the coffeemaker like she'd never seen it before. "God, my brain's not functioning," she said. "I think I'm still drunk from last night. I didn't even go to bed until after three. Don't be an idiot, Sari. You and I went out to celebrate my birthday two months ago. Don't you remember?"

"Oh, right," Sari said. "We went to Bombay Café."

"Why wasn't I invited?" Lucy said.

"You were. You were working late and couldn't come." Sari turned back to Kathleen, who was filling up the coffee carafe with water at the sink. "But you turned twenty-seven."

"I know."

"So why were the twins celebrating their twenty-fifth birthday last night if they turned twenty-seven two months ago?"

"Good question," Kathleen said. She carried the carafe back to the coffeemaker. She had overfilled it, and the water was trickling out, leaving a trail of drips on the wood floor behind her. "The party was a publicity event for their new movie. The twenty-five part is just a lie." Kathleen's sisters had once had a successful sitcom on TV where they played identical twin sisters who confused a lot of people by exchanging places. It ran for six years. When it ended, they started making movies, in each of which they played identical twin sisters who confused a lot of people by exchanging places.

"They always seem younger than you," Lucy said. "Are you sure you're the same age?"

"Yep," Kathleen said. "We popped out all together. In fact, I was the last one out, which makes me the youngest. People just think I'm older because I'm so much taller. Plus I went to school while they were stuck on some set or another being quote unquote tutored so they have the intellect of ten-year-olds."

"Was it a good party?" Sari asked, looking around. "It looks like it was a good party. The house is trashed."

"I honestly don't remember much about it. There was a cute bartender who was extremely talented. He made the best pomegranate margarita . . ." Kathleen poured the water into the coffeemaker. "I talked to him, helped him out by tasting some new variations—" She stuck the carafe in its place and turned to look at them. "I have a bad feeling, though—"

"About what?"

"I don't know. Like I did something last night I shouldn't have."

"Maybe you slept with the bartender," Lucy said. She tore a bagel in half, then carefully dug out the insides with her long, slender fingers. She piled the discarded bread in a neat pyramid on the counter in front of her.

Kathleen shook her head. "No, that would have been a good thing. And it's more that feeling you get when someone's mad at you."

"Maybe the bartender had a girlfriend."

"Will you forget about the bartender?" She pushed the start button on the coffeemaker. "It'll be ready in a few minutes. You guys want to stay in here or move to the family room?"

"Those are our only choices?" Sari said. "Doesn't this house have at least fifty other rooms?"

"Oh, don't exaggerate," Lucy said. "It's a simple little fifteen-thousand-square-foot cottage. Don't make it sound like a *mansion.*" She took a small bite of her bagel shell, then put it down on top of the pile of discards and dusted off her fingers with the finality of someone who has had all the breakfast she intends to have.

"I should get dressed," Kathleen said with another yawn. "But it seems like so much work."

"You poor thing," Lucy said. "You slave over a hot drink all night—"

"A hot bartender," Sari said. "She slaved over a hot bartender all night. The drinks were cold. All fifteen of them."

"I think there may have been fifteen," Kathleen said. She pushed a strand of hair out of her eyes and said wearily, "I've got to cut back."

"What I don't get is how you stay so thin," Lucy said. She reached down to the floor for her knitting bag and pulled out a ball of yarn, two knitting needles, and an attached length of sparkling blue scarf. "If I drank as much as you, I'd be the size of this house. Alcohol's fattening."

Sari said, "Uh, Kathleen? I usually take coffee in my coffee."

Kathleen turned to look. Steaming brownish hot water was dripping into the carafe. "Shit," she said. "I forgot to put in the grounds."

Lucy hooted. "Brilliant."

"I told you I was still drunk from last night." She punched the coffeemaker off.

A young woman walked into the room. They all turned. "Hi," she said. She had an appealingly childlike round face, long, wavy auburn hair, and a narrow body that seemed too small for the size of her head. "Sorry if I'm interrupting."

"Not at all," Sari said. "Hi."

"It's your house," Lucy added.

"Morning," Kathleen said. The other girl didn't even acknowledge her but, with a nod at the other two, walked over to the refrigerator, opened it, took out a bottle of Voss water, then, with another nod and a "Later," left the kitchen.

There was a moment of silence. Kathleen carried the carafe of dirty-looking water over to the sink and dumped it, then refilled it with clean tap water.

"Okay," Lucy said. "Which one was that?"

"I don't know," Kathleen said. "I can't tell them apart."

"Yes, you can," Sari said.

Kathleen reached into a cabinet above the coffeemaker and got out a canister of coffee. "Fine. It was Christa. Does it really matter to you?"

"She always that friendly in the morning?" Lucy said.

Kathleen shrugged as she shook some coffee grounds directly into the filter. "I think maybe she's mad at me about last night."

"Why?" Sari said.

"I told you—I can't remember."

Lucy held her knitting up and studied it critically.

"It's beautiful, Lucy," Sari said. She reached out and pulled the end of the scarf toward her. "This yarn is incredible. I love the way it glitters."

"It's got these metallic pieces woven in . . . It's cool, isn't it?"

"Have you ever made anything besides a scarf?" Kathleen leaned back against the counter where the coffee was finally successfully brewing. "I mean, we've been doing this for years and all I've ever seen you make is scarves."

"I like scarves," Lucy said.

"I've never seen you wear one. Unless you're using them as part of some kinky sex bondage game . . ."

"Scarves are fun to knit," Lucy said. She picked up her needles and started clicking away with them. "You just go on row after row, and when it's long enough, you're done."

"How about some plates here?" Sari said to Kathleen.

The phone started ringing. Kathleen reached up to open a cabinet.

"Don't you need to get that?" Sari said.

"It's not for me—I only use my cell." The phone stopped ringing. Kathleen put a stack of plates on the counter, then reached into the bag and took out a handful of bagels. She was piling them high on a plate when one slipped off and fell on the floor. She picked up the bagel and was about to drop it back with the others when Lucy thrust a hand in the way.

"For God's sake, throw it out. It's got *hairs* on it."

"Picky, picky, picky." Kathleen tossed it into the sink.

Sari pulled a container of cream cheese out of the bagel bag and opened it. "Get a knife, Kath, will you?"

"A clean one," Lucy said.

"And cups for juice," Sari said.

"And mugs for coffee."

"You guys are a lot of work," Kathleen said.

"When you come to my place, everything's already set up," Lucy said. "Sari's, too."

"I'm sorry I'm not Martha Stewart," Kathleen said. "Somewhere around the seventeenth drink last night, I guess I forgot to clean the good china for you."

"Party girl," Sari said fondly.

Kathleen grinned at her. "Working on it."

"Mugs?" Lucy said.

As Kathleen was reaching up to get them, her mother entered the room, flanked on each side by a girl identical to the one who had entered the room earlier. The two redheads made perfect bookends to their blond mother as they all stopped in the doorway. Sari and Lucy swiveled to greet them.

"Hello, Sari, darling," said Kathleen's mother, who, with her regular features and small frame, looked more like the twins' sister than their *sister* did, since Kathleen was tall and dark-haired. "Hello, Lucy. Kathleen, could we please have a word with you?"

"Why?" Kathleen said, turning around. "What is it? Is it about last night? What'd I do?" She seemed more curious than concerned.

"You know what you did," one of the twins said. It was Kelly, but only her blood relatives could tell for sure—Sari and Lucy had no idea which twin was which.

"Yeah," Christa said. "You know."

"Honestly," Kathleen said. "I don't. Last night is kind of a blur."

Christa stepped forward, ruining their symmetry. "Oh, please.

Like you don't remember talking to that *Hollywood Reporter* reporter?"

"Reporter reporter?" Lucy repeated under her breath to Sari.

"Not really," Kathleen said. "I had a lot to drink—"

"Tell us about it," Kelly said with a roll of the eyes. "You were so wrecked—"

"Like you weren't," Christa said to her. "You were all over Munchie's nephew."

"He was all over *me.* Jealous much?"

"The point is," said their mother. "The point is, Kathleen, that you said some unfortunate things last night—"

"And now we're screwed because of it," Kelly said.

"Well, we hope not," their mother said. "Junie's trying to convince the guy it's worth killing the story to have her owe him a favor—but if he decides to go to print, well, then . . ."

"We're screwed," Kelly said, and this time her mother nodded.

"Why?" Kathleen said. "What'd I say that was so bad?"

"What *didn't* you say?" Christa asked. "I mean, you started with our—"

"You let leak some confidential family information," her mother said, cutting her off with a meaningful glance in Lucy and Sari's direction.

Kathleen was still trying to figure it out. "What? You mean about their age?"

"That. And some other things I'd rather we not discuss at the moment."

"Shit, Mom, I didn't say anything that isn't common knowledge. What's the big deal?"

"The big deal is that you've betrayed your sisters' trust," her mother said. "Your sisters who house you and feed you and employ you . . . The least you could do is respect their privacy."

"I was drunk," Kathleen said. "It wasn't on purpose."

"Then you shouldn't drink," Kelly said.

"Neither should you," Christa said to her. "You were as bad as she was."

"I didn't say anything stupid."

"No, but you *did* a lot of stupid things. Your tongue was so deep in his mouth—"

"I think," said their mother, "that Kathleen owes you both an apology."

Kathleen shrugged. "Sorry," she said. "I was drunk. Sometimes I do stupid things when I'm drunk."

"And sometimes even when she's not," Lucy whispered to Sari, who hushed her.

"Oh, come on," Christa said. "At least try to sound like you mean it."

"She's right," their mother said. "Kathleen, your sisters have been nothing but good to you and you don't seem to appreciate it. Everything you have you have because of them, but they get nothing from you in return—"

"What are you talking about? I've been working for them since college."

"Yes, you have," said her mother. "And that steady income you get is something else you owe them."

"If you don't like the way I do my job—"

Kelly snorted. "Come on, Kathleen. All you do is make a couple of phone calls now and then."

"No, really," Kathleen said, standing up straight and squaring her shoulders. "If you guys don't want me around, just say so. I mean, I thought I was doing you all a favor by helping out with the company and keeping an eye on things here, but if you think the favors are all on your side . . ." She looked from one member of her family to another. No one said anything. "Fine," she said then. "Fine. I don't have to stay here. And I won't. I have other options."

"No, you *don't*," said Christa, rolling her eyes.

"Yes, I do."

"No, you don't."

"Yes, she does," said Sari, swiveling the bar stool around to face Christa directly. "I've been begging her for ages to come stay with me and help me out with the rent." She rotated back around. "What do you say, Kathleen? You ready to move in with me?"

"Are you kidding? Just give me ten minutes to pack my bags." Kathleen came around the island.

"Don't be silly," her mother said. "Come on, Kathleen, if you're doing this to prove something, it's not worth it. You know we don't actually want you to *leave*."

"Yeah," said Kelly. "You're making too big a deal out of this."

"We don't want you to move *out*," Christa said. "We just want you to not get trashed and say stupid things anymore."

"Live free or die," Kathleen said, brushing past her. "That's my motto."

"I thought that was New Hampshire's motto," Lucy whispered to Sari.

"It is," Sari whispered back. "But I'll bet you anything *they* don't know that."

II

The twins may have been the ones with a successful television and movie career, but Kathleen had her own flair for the dramatic. She flounced out of the house half an hour later, with two packed bags, a toss of her head, and a haughty, "You can reach me on my cell," leaving Sari and Lucy to murmur awkward goodbyes and follow her outside.

"At least it got her dressed," Sari said as they walked toward the car.

"If you call that dressed," Lucy said with a disgusted nod at Kathleen, who was wearing a pair of old, torn sweatpants and a tank top with no bra. Lucy only left the house in sweats when she was on her way to the gym. And she always wore a bra.

She snagged the front seat of Sari's car while Kathleen was still stowing her bags in the trunk.

Once they were well on their way down the long narrow driveway that led out of the twins' property, Sari said over her shoulder, "Hey, Kath, you know I was just bluffing about the apartment, right? I mean, you're welcome to spend a night or two but you can't actually move in permanently. I don't even have room for *me* in there."

"That's okay," Kathleen said. "I can sleep on the floor."

"There isn't enough space on the floor for you. For me, maybe, but not you." Sari was almost a foot shorter than Kathleen.

"Then I'll take the bed and you can have the floor," Kathleen said. "Problem solved."

"Try again," Sari said.

"I'm kidding." Kathleen was slouched low in the backseat, her knees sticking up at chin height. She hadn't put her seatbelt on. "I'm kidding. I won't stay long. I'm planning to get my own place—there was this guy at the party last night who was bragging that he knows someone really big in real estate. I'll see if he can help me find a cheap apartment."

"You remember that?" Lucy said. She had pulled her knitting back out of her bag and was working on it, right there in the car. "You can't remember what you did that pissed off your sisters but you remember that some random guy at the party had a friend in real estate?"

"I wasn't drunk yet when he told me that."

"She'd only had twelve margaritas by then," Sari said. "Some brain cells were still functioning. So do you have that guy's number?"

"The guy who knew the guy, yeah."

"You should call him soon. Like today soon."

"Do I detect a note of panic?" asked Lucy, eyebrows arched.

"Not panic," Sari said. She looked at Kathleen in the rearview mirror. Their eyes met. Sari smiled. "Not *yet*."

"We'll have fun," Kathleen told Sari's reflection.

"I know we will. But call that guy soon, anyway, will you?"

"Soon as we get to your place."

"Oh, I know what I wanted to tell you guys," Sari said suddenly. "Remember that woman at the knitting store in Santa Monica—the young one with the incredibly long black hair who's always just sitting there knitting, no matter what time you go in there?"

"A knitting junkie," Lucy said. "When good girls go just a little bit bad."

"Do you remember how the last time we saw her I said I thought she was pregnant?"

"No," Kathleen said.

"You don't? I said her breasts had grown since the last time we'd seen her and either she was pregnant or had had a boob job and you guys voted for boob job."

"Oh, yeah," Lucy said. "I remember."

"I still don't," Kathleen said. "But I'm slightly disturbed to know you go around staring at women's breasts, Sari."

"It's all about the envy," said Sari, who was built like a twelve-year-old girl. She was small and slight, with cropped thick hair and enormous blue eyes—the kind of woman who would never get past being called "cute" her entire life. "Anyway," she said, "the point is that I went in there the other day and we started talking and she *is* actually pregnant."

"How old is she?" Lucy said.

"Twenty-eight," Sari said.

"Twenty-eight?" Kathleen said. "That's *way* too young to start having kids."

"No, it's not," Sari said. "The majority of women in this country have babies by the time they're twenty-eight. Just because *we're* incapable of growing up—"

"Hey, hey. Speak for yourself," Lucy said.

"Yeah," Kathleen said. "I left home today."

"Leaving home for the first time at the age of twenty-seven isn't grown-up," Lucy said with a quick hard tug at a strand of yarn for emphasis. "It's pathetic."

"It's not my first time—I went to college for four years."

"And then moved right back in with mommy afterward. Face it—you've only ever lived off your family."

"I wasn't living off of them," Kathleen said. "I worked for them the entire time. Nine to five and all that."

"Getting paid to sit at home and polish your toenails. It's a hard-knock life, isn't it?"

"I didn't say it was *hard*." Kathleen leaned forward, putting a hand on each of the two front seats. She was so tall that her head barely cleared the top of Sari's small Toyota. "You sure knitting in the car is safe, Luce? Sari could hit the brake, and a needle could go right in your eye and—poof—no more hotshot research for you."

"I'm willing to risk it," Lucy said.

"So who was the guy you met last night?" Sari said. She was

stopped at another light, so she tilted the rearview mirror to look at Kathleen. "The one with the real estate connections?"

Kathleen fell back with a thud against the car seat. "No one special."

Sari knocked the mirror back in place. "I know that tone. There's definitely more to this story. Was he cute?"

"People would probably say he was handsome."

"Our age?" Lucy asked.

"Twice that."

"Too old then," Sari said. "Why was he at the party?"

"Oh, for goodness sake," Kathleen said. "It was my father."

"Your father!" they both exclaimed. Sari turned to look at her. "You're kidding!" she said. The light changed, and the car behind them honked. Kathleen automatically raised her hand and gave them the finger without even looking. Sari lifted her own hand in an apologetic wave as she drove on.

"I thought your dad was completely out of the picture," Lucy said.

"Oh, he resurfaces now and then when he needs money. He's such a jerk, it's unbelievable." She wrinkled her nose. "And I had to be the one who looks like him."

"You just said he was handsome."

"Yeah, but who cares? What kind of a freak says to his wife right after she's given birth to *triplets*, 'Sorry, babe, just realized I don't like kids,' and takes off?"

"He came back," Lucy said.

"Yeah, right—once the twins were rich."

"Why was he invited to the birthday party?" Sari asked.

"He wasn't. He just found out about it somehow. He knows that if other people are around, the twins have to act like they're glad to see him or it'll be all over the tabloids that they hate their father." She grinned. "But I'm not famous, so I don't."

"But you said you were talking to him at the party."

"He was talking to *me*. He was going on about having met this real estate guy at a party some bimbo girlfriend of his took him to. I wasn't even paying attention. Oh—by the way—that's why my mother and sisters were so pissed at me. They said I told the *Hollywood Reporter* guy all about Lloyd—how he shows up asking for money and we're always bailing him out of trouble. And I guess at some point I also mentioned the twins' real age."

"Why'd you do that?" Sari asked.

"How should I know? I don't even remember doing it."

"The first step is admitting you have a problem," Lucy said.

"The second step is for you to fuck off."

"Girls, girls," Sari said. "Let's play nice."

They dropped Lucy off at her place, and Kathleen hopped out and got into the front seat, folding up her long legs so she could cram them into the small space. "Let's go do something fun," she said. "See a movie or something."

"Can't," Sari said. "I have like five thousand progress reports I'm behind on. I've got to work."

"Okay," Kathleen said. "I'll just go for a run, then. Best way to get rid of a hangover."

"You do that. And then—"

"What?"

"You'll make that call? To your father? To get the name of his friend?"

"Don't you love me anymore?" Kathleen asked, tilting sideways so she could rest her head on Sari's shoulder. "Don't you want me to live with you?"

"If you make me crash—"

"Fine. Be that way." Kathleen righted herself. "Hey, I'm going to need a new job. You guys hiring at the clinic?"

"You wouldn't last an hour there," Sari said.

"Why not? I like kids."

"No, you don't."

"No, I don't," Kathleen agreed. "But kids with autism don't talk, right? I don't mind kids if they don't talk."

"Some of them talk. And a lot of them hit people and bang their heads and scratch at your eyes and scream all the time."

"Sounds like fun," Kathleen said. "Think I'll skip it." She reached down for the lever that adjusted the seat and reclined the seat as far as it would go, so she was more lying down than sitting, then slipped her feet out of her flip-flops and shoved them against the dashboard, so her knees were way up in the air. She had a Chinese pictograph tattooed above her left ankle but always claimed to have forgotten what it meant. "So what kind of job can I get where you don't have to work all that hard but you make enough money to live in a nice house and hire people to do things like clean and pick up after you? I mean, I don't really want to give any of that up, just because the twins are acting like jerks."

"There aren't jobs like that," Sari said. "Not for someone at your level of expertise, which is none. The only thing you could do is marry someone who's already rich."

"I love that idea," Kathleen said. "I'll marry someone rich. Rich and wonderful—I don't want a rich asshole. Know any wonderful rich guys?"

"Do you think I'd be driving this shitty car and living in that shitty apartment if I did?"

"Possibly," Kathleen said, rolling her head to the side and studying Sari's profile. "The problem with you, my love, is that you raise self-sacrifice to an art. Look at you—you have the toughest job in the world, and you know you'll never make even decent money doing it. You're either an idiot or a saint."

"I vote for idiot," Sari said with a sigh. "I mean, I told you you could move in with me and I just remembered—"

"What?"

"You're a total slob."

"See?" Kathleen said. "That's why I need to be rich enough to hire a maid. I'm a slob."

"No," Sari said, "that's why you need to find another apartment *now*."

"I'm on it," Kathleen said and took her cell phone out of her purse.

III

Kathleen's phone calls were so productive that she was able to land an appointment with the real estate guy early that very evening. At her request, Sari helped her pick out some "responsible" clothes—a pair of dark brown pants and a cream-colored silk shirt. Kathleen even put her hair up in a twist. "Wow," Sari said. "You look almost like an adult."

Sari insisted on driving her back to the twins' house to pick up her car. Kathleen had intended to leave the car behind as a grand gesture to her newfound independence—the twins' production company was leasing it for her. But Sari pointed out that Kathleen would have no way of getting around town without it.

"I could drop you off at work every day and use your car the rest of the time," Kathleen said. "Play chauffeur."

"No, you couldn't," Sari said. "We're getting your car."

They drove up to the house, and Kathleen jumped out of Sari's car and into her own without anyone even coming out of the house. And she was relieved, really—she loved her car. It was a turquoise-colored convertible Mini Cooper that had originally been leased for Kelly—Christa had the same car in red—but the twins had moved on to electric cars at the suggestion of Junie Peterson, who said that people liked their celebrities to be environmentally conscientious. So this one was now Kathleen's baby.

Kathleen was very good at changing her mind when it was expedient to do so, and by the time she had arrived at her destination, she had already decided that there was nothing morally compromising about her using the car, that she had earned it by working for her sisters as long as she had.

She parked the Mini Cooper in front of the address she'd been given, which turned out to belong to one of the high-rise buildings that line Wilshire Boulevard near Westwood Avenue. She entered off the street, through the building's big glass front doors.

Kathleen gave her contact's name—Sam Kaplan—to both the doorman and the security guard at the front desk. The elevator man, who wore a red suit and an air of frosty boredom, took her up to the penthouse floor, gestured toward the only door in the foyer, and closed the elevator doors behind her as soon as she stepped out.

Kathleen wondered if this meant that the penthouse apartment was available, and that Sam Kaplan might offer it to her. It would have to be at a hugely reduced rate, of course. She hadn't saved much while working for the twins—she liked to buy clothes and go out to clubs and bars. So there was no way she could afford a penthouse, except by special arrangement.

The door was slightly open. She knocked on it, didn't hear a response, and went on in, calling "Hello?" as she entered.

The living room was completely—and expensively and beautifully—furnished, and there were current newspapers on the coffee table. Which meant that someone was already living there, so she could forget about moving in.

A man's voice called out, "Come back here, to the kitchen," in reply to her shouts.

Kathleen followed the sound of his voice out of the living room into a wide hallway hung with enormous framed paintings—all of them very modern and graphic—and then on into the kitchen. The owner of the voice stood at a six-burner Wolf range, his back to her.

"I assume you're Kathleen," he said with a quick glance over his shoulder. "You're late. Sit down. Are you hungry? I'm making eggs."

"I'm always hungry," Kathleen said and sat down at the half-round dark green marble table that was attached to a higher and extremely long island made out of the same marble.

Sam Kaplan—she assumed—went back to his cooking. Kathleen craned her neck to see his face again. He was thin in a wiry way, with thick black hair that was graying at the sides and a hawkish face, pursed in concentration at the moment.

"You want toast?" he said after a little while.

"Why not?" she said. "I'm easy."

He made no reply to that, just scraped the eggs onto a couple of plates, pulled some bread out of a toaster-oven, and tossed a slice on each plate, then brought the dishes over to the table. "I've got beer, if you want it and you're old enough. If not, there's orange juice." He foraged through a drawer and transferred a couple of forks to the table.

Kathleen said, "Do you need to see some ID? Or will you take my word for it?"

He glanced at her briefly. "You're old enough."

"Then I'll take the beer."

He nodded at that and extracted two beers from one of two Sub-Zero refrigerators. He also got two crystal highball glasses out of a glass-front cabinet.

"I'm fine with the bottle," Kathleen said. In college, she had left a trail of beer bottles wherever she went. Her roommates once got so sick of her leaving her empties around their dorm room that they built a pyramid of them right in front of her bedroom door when she was asleep, so she had to dismantle it before she could go anywhere. Made her late for class that day.

No, wait—not late—she had just skipped class completely and gone back to bed.

Sam Kaplan said, "In my house, we use glasses."

"Yes, sir," Kathleen said, snapping him a salute.

He raised his eyebrows without saying anything, then flicked the beer caps off with a bottle opener, threw them both in the trash, and poured the drinks. The empty beer bottles went into a recycling bin under the sink. He put one filled glass in front of her and one in front of his own plate, then squinted at the whole presentation. "Have I forgotten anything?"

"Looks good to me," Kathleen said. The plates were large and white without a single scratch, and the flatware was real silver and very heavy.

"Napkins," he said, raising a finger, and turned around to slip two out of a drawer. They were linen and impeccably starched and ironed.

"It goes in your lap," he said, handing one to her.

"Yeah, I've heard that." She spread it across her legs.

"All right," he said. "Now we eat." He sat down at the table, and, for a moment, they ate in silence.

Kathleen looked up to find Sam Kaplan studying her face.

"What?" she said. "Do I have egg on my chin?"

He shook his head. His eyebrows were heavy and dark and his eyes were even darker. "So you need a place to stay?"

"Yeah."

"How much can you afford?"

"Not much. I'm momentarily unemployed."

"Why?"

"I had a falling-out with my . . . employers."

"Whose fault?"

"Mine," she said with a shrug. "I was what you might call indiscreet."

"Meaning what?"

She gave him a big smile. "If I told you, then I'd be even more indiscreet, wouldn't I?"

He didn't seem amused, but he let it go. "Who were you employed by?"

"A small production company." Well, it was true, wasn't it? "I did PR, mostly."

"I assume you finished college?"

She nodded.

"Any graduate school?"

"No." She hadn't considered that for a second, having spent her entire academic career counting the days until she'd be done with school forever. Sitting in a dark classroom on a beautiful day was her idea of torture.

"What did you major in?"

"Economics. And I had a B minus average, if that's what you were going to ask me next. Do you always ask this many questions when you're helping someone out with an apartment?"

"I don't usually 'help people out' with apartments," he said. "I'm in the business of buying, selling, and leasing real estate."

"Well, you should know right now, I can't afford to buy or even rent an apartment."

"Yes," he said. "I'm aware of that. Which is why I'm trying to figure out whether you're responsible enough to house-sit."

"I am." She was glad she had worn her responsible clothes.

"We'll see. So what kind of job are you going to be looking for now? Something else in entertainment?"

"Probably not. I never really wanted to go into it in the first place—"

"Then why did you?"

"I just kind of fell into the job."

"Ah," he said. "So what's next?"

"I don't know. I don't want to jump at the first thing that comes along. I want to figure out what's right for me long term."

"And what have you figured out so far?" He dotted his mouth carefully with his linen napkin, then set it back across his lap. His fastidiousness was more suited to a fancy dinner party than to a couple of people sitting around a breakfast table on a Sunday evening eating eggs and drinking beer.

"I don't know," she said again. "The only thing I liked in college was playing sports."

"Sports? Well, have you thought about coaching kids? Maybe teach PE at a local school?"

"I'd hate that."

"How about professional sports?"

"I'm not in that kind of shape anymore. I run, but I don't do much else."

Sam Kaplan had finished his eggs. He leaned back in his chair. Up close, his face was craggier than it had looked from a distance. He said, "I think I can help you out."

Turned out, there was an empty apartment on the floor right below him, and, for complicated legal reasons, they couldn't put it on the market. "It's all tied up," was all Sam Kaplan would say about it. "And since we've got plenty of other vacancies right now, I'm not even going to show it until things are settled. You could live there for a while, but I can't make any promises for how long, and you might have to vacate very suddenly. You have family around, right? I mean, other than your father? You wouldn't end up on the street?"

"No, it's fine," she said.

"All right, then. The apartment's yours if you want it. We can go see it now if you like."

"I want it," Kathleen said. "I don't even need to see it to know I want it." She pushed her empty plate away, leaned far back in her chair, and stretched. "So," she said. "Now that I've got a place to live, I need a job. Got any ideas?"

"You know," he said, "I just might."

IV

While Kathleen was getting herself an apartment, Lucy was getting herself laid.

Right there, on the lab table, just feet away from the stinky paper-lined cages where the rats chattered and squeaked and ate and shat constantly.

She wasn't planning on having sex when she first headed into work late that afternoon. She was working on a grant proposal, and a lot of the information she needed was in the lab, so she figured she'd just take her laptop and write there. She had left a message for James letting him know that's where she'd be, and he called her back just as she was walking into the building to say, "I'll meet you there with a bottle of wine in an hour—what goes well with rat, red or white?" and so she was smiling as she flipped her phone shut and didn't even hear David coming up the steps behind her until he said, "Hey, world, Lucy Cameron's smiling. This has got to be a first."

She spun around.

"Jesus," she said. "You scared me."

"Imagine how I felt. Seeing you smile. Must be awfully cold in hell right about now."

"You're so funny," Lucy said. "You're just so incredibly funny, David. Has anyone ever told you how funny you are?"

"Frequently," he said. "But I never get tired of hearing it."

"Just too funny for words," she said. They had reached the front door of their building. She waited, and he reached forward and opened the door for her, then gestured her through with an exaggeratedly gallant arm sweep. She walked through and kept going.

"But you *were* smiling," David said, scuttling to catch up with her. He was a small guy and his legs were shorter than hers.

"Was I?" Lucy said. "I must have been thinking about how nice it was going to be to have the lab all to myself. Have you noticed the smile's gone since you showed up?"

"Yeah, I noticed." He hunched into himself as they walked down the hallway, and she wondered if she had genuinely hurt his feelings. Not that she cared. She was annoyed at him for being there. As lab partners went, he was a decent one and she didn't really have anything against him, but just by showing up he was going to ruin her romantic evening with James.

"Why are you here, anyway?" Lucy said as he unlocked the door to their lab and held it open for her. "It's Sunday."

"Picking up my laptop—I left it here last night."

"You were here last night?"

"Yeah." He shut the door behind them. "I had some writing to do and it's quieter here than anywhere else. My roommate had some kind of stomach bug and kept barfing in our toilet. I had to get out."

"Still," she said. "Saturday night, David? No parties? No night-clubs? You're ruining my image of you as a wild party animal."

"Shut up," he said. "What were you doing that was so wild and crazy?"

"Knitting and watching TV."

"Woo-hoo," he said. "Your life is just as exciting as mine. So where was our friend James that you were at home alone on a Saturday night?"

"Our friend James leads his own life. We're not joined at the hip."

"That's not what I've heard." He made his eyebrows go up and down.

"Oh, now that one's clever," she said. "You should write that one down."

He went to his desk. "Good. The laptop's still here. My entire identity is on that hard drive. Without it, I'm nothing."

"Glad you found it then," Lucy said, pulling out her own chair and sitting down. "Don't let the door hit you on the way out."

"Oh, am I leaving?"

"You don't have to on my account," she said. "But it's a beautiful day. You should be taking advantage of the sunlight before it's all gone."

He squinted at her. "Why do I get the feeling you want me out of here? What are you planning, Lucy?"

"Nothing." Lucy shrugged and opened a book. "Stay or go. I don't care."

"Don't worry." He thrust his computer into its carrying case. "I'm leaving. I can't stand the way the rats are looking at me tonight—like they know their hours are numbered."

"Oh, right," Lucy said. "Tomorrow's Monday."

"If it's Monday, it must be rat-killing day. And they say there are no good jobs left in America." He turned to the cages. "Goodbye, my friends. Enjoy your last meal in peace. Have sex, get drunk, say goodbye to the kids—do whatever needs to be done, knowing that tomorrow morning you will be sacrificing your lives for the greater good."

"That would be *our* greater good, not theirs," Lucy said.

"Shh," David said. "Don't tell them that. I had them feeling all good and martyr-y about things. They'll be dreaming of little rat virgins in heaven tonight."

"Just say goodbye to the rats and go, will you?"

"I'm gone. I'll see you bright and early mañana, Luce."

"Bye." He left, and she breathed a sigh of relief. So she and James would have the lab to themselves after all.

James was later than he said. He was always later than he said, but he always arrived with such a flurry of noise and energy that it was impossible to stay angry at him. He had also forgotten the wine, but when Lucy pointed that out, he said he figured instead of having wine there, they'd go out for a nice dinner as soon as—

"As soon as what?" she said when he paused, and he got that grin on his face, like he had heard a joke no one else had heard, and it was the wickedest joke anyone had ever told. And then he was on her like they hadn't had sex in days—which they hadn't, because he had been out of town at a conference where he was lecturing on adrenal insufficiency in rats with the JRL mutation and its implications for humans with Addison's disease—and she was resisting a little, laughing, and only a little and only because resisting made it more fun, meant he had to work a little harder to get her where he wanted her, which, as it turned out, was down on her back on her own desk, books and papers and computer shoved aside, just a couple of pencils left digging into her shoulders, her legs dangling off the desk, James standing between her thighs, busily working on the snap to her jeans and—

"Wait," she said, pushing herself up on her elbows. "Lock the door."

"Why?" he said. "You expecting company? It's Sunday."

"David was here earlier. You never know."

"The more the merrier," he said, but he moved away and locked the door and by the time he was back she had not only unsnapped her snap for him but also unzipped her zipper, and it was clear that the resistance she had put up had been entirely for show, and that she was completely and entirely willing. The grin returned to James's face. His pants came down even more quickly than hers and he was nudging her thighs apart with his own before she had even settled back down in place.

"Go ahead," James whispered in her ear at one point. "Make noise. You know you want to."

She was able to gasp out the words, "Don't. Tell me. What I want." But he was right—James was always right—and soon after that she had reached a place where even the fact that she could be overheard by someone walking down the hallway wasn't a sobering enough thought to control the moan of pleasure escaping from her lips.

As if in response, there was a sudden loud squeal from the other side of the room, which was soon followed by a chorus of squeaks and chatters.

"What the hell—?" James said. He had collapsed on top of her, but he raised his head a few inches off her chest to look around.

"It's the rats," Lucy said hoarsely. "I think they approve."

"Of course they approve. It's your basic biological drive at its best." He kissed her shoulder. "And I do mean at its best." He pushed himself up on his arms and gently pulled out of her. "We've got to stop meeting like this," he added as he reached down for his pants, which were around his ankles. "The rodents are beginning to talk."

Lucy quickly slithered down off the desk and pulled on her own jeans. The lights were on in the lab, and she wasn't comfortable having him see her naked. Residual self-consciousness from her older, fatter days. Of course, in her older, fatter days there were no gorgeous postdocs diving between her legs in the workplace.

"So . . . dinner?" said James before they had even finished adjusting their clothing. Lucy sometimes wondered if James might have a mild case of ADHD, since he always seemed to be moving on to the next thing and lost interest in subjects and activities with frightening speed. Things were always interesting when he was around. They were just never calm or quiet.

As they walked out onto the street together, she looked around, hoping people would see her with him. In college, she would have killed to have gone out with someone who looked like James—sleek and long-haired and thin-hipped . . . None of which she herself had been back then, come to think of it.

Actually, back then she would have killed to have gone out with James himself—she knew who he was because, even though he was also an undergraduate, just two years ahead of her, he was already famous in the department for having co-authored an article with a tenured professor. Someone pointed James out to Lucy at a party soon after, and she was shocked at how young and cute he was. She had assumed the famous James Shields would be your basic science nerd. But the guy was hot.

Unfortunately, Lucy was not. Not back then. She was a junior in college and weighed a good forty pounds more than she should have. The freshman ten had come and stayed for a nice long visit and invited its friend, the sophomore fifteen, to come join the party. And she hadn't exactly been svelte back in high school. So she went around in overalls and sweatshirts and figured she'd be the kind of girl who got by on brilliance instead of looks. Besides, she was still one of only a few females in her advanced bio classes, and guys were interested in her simply because she had breasts and a vagina. A few extra pounds didn't matter to most of them—just added to the mouthfeel.

Of course, the guys who were interested in her back then—fat butt, overalls, glasses, and all—were guys who themselves were . . . well, like David, her current lab partner. That is, perfectly decent guys without an ounce of flair or sexuality. Seeing James Shields in the midst of them all that night was like seeing a shining-coated yellow Labrador in a room full of gray and white mutts.

He was so far out of her league that Lucy hadn't given him another thought until they both ended up on the same research project years later—he was supervising it, and she and David worked under him. She had reinvented herself in the intervening six years, had lost over forty pounds, swapped the glasses for contacts, and learned to dress like an adult. James was no longer out of her league, a fact that he realized almost immediately but which took *her* a little longer to absorb. Even after dating him for a few months, she was still sort of amazed to find herself walking around arm in arm with someone like him.

"Oh, fuck it all to hell!" he said suddenly and dropped her arm.

"What?" Then she saw what he was looking at. "Oh, *shit*," she said.

Someone had thrown a pail of dark red paint over the top of James's Ridgeline pickup. Red had dripped down off the roof and onto all the windows. Scrawled in black spray paint across the doors and hood were the words "Killer," "Murderer," and, "Animals are people, too."

"Jesus fuck it all!" James said, circling the car like an angry animal. "I was inside for less than half an hour. They must have been following me. God *damn* it! Now I'll have to spend all night filling out reports at the police station and trying to get this clean. Those fucking, fucking, cocksucking assholes."

"I'm so sorry," Lucy said. "I can't believe they did it again."

"I should have parked in the garage," he said. "I'm an idiot. I figured I was safe on a Sunday afternoon for twenty fucking minutes."

"I'm sorry. If I hadn't asked you to come—"

He wasn't even listening. "This is the third time this year and the police still haven't caught them. They haven't even *tried* to catch them."

"It's awful," she said.

"We're talking hate crime here," he said. "Punishable by law." He thumped the truck with his fist. "Man, I'd like to see these fuckers locked up for years! Let them take it up the ass in prison for a while before they go around dumping paint on people's cars again."

"Whoa there," Lucy said. "Let's keep it in perspective—these guys aren't skinheads or anything like that."

He turned on her with a pounce. "Are you *defending* this?"

Lucy put her hands up. "God, no! This paint thing sucks. But you have to admit it's not like they're racists or murderers or anything like that. They want to keep animals from being tortured and killed. They're *wrong*, but they're not totally evil."

"Being this stupid is totally evil," he said. "It's worse than evil. Jesus, Lucy, I can't believe you would defend them."

"I'm not *defending* them," she said. "They're stupid assholes for targeting scientists doing valid experiments. But sometimes it takes stupid asshole extremists to get people to really think about what they're doing. When we sac rats it's legitimate, but I don't think cosmetics companies should just go and—"

"Oh, please," he said. "Don't waste my time with that shit."

"I know you're mad about the car—"

"Yeah," he said. "I'm fucking pissed." He unlocked his front door and pulled it open. "I'm going to the police station. You can come with me or not. I don't care."

"If you want the company—"

"I said I don't care."

"Fine, then," Lucy said. "Go by yourself."

And he did.

Lucy spent the evening at home alone. Since they hadn't made it to dinner, she ate an apple and a small piece of cheese, just as happy not to have to face the calories of a full meal, then worked on a grant proposal for a while, but got bored with that after an hour or so and decided she wanted to do something more fun with her Sunday night than write about rat adrenal glands, so she took out her knitting and worked on it while she watched a soapy medical drama on TV.

After an hour or so, she tried the scarf around her neck and decided it was the right length. She bound off the end and held it up to look at it. It needed something more. Fringe. She searched through her leftover bits of yarn and found a deep blue that looked good with the metallic blue of the scarf. She cut it into short, even pieces and pulled several strands through the ends of the scarf about one half inch apart to make the fringe. She was so absorbed in what she was doing she didn't even notice that the TV channel she was watching had switched to showing a late-night rerun of an eighties sitcom she had never liked in the first place.

It took several rings before she realized it was her phone and not the TV set that was ringing.

She put the scarf down and reached for the phone.

"It's me," said James.

"Hey," she said. "How'd it go with the police?"

"Oh, you know. The usual. They took some photos and wrote up a report. Nothing will come of it. I went to the carwash and got most of the paint off."

"That's good," she said.

"I guess . . . So, listen, Luce, I've got some stuff to do tomorrow. And Tuesday I have this stupid thing down at Irvine and won't be back until late. Can I see you Wednesday night?"

"Yeah. Wednesday's good."

"Great," he said. "Sorry about losing my temper today."

"It's okay," she said. "You had every right to be in a bad mood."

"Yeah, and you were saying some pretty stupid things. But it's okay. And by the way, I forgot to tell you I loved what we did earlier—too bad this had to ruin it. We'll try to keep the mood a little longer on Wednesday, okay? Maybe even make it to dinner? I'll call you at the lab, or just come by."

"Okay," she said. "I'll be there all day." But he had already hung up.

She went back to her fringe, and in a fever of industry didn't stop until she had finished it all. She dampened and blocked the scarf and left it to dry on the ironing table. It was already after one when she crawled into bed.

The next morning she woke up with a delicious sense of possibility: she could start a new knitting project. Maybe she'd tackle something more intricate than a scarf this time. Before going into work, she spent an hour online looking through patterns and pictures, trying to find something that inspired her. Pretty soon she realized she was looking almost entirely at men's sweaters.

She and James had been going out for six months. She had never been so in love with a guy before, never felt her body leap to someone's touch the way it did at just the *thought* of James's hand on her.

It would be wonderful to see him in a sweater she had knit, to watch him walk out into the world wearing something that marked him as hers for everyone to see. If she started it now, she could have it done by Christmas.

Online again late that night, she found a design for an oversize man's cabled sweater in dark red. It was the kind of thing James tended to wear, anyway, only if she made it, she'd buy better yarn than he was used to—like a soft wool with a touch of silk or linen in it. It would be wildly expensive, but she didn't mind spending a lot on his Christmas present.

Later, though, it occurred to her that she probably shouldn't buy the wool in dark red. Another color might be . . . better.

V

"Can you take on a new kid?" Ellen asked Sari first thing Tuesday morning. It wasn't really a question, since Ellen never accepted a refusal.

Sari looked up from the desk she shared on a first-come-first-served basis with several other clinicians. It was early and she was the only one there now, so it was all hers. "How many hours a week are we talking?"

"As many as you can give him."

"Then there's no way," Sari said. "I barely have enough time in the day for the workload I've got now."

"Join the club," Ellen said. "You want to call the parents and tell them you can't make time for their kid?"

"Am I allowed to mention that I work for a crazy zealot?"

Ellen laughed. "Come on, Sari. He's your kind of kid—melt-your-heart-cute with big Bambi eyes. Their first appointment's at ten this morning."

"That's in less than an hour," Sari said. "Seriously, Ellen—you said you needed Mary's progress report written up for her IEP this afternoon. I won't have time if I've got to—"

"You'll figure something out," Ellen said. She tossed a file on the table in front of Sari.

"Who did the eval?"

"I did."

"By yourself?" Sari raised her eyebrows. Ellen never had time to do the whole evaluation. She usually just came in at the end.

"Yes, all by myself. I taught *you* how to do them, if you remember."

"You just don't, usually."

"Well, they were desperate, so I squeezed them in late one night last week." She pointed her finger at Sari. "You see? You *can* make more hours in the day, if you try hard enough."

"We can't all be you," Sari said.

"More's the pity," Ellen said with a wink and left.

And Sari sighed and opened the file, because Ellen—whose voice was too loud and who wore skirts that were too tight over torn black stockings and whose hair was too long and too red for someone over fifty-five—Ellen was her hero and her big sister and her best friend and the bane of her existence all rolled into one overwhelmingly dear package.

Sari had left home to get away from her parents and then somehow ended up working in a place where every woman she met reminded her of her mother. They weren't necessarily as pretty and well preserved as she was, but they all flickered with the same nervous terror.

Like the mother who had come in just the week before. The first thing she'd said when she walked in the door with her son was, "I wouldn't even be bringing him if his teacher hadn't made me. All this fuss and bother, just because he has a slight language delay."

She smelled of cigarette smoke and Opium perfume and watched Sari's every movement with a ferocious intensity.

Sari tried to talk directly to the boy—a chubby four-year-old with dark rings under his eyes—but he wouldn't look at her, not even when she stuck a bright pink sticker on her nose and danced in front of him.

She put an M&M inside a cup, showed it to him, then covered the cup with a book. "If you take the book off, you can have the M&M," she said. He sat there, hunched inside himself, and didn't move.

"He's not hungry," his mother said. "He just ate lunch. He doesn't want the M&M."

Sari put two cars in front of him and he lined them up next to each other, but when she took one and made vroom vroom noises, he just shoved the other one off the table with the side of his hand and didn't respond when she asked him to pick it up.

"He doesn't like to play with cars," his mother said. "Everyone thinks boys like cars, but they've never interested him."

The whole exam went like that. She kept making excuses for him.

When Ellen came in to meet with them at the end of the hour, she glanced through Sari's notes and told the mother that the boy had some clear delays in several key areas, areas that might suggest an Autistic Spectrum Disorder. She said they'd like him to return to the clinic for further evaluation and to arrange for a program of interventions.

The mother exploded. "Oh, for God's sake!" she said. "Look at him. He's sitting there quietly, as normal as you or me. But of course you won't admit that." She stood up. "Do you *ever* say a kid is okay? No, of course not—why *would* you? There's no money for you in okay."

"This isn't about money," Ellen said.

The woman dragged her unresisting son by the hand to the door. "It's always about money," she said over her shoulder and left.

Ellen and Sari looked at each other. "That poor kid," Ellen said. "That poor kid."

Sari was used to moms like that. She was used to moms of all types, really—she saw dozens of them at the clinic on any given day. Sometimes both parents came in with the kid, but ninety percent of the time it was just the mother, so it was definitely unusual for Zachary Smith to arrive at the clinic later that morning with only his dad at his side.

Sari rose to greet them, holding her hand out to the little boy, who had dark curly hair and large blue eyes. Ellen was right—

Sari *did* prefer kids who were cute, although it was embarrassing to realize that her boss had noticed.

"Hi," she said. She had to reach down and take his hand, since he wasn't responding. "You must be Zachary. My name is Sari." She turned to the father, her hand still extended. "Sari Hill."

"Jason Smith," the father said, putting out his own hand in greeting.

The name and the face came together and she realized she knew him.

It was too late, though. She was already shaking his hand.

It hit him at the same moment. "Wait," he said as their hands clasped. "That name. Sari Hill. Why does that sound so familiar?"

"High school," Sari said. She withdrew her hand. "We went to high school together."

"Oh, man," he said with delight. "Of course! That's it! Sari Hill. I totally remember your name from attendance. Wow. What a weird coincidence."

"Yeah." She could have passed him a hundred times in the street and not recognized him, but, looking at him now, she thought he hadn't really changed all that much. He had been an athlete in high school, and he still looked fit but not beefy. His hair was still thick, but his face had gotten thinner, so the lines of his cheekbones and the slant of his jaw stood out more than they used to.

He was still just as handsome as he had been in the days when girls used to fall over themselves trying to sit near him in English class.

"So," Sari said. Her voice came out unusually high. She cleared her throat with a little cough. "Excuse me. A lot's changed for you since high school, I guess. Tell me about your little boy."

Jason looked down at his son, who held his hand patiently, staring at the opposite wall, oblivious to their attention.

"Zack's my pal," Jason Smith said. "He's the greatest little guy in the world. Only—" He stopped. "You know."

"Does he have any words?" According to the eval, he didn't talk yet, but it was good to go over the information again, in case the parents had left anything out. Plus it was easier to keep asking questions than to try to process the fact that Jason Smith—*Jason fucking Smith*—was standing in front of her.

"No. I mean, sometimes he'll surprise us by counting or making an animal sound or something, but no real words. He once recited part of the alphabet, but then he never did it again."

"He's very cute."

He smiled. "I agree."

"He looks like you."

"So they tell me."

Sari cleared her throat again. "How's his frustration tolerance? Any tantrums when he can't make his needs known?"

"He cries a lot," Jason said. "But he never throws anything or hits anyone or anything like that."

"Any self-injurious behaviors?"

"God, no," he said.

"Go sit down over there." She gestured to a chair in the far corner of the room. "See if he'll stay here with me." She took Zack's hand while Jason did as he was told. Zack didn't protest, just let her lead him to the corner where the toys were kept in a big cabinet. She spent the rest of the hour trying to see which ones interested him and what kind of candy he liked. They kept all sorts of treats and playthings in the clinic, positive reinforcement of good behaviors being the foundation of their behavioral approach.

Jason had been accurate: Zack didn't have any words that Sari could get out of him in that first session, and the slightest frustration—like having to wait while she took turns with a toy—made him open his mouth and wail. But he liked candy, and there were a couple of noise-making toys that seemed to fascinate him, and both those things were encouraging—it was the kids who didn't respond to anything who were hardest to teach. Zack didn't once strike out at her, no matter how frustrated he got, and that was a relief. She had plenty of bruises and scratches from kids who did more than cry when they were upset.

"So," Jason Smith said when she beckoned to him to come talk to her at the end of the hour. "What do you think? Can this boy be saved?"

"He's really smart," Sari said. "And sweet. He'll learn fast."

His face lit up. "That's great," he said. "You have no idea how great it is to hear that. It's been—" He stopped and then said, "How often can we see you?"

"I don't know yet," Sari said. "It's complicated."

"Ellen said that we should really push forward, not waste any time. She said some kids do as much as forty hours a week and that you can make the most progress when they're young. She said—"

"I know what Ellen says."

"I'm sorry," he said. "I know there must be thousands of people who want your time and it's probably impossible to take care of us all. It's just . . . I want so much for him."

"I understand," Sari said. "And we'll do the best we can for you. But—" She looked down at her hands. "You should be aware that it might not be me who works with Zack. It might be another therapist. Just so you know."

"I hope it's you," Jason Smith said. "You seem so good at this. I think Zack likes you already. And we go back such a long way together, you and I." She looked up again to find him smiling at her. "I won't hesitate to play the old friends card if there's a chance it might help."

"I'll talk to Ellen," Sari said. "We'll figure it out and get back to you before the end of the day."

As they said goodbye, Jason leaned forward and gave Sari a quick kiss on the cheek. Maybe, Sari thought, that was what you were supposed to do when you met someone from high school ten years later. "Sari Hill," he said with a shake of his head. "An honest-to-God miracle worker. Who'd have thought?"

Sari watched him take his son's hand and walk out the door with one last wave. She sank into a chair and let her head fall back.

Even hand in hand with a small child, Jason Smith swaggered when he walked, just like he used to swagger a million years ago in high school—when he and his friends ridiculed and tortured Charlie on a daily basis.

Sari tried to remember the details, but it was all pretty foggy. Funny how hard it was to remember the most painful periods of your life really clearly. Maybe there was a reason for that—maybe that way you protected yourself from reliving them.

Jason Smith was one of a bunch of faces, a bunch of names. They all blurred. Had he ever led the charge against Charlie? Been one of the ones who called him retard and shoved him against the wall? Or was he one of the kids who just stood there and laughed while shit like that went down? Looking at his face—handsome as it was—had made Sari want to throw up, so she knew he'd done at least that.

Some things your gut remembered better than your brain.

Someone had pulled Charlie's pants down during recess, in front of a circle of cheering students. Had that been Jason? By the time a friend had found Sari to tell her, and she'd gone running to help him, it was too late. There was a teacher already there, but he hadn't seen anything, and in the end no one got in trouble because no one would say who did it. It could have been Jason. Or one of his rich asshole friends. It almost didn't matter. Whether you were the one who did the deed or just the one who stood by—applauding—and let it happen—what was the difference, really?

Sari hugged her arms across her chest and rocked, feeling cold and hot at the same time.

All the girls had crushes on him. You'd walk into the bathroom and see his name in a heart with someone else's, or two girls would be sitting perched on the edge of the sinks, talking and smoking, and you'd hear his name over and over again. Even Sari couldn't *not* look at him when he was in the same room. He was that handsome.

He had kissed her on the cheek just now, had said that they were old friends, and she was supposed to—

She was supposed to help his kid. Sari was supposed to help his kid just because Zack had a neurological disorder, and because that's what she *did*. She helped kids with autism learn to talk and behave and overcome the symptoms of their disorder. No matter *who* their parents were.

Sari helped kids with autism get better, and it shouldn't matter to her that Zack's father and all his friends had tortured her brother and ruined her life.

She sat up straight. It wasn't Zack's fault who his father was.

So. She had to help him. It was the right thing to do and she knew it. It wasn't even a choice.

But the finality of that didn't stop her from wondering—did Jason Smith really not remember about Charlie or did he just not care?

Could anyone be that cold?

She crossed to the desk and fished her cell phone out of

her purse. "I have to see you tonight," she said when Lucy answered.

"Meet me at the yarn store," Lucy said.

VI

"Jason Smith," Sari said, as soon as she had greeted Lucy. She had found her in the back of the store, where the wall was lined with diamond-shaped cubbyholes filled with different-colored balls of yarns. Skeins of wool were also piled up in wooden general store bins. Yarn stores usually gave Sari the same feeling that candy stores did when she was little—there was the same rainbow of choices spread out before her and the same anticipation made both wonderful and tense by the knowledge that all these choices had to be eventually narrowed down to a selection. Tonight, though, she barely glanced at the colors around her. "What do you remember about him?"

"Jason Smith?" Lucy repeated. She ran her fingers lightly along a row of blue wool skeins. "Too rough. I want it really soft . . . You mean Jason Smith from high school? Man, I haven't thought of him in years."

"I know. Me neither. What do you remember?"

Lucy thought for a moment as she slid along the wall, fingering more yarn. "Good-looking asshole."

"How big an asshole?"

She plucked out a ball of wool and studied it thoughtfully. "Big. I think. But he kind of had a right to be because he was so hot."

"Debatable," Sari said. She leaned back against the cubbies

and folded her arms. "He was one of the guys who tortured Charlie, wasn't he?"

"A lot of people did that," Lucy said, tossing the skein back and picking up another one.

"I know," Sari said. "But I think Jason Smith was one of the worst ones."

"Maybe. I don't remember. What I do remember is he was always being followed around by a bunch of girls, because he was good-looking and a jock. Why'd you bring him up, anyway?"

"He brought his kid into the clinic today for treatment."

"No way!" Lucy raised the yarn she was holding up to the light. "Pretty, don't you think?" She lowered her hand. "So Jason Smith has a kid with autism?"

"Yeah. And, by the way, I could probably get fired just for telling you that, so keep it between us."

"He's not old enough to have a kid with autism, is he? How old is the kid?"

"Three."

"Babies having babies," Lucy said with a shake of her head. She searched through the bin of wool that matched the color she had picked out. "Do you think there are fifteen balls in here? I need fifteen."

"Don't forget to check the dye lots."

"Oh, right."

"You know," Sari said, watching her sort through the yarn, "we keep doing that. You, me, and Kathleen."

"What? Forget to check the dye lots?"

"No—I mean, we keep acting like no one our age could possibly have kids. We even act surprised when people we know get married. But we're not that young anymore. People our age get married and have kids all the time. People a lot *younger* than us do. At some point, we've got to accept the fact that we're not college students anymore and haven't been for a while."

"I've accepted it," Lucy said, making a pile of the yarn on top of a chair. "I don't like it, but I've accepted it. Okay, that's nine, ten, eleven—"

"It's just . . ." Sari stopped and stared at the growing pyramid. Then she said, "It was really weird seeing this guy. Last time I saw him was probably high school graduation. And here he comes in with a kid and he's a parent like all the other parents I see every day. It was weird. Like he had become a grown-up but I hadn't."

Lucy stopped counting and looked at her. "What are you talking about? You were the professional in the room, and all *he* did to be there was blow some sperm. Any fifteen-year-old can get a girl pregnant."

"I'm not really a professional," Sari said. "It'll be years till I get my license and can practice in my own right."

"Doesn't matter. You were still the expert." She turned back to the yarn and counted it again with little pecks of her index finger. "Twelve, thirteen . . . Shoot, I don't think there's quite enough."

"What are you making, anyway?"

"A sweater."

"For yourself?"

"For James, actually."

"Wow," Sari said. "That sounds serious."

"It's just a sweater," Lucy said.

"Yeah, right. Just hours and hours and hours of work. Hours and hours and hours."

"I know," Lucy said. "That's okay. I like knitting."

"Still, knitting for a guy means you think it's going to last. I wish I knew James better—we've only ever met in passing."

"We should all have dinner together," Lucy said. "Could you do it next Friday night?"

"I don't know," Sari said. "I'd have to cancel my date with this hot guy I've been seeing who gets really jealous when I go out without him. Have I mentioned that he's imaginary?"

"The problem is your job," Lucy said. She scooped up the whole pile of yarn and dropped it back in its bin. "Every guy you meet at work is married."

"Or on the spectrum. Hey, I like that green." Sari picked up a skein and showed her. "Don't you think that would look nice on James?"

"Yeah, I do. Help me check the dye lots." They started to search through the barrel of yarn. Then Lucy stopped. "Oh, wait—I just remembered something else about Jason Smith."

"I'm counting D-44s. What?"

"He slept with Portia Grossman."

Sari looked up. "Shut up! She was our class *valedictorian*."

Lucy nodded. "He did. I'm sure of it. I remember her strutting around, telling her friends during homeroom. They were all so jealous. *I* was jealous."

"You just said he was an asshole."

"I said he was a good-looking asshole. There's no one hotter in the whole world than that, Sari."

"Not to me. There are only twelve D-44s, Luce."

"I think there are enough D-47s. See if you can find one more in there." Lucy watched as Sari rooted through the bin. "There's just a vibe about bad boys, Sari. Like they could get a little angry, a little dangerous, and in bed that would be—"

"Jason Smith tortured my brother," Sari said. "I could never be attracted to him."

"Yeah, all right," Lucy said.

The total for the yarn came to two hundred and fifty dollars. Lucy sighed and paid it.

Sari lay in bed that night feeling lonely. Kathleen had moved into her new place that afternoon, which was a good thing—she took up a lot of space, both because she was so tall and because she was . . . well, *Kathleen*. She had, for example, woken Sari up at four the previous morning because she thought it would be "fun" to bake cookies and talk, and Sari, who had to be up at seven to go to work, cursed at her and pulled a pillow over her own head so she could go back to sleep.

But tonight she could have used Kathleen's company.

For the first few years of her life, Sari had shared a room with Charlie, because the house had only three bedrooms and Cassie had thrown a fit when they tried moving newborn baby Sari in with her. Even at the age of five, Cassie was spending a lot of time alone in her room with the door shut—presumably living out a fantasy life that improved on her real one—and she wasn't about to give up her privacy without a fight. So Sari's crib was set up in Charlie's room, which he accepted without question. He accepted everything without question. Possibly because he didn't have the language then to *ask* a question. But also because he was, by nature, passive and accommodating.

When Sari turned five, they moved to a bigger house, and she got her own room. She was thrilled—no more worrying that Charlie would suddenly decide to empty everything off the shelves or methodically pull every hair out of her dolls' heads as he occasionally had done in the room they shared.

But for years after that, if she woke up during the night because of a bad dream or because she heard a strange noise or because it was raining out—for any reason at all—the loneliness of her own room would become unbearable. She would slip out of her bed and dash across the hallway to Charlie's room. Before she had even reached the threshold, she could hear his snoring—he was already growing fat and had always had allergies, and the combination made him a noisy sleeper.

Sari would crawl into bed next to him, shoving him over to make room for her on the outside half of his narrow twin bed. He often muttered in response but never woke up, and Sari would snuggle up tight against him. He was big and warm and the familiar rhythm of his snores soon put her back to sleep.

In the morning, Charlie would wake up early and roll over her to get out of bed, as if she weren't even there. Sari would huddle under the covers then, still half asleep, and drowsily watch him while he walked in circles around the room, hooting and waving his hands in the air, an alien creature whom she could never completely come to know.

2

Ribbing

1

So what's the apartment like?" Lucy asked, glancing up from her knitting. This morning was the first chance she'd had to start the sweater for James, and she was casting on stitches for the back.

"Big," Kathleen said.

"What is it with you and big?" Sari asked. She lived in a tiny one-bedroom fourth-floor walk-up near Westwood Village and could barely afford the rent. Right now, the three of them were crammed around the one small round table that functioned as both her kitchen table and her desk—she'd had to move her computer and a bunch of papers onto the floor before setting up for brunch. Plates of half-eaten muffins and cups of tepid coffee were jammed in with knitting magazines and uncurling coils of measuring tape. Sari gestured around her. "How come you keep getting to live in these big beautiful places, and I'm stuck here?"

"I don't know," Kathleen said. "Maybe I was nice to cows in a previous life and earned a lot of good karma."

"I *was* a cow in a previous life," Lucy said with a smirk. "Back in high school."

"You weren't fat." Sari squinted at her row counter and flicked another number forward. "You just thought you were. Is it furnished, Kath?"

"Nope."

"Shit," Lucy said, throwing down her needle with the cast-on stitches. "I've counted this three times and I've gotten a different number each time. I feel like I'm losing my mind."

"Here." Sari rested her own knitting on her lap and held out her hand. "Let me try."

"Thanks." Lucy handed it to her and watched as Sari slid the stitches along, one by one, her lips moving silently. "So when are you going furniture shopping, Kathleen?"

"I already bought a couple of airbeds and a few odds and ends. But I'm not going to buy any real furniture or anything. I mean, the guy could kick me out at any minute. No point getting too settled. Plus I'm short on cash."

"How long can you live like that, though?" Lucy said. "It sounds like you'll have this place for at least a few months. You can rent furniture, you know."

"Too much work."

"Well, at least buy some kind of bed frame, so you're not sleeping on the floor with all the bugs."

"There aren't any bugs in that place," Kathleen said. "They can't afford the rent."

"I got sixty-four," Sari said, handing the needle and yarn back to Lucy.

"Good," Lucy said. "I got that once, too." She took her knitting back to her own seat. "You'll need a table and at least three chairs, Kath, for when it's your turn to host."

"Can't we just sit on the floor?" Kathleen said. "Have we gotten so old we need to sit in chairs all the time?"

"*I* have," Lucy said. "It's one thing to be all bohemian and stuff in college, but we're years out of college now. I'm over being uncomfortable."

"But I like having the empty floor space," Kathleen said. "I can run laps in my own apartment. And do push-ups and play soccer—"

"Play soccer?" Sari said. "Your neighbors must love the sound of balls thwacking against their walls night and day."

"No one's complained yet. Except for one old lady but she's the type who'd complain about anything." Kathleen stopped knitting to pull at a couple of strands of yarn that were all tangled up. "Hey, did I tell you guys I've got a job interview tomorrow?"

"You're kidding," Sari said, searching through her bag. "That was fast." She pulled out a skein of white wool, frowned at it, and shoved it back. "What's the job?"

"Nothing exciting. I'd be the assistant to some real estate guy. That's all I know." She reached for her coffee mug and took a sip.

"What's his name?"

"Rats—Sam told me, but I don't remember. Something Porter, I think. Johnson Porter? Jackson Porter? Something like that." She put the mug back down.

"You should probably try to get it right in the interview," Lucy said.

Sari said, "Is he the Porter in those Porter and Wachtell signs you always see on big construction sites? That Porter?"

"I don't know. Maybe."

"If he is, that's a huge company," Sari said. "I see those signs everywhere. How did you get the interview?"

"Through the same guy who got me the apartment. Sam Kaplan." She squinted down at the pattern she was using. "Does anyone know how to do a yarn-over at the beginning of a row? I can't figure it out. It doesn't make sense, does it? Doesn't it have to be in the middle of a row to work?"

"Hold on, let me take a look." Sari put down her own knitting and came over to kneel in front of Kathleen. "Well, first of all, you've gotten it all tangled up," she said.

"Like everything in my life," Kathleen said, watching Sari's hands sort through the tangle. "But you'll fix it, won't you, Sari? That's what you do—you fix everyone's messes."

"This is the slipperiest yarn I've ever seen," Sari said.

"Slipperiest?" Lucy repeated. "Is that even a word?" She looked over. "But I see what you mean. It's all shiny. You might even say blinding. What are you making, Kathleen?"

Kathleen held up her *Vogue Knitting* so they could see the picture. "A tank top."

"A bright gold tank top," Lucy said, shaking her head. "Subtle you're not."

"I like bright colors," Kathleen said. "We can't all be elegant and boring like you."

"I'll accept that as a compliment coming from a girl with bright green toenails."

"They're not green," Kathleen said, stretching out her bare feet so they could all see. "They're chartreuse. It's my new favorite color. When I finish this tank, I want to make a chartreuse tube top. Don't you think that would be cool?"

"If you wear a handknit tube top, don't your nipples poke through?" Lucy said.

"Not if you use a small enough needle and a really fine yarn," Sari said. "I think I got it straightened out, Kath. Let me see the instructions."

"Anyway," Kathleen said, handing them to her. "What's wrong with a little nipple showing? Give 'em what they want, I always say."

"And do, from what I've heard," Lucy said.

"Plus I can always wear it over a T-shirt or tank top."

Lucy wrinkled her nose. "That would look weird."

"You need to experiment more," Kathleen said. "In all kinds of ways."

"I spend my life doing experiments," Lucy said. "It's my job."

"That's so not what I mean."

"I think I've figured this out, Kath," Sari said and, while she explained how to do the stitch to Kathleen, Lucy found her thoughts wandering to her rats and then on to her recent fight with James.

"Hey, Sar?" she said after a moment.

"What?" Sari stood up, took a bite of muffin, then wiped her fingers on a napkin and sat back down to her own knitting.

"Remember Daisy?"

"Who was Daisy?" Kathleen asked.

"Oh, just this incredible bitch we used to know," Lucy said, and Sari laughed.

"You going to let me in on the joke?" Kathleen curled her feet up under her ass and attacked her knitting with renewed determination.

"She was my dog," Lucy said. "When I was in middle and high school. She died like five years ago. She was a great dog, wasn't she, Sari?"

"Yeah, she was sweet," Sari said.

"What kind of dog?" Kathleen asked.

"She was a mix. I think she had some Labrador in her, but she was smaller and furrier than a Lab. I used to pin her ears to the side of her head and say she was an otter." Lucy finished a row and turned her knitting over. "I could do anything I wanted to that dog and she never got mad, just licked me harder."

"Wish I could find a guy like that," Sari said.

"You ever have a dog?" Kathleen asked her.

"For like four weeks. Some therapist told my mother that a pet would help Charlie connect emotionally. So she went out to the pound and brought back the first dog she could find. She didn't even know what sex it was. I totally loved it—just because it was warm and soft and therefore much better company than any other member of my family—but then it bit my father, and after that they kept it in the garage. And a few weeks later my mother said that thing that parents say—you know, how they had taken it to a 'farm' where it could run free and be happy. Even at the age of seven, I knew it was bullshit and that dog was a goner."

"Wouldn't it be funny if all this time parents have been telling the truth?" Kathleen said. "And there's really some big doggy Eden somewhere?"

"I should get a dog," Lucy said. "It would be nice to have a friendly face to come home to at the end of a hard day."

"You work long hours and then you go out at night," Sari said. She flicked at the row counter again. "Don't you think a dog might get a little lonely?"

"I could hire someone to walk it."

"Then what's the point?" Kathleen said. "Someone else plays with the dog you bought. And it would still be alone too much. You'd feel guilty and stressed and—"

"Okay, okay," Lucy said. "So maybe it's not the right time. Someday, though, I'm going to get one."

"When you grow up," Kathleen said. "I like that color green, Lucy. What are you making?"

"A sweater."

"Really? I thought sweaters took too long."

"You haven't heard the best part," Sari said. "It's for James."

"You're making a sweater for your *boyfriend*?" Kathleen said. "You're nuts."

"Why is that nuts?"

"You should only ever knit for yourself," Kathleen said.

"That's the first rule of the single girl's knitting handbook. It's the *only* rule." She put down her work and held up her hand. "You try to knit a guy a sweater, then one of two things will happen"—she raised her index finger—"either he'll break up with you just as you're finishing it, which means you have to destroy all your work or spend the rest of your life trying to find another guy exactly the same size, or"—another finger went up—"even if you *do* get to give it to him, he won't like it or ever wear it and it'll make you so mad, you'll end up breaking up with him. And some future girlfriend of his will find it one day and tear it to pieces. Trust me, you only want to knit stuff for yourself." She picked up her knitting and waved it at them. "Slinky gold tank tops, girls. That's where it's at. Follow my lead."

"Yeah," Lucy said. "Let's follow the lead of the girl who sleeps on an airbed in someone else's empty apartment. She's obviously going places."

"I am," Kathleen said calmly. "Just you wait and see."

II

When Kathleen's job interview went well the next day (once again she wore her responsible clothes, which were starting to seem lucky as well as responsible), she was immediately hired to start that very week, which convinced her she had been right to tell Lucy she was going places.

On the downside, the job wasn't exactly what you might call high-powered. On her first day at work, she discovered that she wasn't the assistant to Jackson Porter, CEO of Porter and Wachtell, as she'd been led to believe in her interview with the head of personnel, but was, more accurately, the assistant to *his* assistant, sixty-year-old Luisa Rivera.

Luisa was Jackson Porter's secretary, assistant, confidante, advisor, personal shopper . . . whatever he needed, she had been, for twenty-five long years. Kathleen was Jackson's twenty-fifth anniversary present to Luisa, the idea being that the new girl would take over any duties Luisa no longer enjoyed.

As it turned out, Luisa was fairly proprietary about her boss and not all that interested in giving up any of her access to him, so Kathleen spent most of those first days fetching coffee, typing the occasional memo, answering the phones, and organizing drawers of stationery supplies.

She considered being disgruntled but decided it wasn't all that bad. For one thing, her job was pretty easy, since Luisa wasn't used to asking anyone to wait on her and didn't like other people to wait on Jackson. For another, the central position of Kathleen's desk—in front of the wall outside Jackson's office—allowed her to observe and eventually meet anyone at the firm who caught her interest.

Kathleen was good at meeting people. The first few days she was there, she wore bright-colored silk tops and called out cheery hellos to anyone who came within a few feet of her desk. It wasn't long before a lot of the guys at Porter and Wachtell were finding excuses to wander by the new girl's desk. Even the women were happy to discover there were new and enthusiastic ears to pour old rumors into.

She learned very quickly that three of the top businessmen who were always rushing around in suits and ties were not just Jackson's employees but also his sons. And that, while the older two were married, the youngest one was not. "And he's the nice one," one of the secretaries had added before tossing down her third Ultra Slim-Fast chocolate shake of the lunch break.

"Is he straight?" Kathleen asked.

"Why wouldn't he be?" The secretary sounded almost insulted, so Kathleen quickly said, "No reason. I just dated a guy once who turned out to be gay."

"I guess that can happen," the woman said. "But Kevin Porter's had tons of girlfriends since I started working here. And"—as if it settled the subject—"they're always *very* pretty."

Well of course they were, Kathleen thought. The guy was worth hundreds of millions—he could pick and choose. And if Kevin Porter were the kind of guy who cared what a girl looked like, Kathleen was the kind of girl who was realistic enough to know that meant he was bound to notice her sooner or later.

It was sooner. Kevin came walking up to her later that same day to introduce himself and welcome her to the team. (*Literally*—that's what he said—"Welcome to the team.") He had a nice face and good posture and met her eyes when he talked to her. Kathleen had gone out with far less appealing men. And he was wildly rich. Hadn't Sari told her that a rich guy was her fastest path to a happy future?

Which made her think she was really growing up—here she was, thinking about her *future*. What better sign of maturity than that?

III

Sari had a less pleasant week.

Monday morning she was woken up by a phone call and there was her sister, Cassie—who hadn't spoken to her in over three years—saying, "Sari? You're up, right? I couldn't remember the time difference, but I figured you're probably the early-bird type."

It was four in the morning and of course Sari had been asleep. She had spent the previous day wrestling a kid who liked to scratch people's eyes and then had stayed up until one working on some progress reports—no matter how much she wrote, she never caught up with the paperwork. She was still trying to get out some sort of coherent response, when Cassie cut her off. "I woke up early and couldn't get back to sleep," Cassie said. "I was thinking. Sari, you have to promise me. *Promise me.*"

"What?"

"Never to have children. Never. I mean, look at our family. We can't do this to anyone else. Neither of us can have kids. Ever. *Maybe* we could adopt. No, not even that. Not even adopting. Promise me, Sari."

"Cassie—"

"No, listen. I'm right about this. I haven't slept all night. I won't ever sleep again unless you promise me this right now. I mean it."

"I can't *promise*," Sari said, her voice hoarse with sleep. "I mean, I don't even know what—"

"Fine," Cassie said. "If you're going to be like that. But you're wrong. You're so wrong, I can't believe it. Why am I the only sane one in the family? Do you know mom actually asked me once when I was going to get married and have kids? Like she thought it was a good idea?"

"That's not such an awful—"

"Oh, fuck this," Cassie said. She hung up and Sari couldn't get back to sleep.

So when she walked into the clinic that morning, she was too exhausted to put up much of a defense when Ellen cornered her and said she had been assigned to work with Zachary Smith.

"You started with him," she said, as if the original choice had been Sari's and not hers. "You started with him, and the first session went well. The father requested you, and you had chemistry with the kid. I want you to stick with him, at least for the first few months. Then we can reevaluate."

Sari could have argued, but she had never once won an argument with Ellen. Besides, she had already vowed that she would help Zack, if asked. So she called up Jason Smith and scheduled time for Zack—four sessions a week, three of them at the clinic for an hour and a half, and then four straight hours at his house on Friday afternoons. She would have to cut way back on intake work, but Ellen was already training someone else to do evaluations. There was no one to take over her grant proposals or progress reports—they were all overloaded on that stuff—so she'd be working late at night and early in the morning just to keep from falling too far behind.

None of that was really a problem. It wasn't the first time she had devoted herself to a kid for a few months and had to scramble to keep up with everything else in her life.

No, the real problem was trying to reconcile her past and present every time Jason Smith walked through the door. Which was a lot, since he came every time. The mother never showed.

When she came to their house that first Friday afternoon, a housekeeper let her in. Jason wasn't home, which was a relief at first. But Maria the housekeeper came with her own set of problems. Her job, as she saw it, was to keep Zack from getting upset.

And upsetting Zack was basically Sari's job description.

Sari had to teach Zack that communicating with words was a more efficient way of getting what he wanted than screaming and crying, but the only way to make that point was to let him cry without giving him what he wanted. At first, if she held up a piece of candy and told Zack he needed to say "candy" if he wanted it, Zack would cry and scream for an excruciating *ten minutes* in the hopes that this new lady in his life would just go ahead and give it to him—all his life, people had given him stuff when he cried.

Sari knew—having done this hundreds of times with dozens of kids—that if she ignored the screams for long enough Zack would eventually stop sobbing and take a stab at saying "candy." The instant he did, she would hand him the candy. And, over time, he would learn that saying words actually worked *better* than crying at getting him what he wanted, especially if all the other adults in his life waited him out the same way.

Already, within the first week, he was showing signs of progress. He was making some of the beginning sounds of words. He was *trying*. Pretty soon, Sari knew, he'd really get the idea, and then words would start coming like crazy.

But not if—as happened that first Friday in Zack's house—Maria was going to come racing into the room the second she heard him scream, and—one hand outstretched, the other clutched to her heart—cry out, "Oh, my love, my life! What's wrong? What has she done to you?"

"Nothing's wrong, nothing's happened," Sari said.

"Is he hurt?" Her hands on his shoulders, she was scanning his face—apparently looking for bruises.

"He's fine," Sari said. "He just needs to stop crying and try talking if he wants this cookie."

"He's a good boy," Maria said. "No trouble with *me*." Zack buried his face in her shoulder.

Sari said, "I know it's hard to hear him cry like that, but it's really just out of frustration and soon he'll—"

"He never cries with me."

"Well, then, you're going to have to start letting him," Sari said. Maria didn't even bother responding to that. She wrapped her arms around Zack and rocked him, crooning softly, until Sari gave up and left the house.

Sari hated to get anyone in trouble, but something had to change, and she told Jason that when he came to the clinic on Monday.

"As long as she comes running whenever he cries, he'll keep crying," she said. "And it's not just a problem when I'm there. It's a problem *all* the time, if she's soothing and cuddling him when he's behaving badly. All she's doing is rewarding the bad behavior—which means it will continue no matter what I do."

"Should I fire her?" Jason Smith said. "Because I will, if you tell me to. Actually," he said, "I'd do anything you told me to."

Sari said, "Don't fire her. Of course, don't fire her. We want Zack to feel loved and secure right now. But talk to her for me. Tell her she's got to change how she deals with him."

"I'll try," he said. "Maria and I aren't exactly in the habit of talking a lot." His mouth twisted. "The truth is, I'm scared to death of her. We kind of keep our distance, take our shifts with Zack . . . Denise was the one who hired Maria in the first place. She likes her because she's so competent and take-charge about everything, but now that it's just me at home, I'm the one left dealing with her, and all that competence terrifies me. I don't think I live up to her expectations." He tried to laugh, but it ended in a sigh. "This single dad stuff is all new and strange to me."

So he was divorced. Or at least separated. Not that Sari cared. She said, "If you could just make sure she's busy doing something else when I come on Fridays, that would help a lot. And please tell Maria not to give him what he wants whenever he cries, but to wait until he's asking appropriately. We all have to be a little bit tough with him right now."

"Cruel to be kind?" Jason said.

"Exactly."

Later, when they were shaking hands goodbye, Jason Smith said, "I've been wanting to say—what you've been doing with Zack is amazing. *You're* amazing."

"It's all pretty simple, really," Sari said.

"I know. That's the beauty of it. I watch you and you make it look so easy. But he's actually starting to say words. I didn't think I'd ever—" He stopped. They both looked at Zack, who had turned a toy truck upside down and was using his index finger to make one of its wheels spin. After a moment, Jason said, "I feel like I'm seeing him for the first time. You know what I mean? Like the real Zack is starting to come out."

"All of him's the real Zack," Sari said. "We're just encouraging him to talk and be social. But he's all Zack all the time."

"Yeah, of course," Jason said. He was wearing jeans and a plain white T-shirt that hung straight down from his broad shoulders. He looked like a jock. He'd look like a jock in footsie pajamas.

He was still talking. Sari made herself focus. "I've always loved him, but now it feels like he's turning into a friend. It's incredible. He actually asked me for juice today. I couldn't believe it. He came right up to me and said, 'Joo, joo.' "

"Maybe he just thought you looked a little Semitic," Sari said.

He laughed and then said, "It's weird that you're funny. I remember you as being really serious. I mean, in all honesty, I don't remember you all that well, but I have this mental picture of you always being in the library."

"I'm amazed you remember me at *all*," Sari said. "I didn't hang around with your crowd much."

"My crowd?" he repeated. "I didn't have a crowd."

"Sure you did."

"I had a few friends. Not that many."

"You had an *entourage*," Sari said. "Which was appropriate, what with you being the king and all."

"Was I voted king?" he said. "Funny that I don't remember that."

"People don't vote you king," Sari said. "You're born to it."

He shook his head. "Not me. I was just trying to survive, like everyone else."

It blew her mind that he could say that, that he could act like his high school experience was anything like hers, like he hadn't *ruled* the place and dealt out favors and cruelties with equal generosity.

IV

Dinner Friday night didn't go as well as the girls had hoped.

It started off fine. Kathleen was late, of course, but the girls knew that Kathleen never paid much attention to time, so they went ahead and ordered drinks without her. For a while, they drank and chatted about restaurants and movies, and James seemed fairly relaxed for once, his arm draped around Lucy's shoulders, his long legs stretched out under the booth they shared.

Then James asked Sari what she did for a living and she told him.

He was already shaking his head before she had finished speaking. "I know you don't want to hear this," he said, "but it just kills me when I hear about these autism clinics popping up everywhere. Like they're going to make a difference."

"Excuse me?" Sari said, blinking.

"How many kids do you see in a day?"

"Me, personally, or at the clinic?"

"At the clinic."

"Roughly thirty, I guess. Some evaluations, but mostly ongoing therapy."

"Which means most of the kids are repeat visitors, right? So it's not like you're seeing thirty different kids every day."

"Yeah, right," she said. "So?"

He was shaking his head again. "It's a waste, that's all. A drop in the ocean. It's like a doctor putting calamine lotion on *one* kid with chicken pox instead of vaccinating all the kids in his practice."

Sari shifted uncomfortably in her seat. "We help every kid who comes through our clinic."

"So you patch up a few kids," he said with a shrug. "At a huge expense, right? Meanwhile, that money—and intelligent clinicians like you—could be put to far better use pursuing scientific solutions to the problem." He picked up his beer glass with his free hand, the one that wasn't around Lucy's shoulders. "Autism isn't going to go away because some kids learn to say a word or two. We've got to find a real biomedical solution to the problem. The only way to do that is to take all the money we've got and put it directly into reputable scientific research." He took a sip and put his glass back down.

"I'd be thrilled if someone found a biomedical solution," Sari said. "But no one's come knocking on our door with one yet. Behavioral interventions are all we've got that *work*—"

"One kid at a time," James said. "And each kid requires—what?—hundreds of hours of one-on-one intervention, right?

Come on, Sari, it's a waste. All those man-hours, all that money . . . Put them to use, I say. Stop playing around with one or two kids and set your sights higher."

"You want to come to the clinic and tell our parents that?" Sari said. Her cheeks had turned red. "You want to come tell them we're closing down and not helping their kids anymore because maybe someone someday will find a better solution? 'Sorry, folks, your kids aren't going to learn to talk but, hey, if we find a magic pill, we'll be sure to call you'? Like that?"

"Whoa, there," James said, removing his arm from Lucy's shoulder so he could put up both hands in surrender. "Calm down, buddy. I'm on your side. It's just that I come from a hard science background—I deal in research and real solutions."

"Our approach is completely research-based," Sari said. "This is science, too. Behavior mod can change people's brains at the chemical level."

"Not as fast as chemicals can," James said. "But let's not argue. It's great that you want to help kids. Really." He slid out of the booth and stood up. "Excuse me, guys—got to make a quick trip to the men's room. I'll be right back." He left.

The girls sipped their drinks and didn't meet each other's eyes. "I'm sorry," Lucy said after a moment. "I didn't know he'd—"

Sari waved her hand. "Don't worry about it. A lot of people feel that way."

There was a flurry and a blur and suddenly Kathleen was sitting next to Sari. "Sorry I'm late! Where's James?"

"Men's room," Lucy said.

"I miss anything?"

"Yeah," Lucy said. "James was a jerk and now Sari hates him."

Sari rolled her eyes. "I don't hate him."

"Why does she hate him?" Kathleen asked. She was wearing a red handkerchief top and tight jeans and looked pretty spectacular, the way Kathleen always did when she got out of her sweats and made an effort to dress up.

"I don't hate him," Sari said again. "We had a polite disagreement about something."

"Whatever," Kathleen said. She put her fingertips to her neck. "My throat's killing me. It's been hurting all day."

"You should take some vitamin C," Sari said.

"You know, there's no actual scientific evidence that that works," Lucy said.

"Don't *say* that. Haven't you heard of the placebo effect? Which you've just ruined for me?"

"I'll try anything right now," Kathleen said. "I so don't want to get sick. There's lots of vitamin C in orange juice, right?" She signaled to a waiter and ordered a screwdriver when he came over.

James came back to the table a minute later. For the rest of the meal, they stayed away from the subject of autism clinics, and James went out of his way to be charming and friendly. But no matter how pleasantly Sari smiled, Lucy *knew* she had to be pissed off that James had called the career she loved a waste of time.

James and Lucy left soon after ten—he was worn out from all the traveling and lecturing he'd been doing—but Kathleen and Sari lingered over slices of flourless chocolate cake.

"Lucy's lucky," Kathleen said. "She's going home to have sex."

"Remind me what that is again," Sari said.

"Sort of like this chocolate cake, only better. You shouldn't go so long between guys, Sar."

"It's not like I *want* to."

"No, but you don't actively go after them, either. Let's go to a bar and I'll show you how to pick someone up. Just for practice."

"I don't do that," Sari said.

"But you should."

"I don't know how to go after guys, anyway," Sari said. "They didn't teach that where I went to school."

Kathleen squished a crumb of chocolate cake with her index finger then licked it off. "You just find a cute guy and listen to him talk like he's interesting—whether he is or not—and smile a lot and touch his arm and make it clear that you're available. The rest just kind of follows."

"It just kind of follows for *you*," Sari said. She had moved to the other side of the booth when Lucy and James had left so they could face each other, and now she gestured across the table toward Kathleen's face. "You're gorgeous. Guys fall all over you. It's not like that for me."

"It could be," Kathleen said. "You're the cutest girl around, Sari. You just have to stop acting all sweet and shy like the girl next door and put a little slut into your moves."

"That works for you, huh?"

"Almost always." She took a sip of water and grimaced. "Hurts to swallow. Hey, Sari, remember how you said the best job for me would be to marry someone rich? I've been thinking you may be right about that."

"I was joking," Sari said. "Marrying a guy just because he's rich is a bad idea."

"I know that," Kathleen said. "But what if he's rich and nice and you actually *like* him?"

"That's a lot of ifs."

"I'm suddenly really tired," Kathleen said and pushed the cake away. "Fuck, Sari, I don't want to get sick."

V

You look like shit," Sam said when he opened the kitchen door for Kathleen the following night.

Kathleen had come up the back way to the service entrance, which was how she almost always came up to Sam's place, once she'd discovered that the back stairs took her directly from her kitchen to his. At first, she came when she needed something, like a pair of scissors or a cup of coffee. But sometimes she came just because the silence of her bare apartment made her desperate for company and she knew that Sam was likely to be there when he wasn't at work.

"I'm sick," she said. "My head hurts and I can't stop shaking."

"And you had to come *here*?" He was backing away already. He was terrified of germs. Once Kathleen had wiped her mouth on his napkin, and he had freaked out when she pushed it back over to him. He had threatened to start locking her out if she ever did anything like that again.

"I need some medicine," she said. "You've got to have something in that drugstore you call a bathroom."

"Just go back downstairs to bed and sleep it off. Best thing for you."

"Can't," Kathleen said. She pressed the palms of her hands against her cheeks, which felt hot. "There's a big company party tonight. My first. I have to go and impress people."

"Oh, for God's sake, you're an assistant. No one cares if you go or not." He retreated farther. "They certainly won't thank you for going if there's a chance you're contagious. You start sneezing, and you'll just make them all hate you."

"No one will know I'm sick," Kathleen said. "I haven't

really been sneezing. I just need something to make my throat and head stop hurting. Tylenol, Advil, anything like that. Or that aspirin stuff that has caffeine. I could use some. I feel so tired."

"If I give you something, will you leave?"

"I swear."

He led her to his bathroom and opened the medicine cabinet. Kathleen reached over his shoulder, grabbed a prescription bottle and peered at it, pretending to read, in mock surprise, "Viagra? I'm shocked, Sam. And a little intrigued."

"Very funny," he said, snatching the bottle away. He plucked another container off the shelves and thrust it at her. "Take this and get the hell out of here. You're infecting the whole place."

"It's a *cold*, Sam—not the Avian flu." She shook a couple of pills into her hand, tossed them into her mouth, then bent down and drank some water straight out of the faucet, shoving her head sideways into the sink. She stood up again, and swiped at the drops around her mouth with the back of her hand. "How long do these take to work?"

"Didn't anyone teach you any manners at all?" He threw her a towel.

"They tried," Kathleen said. "But it was no use." She dropped the towel and suddenly grabbed on to the sink. "Yikes. Dizzy."

"You don't *have* to go to this thing," he said and sat down on the edge of the bathtub. "You *want* to."

"Yeah, I want to. Man, my head's spinning. I want to see everyone from work get drunk and act silly. And I want to see if Kevin Porter has a girlfriend."

"Why do you care?"

"I'm curious is all. Oh, and the food should be good. If I don't throw up, which right now I think I might."

"Not here," Sam said. "I am not cleaning up after you, Kathleen, so if you're feeling sick, get out now or be prepared to mop it up yourself."

"Boy, and I thought my *father* was a jerk—"

"Get out," Sam snarled, and she fled.

The cold medicine kicked in, and by the time Kathleen got to the party an hour and a half later, her head wasn't throbbing so much, although she still felt kind of shaky and strange—which could have been the virus or the drugs or a combination of the two.

She looked a lot better, too. She had washed her hair and blown it dry, so it was straight and glossy, and had covered up the shadows under her eyes with concealer, then applied her evening makeup with a skilled, if slightly heavy, hand. She chose a black dress tight enough to flaunt the strong V-shape from her shoulders to her waist and short enough to make her long legs look about a mile long, especially once she had also strapped on a pair of spike-heeled sandals.

As soon as she entered the banquet hall, a waiter was at her elbow with a choice of white or red wine. She chose red and strolled through the room while she sipped it slowly. There was a string quartet quietly playing lively music in one far corner and lots of waiters wandering around with trays, passing out drinks and offering hors d'oeuvres. The general atmosphere was fairly subdued and genteel, but, given the ubiquity of the alcohol, Kathleen suspected—and hoped—that things would get a lot more interesting before the end of the evening.

There were open French doors at the far end of the room, and through them you could see a balcony and, beyond that, the ocean. The hotel was right on the beach in Santa Monica. Kathleen didn't feel like making small talk with anyone yet, so she walked through the room—smiling and waving at a couple of semi-familiar faces—and out onto the balcony. There were a few other guests out there—mostly couples who were holding hands and watching the sunset.

There was one guy standing alone by the railing, apparently captivated by the play of light on the waves. Kathleen stepped forward so she could see his face. She smiled.

She came and stood next to him and joined him in looking at the water.

"It's pretty amazing," she said after they had stood side by side in companionable silence for a moment or two. "Too bad you can't bottle and sell it."

He shook his head. "That's what makes it so great. It only lasts for as long as you're there to look at it. And it belongs to everyone."

"No admission charge."

"The best things in life are free."

"So are the worst, but no one goes around pointing that out."

He laughed and turned to look at her. She smiled back at him, assessing him in this light as she had back in the office. Not gorgeous, Kevin Porter, but attractive, helped by the glow of good health and comfortable living, though he was starting to swell a little at the waist and chin. Slightly better than average looks, but when you added in the bank account, he became gorgeous, because how many men in that price range could even come close?

"I'm sorry," he said. "I know you're Luisa's new assistant, but I've forgotten your name."

"Kathleen." He wouldn't ever forget it again, she'd make sure of that.

He leaned back against the railing, the ocean view put aside for the moment in favor of the closer eye candy. "So, Kathleen . . . How's it going? Are you enjoying working with us?"

"Sure. Everyone's been very nice to me."

"I'm glad to hear it," Kevin Porter said. "How'd you happen to come interview in the first place?"

"A friend referred me. Sam Kaplan."

Kevin looked surprised. "Sam's a friend of yours?"

"Sort of. I only met him a few weeks ago. But he got me this job and a free apartment, so he's definitely on my good guy list."

Kevin Porter smiled. "Biggest shark in L.A."

"You're kidding."

"My father adores him. The only guy in town who's tougher than he is."

"Really?" She filed that piece of information away. Interesting.

There was a pause, then Kevin said, "Are you a runner, by any chance?"

"I am," Kathleen said. "How did you know?"

"You just looked like you might be." They both knew it meant he had been looking at her legs. And they were both okay with that.

"How about you?" she said. "Do you run?"

"I like to. But only if I have company. I get bored running alone."

"Ah," she said. "That's where the iPod comes in."

"Music?" he said. "Not enough of a distraction—I still know I'm running."

"Well," she said. "If you ever need a partner—"

"Let me buy you a drink," he said immediately.

"I think you already did," she said, putting her empty wineglass down on the edge of the railing. But she let him walk her back into the party.

* * *

That night in bed, after spending the whole evening talking and dancing with Kevin, she pictured a future in which *she* would be the one buying the cars for her mother and sisters.

Maybe she'd even get them all a beach house. She had liked looking at the ocean that evening, and the twins didn't own a beach house yet. She could lead the way.

One day, Christa and Kelly wouldn't be cute anymore, and their earning potential would just shut down, but if she married Kevin Porter, Kathleen would always be rich. And then they would come to her, begging her for money. And she'd give it to them. She would be very generous when she was rich.

When Kathleen got bored with picturing herself as the bulwark of her family, she wrote herself an even better scenario. One day, she decided, she would stroll into Sam Kaplan's place and let him know that the moment her apartment was cleared of all legal hurdles, she was prepared to buy it. With cash. "You see?" she would say to him, "I *did* figure out my future after all." He would, for once, be speechless.

And that thought was so delicious, she kept running the scene through her head until she fell asleep, a smile on her face.

VI

"You've got to wake up," Lucy said.

James just burrowed more deeply into the pillows. Lucy pounded on his back. "I mean it," she said.

"Why?" he said, half opening one eye to squint up at her. "It's Sunday morning, isn't it? I get to sleep late."

"I told you last night. The girls are coming over to knit at ten. It's already nine-thirty. You need to shower and go."

"Oh, yeah." He rolled onto his back and rested his arm over his forehead. "You really serious about this knitting shit?"

"Why wouldn't I be?"

"I don't know. Knitting. It sounds like something old ladies would do."

"It's fun. We sit and knit and talk and eat and it's fun."

"Bet *you* don't eat. You never eat."

"Get up, James."

He reached an arm out to the side and nabbed her around the legs. She was wearing a big T-shirt and not much else. His hand slid up her thigh. "Why can't I stay and watch? Is it so you and the girls can talk about me?"

"Maybe. Hey, watch that hand, mister."

"Why? Don't you like it?"

"I like it," Lucy said and let him pull her down on the bed next to him. He rolled on top of her, pinned her with his arms and then rolled again onto his back so she was lying on top of him. The sheet was between them, but she could feel him hard against her pelvis through the fabric. He held her tight like that for a moment, his eyes shut, his breath so regular it sounded like he was going back to sleep. "You want me to do all the work, don't you?" she said then.

"I'm still a little sleepy." He was pretty cute in the morning, his long hair rumpled, his face all round and smooth and childlike.

She set to work unpeeling the sheet from his body.

"Ah-ha," she said when he was unwrapped. And then made another similar-but-different sound when she straddled him.

It was, she thought, a nice way to start the morning. So long as he was gone by the time the girls came.

"Who wants more coffee?" Lucy said, entering with a fresh pot.

"Why do we always ask that?" Sari said, looking up from her knitting. "Has any one of us ever once said no to coffee?"

"It's like asking Kathleen if she wants an alcoholic beverage," Lucy said.

"Very funny," Kathleen said. "You offering?" She sat down next to Sari and pulled out her work. She was sewing together the finished pieces of the tank top. "What are you working on, Sari? It looks new."

"Yeah." She held it up so they could see. "I just started this. It's a blanket for Ellen's granddaughter—her son's wife is due next month."

"Oh, it's so soft," Kathleen said, reaching out to touch it. "I like the color, too. Usually baby stuff is so friggin' pastel-y."

"I know," Sari said. "That's why I went for midnight blue."

"You rebel."

"Isn't Sari breaking your only-knit-for-yourself rule?" Lucy asked Kathleen as she refilled her coffee cup. "Don't you have a problem with that?"

"Babies are different," Kathleen said. She put her knitting pieces in her lap and poured half the pitcher of cream into her coffee. "They'll wear anything you make them and they rarely have girlfriends who rip things apart." She reached for the sugar bowl.

"Speaking of girlfriends and boyfriends," Sari said, "what did James think of us, Luce?"

"He liked you guys." What he had actually said was, "Man, that Kathleen's a total babe," and Lucy had said, "You want me to set you up with her?" and he had grinned and said, "She's hot but she looks like trouble. I'll stick with what I've got." "And what did you think of Sari?" Lucy had asked. "Very cute and likable, even if she's wasting her time on a pointless career," was James's summation.

"I'm sorry he said all that stuff about the clinic, Sari," Lucy said. "He's just been in a bad mood lately because of these animal rights lunatics. They've been stalking him, leaving him notes and messing up his car and stuff. It's driving him nuts."

"That's terrible," Sari said. "Why?"

"Everyone knows he uses a lot of animals in his research. He talks about it openly. Most people are more circumspect about that stuff." She set the coffeepot on a trivet and sat down. "Anyway, the point is that James isn't usually that annoying."

"He sure is purty, though," Kathleen said.

"Isn't he?" Lucy said. "Makes it hard for me to stay mad at him."

"Why do we care?" Sari asked, her needles clicking emphatically against each other. "About looks, I mean? Wouldn't it be better if we didn't?"

"It's not a question of what's *better*," Kathleen said. "It's just the way it is. Some guys are more appealing to us than others, that's all."

"Yeah. But remember that guy I went out with last year? Jeff Fleekstra?"

"Yeah, I remember him," Kathleen said. "Yuck."

"Hey," Sari said.

"Sorry. But you know what I mean."

"He was a good guy," Sari said. "He was doing some really interesting autism research and—"

"He was gross," Kathleen said.

"Don't be obnoxious," Lucy said. She picked up her knitting.

"Sari went out with the guy for months. You'll make her feel bad if you point out how incredibly *revolting* he was."

"You're right," Kathleen said. "I'll try not to bring up the fact that Jeff was an unpleasant little troll."

"Good," Lucy said. "And, whatever you do, don't remind Sari about how he used to spit when he talked and food would come out of his mouth when he laughed."

"I'd have called it more of a giggle than a laugh," Kathleen said.

"Are you guys done?" Sari said. "May I continue?"

"I guess so," Lucy said.

"I could go on longer," Kathleen said.

"Well, don't," Sari said. "Anyway, Jeff was a nice guy doing the kind of work I admire. And he treated me really well. But I couldn't get past his looks. Doesn't that make me shallow?"

"It makes you *human*," Kathleen said. "Even you—awesome and saintly as you are—"

"You are, you are," Lucy echoed.

"—even *you* want a guy who's hot enough to give you the shivers. Nothing wrong with that."

"And besides," Lucy said, "guys have been judging women on the basis of their looks forever."

"Yeah, but just because men are superficial doesn't mean we have to be," Sari said. "Can't we be more evolved than they are? I mean, there are more important things in life than looks."

"There are equally important things," Kathleen corrected her. "But if the attraction isn't there, forget it. Nothing else can make it work. Anyway," she added, "Jeff was kind of gross."

"I know," Sari said with a sigh. "And that's why I broke up with him."

"That's not being shallow," Lucy said. "It matters. Sexual attraction matters."

"But so do other things, right?" Sari said. "Like good values and intelligence?"

"And money," Kathleen said.

"You're not helping my argument."

"Sure, I am," Kathleen said. "Every guy is a package. What matters is how it all adds up." She raised her eyebrows twice. "And how big the package is, if you know what I mean."

Lucy threw a ball of yarn at her and that was the end of that conversation.

VII

So . . . no Maria?" Sari said, looking around. The Smiths' house was small, but lovely, on a quiet cul-de-sac in Brentwood. From the little she knew about real estate, she guessed it was worth at least a couple of million dollars, even though it was just your basic cozy Mediterranean.

"No Maria," Jason said. "I fixed it—she's going to baby-sit Friday nights, instead of during the day. So the good news is I can now go out on Friday nights."

"Is there bad news?"

"Yeah—I have no one to go out *with*."

Sari decided to ignore that. "Did you talk to her about letting Zack cry?"

"Uh—" He looked down, shuffled his feet.

"You really *are* scared of her, aren't you?"

"I told you."

"Seriously," Sari said. "You've got to get her onboard with this, or it's going to hurt Zack's progress."

"I know. I will." He took a deep breath. "Sometimes it's all just so *hard.*"

Sari narrowed her eyes. What did he want from her? Sympathy?

Fortunately, Zack poked his head into the hallway at that moment.

"Hey," Sari said. "I see you there, mister. We're going to have fun today."

Zack immediately went running in the opposite direction.

"I'll get him," Jason said and took off.

He scooped Zack up and trotted back with Zack tucked sideways under one arm. "He's running for the goal," Jason said, his free hand held out, running back style. "He's at the thirty-yard line, he's at the twenty, the ten, and he's almost there, and he— Touchdown! Woo-hoo! The crowd goes crazy! Victory dance for the good guys!" He lifted Zack up high in the air and then tossed him a couple more feet up before catching him again. Zack laughed out loud—he had a great laugh, bubbly and unforced and infectious—and as soon as Jason set him down, he tried to climb back up into his arms.

"Oh, so you want me to do it again, do you?" Jason said, picking him up and tossing him high. Zack came back down shrieking with laughter.

"Wow," Sari said. "He really likes that."

"Loves it," Jason said, a little smugly, holding Zack against his chest. "Always has. It's a guaranteed Zack-pleaser."

"Perfect," Sari said. "Let's make him ask for it."

"Ask for it?" Then he realized. "Oh, no. Do we have to?"

Sari shrugged her backpack off her shoulder and tossed it on the floor. "All he's got to say is 'up.' But you can't give in until he does. No matter how much he cries."

He heaved a big theatrical sigh. "All right. You're the boss."

He put Zack on his feet then held out his arms. "You want to go up, Zack? Say 'up!'"

Zack grabbed at his arms, and Jason raised them out of his reach. "No, pal. You have to say the word. Say 'up.'" He looked at Sari. "Am I doing this right?"

Zack let out a scream of frustration.

"You're doing it right," Sari said.

Getting him to say "up" the first time was tricky—the first time always was with a new word—but once Jason had prompted the word about twenty times, pantomiming the action, Zack did finally make an "uhh" sort of noise, and then Jason quickly grabbed him and tossed him. Five minutes after that, Zack was saying "up" with just a reminder or two, and about five minutes after that, he was saying it without one. And about five minutes after *that*, Jason said, "My back is breaking, Sari. I've got to take a break."

"All right," Sari said, "I think you've earned one." Only then Zack said, "Up! Up!" so she said, "Just one more time? Please? He said it so perfectly that time."

Jason moaned but tossed Zack up. Then he said, "No more." He set Zack down on the floor and arched his back, digging his fingers into the muscle above his waist.

"Up, up!" Zack said and tugged on Jason's pants.

"I can't, buddy. Daddy's in too much pain."

"Up? Up?"

"Good job, Zack," Sari said, squatting down in front of him. "But there's no more where that came from right now. We'll do more up tomorrow."

"Up, up!" he said, trying to climb Jason's leg.

"No more up," Sari said.

"More up?" he said.

Sari lost her balance and had to grab at the wall to steady herself. "What did you just say, Zack?"

"More up? More up?"

"My God," Sari said. "That's a sentence. You just made a sentence, Zack. He just made a sentence," she said to Jason.

"Well, not really a sentence," he said. "I mean, technically—"

"Okay, fine, it's a phrase, not a sentence. But he put two words together. On his own. That's huge. That's bigger than huge. I've never had a kid do that on his own before." Sari hugged Zack. "You're incredible. Did you know that you're incredible? Because you're incredible."

He pushed her away. "More up," he said.

She looked at Jason. "You *have* to."

"But it hurts."

"More up?"

"You *have* to," Sari said again. "You've got to reinforce this. Please, Jason. You have no idea how huge this is."

"All right," he said. "But you better have a hot towel waiting for me when I'm done."

"You've got it," Sari said. She felt giddy. She didn't get a lot of sudden breakthroughs like this. Most of her work was slow and frustrating. But this—this was the kind of thing she dreamed about. "A hot towel and anything else you want. On me."

"Anything?"

"You name it."

He raised his eyebrows. "You *are* a dedicated therapist." He held his arms out. "More up, Zack. Come and get it."

* * *

Sari really did get him a hot towel afterward.

She let Zack take a few minutes to play by himself—he'd certainly earned it—and ran off into the kitchen, returning a short while later with a towel she'd soaked with insta-hot water.

When Jason saw what she held in her hand, he laughed. "All right," he said and turned so his back was to her. "Put it on. You owe me." He hitched up his shirt, exposing the area above his narrow waist.

Sari pressed the towel against his back.

He yelped and said, "It's hot!"

"I thought that was the point."

"Yeah, it was." And then he relaxed and said, "Aah. Now it feels good." Then, after a moment: "Can you put it a little higher?"

Sari pushed his shirt up over his shoulders, baring his whole back, and pressed the towel against it. The skin there was smooth and hairless. When he shifted, even slightly, muscles moved and tightened below his shoulders. Sari tried not to think about how she could, if she wanted to, simply run her hands around his waist and up to his chest.

His eyes were half closed with pleasure. "They should offer this at all the spas."

And suddenly Sari remembered girls—high school girls, their classmates, giving Jason Smith massages out on the low wall behind the cafeteria, where everyone sat during free periods. He'd be sitting on the wall and they'd stand behind him and rub his shoulders through the light fabric of his shirts—usually the polyester top to some team uniform—and laugh and coyly let their fingers slide in against his neck and up into the curly hair above his collar. And he would wink at his friends and make little grunts of satisfaction like he was doing now.

Sari took an abrupt step back. She gathered up the towel in her fist and jerked his shirt back down into place with her other hand.

Jason turned his head. "You're done?"

"I should get back to Zack."

"Oh, okay," he said. "Well, thanks. That felt great."

"If it's still sore later, you could take some Advil," Sari said and went back to the kitchen, where she dropped the now cool towel on the counter like it was burning her fingers.

After that day, she would find Jason looking at her in a whole new way.

She'd be running with Zack outside, playing some kind of chasing game, and she'd glimpse Jason standing by the French doors, watching them with this new, curious, eager look on his face. Or, at the clinic, she'd be tickling Zack while they were playing a game and he'd try to tickle her back and she would roll a bit on the floor with him and then realize that Jason wasn't reading a book in the corner of the room like she thought but was just sitting there watching them, his head thrust forward, that look on his face again. And she'd scramble to her feet, suddenly uncomfortable in the room where she spent hours every day.

"I think Jason Smith is interested in me," Sari said. She and Lucy were sitting on her bed, cross-legged, knitting, homemade Manhattans in lowball glasses on the night table beside them. They were both a little buzzed but not completely blotto. Not yet.

"Of course he is," Lucy said. "How could he help but be? You're incredibly cute, and you're fixing his kid—"

"Zack Smith isn't *broken*, Lucy."

"You know what I mean. Substitute whatever politically correct term for it you want. Hey, do you have a measuring tape?" Sari fished one out of her knitting bag and handed it to Lucy, who spread her knitting on the bed and measured it. "Shit. It's nowhere near twenty inches yet. This sweater's going to take me the rest of my life." She rolled the tape back up, concentrating carefully as if the task were a challenging one, which it was, since she was tipsy. "Married guys must come on to you constantly when you're at work."

"It happens," Sari said, reaching over to the night table and picking up her glass. "Usually they're just kind of sad and pathetic and I ignore the whole thing and eventually they give up." She took a sip. "But this is different." She put the glass back down.

"Because he's cute?"

"No. No." She almost said "No" a third time, but she stopped herself.

"He's married, right?" Lucy leaned back against the headboard and resumed her knitting.

"Divorced. Or maybe just separated. I'm not sure. His wife was at the evaluation, according to the report. But I haven't seen her since then and he's said stuff about being a single dad." She poked at her knitting but didn't pick it up.

"What does he do for a living?"

"He told me once he's trying to be a screenwriter but I don't think he's ever sold anything. I know he coaches kids basketball at their local rec center."

Lucy snorted. "And you say he's not one of the pathetic ones?"

"He comes from money. And I assume his wife works. He doesn't *have* to earn a living."

"I still say he's kind of a loser. I mean, compared to what he was like in high school."

"Still good-looking, though. Even better-looking, actually."

"So why not go for it?" Lucy asked. "I mean, he's good-looking and available and you think he's interested. And he's definitely a huge step up from Jeff."

"He's an asshole, Lucy. Remember?"

"I didn't say you should marry the guy."

"Did we decide to stop having standards in our love lives?" Sari asked, hugging her knees to her chest. "Because I didn't get that memo."

"It's not about standards," Lucy said. "It's about having fun. The guy's good-looking, right?"

"What he and his friends did to Charlie—almost on a daily basis—" She couldn't even finish the sentence.

"All right then," Lucy said after a moment. "So let's remember that. That he was an asshole and worse to Charlie. So here's my super-brilliant idea: you sleep with him and break his heart afterward."

"Oh, please—" Sari said, but Lucy didn't let her finish.

"I'm serious. You make him fall in love with you and when he's good and overwhelmed and madly in love with you—because I think any guy would be if you gave him half a chance—you tell him you remember everything, and you tear his heart right out of his body and you leave him open and bleeding on the floor."

"That's a beautiful thought."

"It is, isn't it?" Lucy said without a trace of sarcasm. She put down her knitting and took a big gulp of her Manhattan, then gestured with the glass. A few drops flew out and onto her quilt. "You get it all then, Sari. You get to sleep with the best-looking guy who ever went to our high school and you get revenge for everything you and Charlie ever suffered. Tell me you wouldn't have dreamed about that ten years ago. Tell me that isn't everything you ever wanted."

Sari lay in bed that night, thinking about what Lucy had said, wondering if she could really do that—sleep with Jason Smith and then break his heart.

All her life she had tried to make up in some way for everything Charlie had suffered. The struggles he'd had just to communicate. The loneliness he must have felt when kids wouldn't sit next to him on the bus. The times he tried to smile at someone or worked hard just to say hello and only got a "What's your problem, retard?" in response.

Every choice she had made as an adult was about Charlie. And, in a weird way, about Jason Smith and all the Jason Smiths who had ever shoved Charlie or laughed at him or made Sari hate her own brother for letting himself be made fun of.

She once got so angry at him for always letting them humiliate him that she went after him herself—hit him as hard as she could, clawed at him with her fingernails, screamed at him that he had ruined her life by being autistic. She could remember him backing away from her, terrified, even though he was twice her size. All that night, she couldn't sleep, sick with shame and self-loathing. In the end, she had crawled into bed with him, hugging him and crying, hugging him and crying.

Her anger and her guilt—all the fault of Jason Smith and his friends.

She lay in bed now and wondered: would there truly be any comfort in revenge?

And immediately knew the answer. Of course there would. *Of course there would.*

3

Patterns

1

Sign me up," Kathleen said. "It's perfect." She hoisted herself, ass first, onto the edge of Lucy's kitchen table and sat there, long bare legs dangling—she was wearing shorts, a tank top, and flip-flops, even though it was a fairly cool October morning. "Tomorrow at work, I'll ask Kevin to sponsor me for Sari's autism walk, and then I'll try to get him to ask to come with me, and he probably will, but even if he doesn't, it'll still make me look all noble and caring."

"How gullible *is* this guy?" Lucy asked. "And get off my table. You'll break it."

Kathleen jumped down. "I need to jump-start this thing. I mean, it's not like we're *not* spending time together—so far, we've gone running twice, and he flirts like crazy. But he's got this girlfriend to get rid of and he's too nice a guy to just dump her. But if I take him on Sari's autism walk thing, I'm pretty sure I can clinch the deal."

"How romantic," Lucy said. "How long is the walk, Sari?"

"Five K. And afterward, they give us lunch. In-N-Out Burgers. And there's supposed to be Krispy Kremes and coffee in the morning before the walk."

"Woo-hoo," Kathleen said. "Krispy Kremes? I'm so there."

"I'm coming late and leaving early," Lucy said. "I don't want to eat that stuff but I will if it's right there in front of me."

"No, you won't," Kathleen said. "You never do. You only eat self-denial. What does that taste like, anyway?"

"Like chicken," Sari said.

"Yeah, well we can't all have your metabolism," Lucy said to Kathleen. "Or lack of willpower."

"Haven't you heard?" Kathleen said. "Willpower's out. Self-indulgence is the new willpower."

"That doesn't even make *sense.*"

"See if you can dig up anyone else to come, guys," Sari said. "They want as huge a crowd as they can get."

Lucy said, "I'll ask my lab partner. David. He's always doing charity stuff. I bet he'll go."

"Great," Sari said. "I've always wanted to meet him."

"You *have* met him," Lucy said. "You came to get me at the lab once a few months ago and met him. You guys talked for like ten minutes."

"Really?" Sari said.

"That's David's most remarkable quality," Lucy said. "He's completely forgettable. I work with him every day and *I* can barely remember him."

"Oh, wait—is he Asian?"

"Half Chinese, half Jewish."

"Okay. It's coming back. I do remember him. He's a nice guy."

"He's a nerd," Lucy said. "A nerd who's very good at killing rats. Not as good as I am, but very good."

"Excellent," Sari said. "It's a relief to know we'll be covered if any small animals attack us during the walk."

11

Back at her own place later that day, Kathleen let herself slide into a delicious Sunday afternoon nap on her airbed but was woken up by the buzzing of the intercom. Sam's state-of-the-art intercom was built into his phone system, but Kathleen hadn't bothered to get a line installed since she had her cell. Fortunately, the building's original buzzer system from the seventies still worked. Very loudly.

Since she rarely had visitors to her unfurnished apartment—and never before an unexpected one—Kathleen quickly shook herself awake and ran over to the speaker.

"Your father's here to see you," the doorman said.

"Oh, shit," she said, right into the intercom. "Send him up, I guess."

She turned and surveyed her living room. It stretched out in all directions, an enormous room with high ceilings and magnificent moldings, furnished with only a single twin airbed. Actually, Kathleen owned two airbeds, both bought at Bed Bath & Beyond for ninety-nine dollars each. One was in her bedroom and therefore her designated bed. This one was in the living room, so it served as a sofa and a place to nap. She also sat on it to eat, so it was her de facto dining room, as well. The actual dining room served as her soccer and field hockey playground. She had recently purchased a set of orange cones, which she used as goals for whatever sport she felt like playing and were currently arranged for soccer. Balls, pucks, bats, and hockey sticks lay scattered on the floor.

There was a knock on the door. Kathleen opened it.

Lloyd Winters wasn't alone. There was another guy with him, a younger one, with big brown eyes and longish hair. He wore an oversize sports jacket over a yellow mock turtleneck.

"There she is. My gorgeous baby girl." Lloyd approached her with his arms out. Kathleen crossed her own tightly across her chest and took a step back. He gave up on the hug but did manage to kiss the air near her cheek. "Kathleen, my beauty, this is Jordan Fisher. Jordan is not only a friend of mine, but one of the hottest young talent agents in Hollywood."

"Please, Lloyd," Jordan said, holding up a thin, self-deprecating hand. Then, to Kathleen with a smile: "He exaggerates." He held the hand out and Kathleen shook it briefly.

"Modest," Lloyd said, draping an arm across Jordan's shoulder. "Not like most of those conceited bastards. They'll sell you a line, but not this guy. Are you going to let us in, Kathleen?"

"I don't have any furniture," she said. "You'll have to stand. Or sit on the floor."

"Only Kathleen," Lloyd said with a laugh, steering the other man through the door and closing it. "She's an original."

"How would you know?" Kathleen said. "And why are you here?"

"To see you," Lloyd said. "Doesn't she look just like me, Jordan?"

"Just like," he said.

"The features are almost the same, but on her they make something beautiful."

"They really work," Jordan said.

"You haven't answered my question," Kathleen said.

"Can't a father come see his—"

"No, really," she said. "Why are you here?"

Jordan tossed his long hair. "You really cut through the crap, don't you, Kathleen? I admire that." And you really dish it out,

Kathleen thought, without any admiration at all. "Your father's been telling me a lot about you. A lot of very interesting and wonderful things. Do you know what he says about you?"

"That we barely know each other?"

The men laughed as if she had said something witty. "The greatest regret of my life," Lloyd said gallantly. He had gotten his hair cut very short recently—buzzed, really. It was starting to recede, and Kathleen suspected that this was his attempt to hide it.

Jordan put his hand on her arm. "Let me tell you what he says. He says that you're the true beauty of the family. The true talent, too. Not to disparage your sisters, who are lovely, lovely ladies. But we all know that the fact that they're identical twins has a lot to do with their success and—uh, may I be completely frank here?"

"Just get through it," Kathleen said, shaking off his hand.

"I think their identicality"—Was that even a word? Kathleen wondered—"blinded people to everything else. It was all anyone noticed about them—about all three of you, if you don't mind my saying so. And, in the end, I think their twinness overshadowed something far more appealing. Or should I say *someone*?"

"Someone, as in me?" Kathleen said.

Jordan smiled, showing teeth all the way back to the corners of his lips. "Exactly. She's quick, isn't she?" he said to Lloyd.

"Of course. She's my daughter."

"It really is astonishing how much she looks like you. She's tall like you, too, the lucky girl."

Kathleen walked over to a basketball that was lying nearby. She scooped it up and dribbled it a few times. It made a loud thud each time it hit the hardwood floor and the men turned to look. "Oh, sorry," she said, catching the ball. "I didn't mean to interrupt."

"You're probably wondering what the point of all this is," Jordan said.

"Not really," Kathleen said. She tossed the ball away and turned back to them. "I'm pretty sure I've figured it out. You think I should become an actress and you want to represent me."

"A star," he said. "Not just an actress. A star. Kathleen, I could take you places you never dreamed of. Features. TV series. TV movies. *Indies*. You name it, and together, we'll conquer it."

"Adult movies?" Kathleen said.

"Excuse me?"

"Oh, I just got the sense that with you at my side I'd end up in adult movies. Pornography."

Jordan looked thoughtful. "If that appeals to you . . . I mean, Jenna Jameson has certainly proven that's one road to stardom and while I don't know that world as of yet, I'm certainly open to—"

Lloyd cut him off. "Jordan's totally legit, Kathleen. He represents tons of actors. Kimberly Sostchen. Jersey London. Just to name a couple."

"I've never heard of them."

"Then you're not watching enough TV. They're both on major series and very hot right now."

"Good for them," she said with a yawn. "What agency are you with, Jordan?"

"My own. I started with William Morris but decided to go into business by myself. I just didn't feel like we were servicing our clients well enough there—there was too much bloat at the company. Know what I mean?"

"Uh-huh." She bet he had served coffee at William Morris.

And gotten kicked out for not remembering the sugar. No way this guy was a real player. Not with that turtleneck. Not if he was hanging out with Lloyd and coming to her apartment to try to convince her to do something she had no interest in doing, all because she had the same last name as her moderately famous sisters. She moved toward the door. "Well, thanks for all the compliments, but I don't want to act. Sorry. Better luck next time."

The men exchanged knowing smiles. Lloyd said, "I told you she'd take some persuading." He rubbed his hands together. "Fortunately, we both love a challenge, don't we, Jordan? So how about we go get something to eat? We can talk about it more over dinner."

"No, thanks," Kathleen said. "I'm exhausted."

"You're too young to be exhausted," he said. "Come on, sweetie—it'll be lady's choice—whatever you want. So what do you like? Sushi? Indian?"

"None of the above. I'm tired."

"I hear you. We'll do takeout." He gestured toward her shorts and tank top. "No need to worry about how you look."

"I'm not hungry," Kathleen said. "I just want to go to bed."

"I know what that made me remember!" Jordan said suddenly.

"What what made you remember?" Lloyd asked.

"That basketball. It just came to me. Someone told me recently about this huge movie they're doing. About a women's soccer team. Sort of an American *Bend It Like Beckham*, with a dash of *League of Their Own* thrown in. And they want to cast unknowns. You'd be perfect, Kathleen. With your athleticism and grace . . . I mean, *wow*."

"Now we're getting somewhere," Lloyd said. He took a step

toward the door. "I'll get us a bottle of wine. A bottle of wine and something to go with it."

"I could really go for some Mexican right now," Jordan said. "But not the greasy kind. Tacos al carbón. Something like that." He slapped his skinny stomach. "Got to watch my figure."

Kathleen said, "I don't—"

"If it's Mexican, I think I should get beer instead of wine," Lloyd said to Jordan.

"Oh, absolutely," Jordan agreed. "There's a place down the block—"

"Hold on," Kathleen said, but the men were discussing brands of Mexican beers and didn't seem to hear her. So then she said, "Excuse me," and dashed down the hallway to the kitchen and through the kitchen to the back stairs. She ran up quickly.

Sam's kitchen door was unlocked, as it usually was these days. She shouted for him as she stuck her head around the door.

"I'm right here," he said. "You don't need to yell." He was cooking at his stove. Something with onions and butter. It smelled good. He peered over his shoulder at her. "What do you want?"

"Help," she said, coming into his kitchen. "I need help."

"Why? What's wrong?"

"My father showed up with a creepy agent type and they won't leave me alone. They want to put me in porn. I can't get rid of them."

"Just tell them to leave."

"I've tried. They won't."

"So go be in porn. You wanted a career."

"Come on, Sam. Please. Help me."

"Do I have to?"

"Yes."

He sighed. "All right." He turned the burner off and shoved the pan across to a cool one. "I don't remember signing on as your personal bodyguard when I agreed to let you house-sit."

"I didn't know my father was going to start bringing creeps over to my place."

"You should never have given him your address."

"I didn't," she said, heading back down the stairs, with him following. "He's sneaky."

He followed her back through her kitchen and down the hall into the living room, where they found the two men kicking the basketball back and forth without much enthusiasm or ability. Sam said, "Hello, Lloyd."

Lloyd looked up and immediately strode forward, neatly sidestepping the rolling ball. "Sam Kaplan! Where the hell did you come from?"

"Upstairs." The two men shook hands.

Lloyd said, "Sam, Jordan Fisher. Jordan, Sam Kaplan. Sam's the real estate guy I was telling you about. Very big."

"Pleased to meet you," Jordan said. "*Very* pleased to meet you. Do you live here?" He looked at Kathleen. "With her? Are you—"

"No," Sam said. "I live upstairs and Kathleen just ran up because she wanted me to ask you both to leave."

"Excuse me?" Lloyd said.

"Kathleen's not interested in representation at this time."

Lloyd looked back and forth between them. "I don't know what Kathleen's been telling you, but we just wanted to have dinner and talk. No one was putting any pressure on her."

"You wouldn't leave," Kathleen said. "I told you I didn't want any dinner but you wouldn't leave."

"I'm sorry if you felt we were wasting your time," Lloyd said.

"I thought we were having a pleasant chat. I'm not sure why you felt the need to misrepresent the situation to my friend Sam here."

"Me neither," said Jordan.

"I apologize," Lloyd said to him. "I thought my daughter had manners. And some intelligence. Clearly, I was mistaken on both accounts."

"Yep, you were," Kathleen said. She opened the door and gestured toward it. "Now you'll know better. Goodbye."

As they went through the doorway, Lloyd turned and said, "I think you at least owe us an—"

She slammed the door in his face. "Idiots," she said. She turned and looked at Sam. "Thank you."

"You're welcome." As he headed back toward the hallway, he gestured around the living room. "I love what you've done to the place."

"It suits me."

"It also explains why you're always coming up to *my* apartment. Good night, Kathleen. I'm going back to my cooking. Unless you're expecting some more surprise visitors."

"How can you expect a surprise visitor?"

He laughed, then said, "Back to my onions." He crossed through the kitchen to the back door. Kathleen caught the door before it closed and held it open. Sam paused on the stairs to look back at her. "What?"

"I'm hungry."

He waited, his eyebrows cocked expectantly.

"It smelled good, what you were cooking."

There was another pause. He sighed. "Come on up, then."

She bounded up the steps to his side. "So," she said. "What are we having for dinner?"

III

"Well?" Lucy said. "What do you think of him? Kathleen's rich guy?"

"He seems nice enough," Sari said. She and Lucy were walking side by side along a dirt path, surrounded by scattered trees and bushes. A field to one side of them sloped down to a small man-made pond.

"Nicer than I expected," Lucy said.

"Kathleen wouldn't go out with a jerk. She may be mercenary—" Sari stopped herself. "I don't even think she's mercenary. Honestly."

"You just don't want to think badly of her. She's been pretty honest about what she's going for."

"Maybe she likes him," Sari said. "Maybe she really likes the guy, but it's easier to pretend she's only interested in his bank account—so she's not setting herself up to get hurt or embarrassed if it doesn't work out."

"The excuses you make for her—" Lucy gave a sudden lurch and swore, grabbing at Sari to steady herself. "Ouch, my ankle. Why didn't you tell me to wear sneakers?" She reached down to adjust her shoe, which had a narrow two-inch heel.

"I figured you'd know," Sari said. "It's a walkathon, for God's sake."

"Sneakers are for the gym," Lucy said. "I need a heel if I want my legs to look halfway decent."

"I've never seen Lucy in flat shoes," David said, coming up on Sari's other side. He had fallen briefly behind to look at a spiderweb. "She always dresses like she's on her way to a job interview."

"You should have seen her in high school," Sari said.

"No, he shouldn't have," Lucy said. "No one should have."

"Give me a break," Sari said. "You were adorable. She wore overalls every day," she told David.

"Overalls?" His eyebrows shot up.

"If you tell James that, I'll kill you," Lucy said. "And you know I can do it, because you've seen me sac a lot of rats. Sari, your days are numbered."

"I'm trying to picture Lucy in overalls," David said. "I just can't. It doesn't compute."

"It wasn't a pretty sight," Lucy said. "I was fat then and I guess I thought the overalls would hide some of it."

"You weren't fat," Sari said.

"Did she actually eat food back in those days?" David said. "Because she seems to have sworn off the stuff in recent years."

"I just choose not to eat around you," Lucy said. "The way you eat could take away anyone's appetite."

"Ouch," David said. "That one almost hurt."

"Don't be mean, Lucy," Sari said. "Not after David was so nice about coming today."

"I'm happy to be here," David said. "You couldn't ask for a more beautiful day."

Sari agreed, but Lucy said, "All right, you've successfully bored me out of here. I'm going to go see if I can get a feel for Kathleen's rich boyfriend."

"A feel for him is fine," David said. "A feel *of* him might annoy your friend."

"That was an example of the fine wit I get to enjoy for hours every day," Lucy said to Sari.

"Lucky girl, isn't she?" David said.

Lucy snorted and fell back to wait for the others, while David and Sari walked on.

"You guys always go at each other like that?" Sari asked.

"We're alone in the lab a lot. Shooting the shit helps to pass the time. It's all supposed to be good-natured." He shrugged. "But sometimes I think she gets a little pissed off at me for real."

"Lucy can be a little . . ." She groped. "High-strung. But she's a good guy deep down."

"Yeah, I know," David said. "She's definitely—" He stopped and left the sentence dangling.

After they'd walked for a little while longer, Kathleen came running up to join them. "Help!" she said. "Lucy's giving Kevin a hard time about some project his company's doing that she says is bad for the environment."

"Do you want me to go stop her?" Sari asked.

Kathleen fell into step with them. "Nah. I just wanted to escape. Kevin's fine. He can hold his own. And if he can't, maybe she'll make him think twice about destroying the environment, and it's not like that's a bad thing, right?" She reached up and pulled out her hair elastic and redid her ponytail without breaking stride. "Hey, either of you guys know why James didn't come?"

"I'm sure he doesn't approve of the organization," Sari said. "They support a lot of behavioral research and we all know what he thinks of *that*."

"Still," Kathleen said, "he could have come for Lucy. I think—" She was interrupted by a new voice calling Sari's name, and they all stopped and turned.

Jason Smith came running up, pushing Zack in a stroller. "I was hoping you'd be here," he said, a little out of breath. "We were late. I've been looking all over for you."

Sari stared at him for a moment. Then she realized everyone was waiting for her to say something, so she forced a smile, greeted him, and introduced him to the other two. Kathleen stared at him with frank appraisal, then caught Sari's eyes and pursed her mouth in a silent wolf whistle. Sari pretended not to see it.

Lucy and Kevin caught up to them as they stood there, and more introductions were made.

"Nice to meet you," Jason said, and Lucy said, "You've met me before. We went to high school together."

"Oh, right," he said uncertainly.

"I looked different then," Lucy said.

"She wore overalls and was fat," David added.

"Shut up," Lucy said.

"You said so yourself."

"I know I did. Shut up anyway. You look exactly the same, Jason."

"I'm a lot older," he said. "And I have this." He gestured down.

"A stroller?" Lucy said. "You must be so proud. Oh, wait, there's something in there." She bent down and peered in. "He's cute," she said.

"Thank you."

"What's your connection to the cause?" she asked, as if she didn't already know.

"Zack has autism," Jason said. "And Sari's working with him."

"*Are* you now?" Lucy asked her with deliberate staginess.

Sari could have killed her. "Yes, I am."

Kathleen said to Jason, "You're lucky. I bet Sari's amazing at what she does."

"She's better than amazing. She's a lifesaver."

"That sounds like our girl." Kathleen took Kevin by the arm. "Shall we walk?"

"I'd love to," he said, and they strode off together, well matched, both of them tall and healthy and good-looking.

Lucy watched them go and said, "I just can't get a sense of what he's really like."

"Maybe he's an android," David said. "Looks human but has no scent."

"Wow," she said. "You've actually reached new heights of nerdiness. And just when I thought you had no place to go but down." She beckoned to him. "Come on—let's you and me go smell Kevin, just in case." As they moved forward, she glanced back over her shoulder. "Hey, Jason, stick around after the walk. I want to see what you're like now. You were a real asshole back in high school, you know."

She took off, her heels leaving small neat holes in the dirt path. David shrugged apologetically at the other two and followed her.

There was a pause and then Sari said, "Uh," at the same moment that Jason said, "So I guess—" They both stopped and said, "Excuse me?" at the same moment.

"Let's keep walking," Jason said then, with a jerk of his head.

Sari nodded and moved forward, trying to conceal her discomfort. She knew her friends had deliberately left her alone with him, and she could have slit their throats for doing it so obviously.

After a moment, Jason said, "The funny thing is, 'Fat and wore overalls' did it for me. I remember her now."

"She wasn't that fat," Sari said, a little wearily.

"It was probably just the overalls. She's certainly not fat now. Not an ounce on her."

"No."

"Was I really an asshole?" he said. "Is that how people remember me?"

Sari searched for a response. "Do you care?" she finally said.

He gave a short laugh. "That answers that." She was silent and he said after a moment, "I mean, I know I wasn't a saint, or anything. I probably did some pretty shitty things. But it was high school. Who *didn't*? We were all just trying to impress each other, right? It was a crazy, awful time for everybody." Sari stayed silent. This wasn't a conversation she wanted to have with him. So she didn't say anything, just let him stumble along for a few moments and then gradually fade into silence.

The park was mostly empty, except for the autism walkers, who were strung out along the path. Ultimately, they would make a big circle, ending up back at the same wide grassy field where they had cut the ribbon to start the walk—which seemed very appropriate to Sari. Years had gone by and here she was, right back where *she* had started, hating Jason Smith and being aroused by his very presence.

Her silence went on for too long, and Jason said, "Everything all right?"

"I'm fine," she said. "I'm glad it didn't rain. We got good weather for the walk."

"I don't even know who the money's going to," he said. "And, to be honest, I didn't have time to get any sponsors. It's just . . . I saw a flyer at the clinic. So I asked Shayda if she knew whether you were going, and she said she thought so. So I came."

"It's a good excuse to take a walk," she said.

"It's a good excuse to see you away from the clinic."

Another silence. Then Sari said, "Zack's been awfully quiet."

Jason glanced down. "He gets that way in the stroller. Very mellow and relaxed. Sometimes, when the day feels like it's been endless, I just throw him in and we walk for hours."

She craned her neck to see into the stroller. "I think he might be asleep."

"I wouldn't be surprised. He was up at four this morning."

"Oh, man," she said. "That's too early. Did he go back to sleep?"

"Neither of us did."

"Does that happen a lot?"

"Constantly."

"You should have told me he was having sleep issues. We have some strategies for dealing with them."

"Really? Like what?"

"Like not letting him nap during the day," she said.

"*Now* she tells me." There was a pause. "I wasn't even supposed to have him today. Denise was. But she said she had to work. On a Saturday morning, she has too much work to—" He stopped.

"I'd like to meet Denise," Sari said. "Show her what we're doing with Zack."

"I tell her what I can," he said. "She's not with him enough for it to matter."

"Why isn't she?" Then: "I'm sorry. If you don't want to talk about it—"

"Are you kidding? I'm desperate to talk about it. I'm just afraid that if I start, I won't be able to stop. You may run away from me screaming."

"I doubt it." She instantly regretted saying that because it sounded flirtatious. But she was curious.

"We'll see," he said. "Anyway, the thing about Denise is . . . How do I describe her?" He thought for a moment. "Perfect. She's perfect."

"No one's perfect."

"Not her, then. Her life. Her *life* was perfect. Up until this"—he gestured down at the stroller—"everything in her life was perfect. First of all, she's really beautiful. We met in college and she was just the most—" He stopped. "Doesn't matter. She's beautiful, is all. And smart and talented and athletic and funny and basically just good at everything. So she figured she'd be good at the mommy thing, too. Better than anyone else. Meanwhile, I didn't even *want* a kid. That's the real joke of this whole thing. I didn't think I was ready." His mouth curled briefly into a humorless grin. "I'm sure you'll be shocked to hear I'm not the most mature guy in the world. Before we had Zack, I was still getting drunk a lot on the weekends and my career wasn't working out, but I kept thinking what the fuck, I was still young, I didn't have to grow up yet. But Denise just kept moving ahead. In every way she could."

"What does she do?"

"She's a TV executive. She started as someone's assistant right out of college and kept getting promoted like every six months. And now she has her own assistant. And treats him like shit, I might add." He swatted at a fly near his face. "Anyway, she talked me into having a kid. She said any child of ours would be amazing, and it seemed—well, it's obnoxious to say, but it seemed like a kid of ours probably *would* be."

"It's not obnoxious," Sari said.

"Yeah, it is. At any rate, she talked me into the whole thing. And when she got pregnant, she was totally into it. She did yoga and drank milk and basically just did everything right. And then Zack was born and he was a really cute baby—"

"He's still amazingly cute."

"Yeah, I know. But pretty soon things started being weird with him." He glanced at her. "You know how the story goes. And Denise just couldn't deal." He thought for a moment, the two of them walking in rhythm, his fingers tapping on the stroller handlebar like he was typing. Then he said, "No, that's not fair. She *tried* to connect to him at first, but he kept getting worse and eventually it was easier for her to just go to work and let me or Maria take care of him. And when he got diagnosed, I think it just—" He shrugged. "You know. She had always been this golden girl and now she was failing at something."

"It's not a question of failing," Sari said.

"Strangely enough, I got that," Jason said. "I didn't feel like I had failed. I just felt like I wanted to make it better. As soon as possible. But she . . . You know what she said to me before she moved out?"

"What?"

"She said she was too sensitive to stay. That it hurt her too much to look at him and know he'd never be like the other kids and that's why she *had* to go. Like the only reason *I* could stay with him was that I didn't care as much as she did."

"That's kind of bullshit," Sari said.

"Thank you for saying that. I've never— Uh, excuse me?" This last was to a guy who was kneeling on the pathway in front of them, tying his shoe. The guy jumped up.

"Sorry," the guy said. "Didn't see you. Oh, hey, Sari!"

"Jeff," she said, her heart sinking at the sight of her ex-boyfriend. "What are you doing here?"

"Same thing as you, I assume. The autism walk, right?" He kissed her on the cheek. "I was hoping I might see you here." He looked pretty much the same as the last time she'd seen him, his back shaped like the letter C, his hair still badly cut and combed all wrong—there was even a familiar sheen of greasy perspiration on his forehead. Fortunately, he no longer looked like she had just socked him in the stomach the way he had the last time she saw him, when she had broken up with him.

It was hard not to compare him to Jason, who stood a head taller, his shoulders wide under a simple V-neck black sweater, his thick hair tousled and wavy. When his eyes caught the sun, they were this unbelievable shade of blue . . .

Sari suddenly realized that both men were watching her, waiting for her to say something. "I didn't know you were involved with GRAY," she said quickly. GRAY stood for Get Rid of Autism Yesterday, the name of the organization sponsoring the event.

"Are you kidding?" Jeff said. "They've funded most of our research. I'm fairly certain I told you that." He had an aggrieved tone to his voice, like she owed him that at least—to remember things he had told her back when they were still going out.

"Oh, right," she said.

"So." Jeff stuck his hands in his pockets and looked at Jason. "What brings *you* here?"

Sari realized she had to introduce them. "Jeff, this is—" She hesitated. "My friend. Jason Smith. Jason, Jeff Fleekstra."

The men nodded at each other and then they started walking again, Sari sandwiched between the two of them and wildly furious at herself. Why had she made that little pause at the word "friend," the pause that everyone knew meant someone was more than a friend? Why didn't she just say that he was a dad at the clinic?

More important, why oh why was she so desperate for Jeff to leave them alone so they could talk more?

It was wrong, all wrong, and she knew it. So, while the two men exchanged pleasantries, she worked on pulling herself out of the daze she'd been in. Remember the history, she told herself. Remember who he is.

And, so, for the rest of the walk, she made herself remember.

IV

Arriving back at the field where they had started, Sari spotted Kathleen and Lucy settled under a shady tree. She headed their way, accompanied by Jason and his stroller. Jeff had split off at the finish line.

"Where are David and Kevin?" Sari asked when she reached the others.

"Getting food," Kathleen said with a nod toward the distant In-N-Out Burger truck.

Jason looked at Sari. "Should I go get something for us?"

"Don't feel you have to," she said. "If you need to take off or anything—"

"I've got time."

You could tell he was waiting for Sari to give him some kind of clue, let him know if she wanted him to stick around or not. But even her friends, who thought they knew Sari pretty well, couldn't figure out what the blank look on her face meant.

Sari said, "If you want a burger, you should certainly get one."

That seemed to be encouragement enough for Jason. "Actually, I'm starving. I'll go see what I can find." He left, still pushing the stroller.

Sari sat down on the grass and hugged her knees to her chest.

"God, he's cute," Kathleen said, watching him walk away. "Totally built. But he's got a kid. Does that mean he's married?"

"Divorced," Sari said. "About to be, anyway. But it doesn't matter. I'm not interested."

"Why not?"

"Lucy knows. He was a jerk to Charlie. Back in high school."

"Really?" Kathleen said. "He doesn't seem the type."

"Well, he was. I was thinking about it all just now, during the walk—about all the awful things they used to do. Like shove the food off of Charlie's tray at lunch. Or bump into him when he was carrying something and make him spill it on himself. Or stick his stuff in someone's locker and lock it in there. They'd throw water at his crotch and act like he'd pissed himself. Stuff like that."

"Assholes," Kathleen said.

"And they all called him 'retard.' Every one of them. Like it was his name." She imitated a guy's voice. " 'Hey, retard, you pissed yourself again.' "

"Fucking *assholes*."

"Once there was this assembly," Sari said. Now that she had started talking about it, she couldn't stop. "They brought out the kids with special needs—they were different ages but all went to class in the same room because that's just how they did it back then—anyway, they brought them out to sing a song. It must have been Christmas or something. So they bring them out and they're singing away and Charlie really loved to sing. Even before he could talk, he could sing. So I'm there with all the other kids, and I hear someone do this fake cough. You know—" She pretended to cough into her hand but the cough was the word "*retards*." "And then someone else does it and then pretty soon, all the kids in the whole auditorium are coughing 'retards' into their hands. And laughing. Even the kindergartners are doing it and they don't even know what they're *saying*."

"What happened to the kids onstage?"

"They just kept singing," Sari said. "Charlie was up there smiling and singing away. He didn't even notice what was going on."

"So maybe it wasn't that bad for him," Lucy said. "If he didn't notice—"

"Yeah," Sari said. "Maybe it wasn't that bad for him." She clasped her hands together below her knees. "But I was down there in the audience. I was down there in the middle of it. And I kept trying to get them to shut up and stop and everyone just laughed at me and kept doing it."

Kathleen shifted forward so she could put her arms around Sari. She hugged her close. "Fucking morons," she said. "I wish I'd gone to your school. I would have punched out every one of their fucking faces."

"You can't fight everyone," Lucy said.

"Where were you during all this?" Kathleen said, turning on her. "Why weren't you helping her make them shut up?"

"I wasn't even there," Lucy said. "I always tried to go late on assembly days. My mother was very understanding about that stuff."

"You were the smart one," Sari said. "Anyway, this guy—Jason Smith—he was one of them. I swear I can see him sitting there, coughing into his hand. That's why it doesn't matter how good-looking he is. He was one of them. And that's all he'll ever be, as far as I'm concerned."

The other girls were silent, but when Jason came back, long after the other two men had returned, all three of them watched him struggle toward them with the stroller and the bags of food and the cups of soda and not one of them moved to help him.

Kevin eventually noticed and jumped up to give him a hand.

V

Thanks for coming today," Kathleen said to Kevin, after he had walked her to her car. "You've officially achieved good-guy status with my friends."

"It was a pleasure," he said. "Really."

There was a pause. "Saturday afternoon," Kathleen said, glancing vaguely around the parking lot. "It feels like it should be later than one."

"All that walking," he said. "I was going to ask you to go running with me, but I'm too wiped out."

"I don't *just* run," she said. "I do other things, too."

"Ah," he said. "I'm glad to hear it. Do you go to movies ever?"

"All the time."

"And to dinner?"

"A girl's got to eat."

"Dinner *and* a movie?"

"Even better."

"I don't suppose you're free for something along those lines tonight?"

"I am," Kathleen said. "Are you?"

"Definitely."

"A week ago, you had a girlfriend. You mentioned it in passing."

"Yeah, well, a week ago, I did."

She waited.

He smiled. "Not anymore. Not as of last night."

"That worked out well," Kathleen said.

"It's not a coincidence." Then he said, "Those times we've gone running—"

Again she waited.

"I haven't wanted to stop."

"Well," she said. "It's good exercise."

"That's not what I meant."

"I know. So dinner and a movie tonight?"

"At least," he said.

That evening, after they had finished their entrées and were relaxing at the table, trying to decide if they were hungry enough to order dessert, Kevin asked Kathleen about her family and was genuinely surprised to hear she was related to the famous Winters twins. "I can't believe you never mentioned it before," he said. "You'd be an instant celebrity at work."

"And for all the right reasons," Kathleen said.

"Life is boring. People need thrills." He gestured to a waiter, who immediately came running over. Kathleen wondered if it was something they taught you in rich kid school—how to flick your finger just *so*. "Another bottle of wine," Kevin told the waiter. "Same kind." He settled back down in his chair. "So what's it like being a triplet?"

"Weird for *me*, because they were identical twins and I was the different one."

"Did you hate that?"

"Sometimes. My mom dressed us all alike when we were babies, and then one year I had different clothes but Christa and Kelly still matched. So I asked what happened and my mother said, 'Oh, honey, it's so cute on them but on you it just looks *wrong*.'"

"Ouch," he said.

"No, it was probably good, in the long run. If I had twins, I wouldn't dress them the same, anyway. People couldn't ever tell my sisters apart, and sometimes that really bothered them."

"How did they get into acting?"

"This agent stopped my mother at Target one day and asked her if she had any idea how valuable identical twins were in Hollywood. Especially ones that were small for their age."

"What makes twins so valuable?"

"It has to do with the child labor laws. Any individual kid can only work a certain number of hours, but if you have identical twins, they can both play a single role and double the number of working hours."

"Cool. But what was that about being small?"

"It just means they can play younger roles as well as their age."

"It's hard to believe," Kevin said, "that you have sisters who are on the small side."

"I know," Kathleen said. "But my dad's like a foot and a half taller than my mom and I look like him and they look like her. Kind of like if a Great Dane mated with a Chihuahua."

He laughed. "Sounds a little painful . . . Do you get along with your sisters? Does the Great Dane play nicely with the Chihuahuas?"

"Yeah, I guess so. They've actually always been pretty generous to me. They paid for me to go to college even though they didn't get to go."

"Why not?"

"They were stars already. No point. And they had been tutored—badly—on sets for most of their lives, so I think college would have been a disaster for them, anyway." She looked at him sideways. "How about you? Do you and your brothers get along? It's got to be complicated, working together every day like you guys do."

He dismissed the question with a quick wave. "It's fine. We get along fine."

The word around the office was that Kevin's relationship with his brothers *wasn't* fine, that the two of them had allied in a way that froze him out, left him an outsider in his own family's business. There were meetings he wasn't told about, client dinners he wasn't invited to, projects he never had a chance to weigh in on, information he was never given and looked foolish without. When Kathleen heard all this—Kevin had the office assistants' loyalty, if not his brothers'—she thought she'd found something they had in common. He, too, was the odd man out. Only now it seemed he wouldn't admit it.

Not *yet*, she reminded herself. It was just a first date. There would be plenty of time for confidences in the lengthy future she was planning for their relationship. She had to be patient—something, admittedly, she wasn't all that good at.

The waiter came over with their wine. He showed Kevin the label. "It's fine," Kevin said, without a glance. "Just pour it. I don't need to taste it this time."

The waiter moved off. Kathleen took a sip of wine and looked up to find Kevin studying her. She was wearing the gold tank top she had recently finished knitting and her hair was loose and wavy.

He said, "So what sports did you play in college?"

"Soccer mostly. But I swam during the off-season."

"For the school?"

"Just intramurally."

"When was the last time you swam?"

"Not since I moved out of the twins' house. Why?"

He leaned forward. "I was just thinking . . . I keep the pool heated at my place all year round. We could—" He stopped. "What was your fastest time?"

"Excuse me?"

"Your fastest freestyle time."

"Oh." Kathleen had to think about it. "I broke a minute in the 100. Once. I don't think I still could."

"That's pretty fast," he said. "And you look like you've stayed in better shape than I have."

"Are you asking me to *race*?"

He just smiled at her and beckoned the waiter over. Without taking his eyes off of Kathleen, Kevin said, "Check, please."

So they never finished the second bottle of wine, barely touched it in fact. Kathleen loved that he had ordered it but didn't care whether they actually drank it or not. The wastefulness of the gesture sang of wealth and power and indifference to the kinds of things other people spent their lives worrying about.

Kevin's house was smaller than the twins', but more impressive. The lot was so big, you couldn't even see his neighbors' houses once you had gone up the driveway. Inside, all the details were pricey, from the perfectly straight lines of the ceilings and walls—no moldings to cover mistakes and no mistakes to cover—to the vintage Eames furniture. It was clean and modern and architectural, manly and unfussy.

In the foyer, Kevin watched her as she looked around the place. "It's fantastic," Kathleen said.

"You really like it?"

"It's fantastic," she said again and meant it.

"Come see the backyard. That's my favorite part." Once he had led her through the house and out back, she could see why. The yard stretched in all directions, at least as far as she could see in the dark. Tiny lights were hidden among the bushes and trees, sparkling here and there like lightning bugs. "Hear that?" Kevin said. There was a faint tinkling-whooshing sound when Kathleen stopped to listen. "There's a creek down below—it's part of the property."

"Nice. We're not swimming there, though, right? You mentioned a heated pool."

"This way." He led her to a fenced-off part of the yard and opened up the iron gate. "My sister-in-law made me gate it," he said. "It kind of ruins the way the backyard looks, but she has little kids and wouldn't come visit until I did."

"Couldn't she just tie her kids to a tree when she comes over?"

"Somehow I don't think she'd go for that."

"You're just too nice to suggest it." Kathleen walked over to the edge of the water and knelt down. She put her hand in. "Warm."

"Eighty-eight degrees. It feels even better when you get your whole body in."

"Which reminds me." She stood up, wiping her wet fingers on the side of her black silk pants. "I don't have a suit."

"Hold on." He walked down the length of the pool to a row of small cabanas at the far end. He opened the door to one and vanished inside, then reappeared with something dangling from his fingertips. "It's a bikini. Those are one size fits all, right?"

"Not exactly," Kathleen said. She took the scraps of fabric from him and held them up to the moonlight. "But I think it'll work. Slightly better than being naked, but not much." She dropped her hand. "Someone wasn't afraid of a little exposure. I don't think I want to ask whose it is."

"My ex-girlfriend's," he said. "Does that bother you?"

"Not nearly as much as it would her," Kathleen said with a grin. "Come on. First race is to see who can get changed faster."

They emerged from separate cabanas at around the same time. Kevin was wearing longish board shorts that came down to about his knees. His stomach was slightly soft above the waistband but otherwise he looked good. He wasn't too hairy or anything disgusting like that, and his legs and shoulders were strong. Kathleen definitely approved of what she saw, and, from the expression on his face as he checked her out, she was pretty sure he did, too. It was a pretty skimpy bikini, and she knew she filled it well.

"Okay," Kevin said, gesturing to the pool. "We freestyle to the shallow end, push off, and breaststroke back. First person to touch the wall wins."

"Got it," she said. "Ready, set, go." She dived in neatly and beat him back by a couple of seconds. She clung to the pool edge, catching her breath, as he emerged.

"No fair," he said. "You dived before I was even ready."

"Excuses, excuses. I'm just faster than you." Her legs cycled gently in the warm water. The cool air tingled on her dripping hair and face. The moon was almost full, and she could see Kevin's face clearly.

"I get another chance," he said.

"I'll beat you again," Kathleen said.

"No way," he said. "No way a girl can beat me if I'm ready."

"Those are fighting words."

"I know." He grabbed on to the wall. "That's the point. And I call 'ready, set, go' this time."

"Fine," she said. "I'll still win."

But she didn't. He won by a full body length. As she emerged, he was already at the edge, his free arm raised in victory, the moonlight shining on the drops of water along his shoulders. "Oh, yeah, baby! Now who's the better swimmer?"

"Best two out of three," Kathleen said.

He won again. "God, victory is sweet," he said. "You wouldn't know, of course."

"Do you always gloat?" she asked.

He faced her. They both clung to the wall, their hands a few inches apart, their breath coming in gasps. "Only when I have to fight this hard to win."

"Made you work hard, huh?"

"Yeah," he said. "But it was worth it. I won, didn't I?"

"Just a race," she said. Their bodies moved closer in the water.

"Just a race," he agreed. He reached his free hand out for her and she let herself float toward him. For a moment, they stayed like that, his hand against the small of her back, their legs moving in the water, hitting each other softly. It was so quiet, they could hear the sound of the tiny waves they were making just from treading water.

His hand moved higher up her back and slid under the string of the bikini top, then stayed there, growing warm against her skin. Kathleen let the water carry her against him. She tilted her face up and he put his mouth against hers. The taste of chlorine disappeared into the sweeter wetness of their mouths.

A few minutes later, Kevin lifted his head from hers. His eyes caught the light and glinted.

"Come on," he said, his voice thick. "It's time to get out and dry off."

VI

James called Lucy on her cell around nine that evening. "Dinner?" he said.

"I ate already." Actually, she had eaten a carrot and nine cashews, which, she realized, was only a dinner by her standards (she counted the nuts as protein), but she didn't really want to open the door to eating again. No temptation, no risk of giving in. She was always aware of those forty extra pounds, which, she was sure, were just biding their time in some kind of fat limbo, waiting for her to let down her guard so they could reconvene around her ass and thighs.

Besides, it was kind of late for James to call about dinner. She didn't mind being alone on a Saturday night, but she did mind his assuming she was sitting around waiting for him.

"Okay," James said cheerfully enough. "But can I come see you?"

"Yeah, okay." She was definitely up for some sex.

"And can I bring a pizza?"

"If you want." She wished he wouldn't though—she liked pizza and wasn't sure she'd be able to resist it completely.

Maybe she'd just chew on his crusts.

As soon as she'd hung up, she threw herself into the shower, scrubbed herself down, shaved her legs, underarms, and bikini area, shampooed and conditioned her hair, dried herself off, moisturized her skin, plucked her eyebrows, dried her hair, put on a little makeup, and donned a silk camisole and lounge pants outfit that was both elegant and sexy.

Men, she thought, regarding herself critically in the mirror, were a lot of work.

James, of course, blew in wearing a pair of old jeans and a T-shirt—clearly the same clothes he'd had on since that morning—and sporting some five o'clock shadow. It wasn't fair, Lucy thought and not for the first time.

Still, he looked all right. The stubble suited him. He had the scruffy urchin thing going for him.

"Where's the pizza?" she said as she let him in.

He hit himself in the forehead with the palm of his hand. "Oh, shit, I forgot it. I'm starving, too. Anything here I could eat?"

"Let me see." She went into the kitchen and opened the fridge. There wasn't room for both of them in there, so James leaned against the door frame and watched her. "Eggs. Oh, and leftovers from the Chinese food we had last week."

"Do you think it's still good?"

"I don't know." She opened a container and sniffed. "Smells okay."

"You know how to make an omelet?"

"Of course."

"Heat up the stir-fry, toss it into the omelet, and we'll call it a dinner." He rapped his knuckles against the wall. "So how was the walk this morning? Sorry I couldn't make it."

Lucy put the carton of eggs on the counter. "Couldn't? Or wouldn't?"

He smiled, unashamed. "Let's just say didn't."

"It was fun. Free food, too."

"Did they make a lot of money?"

"I don't know," she said. "Do you care?"

"If it's money that would otherwise have gone to research, possibly."

She got a bowl out, cracked four eggs into it, tossed the shells into the sink. "David came, you know."

"To the walk?" He shrugged. "I'm not surprised. Probably didn't have anything better to do."

"Don't be so sure. He's got a girlfriend now."

"Really?"

She nodded, whisking the eggs. "He said he was going out with a girl tonight."

James laughed. "That's a date, not a girlfriend. And after she spends an evening enduring the famous David Lee sense of humor, she'll be running for the hills." He shifted against the wall, then reached into his pocket and started rattling his change.

Bored already, Lucy guessed. "You want to watch TV while I finish this up?" she asked, as she turned back to the refrigerator for the margarine.

"Sure." He was gone.

By the time the eggs were done, he had already moved on from watching TV to checking his e-mail on her computer.

"Anything interesting?" she asked, putting the plate down at his elbow and resting her hand on his shoulder.

"Just the usual hate mail about how I'm some kind of crazy serial killer."

"I think it's sweet your mother keeps in touch."

"Seriously, look at this." He gestured at the screen. "Apparently I'm going to hell because I don't know that animals have souls."

"That's only one of the reasons you're going to hell," Lucy said.

"Do you think they'd feel differently if I told them I don't think humans have souls, either?"

"Probably not."

He signed off and turned toward her. "I keep changing my screen name, but they find me every time. It's got to be someone with university access. I'm sending this to the police, see if they can trace it."

"Is it really worth all that?" she said. "It's just a stupid e-mail."

"It's a hate crime. Punishable by law."

"Poor baby," she said, ruffling his hair. "The object of hatred wherever he goes. What is it about you that makes people hate you so much?"

He trapped her hand in his, and pressed it against his cheek. "I don't know. I think I'm pretty lovable. How about you? Do you think I'm lovable?" He pulled her down onto his lap. "Give me a kiss, Luce. I need someone to be nice to me."

She struggled to sit up. "Eat your eggs before they get cold."

"Yeah, all right, I'll eat the eggs. But after that . . ."

She slid off his lap. "After that, what?"

And there was that grin again, the grin that made her face turn hot and her hands cold.

Fortunately, he was a fast eater.

VII

"What, no wedding band?" Lucy said when Kathleen finally swept in the next morning, over an hour late, to Sari's apartment. "When you didn't show up, I figured you were off in Vegas sealing the deal."

"I sealed the deal," Kathleen said. "It just depends on how you define the deal."

"There was sealing?" Sari said, looking up from her knitting.

"Lots of sealing," Kathleen said. "We had a blissful night of nonstop sealing."

"You guys are too cute for words," Lucy said.

"Clearly, someone here needs a good sealing," Kathleen said to Sari, who laughed.

"If you're referring to sex," Lucy said, "I've been there, done that. Very recently, in fact."

"Just rub it in, why don't you both?" Sari said.

"Sorry, Sar," Kathleen said. "So what is there to eat? I'm starved." She pounced on the dining room table. "Oh, good—muffins. Are these banana? I love banana." She bit directly into the top of the muffin without even peeling off the paper. "Yum. Sealing makes me hungry. So how is everyone? What'd I miss?"

"Do you talk with your mouth full when you're with your millionaire?" Lucy asked.

"Sure," Kathleen said. "But not when it's full of *food*."

It took a moment and then Sari dropped her knitting so she could throw a sofa cushion at Kathleen. "You're disgusting."

Kathleen blocked the pillow with her right arm. "She asked."

"There's something seriously wrong with her," Lucy said. "Hey, Sari, can you help here? I'm finally starting on the front of the sweater, but the pattern's not coming out right."

"Let me see." Sari put her own knitting down on the sofa and went over to squat by Lucy. Kathleen wandered over, unwrapping her muffin, and looked at the knitting Sari had just put down. "I love this," she said. "This shade of blue. That's going to be one lucky baby." She stuck another piece of muffin in her mouth.

"Don't get crumbs on it," Sari said, looking over her shoulder. "Where's your knitting?"

"I don't have it with me. I came straight from . . . not home."

"You should keep it in the car so you always have it," Lucy said. "That's what I do. You never know when you're going to have to waste time waiting for someone at a restaurant or something."

"Kevin drove," Kathleen said. "He dropped me off here, so I don't have my car, anyway. But, you know, you're right—I should have just brought it to dinner last night and knitted all through dinner and then taken it with me to Kevin's house. I could have kept it right there on the night table when we were having sex. That way, if I got bored while he was, you know, pounding away—"

"You don't think Kevin might have taken offense?" Lucy said.

"Probably wouldn't even have noticed. He's a guy, isn't he?"

Sari was still looking back and forth between the instructions and Lucy's knitting, trying to figure out what was going on. "You know, Luce, as far as I can tell, you *are* doing this right."

"It looks weird."

"Yeah, but maybe it will look right after a few more rows. Sometimes it takes a while for the pattern to make sense."

"Or to see that you've been doing it all wrong from the start," Kathleen said.

"Right," Lucy said. "That's what I'm afraid of."

"Have faith," Sari said. She sat back down and picked up her own knitting. "Sometimes you just have to keep going and hope it's all going to come out right."

"Sounds like a philosophy for life," Lucy said.

"Nah," Sari said. "In knitting, you know someone made the pattern, so a little faith is justified. In life"—she shrugged—"not so much."

VIII

You ever wonder what it would be like to have that much money?" Kathleen asked. She let the Sunday *New York Times Magazine* slide from her hands to the floor and stretched out full-length on the sofa.

Sam peered over the top of the Business Section at her and said, "I know where you're going with this and you might as well stop right there."

"Why? Nothing wrong with a little harmless daydreaming, is there?"

"There's nothing harmless in what you're doing. You're thinking maybe you really could snag Kevin Porter and his bank account, and I don't see any good coming out of that train of thought."

"I am not," Kathleen said. She reached down and picked up the magazine again but only flipped through it idly, looking at the pictures. Sam's sofas were exceptionally comfortable, and Sunday afternoons, after the knitting circle, she often made her way up to his den, where she could leaf through the *Times* and doze comfortably on some real furniture. Sometimes she even brought her knitting with her and settled in for a good long stay. Sam had a large flat screen TV and a satellite feed. "A nice guy with a lot of money is not a bad thing," she said after a moment.

"They should stop telling little girls the story of Cinderella," Sam said. He turned a page. "It ruins them for life."

"My mother married for love," Kathleen said. "It was a disaster. I'm not going to make the same mistake she did. If I ever get married, it'll be for the right reasons."

Sam lowered his paper. " 'The right reasons'? You mean like because he's loaded? Oh, that's noble." He rolled his eyes. "Kathleen, just because your mother was too stupid or too young to realize that Lloyd Winters was an ass doesn't justify your chasing after men for their money."

"I'm not chasing after anyone," Kathleen said. "I'm sitting here—"

"*Lying* here, with your filthy feet on my sofa—"

"Sitting here, very relaxed, having a conversation with my upstairs neighbor. All I'm saying is that it's good to be practical about these things."

Sam folded the Business Section neatly in half. "Have you ever met Kevin's sisters-in-law?"

"Briefly," she said. "They come by the office sometimes."

"And? What are they like?"

"Pretty awful. They boss people around and always look like

they just ate something bad and can't get the taste out of their mouths."

"Do they seem happy?"

"God, no."

"Doesn't that tell you anything?"

"Yeah," she said. "Cinderella's got built-in evil stepsisters."

"Maybe they weren't always evil," Sam said. "Maybe they're just so miserable, they've forgotten how to be pleasant."

Kathleen considered that. And rejected it. "Nah, I think they were probably miserable to begin with."

"I see. So you would be different if you married into that family?"

"Of course I would. For one thing, I wouldn't spend all my time shopping. From what I've seen, that's all they ever do. And even *I* know there's more to life than that. I mean, it's important, but there's more to life."

"You think that's why they're unhappy? Because they shop too much? You think it has nothing to do with the men they married?"

"Kevin is nicer than his brothers. Everyone says so."

"Sure, he is," Sam said. "Nothing like them at all. Why would he be like those guys just because he shares their genes and was raised in the same household and works with them on a daily basis? So . . . You're not shopping all day long. What *are* you doing with the Porter fortune and all your free time?"

"I don't know," Kathleen said. "Maybe using it to help people somehow." She wasn't sure she believed that, but Sam had a way of getting her to say things in self-defense that she wouldn't normally say.

"Kathleen Winters, philanthropist? Patron of the arts?"

"I wouldn't use those exact words, but, sure, I'd be interested in supporting stuff. Why not?"

"Well, the fact that I've never known you to set foot in a

museum or concert hall, for one thing. You're like every other kid in your generation—you think because you've seen a couple of independent films, you're the artsy type. But you're really a philistine. You have no genuine interest in 'stuff.' "

"I never claimed to be artsy," Kathleen said. "Or classy, or anything like that."

"Good," he said. "Because classy and gold-digging don't go together."

"I like the sound of that," Kathleen said, wedging a pillow under her neck and closing her eyes. "Gold-digging. It sounds so twenties. Speaking of which, weren't you in college right around then?"

"Grade school," he said. "If you're going to fall asleep, Kathleen, go back to your place. Last week, you drooled all over the sofa and the cleaning lady couldn't get the stain out."

"No, I didn't."

"See for yourself—it's still there. Get out before you do it again."

She sat up and swung her bare feet around, which were admittedly—as Sam had pointed out—not as clean as they might have been. "You keep throwing me out of here and I'm going to think you don't want me around."

"Gee, that would be a real shame." He picked up another section of the newspaper and unfolded it with a snap. He didn't even glance up when Kathleen said goodbye. Then again, he never did.

But this time she stopped in the hallway that led to the kitchen, turned around, and came back toward him. "For your information," she said, "I really like Kevin Porter. I wouldn't be going out with him if I didn't. I'm not like that."

"You keep telling yourself that," Sam said and turned another page of his newspaper.

4

Increases

11

The following week, whenever Jason Smith brought Zack to the clinic to see her, Sari did her best to ignore him without being unprofessional about it. Whenever they arrived, she looked only at Zack, waving Jason off into the corner of the room. Before they left, when she had to go over with him what they had worked on, she spoke quickly and didn't let him pull her into any small talk.

She could tell Jason was hurt by her behavior—but then he had walked in already hurting on Monday because she, Kathleen, and Lucy had all but frozen him out at the post-walk picnic lunch, wouldn't look at, acknowledge, or talk to him, until he had finally excused himself and set off toward the parking lot, struggling to push the stroller over the uneven grass. Which kind of broke Sari's heart when she thought about it. So she didn't think about it, because she didn't want to soften toward him.

There was one moment, on Tuesday, when Zack said, "Look, Sari! Jumping!" and pointed to a picture of a leaping frog in a pop-up book, and she was so excited that she turned to grin at Jason in triumph before the quickening in his eyes made her regret it. She turned back to Zack and said quietly, "Way to go, buddy. The frog *is* jumping."

* * *

That Friday afternoon, when Jason opened the front door to let her in, she barely greeted him before asking for Zack.

"He's out back," Jason said. "I was trying to get him to play basketball with me."

"That's good," Sari said. "The more regular boy stuff like that he does, the better."

"Yeah, only he won't do it. He's terrified of the ball. Every time I try to show him how to hold it and shoot, he hides his face and cries."

"Maybe it's too hard," she said. "The ball, I mean. Basketballs can really wallop you. You should try something softer, like a Nerf ball."

"I have. It doesn't help. He's still scared."

"Let me work with him on it. It would be good for him to play a sport."

"You really are a full-service establishment," Jason said. "Language, behavior, leisure activities . . . Is there anything you *don't* do?"

She just shrugged and moved toward the back of the house.

Jason followed her. "You know I coach basketball, right? At the rec center?"

Sari nodded and kept walking.

He sped up to be by her side. "Well, there's this kid who comes on Saturday mornings. He's not even five yet, but he totally gets the game. Totally gets it. He can pass and dribble and consistently make baskets—he's the only kid his age I've ever met who can do all that. He's amazing." They had reached the back door. Jason tugged it open and held it for her.

Sari walked through and looked around. Zack was spinning

slowly in circles on the driveway at the side of the yard. There was a basketball hoop over the garage door.

Jason was next to her again. "Anyway, I thought Zack would be like that. I thought he'd be great at sports. Denise and I both played a lot in high school and college. So I figured a kid of ours—" He stopped.

"He'll learn," Sari said.

"I don't even know why I care so much about whether or not he can play sports," Jason said. "It's stupid. I mean, the kid can't even talk or look people in the eye. What difference does it make if he can throw a ball or not?"

"Different things matter to different families," Sari said. It was disturbingly easy to talk to Jason when she didn't have to look at him. "I was working with a kid once and he couldn't talk, wasn't toilet-trained, spat at people—was just a mess. And his mother said to me, 'Please, *please* can you teach him to sit through a movie'? She had always pictured herself taking her kid to Disney movies, only he was scared of sitting in the dark. She wanted that before anything else. It just mattered to her. It's okay if basketball matters to you."

"Everything matters to me," Jason said. "I want him to play basketball and I want him to play soccer and I want him to talk like other kids and I want him to go with me to Disney movies. And about fifty million other things. I'm greedy, I guess."

"Be greedy," Sari said. "Want things for him. It's the greedy parents whose kids progress the most."

"Look at him," Jason said. "Balls and games all around him, and he just wants to turn in circles. I've tried taking him to some of my classes, but he always pulls shit like that, and the other kids think he's weird. And I end up mad at him. That's pretty awful, isn't it? I get mad at my own kid for being autistic. Like it's his fault."

Sari wished she didn't know what he meant, but she used to get furious with Charlie because she couldn't make him understand that if he just acted normal, other kids would leave him alone.

"Give him time," she said to Jason. "He'll learn to play just like the other kids."

"It's funny—" There was a red playground ball on the ground near Jason, and he rested his heel lightly on it. "Here I am, desperate for him to be like other kids. But if you'd asked me before he was born, I'd have said I wanted my son to be different from everyone else, to stand out in a crowd." He rolled the ball under the arch of his foot. "Be careful what you wish for, I guess."

He suddenly kicked the ball as hard as he could. It flew over the grass of the backyard and hit a tree, which shook from the impact.

The sudden violence of the kick startled Sari, but she tried not to show it. "I'll see if I can get him interested in making a basket," she said.

"Can I help?" Jason said.

"No, thanks. We're fine." She walked away from him and went to Zack.

Later that afternoon, Sari tried to convince Zack to touch his tongue to a piece of steak.

Maria had arrived at five and set to work preparing Zack's dinner—pasta with butter. Sari, who had been just about to leave, stopped to ask some questions about Zack's diet. Under questioning, Maria reluctantly admitted that toast, pasta, bagels, and Cheerios were pretty much all he ate. Sari asked if Maria ever offered him other foods and she said she used to, but he never ate any of them, so she had stopped trying.

"We've got to work on this," Sari said.

"He eats healthy," Maria said. "He drinks milk and juice. And not too many cookies. I don't give him too many cookies or candy."

"That's great," Sari said. "But he needs to be eating meat and chicken and cheese and fruits and vegetables. How much of those does he eat?"

"Not *so* much," Maria said. "Bananas, sometimes."

The kitchen smelled good—far better than boiling pasta ever did—and Sari looked around, sniffing. "What else are you cooking?"

"Steak," Maria said. "For my dinner." Adding quickly, "It's fine with Jason."

"I'm sure it is," Sari said. "When it's done, I'd like to have Zack taste it. From now on, I don't want you to give Zack the food he already likes until he's tried a taste of something new. It's enough for him just to put his tongue to it. But he's got to try."

"He eats healthy," Maria said again.

"Tell me when the steak's done," Sari said and planted herself at the kitchen table.

Zack had been standing in the doorway humming to himself during the exchange and now came into the kitchen and climbed into the chair across from her. His right hand came to rest, palm down, on the table. Sari leaned forward and put her hand on top of his. Zack instantly moved his hand away. Sari covered it again. This time, Zack gave a little giggle and when he moved his hand, he glanced quickly at her. Sari covered his hand again with hers. Zack chortled. They did this a few more times and then Sari put *her* hand flat on the table. "Your turn," she said. She waited. Zack looked at her sideways, then darted his hand forward and put it on top of hers. She covered it with her free hand. "Got you!" she said, and he exploded in laughter.

"That's good."

Sari looked up to see Maria standing next to them, watching, a plate in her hand.

"It's nice to see him laughing with you," the housekeeper said. She put the plate down in front of Sari. There was a small piece of steak on it. Maria also handed her a fork and knife and napkin.

"Thank you," Sari said, arranging it all on the table. "This is perfect."

"He won't eat it," Maria said. "Meat makes him do this—" and she made a retching sound.

"Oh, good," Sari said brightly. "Let's model gagging for him."

"I'm just telling you."

"Well, *don't*. Not in front of him." She turned to Zack. "Okay, my friend." She cut off a tiny bit of steak, then stuck a fork into it, and held it up like a steak popsicle. "One taste of this and you get a plate of delicious hot buttered pasta. You want pasta, don't you?"

He grunted and rocked.

"I'll take that as a yes. Taste the steak and you get your pasta." Sari held the fork out to him and he didn't move. "Come on, Zack. One little taste. Just a lick." She moved the steak closer to his mouth but he clamped his lips shut and pulled his head back, away from the fork.

That's when Jason walked in. Sari hadn't seen him since dismissing him from the basketball court. He stopped at the sight of her. "You're still here?"

"I wanted to help with dinner," Sari said.

There was no mistaking the look of renewed hope on his

face. He came closer. "Is that steak? Zack won't eat that. He hates meat."

"He'll learn to eat it," Sari said. "But not if people keep reminding him he doesn't like it."

"Sorry."

"It's okay. But I do want to see him trying new foods. The best way to get him to do that is to wait to give him what he wants until he tastes something he doesn't usually eat. I'll show you what I mean." She turned her attention back to Zack. "Lick the steak, Zack, and then it's pasta time." She put the steak lollipop close to his lips. This time, he gagged audibly. "Come on, buddy. One little taste." She pretended to put it in her own mouth. "Like this. And then you'll get your pasta." Zack shook his head.

Jason was watching intently, standing right next to her. He smelled like a mixture of musk and fresh sweat.

It wasn't a bad smell.

Sari snuck a covert glance up at him. His T-shirt was damp at the armpits and chest, and his arms looked even more cut than usual. He must have been working out somewhere in the house.

He was frowning down at his son. "I don't know why Zack chose to become such a determined vegetarian. I'm sure it was for some deep, spiritual reason."

"Maybe he's just worried about mad cow disease," Sari said.

"Ha. That's one of Denise's nightmares. She ate a hamburger in London years ago and whenever she has trouble remembering something, she's convinced her brain is turning to soup."

"Does she still eat meat?"

"Only if it's grain-fed and organic and all that." He went over to a cabinet and opened it. "It's cocktail hour, isn't it? Anyone care to join me? Sari? Maria? Zack?"

"Hear that, Zack?" Sari said. "If you lick the steak, Daddy will give you a martini."

"I wish you'd stop saying 'lick the steak.'" Jason poured some vodka straight into a small glass. "It's the closest I've come to having sex in months."

Sari laughed out loud before she could catch herself. No one said anything after that for a moment. She looked at Maria to gauge her reaction, but the housekeeper was just standing at the counter, stolidly cutting and chewing her steak.

Jason went over to the refrigerator and pressed the ice button. Two pieces of ice slipped out; Jason caught one, but the other landed on the floor. Jason ignored it, just dropped the one he'd caught in his glass and sat down at the table with Sari and Zack. Behind him, Maria walked over, picked up the piece of ice off the floor, and threw it in the sink.

"Maria?" Sari said. "Would you please get Zack's bowl of pasta ready and bring it over? Maybe he'll be more inspired with it in front of him."

The incentive worked, in a way. Zack was so eager to eat the pasta that he screamed for a minute in pure frustration when Sari held it out of his reach and continued to insist he put his mouth to the steak. Finally, furiously, he touched his tongue to the steak, then retched violently.

"There you go," Sari said. "And here's your pasta." She set it down in front of him and his fury instantly vanished. He plunged happily into the pasta, tears still wet on his face.

"He couldn't really have *tasted* that," Jason said.

"You'd be surprised," Sari said. "Each time you offer him something, he'll be a little more comfortable with the idea, and he'll let himself taste it a little more. At some point, he may even decide he likes it. If you keep it up, I promise you his diet will expand. You just have to insist for a while." She looked over her shoulder to include Maria. "You *both* have to."

"We will," Jason said.

"Remember—he doesn't get anything he already likes without trying something new first." Sari pushed her chair back and stood up. "I've got to go."

Jason followed her to the front door and, as she shouldered her backpack, he said, "Look, I don't know how—" He stopped. "I was just wondering—" He stopped again with a short awkward laugh. Then he said, "It's just that Maria's here for the rest of the evening, and I don't have any plans. I was wondering—hoping—that maybe you'd come get a drink with me. Or dinner. Whatever you want. Would you? Please?"

Sari felt a flash of pleasure and triumph. Jason Smith was asking her out on a date. And he was nervous about it. Her fifteen-year-old self squealed with joy. Then she remembered she wasn't fifteen anymore.

She said, "Thanks. I can't." She sounded rude. She decided that was a good thing. "Goodbye," she said and reached for the doorknob.

Jason put his hand flat against the door so she couldn't pull it open. "Wait," he said. "I'm sorry. But I just have to ask. Did I do something to make you angry? I feel like maybe I said or did something—" He paused, took a breath, started again. "Maybe at the walk? Please tell me. The last thing I'd want to do is offend you in some way."

It almost came out then. Did he really want to know how he had offended her? She thought of the stories she could tell, of the times Charlie had been humiliated and insulted and hurt in a million different ways by Jason and his friends.

But if she told him that, he would probably apologize, say he was sorry he'd ever been such a stupid kid. Then she would end up saying something conciliatory, like it was okay, she understood, it was all in the past . . . She didn't want to be conciliatory. She wanted to be angry. She *needed* to be angry.

So she smiled at him and said, "Don't be silly. You haven't offended me at all. And I don't want to offend you, either, so please understand—this kind of thing happens to me all the time. In fact, it happens to everyone who works at the clinic. Sometimes, unfortunately, people misinterpret our concern for their kids—read more into it than is actually there." She tilted her head with a little sigh. "It's no one's fault. Just a little misunderstanding."

"Oh," he said. His face was turning red. "I'm sorry. I thought—" Once again he stopped.

"You don't have to be sorry," she said. "And please don't be embarrassed. Like I said, it happens all the time. And, really, I think it's very sweet of you to ask me out." She knew the word "sweet" would kill him. "But this is just a job for me. Even though I come to your house. You get that, right?"

"Of course," he said, stepping back from the door. "Of course."

"All right then," she said with a deliberately fake heartiness. "I'm glad we got that all out in the open."

He just nodded, not looking at her.

"So I'll see you Monday?" she said.

"Yeah, all right."

He couldn't close the door behind her fast enough.

She had totally humiliated him. She should feel good about that—revenge was supposed to be sweet, wasn't it?

But it was Friday night and she had no plans. She'd end up knitting row after row of that stupid baby blanket while she watched crappy TV and sipped at a glass of cheap wine. All by herself.

That really sucked.

11

Kathleen wasn't spending much time in her apartment. After work, she was either out with Kevin or at his house. She stayed over a lot of nights, and even when she bothered to come home, it was only to sleep.

It wasn't until she ran into Sam Thursday morning in the parking garage of their building that it occurred to her it had been a couple of weeks since she'd last seen him. He was dressed in a suit and tie and looked tired and grim as he walked toward his car.

Kathleen was heading *into* the building from the opposite direction, wearing the same tight electric-blue dress she had worn the night before to a club—when it had made sense to be wearing a low-cut dress that showed an almost indecent amount of her long lean thighs. She ran to catch up with Sam.

"Hey," she said from behind as she reached him.

Sam turned around. "Kathleen," he said. "Now I understand why I haven't seen you in a while." He nodded toward the dress as if it explained everything.

Kathleen put her chin up and said, "I've been busy."

"I can see that. Are you going into the office later? Or have you stopped doing that?"

"Of course I'm going in," she said. "I'm still working."

"Oh, I didn't say you weren't *working*," he said. "You're clearly working hard." He inclined his head politely and walked off.

That night, she and Kevin had a quiet tête-à-tête at a small, extremely expensive Italian restaurant in West L.A. where everyone who worked or ate there seemed to know him by name, and then they went back to his house, where they soaked in the hot tub for a while, which of course ended with them wrestling under the sheets together, and then Kathleen told him she had to go back to her apartment. "I need a good night's sleep," she said, sliding off the bed and on to her feet. "And some clean clothes."

"You should leave stuff at my place," Kevin said. He was sprawled on the bed, where the rumpled Frette sheets bore witness to their recent activity. "I've got a whole second closet I only use for tuxedos and ski clothes. It's mostly empty."

"Thanks. I'll think about it." Kathleen pulled her dress over her head.

"Want me to come with you?"

"You don't want to. The place is just a big empty mess."

"How can it be empty *and* a mess?" he asked.

"I don't know," she said. "It just is."

When she got home, it was even worse than she had remembered. Since she'd mostly been using the apartment as a big walk-in closet, clothes were tossed all over the place. A lot of them were dirty—after years of living with a housekeeper, she was having trouble getting used to doing her own laundry.

She pushed enough stuff off of her "bed" to clear some space for herself and went to sleep.

She woke up early the next morning, hurled herself into the shower, threw on a pair of decent black pants and a sweater (worn once or twice since the last dry cleaning, but not noticeably dirty), and raced up the back stairs. Sam's kitchen door was locked. She pounded on it. He might have already gone to work, she thought, and pounded harder.

Suddenly, it opened.

"What do you want?" He was wearing plaid pajama bottoms and a T-shirt. "It's eight o'clock in the morning."

"I thought you left for work early," she said. "You were already heading out this time yesterday."

He ran his fingers through his rumpled gray and black hair. "I had an early meeting yesterday. And it almost killed me. I'm not a morning person."

"I'm getting that sense," she said. "Anyway, you're up now. I'll run out and grab us some bagels and coffee."

"Are you treating?" he said.

"Sure."

He yawned. "Be careful, Kathleen. Don't go spending money you don't yet have. The prenup alone could cost you all sorts of setbacks and legal fees."

"You know what?" Kathleen said. "I'm sorry I asked. Forget it." She turned around and headed back down the stairwell.

"Sesame bagel and black coffee," he called after her. "Very hot."

By the time she returned, he had showered and put on his suit pants, socks and shoes, and a crisp white shirt.

He seated himself at the marble half-circle table and Kathleen thunked down the cardboard cups of coffee and two paper-wrapped bagels in front of him. She sat down. Sam immediately got up again with a sigh of disgust. He went to the cupboard and took out two plates, then made a big show of unwrapping each bagel and arranging it on a plate. He frowned when he unwrapped his. "Jesus, Kathleen, what the hell's on this?"

"It's lox spread," she said. "I thought you'd like it. I do."

"Disgusting," he said. "Nitrates mixed with fat."

"It tastes good. But if you don't like it, scrape it off."

"Not worth it. I'll eat something at work." He dropped the bagel on the plate and left it on the counter, picked up his coffee, removed the plastic top, and threw it out in the wastebasket under the sink, then poured the coffee into a mug. He threw out the paper cup, returned to the table, sat down, and finally took a sip of coffee. "You're quiet," he said.

"I'm waiting for you to drink your coffee. There doesn't seem to be much point in trying to make conversation until then."

"True." He took a few more sips, then looked at her over the top of his mug. "So," he said. "Everything going well?"

"Fine."

"I'm assuming that your continual absence in your own apartment reflects well on the success of your current pursuit?"

She shrugged. "I go out with Kevin a lot, if that's what you mean. In fact, tonight we're supposed to go to some big fund-raiser. His dad's being honored."

"What's the charity?"

"I don't know."

"Good for you," he said. "Girls shouldn't worry their pretty little heads with boring details like that."

"Oh, who cares?" Kathleen said. "One charity is pretty much the same as another."

"Your embrace of your own ignorance never ceases to impress me," Sam said and took another sip of coffee.

"Don't be such a dick," she said. "I need your help. You're a bigwig type—"

"Says who?"

"Kevin. He says you're a shark."

"Really?" He looked pleased.

"I bet you go to things like this all the time. Tell me what I should wear—I'm going to be sitting with the Porters and I don't want to make a fool of myself."

"Now *that's* what your pretty little head should be worrying about. What to wear."

"It said 'black tie' on the invitation. Does that mean I have to wear like a ballgown? Or just a really nice dress?"

He flung out his hand. "How the hell would *I* know what a girl your age should wear when she goes out at night? Go pick up a copy of *Cosmopolitan*."

"You could be a little more helpful," Kathleen said.

"No, I don't think I can." He took another sip of coffee. "Anyway, why worry? Your fairy godmother will take care of the dress for you."

"Actually," Kathleen said. "When you think about it, *you're* my fairy godmother. I mean, you gave me the apartment and the job. And that's how I met Kevin—"

"Your Prince Charming."

"The shoe fits," she said. "No, wait, it's Cinderella's shoe that fits." She shrugged. "Whatever. You know what I mean."

Sam shook his head. "I can't wait for your happily-ever-after," he said. "It's going to be so fucking miserable." He raised his coffee cup and smiled. "Cheers."

III

It was rare for Lucy to spend the night at James's apartment, because he lived like a slob and Lucy had standards about that kind of thing, but they had dinner on Thursday night together at a Cuban restaurant that was close to his place and served extremely strong mojitos, and after a few of those they staggered back to his apartment and fell into bed together and had some drunken sex and then more or less passed out for a while, and by the time the alcoholic stupor had worn off and she had woken up again, it was three in the morning and Lucy wasn't about to get into her car alone in Larchmont Village at that hour, and since James was sound asleep and snoring, she just sighed and tried unsuccessfully for several hours to go back to sleep.

Finally, there was daylight, and Lucy slipped out of bed.

James's bathroom was just this side of disgusting—she suspected he cleaned it about once a year—but the shower was nice and strong. Since she had to wear her clothes from the night before, she was glad she had changed right before dinner—the plain black pants and dark blue silk shirt she had worn to the restaurant were unstained and fine for work.

It was still pretty early, so she stopped at Starbucks. She looked wistfully at the scones behind the glass as she poured a thimble of nonfat milk and a package of Splenda into her coffee.

She parked in the garage under the building. For once she would beat David to work—normally he was there when she walked in, already pounding away at his computer or changing the rats' litter. Whenever he pointed her relative tardiness out to her, she, in turn, always pointed out that he wore an old T-shirt and jeans to work every single day and that she actually made an effort with her own appearance, which took time. "Yeah, well there aren't enough hours in the whole year to make *me* look decent," he said once with a sigh and that successfully silenced her.

Lucy rode the elevator up from the garage and headed toward their corridor. She rounded the corner and saw someone at the lab door. Her first thought was that it was probably some kind of delivery that she'd need to sign for, so she was already speeding up when she realized that no, it wasn't a package, that the girl was putting something on the door, and then the girl had turned and seen her and there was a moment when neither of them moved, and then something about the panic in the girl's eyes made Lucy realize she couldn't just let her go, so she ran toward her and the girl scrambled away in the opposite direction—only then she must have realized she'd left her messenger bag leaning against the door because she hesitated and looked back, and in that moment Lucy had already caught up to her and didn't even need to see the "THERE'S BLOOD ON YOUR HANDS" sign hanging crookedly—the girl had only succeeded in tacking up one corner—to know she had just captured the *Enemy*.

The Enemy was short, blond, a little on the pudgy side, and about twenty years old.

"You hurt my arm," she said, cradling her elbow against her chest. She was sitting in a chair in the lab all hunched up inside the big black man's peacoat she was wearing.

She had twisted and fought when Lucy first grabbed her arm, and, since she was both frantic and determined, had succeeded fairly easily in breaking free of Lucy's grip—but Lucy had the foresight to turn and snatch up the girl's bag, and the girl stopped a few steps away, torn between escape and retrieval. Lucy had said—in as reasonable tone as she could muster between gasps for breath—"I'm going to know your name and where you live in a minute, so there's no point in running away," and so, with a heavy step, the girl had followed her into the lab and waited, sullenly, for whatever was going to happen next.

Lucy dumped the contents of the girl's bag onto the desk. Papers, Sharpies, tubes of lip balm, keys, tissues, loose coins, and a wallet all fell out, followed by a can of spray paint, which then rolled off the desk and onto the floor.

She opened the wallet. "Hey, look—a student ID. That's helpful." She studied it briefly, then looked up. "So how are you liking UCLA, Ashley? I see you're living off campus." No response. "So what kind of name is Skopinker, anyway? Russian?" The girl was silent. "Ukrainian?" Ashley just glared at her. "Polish, maybe? Am I at least right to focus on Eastern Europe?"

"You can't do that," the girl said. "That's my stuff. It's illegal to go through someone's stuff without a search warrant."

"It's also illegal to pour paint on people's cars and send hate mail through the Internet," Lucy said. "Maybe you and I should cut each other some slack."

"You don't need to cut *me* any slack," Ashley said. "I'll be fine. It's the rats I'm worried about. Look at them, locked up in those tiny cages. Waiting to be slaughtered. Don't you have a heart? Or at least a conscience?"

"They love their cages," Lucy said, with a brief glance over in that direction. "They're fed, they're warm, they have company—"

"Until you kill them."

"It's a very fast, painless death. It's not like life is so great for a rat on the street, you know."

"I bet they'd be willing to take that chance," the girl said. "How about we set them all free and see whether or not they come back to their cages?"

"They'd die in a couple of days," Lucy said. "Their adrenal glands don't function."

"Holy shit," the girl said. "What have you *done* to them?"

"They were born that way."

"Bred that way, you mean." The girl shook her head and her long blond hair swung first one way and then the other. It really was beautiful hair, Lucy thought. Too bad she was carrying around some extra weight, because the girl had potential. If she just lost twenty pounds and did something about her skin . . .

"It's scientific research," Lucy said. "Ever heard of it? It's led to a lot of cures for a lot of people. For animals, too. In fact, Addison's disease is more common in dogs than in humans, and it's one of the—"

The girl cut her off. "There are ways of doing scientific research without torturing and killing harmless animals."

"You're right," Lucy said. "We could use college students instead. You want to be our first volunteer?"

The girl got up from her chair and walked over to the cages. "Poor little things," she said. "What kind of a creature is man that he can do this to other animals without even feeling guilty about it? *We're* the ones without souls, not them." She poked a finger in one of the cages and made little cooing noises for a while. Then she turned back to Lucy. "Have you ever bothered to get down on their level and look them in the eyes, ever even *tried* to see the intelligence and the humanity—for want of a better word—that's in there?"

"Actually," Lucy said, "believe it or not, I'm what you might call an animal lover. But I'm also a realist. Sometimes you have to kill a rat to save a human life, or two, or three thousand, and that's a choice I'm willing to make."

"Easy for you to say. You haven't asked *them*." She gestured toward the rats.

"They're welcome to perform medical experiments on humans, as soon as it occurs to them to do so. And they get a grant from the NIH."

"How can you say you're an animal lover? You think because you pet dogs now and then, that means you care?" She shook her head in sincere disgust. "If you really loved animals, you wouldn't just go and kill a few every week without even thinking twice about it—"

"No, not without thinking about it," Lucy said. "I think about it all the time. And then I go ahead and I kill them because it's ultimately the right thing to do."

"How can you say that?"

"Because it is. Choices aren't always easy, Ashley."

Ashley snorted. "That's what evil people always say. You start with small animals, then why not kill bigger ones? And while you're killing bigger animals, why not kill off sick or weak humans? And, if you're going to kill *them*, why not kill the ones you decide are inferior to you? Because they're like a different race or religion or something? And then, of course, you'll have to kill anyone who doesn't agree with you—"

"Don't tempt me," Lucy said.

"It's not funny," Ashley said. "Life is valuable. *All* life. Can't you see that?"

Before Lucy could respond, the door opened and David walked in. "Did you see the sign on the door?" he said. "I was thinking we should leave it up there for a while just to— Oh, hi. Who's this?"

"This is Ashley," Lucy said. "She's the one who put the sign there."

"Ah," David said. "Is she also the one who's been dumping paint on James's car?"

"I'm guessing," Lucy said. They both looked at Ashley. She folded her arms tightly across her chest and stared at the wall.

"It's not that I don't think James deserves it," David said, sitting down at his desk. "For all sorts of reasons. Like—see that coffee cup over there? He left that, right on my papers and they're all stained now, thanks to him. A slob like that deserves to have some paint thrown on his car. But he doesn't deserve it because he does animal research. That's to his credit."

"Are we done?" Ashley asked Lucy. "I'd like to get out of here. Can I have my bag back, please?"

Lucy appealed to David. "What do you think? If James were here—"

"He'd want her head on a platter," he said. "But it's kind of a young head. And James can be a little . . . overreactive."

"Yeah, I know." Lucy turned back to Ashley. "Listen, if I let you go right now, will you promise to leave us all alone and go bother someone else?"

"Preferably in a different building," David said.

Ashley scowled. "I haven't admitted to anything yet. Maybe I don't even know what you're talking about."

"Okay," Lucy said, pulling a pad of paper toward her. "Here's the deal, Ashley. I'm writing down your name and address. If I find more signs or any of our cars gets covered with paint again or if we receive any more nasty e-mails, I will call the university administration and the police and tell them who's responsible. Do you understand?"

"You don't have any proof," Ashley said. "And even if you did, I'd have to do what's right, no matter what the risk."

"Yeah, well, if I were you, I'd make sure vandalizing research labs really *is* what's right before I went and got myself arrested for it." Lucy tossed everything that had fallen on the desk back in the bag, then bent down and picked up the can of spray paint off the floor. "This, I'm not giving back to you," she said and threw it in the trash can. "No good can possibly come of your having a can of spray paint. But you can take the rest and go."

Ashley warily darted forward, snatched at the bag, and ran to the door. "Think about what you're doing," she said. "Think about the pain you're causing these animals just because you're bigger than they are. Think about how you'd like to be treated if—"

"Think about the police coming to your door," David said.

She shot him one last look of pure hatred and then was gone, slamming the door behind her.

David raised his fist in the air. "Vive la résistance!" he said cheerfully.

"Yeah, right," Lucy said. "Do you think she thinks she's some kind of hero?"

"Definitely."

"Someone should tell her about rats and the bubonic plague."

"Someone should *give* her the bubonic plague." He stared at the closed door. "Although, it was kind of a relief meeting her—she wasn't exactly an angry mob, was she?"

"She could have friends."

"Or just crazy nuts on the Internet who encourage her to do this shit." David leaned comfortably back in his chair and crossed his ankles up on top of his desk. "So . . . do we tell James?"

"Better not," Lucy said, feeling a little guilty even as she said it. "We can always tell him if she does something else."

"Do you think she will?"

"Now that we have her name and know she goes to school here, she'd have to be pretty stupid to target us again." Lucy bent down and opened up one of her desk drawers. "Want some dried cranberries?"

"Sure." She carried the bag over and poured a bunch into his outstretched palm. "It must be nice," he said, gazing absently at the berries in his hand.

"What?" She put a single cranberry in her mouth.

"To be like that girl. To feel like you're one hundred percent right and everyone else is wrong. To be willing to sacrifice yourself for a cause without ever questioning whether it's really worth sacrificing yourself for." He tilted his hand and let the cranberries fall into a pile on his desktop. "Nothing ever seems that clear-cut to me."

"I know," she said. "To me, either."

They chewed away in thoughtful silence and finished off the bag of cranberries before getting down to work.

IV

Kathleen settled on a cocktail-length, thin-strapped, body-hugging black dress for the fund-raising event that night.

"Wow," Kevin said when she slid into his car. "You look amazing." He leaned over and kissed her hard on her open mouth. Lingered there a moment. He sat back and took a deep breath. "Maybe we should run upstairs. Think I could leave the car here?"

"Not without getting towed." She pulled the seatbelt across her body.

He drove away from the curb with a good-natured sigh of acceptance. He glanced at her a couple of times as he drove along Wilshire. "You have truly beautiful breasts, you know that?"

"They do what they need to."

"Except . . . something's missing."

She looked down at herself. "One. Two. Same as always."

"Dress like that needs a necklace. And I know where to get one." And, with those words, Kevin Porter drove straight to Rodeo Drive and Tiffany & Co., where he bought Kathleen a beautiful and delicate necklace that was, admittedly, sterling silver and not diamond-encrusted, but still cost several hundred dollars and was, for a spur-of-the-moment kind of thing, a touching gesture.

Kathleen was pleased. The only tiny—minuscule really—jarring note for her was that Kevin had chosen to take her to Tiffany, which was where Jackson Porter bought all the gifts for his mistresses. The man actually kept a cache of filled small blue boxes in a locked drawer in his office for ready access.

And that nagged at her. Surely there were other decent jewelry stores in Los Angeles.

When they arrived at the fund-raiser—held in the biggest ballroom Kathleen had ever seen, in one of the swankiest hotels in Beverly Hills—Kevin led her to where his family stood in a knot. They all said hello and then ignored her.

Which left Kathleen free to sip some decent champagne and absorb everything that was going on around her. She and Kevin were among the youngest people at the event. No surprise there, since the honoree that evening was Jackson Porter, who was nearing seventy, and most of the guests were his contemporaries. Besides, a single ticket cost five hundred dollars, and a table went for five thousand, and Kathleen couldn't think of a lot of people her age who could afford to spring for something like that, even for a good cause.

Assuming tonight's charity *was* one, of course. She still didn't know what it was. The signs that hung around the room all read, "In a Parallel Universe . . ." which didn't enlighten her at all.

Kevin's two sisters-in-law were gorgeously turned out that evening, one in Armani black, the other in Prada crimson. Their dresses were almost severe in their simplicity, but tailored and draped beautifully, and the extravagance of the jewelry they wore complemented the spare lines of their dresses. In the past, Kathleen had thought both women were too thin—scrawny, really—but tonight their evening finery made the prominence of their bones seem elegant rather than sickly.

While she was standing there, she heard the sister-in-law in black say to the sister-in-law in red, "You are so brave to wear that color. You know—this year, when no one else is."

The other narrowed her eyes and said, "Oh, I just grabbed

what I could. The kids don't give me a second to get ready. I'm *sure* you'll understand someday. I mean, I *hope* so." From this, Kathleen inferred the one in black was having fertility problems.

Kevin's brothers greeted him with pleasant enough claps on the shoulder and then immediately took their father aside and started whispering to him, freezing Kevin out of the discussion. Kevin just smiled affably at their backs and made some comment to his mother about the turnout. She dipped her head an inch—a nod of agreement, Kathleen assumed. That done, Caro Porter retreated back to silence, smiling vaguely at some distant object while she clutched her champagne glass to her chest with one bony hand.

The fog in her dull blue eyes and her halting speech hinted at artificial sedation. Kathleen, who waved goodbye to Jackson Porter every day as he strode out of the office at noon, reeking of cologne and often tucking one of those small blue boxes into his breast pocket, had nothing but sympathy for Caro's choice to reject clarity.

After an hour or so of this standing around and drinking, someone flashed the lights in the room. None of the guests paid any attention to it. The lights flashed again. This time, there was a subtle murmur throughout the crowd—which then went back to talking and drinking. A waiter refilled Kathleen's glass.

Then someone—hotel staff, Kathleen assumed—called out a personal appeal for people to move toward the dining room. He was ignored, but a little while after that a guest with a booming voice called out that they were already way behind schedule and wouldn't be out before midnight at this rate, and the threat of that finally got people moving.

When they reached their table, Kevin and Kathleen sat down, but Kevin's brothers waited, standing, until their father joined them, and then they maneuvered him into a seat between the two of them. Caro sat down on Kathleen's empty side and the two wives sat next to their husbands. Wine was poured and Caro raised her glass.

"To the poor children," she said wearily, and they all drank.

Kathleen thought Caro meant her own kids for a second, and then realized that she was referring to the recipients of that evening's fund-raising efforts.

Kathleen had been to many social events in her life, but never one that reeked of wealth the way this one did. There were at least three waiters to every table and they were always hovering, refilling glasses and clearing and bringing plates. The room was decorated with wreaths of flowers and candles that cast a flattering warm glow and made the ropes of jewels on the women all around her sparkle brightly.

Cinderella was at the ball.

Funny thing—so was the fairy godmother.

There was a steady stream of tuxedoed men paying their respects to Jackson all during dinner, so at first Kathleen didn't even look up when one more came—and then she heard his voice. And there was Sam Kaplan, clasping Jackson's hand and saying something she couldn't quite catch that had Jackson shaking his head with a rueful smile.

Kathleen was surprised and a little annoyed. Sam hadn't told her he was coming, even after she'd mentioned the event that morning.

Kevin had once said something to her about how his father admired Sam, and there seemed to be some truth to it: Jackson had risen to his feet and was listening intently to whatever Sam was saying. He nodded his head in agreement at the end. They did that guy thing of shaking hands while clapping each other's upper arm, and then Jackson gave him a little salute and sat back down between his older sons.

Sam greeted the rest of the family as he circled around the table, kissing the air close to all the women's cheeks and shaking all the men's hands. "Just wanted to say hello," he said when he reached Kathleen and Kevin. He and Kevin shook hands. "Kathleen," he said with a nod of greeting. Apparently she didn't rate an air kiss.

"Oh, right," Kevin said, leaning back in his seat to include them both. "I forgot—you two already know each other. You're how we *got* Kathleen."

"I'm how she came to work at Porter and Wachtell," Sam said. "You got her all on your own, buddy."

Kevin smiled.

Sam said, "You must be proud of your father this evening." Kathleen was so used to his armchair insults that it was a surprise to realize he could actually be as polished as the next guy when he was out at a social function.

"I am," Kevin said. "I absolutely am."

Sam raised his hand. "Have fun, kids," he said and walked away. He shook a couple more hands and cuffed a few more shoulders before returning to Table Eight, where he sat down next to a young woman with roughly cropped hair that was dyed a bright copper orange. The girl immediately leaned over and whispered in his ear.

Kathleen stared at them. She had been living under Sam's apartment for several months but had never once seen a female go in or out—and here he was at a major social event with a total babe.

A waiter placed a salad in front of her, blocking her view. She quickly devoured the small salad, and then noticed that none of the other women at her table had eaten theirs.

She felt Kevin's hand on her leg under the table and smiled at him. He turned and said, "Hey, Mom, did you know that Kathleen's a triplet and her two sisters are movie stars?"

"How nice," Caro said, and raised her wineglass to her lips.

"Yeah," Kevin said. "Christa and Kelly Winters. They're huge."

"Really?" Caro said. "How interesting."

From her other side, the sister-in-law in red said, "I've heard of them."

"Have you?" Kathleen said.

"Yes. My little girl made me take her to one of their movies once." One eyebrow was crooked derisively, daring Kathleen to ask her whether she liked it, but Kathleen knew better and was silent.

The waiters cleared the salad plates. Kathleen shifted restlessly in her seat. She looked over at Sam's table. He was saying something to the girl next to him. She tilted her head in consideration, and long, heavy earrings flashed at her neck. A few minutes later, Sam rose to his feet and moved across the room. He stopped at a table to talk to someone.

Kathleen pushed her own chair back abruptly. "I need to go to the ladies' room," she said.

"Do you know where it is?" Kevin said.

"I'll find it."

He rose as she stood up. He was polite that way.

She said, "Excuse me," to the rest of the table, but no one seemed to notice.

She made her way across the room, and after Sam had finished chatting with the people at Table Twenty-seven, she darted forward and cut him off before he could go back to his own seat.

"Kathleen," he said and gave her a quick up and down look. "Nice dress."

"Why didn't you just tell me you were coming to this, you jerk?"

"You didn't ask. Are you having a good time?"

"It's okay. You let me go on and on this morning—"

"How much wine have you had?" he asked.

"I don't know. A glass or two." Or three or four. "Why?"

"You look drunk. Your face is red."

"Whatever," she said. "*You* certainly look like you're enjoying yourself."

"Do I?"

"Who's the girl at your table?"

"The girl?"

"Sitting next to you. With the bright orange hair—she's kind of hard to miss."

"Oh, her. Beautiful, isn't she? She usually comes with me to these kinds of things. Takes pity on an old man."

"What's her name?"

"Joanna," he said and Kathleen could have kicked him. Or herself. Joanna was his daughter. She had seen a couple of photos of her around his apartment, but they were all at least several years old, and most of them were of her as a little girl. And she didn't have copper hair in any of them. Kathleen had stupidly assumed she was still an adolescent with undyed hair.

She glared at him. "Why didn't you just say that in the first place?"

"And ruin your excitement? You were so sure you had discovered some hidden scandal in my life—ancient Sam with his little thing-on-the-side."

"You're not married," Kathleen said. "You can't have a thing-on-the-side."

"Whatever," he said, just like she'd said it a few seconds earlier. Making fun of her.

"Can I meet her?"

"If you like." He led the way back to his table.

Up close, Kathleen could see a tiny bit of a resemblance—her nose was long, like his, and she was thin like him, too. She was prettier, though, than you would have expected Sam's daughter to be—not that he wasn't a handsome-enough man in his own hawky, severe way, but she had a delicacy about her features that definitely came from some other source.

Sam introduced Kathleen, and Joanna said, "Oh, the girl who's staying downstairs." Her eyes were light blue—another surprise, since Sam's were so dark—and heavily made up in shades of bright green. Her ears were pierced in four different places. The tarty look suited her, made her look oddly more innocent underneath it all. It helped that she was so young. She gestured at the room. "This is nice, isn't it?"

"Kathleen is here because she cares so deeply about the cause," Sam said. "Have you figured out what it is yet, Kathleen?"

She shrugged. "Something about poor kids."

"'Something about poor kids'?" he repeated with a snort.

"Don't let him get to you," Joanna said. "He's always trying to make me feel like a moron, too."

A woman on the other side of Sam's chair cleared her throat, and he stepped back to include her. "Oh, excuse me. Kathleen Winters, Patricia Kaplan."

"Also known as my mother," Joanna put in helpfully.

Patricia held out a beautifully manicured hand, and Kathleen shook it, a little surprised. She hadn't realized Sam still saw his ex-wife socially. "How nice to meet you," Patricia said. She was a handsome woman, an older version of Joanna, really, with a smaller build and a more elegant presentation. She wore her honey-blond hair in a simple twist at the back of her neck. "Sam was just telling us about your apartment."

"He said you don't have any furniture and you play soccer on the empty floor," Joanna added.

"It's not as crazy as it sounds. I didn't know how long I'd be there so I never really moved in. And with all that extra space—"

"Might as well play ball?" Joanna said with a grin.

"I should have gotten a security deposit from you," Sam said to Kathleen. "It just occurred to me you're probably destroying the floors. I'll have to get them refinished."

"They're fine." She had no idea if that was true or not—she wasn't the kind of person who went around examining floors for scratches.

Several waiters converged on the table with trays of food.

"I should go back," Kathleen said, and the women said goodbye.

Sam walked a few steps with her. Kathleen looked across the room. Back at her table, Jackson was shaking his head with an impatient frown at something the oldest brother was saying, and the middle brother was looking triumphant. Caro was smiling pleasantly at a distant wall sconce. The sister-in-law in black had completely turned her back on Kevin, who was playing with his fork, pushing down on the turned-up tines so the other end rose up like a seesaw.

"Have a nice evening," Sam said and turned to go.

"Wait," Kathleen said.

"What?"

"Don't you think it's a little weird?"

"What?"

"Hanging out with your ex-wife. People aren't supposed to go out with their exes."

"Why the hell not?"

"It's just weird, that's all," she said. "My parents are divorced and they can't stand each other."

"Right," he said. "Your parents. Those stellar examples of a healthy lifestyle."

"People get divorced because they don't want to be together."

"I married Pat because I enjoyed her company," he said. "That hasn't changed."

"Then why'd you divorce her?"

"That's the topic of a much longer discussion than I'm prepared to have at this moment," Sam said. "Or probably ever, with you."

"You don't have to be a jerk about it," she said. "It was a legitimate question."

"Good night, Kathleen," he said. "I suspect I'll see you soon."

He put out his hand, but Kathleen just walked away without taking it. She didn't know why she was so annoyed at him, but she was.

She came over to the table and collapsed ungracefully into her seat. Her main course was already there and waiting for her, the chicken and rice steaming gently.

Kevin picked up his fork and said, "You were gone forever."

"Long line," she said and stabbed her knife savagely into the chicken breast.

V

"So, what do we think?" Kathleen held the necklace up for general inspection.

Lucy immediately dropped her knitting and jumped up to look. She slid her palm under the chain and pulled it closer to her eyes. "Silver?" she said. "Or white gold?"

"Silver," Kathleen said. "Which I happen to like."

"I didn't say anything negative."

"You were about to."

"I think it's pretty," Lucy said with a shrug, letting the necklace slip away from her fingers.

Kathleen brought it over to Sari. "What do you think?"

"It's beautiful," Sari said. "So Kevin just up and took you to Tiffany's, huh?"

Kathleen put the necklace back in its velvet box and closed it with an audible pop. "Yep. He said, 'You need a necklace,' and right to Tiffany's, just like that."

"Next time, point out you could use a new car," Lucy said, sitting down and picking up her knitting. "See what happens."

"Right to BMW," Sari said. "Just like that."

"Oh, please," Lucy said. "No one drives BMWs anymore. It's all about the Audis. Or, if you're really cool, a hybrid."

"I'd take a Lexus convertible," Kathleen said. "That's what Kevin drives."

"That's so open-minded of you," Sari said as she carefully slipped a bunch of stitches from one needle to the other. "Being willing to settle for a Lexus."

"What can I say?" Kathleen threw herself into a dining room chair and pulled the bowl of bagels toward her. "I'm a saint." She started flipping through the bagels.

"Can you please just touch whichever bagel you're planning to eat?" Lucy said.

"Maybe I'm planning on eating them all." She extracted a poppy seed one. "I can't believe you're almost done with that blanket, Sar."

Sari said, "I have no life. That's why I get so much knitting done. Every night, while the two of you are out being social and having fun—and probably having sex—"

"Definitely having sex," Kathleen said.

"I'm sitting in front of the TV, knitting. It's pathetic."

"At least you're making something useful," Kathleen said.

"Yeah," Sari said. "I could probably knit this baby five blankets before it's even born. I could knit one for a king-size bed with the time I have."

"You want me to ask Kevin if he has any great friends?" Kathleen said.

"Why? You think they need blankets?"

"No, I mean to date."

Sari thought about it. Her needles clicked and their metal ends flashed. "Yeah, I guess," she said after a moment. "Why not?"

"Make sure they're rich," Lucy said to Kathleen. "If yours is rich, I think it's only fair that Sari's be rich, too."

"Amen to that," Sari said. "Hey, guys, either of you have any good ideas for a Halloween costume?"

"You going to a party?" Kathleen asked.

"No. I have to get dressed up for this thing we do at the clinic. Most of the kids are scared to trick-or-treat for real, so they come in costume and we hand out candy. Usually I just wear scrubs or something easy like that, but Ellen yelled at me for being lazy about it last year."

"You could be a sexy cat," Kathleen said.

"Or a very wicked witch," Lucy said. "In one of those tight black dresses that lace over your boobs."

"Or a sexy little French maid," Kathleen said. She batted her eyes, her hand to her chest. "Oh, but, monsieur, madame—she weell find out!"

"Uh, guys?" Sari said. "I'm going to be handing candy out to a bunch of four-year-olds with autism. Call me crazy, but I really don't think I have to be all that *sexy*."

"You're crazy," Kathleen said. "It never hurts to be sexy."

"I've got a good idea," Lucy said. "Let's go to a costume store right now and we'll help you pick something out."

"You really don't have to," Sari said.

"It'll be fun. You free, Kathleen?"

"Kevin and I were supposed to go to the beach with some friends of his this afternoon, but I'd rather do this."

"She's already losing interest," Lucy said to Sari. "What's it been? Two weeks? Three?"

"That's our girl," Sari said.

"I'm not losing interest," Kathleen said. "I just don't feel like I have to spend every minute of the day with him."

"Kathleen, you always lose interest after a few weeks," Lucy said. "You've got relationship ADD."

"That's because it's always just been about having fun before," Kathleen said. "No one can sustain *fun* forever. But this is about more than that. This is about stability and friendship and—"

"She's bored out of her mind," Lucy said to Sari.

"How come you don't get bored with us?" Sari asked.

"It's the sex," Lucy said. "She gets bored having sex with the same guy over and over again. Since she doesn't have sex with us—"

"Shouldn't that make you even more boring?" Kathleen asked.

"No, because you actually bother *talking* to us," Lucy said. "If you ever found a guy you liked talking to instead of just having sex all the time, you might last more than a few weeks with him."

"Don't blame me," Kathleen said. "There isn't a guy out there who's willing to sit around and talk when he thinks he could be having sex."

* * *

It was Kathleen's idea to take Sari out for a drink before going to the costume store, but Lucy immediately seconded the motion.

"You'll be more open to our suggestions if you're tipsy," Kathleen said.

"You mean you're going to force an outfit on me when I'm too drunk to argue," Sari said.

"We're your friends," Lucy said. "If you can't trust us—"

"You're my friends," Sari said. "And I don't trust you at all." But she let them drag her into a bar half a block from their destination.

When the bartender brought them their drinks, Kathleen said to Lucy, "I can't believe you drink straight scotch."

"It's not straight," Lucy said. "It's on the rocks."

"You know what I mean."

"I like it. It's a manly drink. And it's lower in calories than those girly cocktails everyone else drinks, but gets the job done faster."

"I'm drinking a beer," Kathleen said. "That's just as manly as scotch."

"No, it's not. It's a frat boy's drink. A whole different thing."

Sari frowned at her glass of white wine. "Clearly, I lose this particular contest. But why exactly do we *have* to be manly in our choice of alcoholic beverages?"

"It's just cooler," Lucy said.

"Scotch tastes like medicine," Sari said.

"I like it," Lucy said and drank it slowly, but with real pleasure. She stopped after one—she was driving, and scotch was strong stuff—but the other two had another round, so when they finally got to the costume store, they were all pretty looped and giggly.

Sari was relaxed enough now to try on a sexy cat costume. When she walked out of the fitting room, Kathleen let out a loud wolf whistle, and everyone in the store turned to look.

"For God's sake, Kathleen!" Sari grabbed the fitting room

curtain and pulled it across her body. "Do you have to completely embarrass me?"

"What are you talking about?" Kathleen said. "You look fantastic. Every other woman in this store would kill to look that good in a leotard."

Lucy said, "She looks good, but the black cat thing's a total cliché—everyone does it. Try this one." She handed Sari another outfit.

When Sari reemerged, Lucy said, "Now that's perfect. It totally fits with the theme."

"A nurse's uniform?" Kathleen said.

"Yeah. I mean, she's working with sick kids—"

"They're not sick, they have autism," Sari said. "And it's made out of *vinyl*, Lucy. I can't wear white vinyl to work. That's just wrong."

"Why not?" Kathleen said. "It wipes off easily." For some reason, this struck all three of them as hysterically funny, and they laughed so hard that Kathleen had to crouch down to keep from falling over.

A saleswoman came over and eyed them suspiciously. "May I help you?" she said.

"No, thank you," Sari said, just as Lucy said, "Yes, you can. We need a costume for our friend here that shows off her assets, but doesn't go over the top. You know what I mean?"

"Yeah," Kathleen said, clambering to her feet. "It should say, 'I could get any man I want but I don't *need* a man to be happy and just because I'm letting you look doesn't mean you should even *dream* about touching.' Oh, and kids should think it's totally super-cool."

The saleswoman was in her mid- to late fifties. She had short gray hair and wore half-moon reading glasses on a chain around her neck. She looked back and forth between them for a moment, her eyes narrowed, her lips pressed together in a hard line.

"All right," she said. "I'll see what I can do. Wait here." She disappeared down an aisle.

"Vinyl," Sari said, looking down at herself. "I can't believe you guys."

"What do you think she'll come back with?" Kathleen asked Lucy.

"I don't know. It just better not be another damn cat." They all dissolved into giggles again.

The saleswoman returned with a costume.

"What is it?" Lucy asked.

"A warrior princess. Guys go crazy for this one. But it's not *too* revealing. Try it on." She pushed it at Sari, who obediently disappeared inside the fitting room. She soon came back out in a tight fake leather and metal miniskirt and an even tighter bustier top made out of the same materials.

"Plus there are wrist cuffs," the saleswoman said, holding them up.

"You know who you are, Sari?" Kathleen circled around her. "You're Xena—the coolest woman ever! It's *perfect.*"

"You're totally hot," Lucy agreed, "but not indecent. The kids will just think you look like a superhero, but the dads will think they've died and gone to heaven."

"What do you think?" Sari said, appealing to the saleswoman. "Would *you* wear this to a Halloween party for kids?"

"Honey," the saleswoman said, "if I looked as good in that as you do, I would wear it to Sunday dinner at my in-laws." She handed them the hanger and wrist cuffs and went off after another customer.

Kathleen stared after her. "I think I'm in love," she said.

"There's an age difference," Sari said.

"Love knows no boundaries."

"We need tall black boots to complete the outfit," Lucy said.

"Do you have anything like that, Sari? With high heels? Really high heels?"

Sari rolled her eyes. "What do you think?"

"I have some that would be perfect," Kathleen said.

"And twelve sizes too big," Lucy said. "There's a Shoe Pavilion down the street—we'll find something there."

Sari was studying herself in the mirror. "Are you sure this isn't too much?" she said. "I mean, look at my breasts."

"I can't take my eyes off of them," Kathleen said. "How'd you manage to hide them all these years?"

Lucy was still eyeing Sari critically. "I wish your hair were longer," she said. "Why'd you have to cut it so short?"

"Because I worked with a kid who kept pulling on it," Sari said. "He was yanking it right out of my head."

"Doesn't that piss you off?" Lucy said.

"Nah. It wasn't his fault. He didn't know how else to get my attention. But he's doing really well now—he can say a lot of words and isn't nearly so frustrated."

"I still don't think I can forgive him," Lucy said. "I mean, your *hair*."

"I think the short hair actually works with this," Kathleen said. "Just make sure you chop it up with gel or mousse or something, Sari. Xena shouldn't be fluffy."

"Xena had long straight hair," Lucy said.

"Yeah, but the little blond chick on the show cut hers short and after that looked even hotter than Xena."

Sari bought the costume and they threw the bag into Lucy's car, then left it there while they walked the thirteen blocks down Wilshire Boulevard to the shoe store. It was a beautiful afternoon, and they were all still drunk enough to feel giddy and laugh a lot for no reason. People turned to look at them—men, especially—because they were pretty girls who were laughing and chatting and who weren't *trying* to catch anyone's eye—were, in fact, completely uninterested in any company except one another's.

At the store, Kathleen sashayed toward the others on a pair of shoes with high, spiky heels. "What do you guys think?"

"Jesus," Sari said. "You're like this Amazonian *thing*."

"You could whip Xena's ass," Lucy said, looking up from a stack of shoe boxes she was scanning for Sari's size.

"Yeah?" Kathleen loomed over Sari. "Well, then, I challenge you, warrior princess. Kathleen the Amazon will smash you into dust."

"Do it in the mud, and we can charge admission," Lucy said. "Guys'll pay a fortune to see two girls fight in spikes and leather. I can't find a seven in these, Sari. Will seven and a half work?"

"Probably not."

"That's the spirit. Sit down. You're trying them on."

Lucy extracted the box she wanted as Kathleen went lurching back in her high heels to the aisle where she had found them. "I wonder why she likes to wear such high heels when she's already so tall," Lucy said. "I mean, I know why *I* do it—it's the only way to make my legs look halfway decent. But the last thing she needs is more height."

Sari sat down on the floor and pushed off her Crocs. "People notice her," she said. "I think she likes that. First time I met her, she walked into this party—at Laurie Wong's house, actually—remember her?—and everyone immediately turned to look at her because . . . well, you basically couldn't miss her. I thought she was a model or actress or something and I figured she'd be all stuck-up and full of herself." Lucy handed her a boot and she pulled it on and held out her hand for the other one. "But she was Kathleen. She threw herself down next to me and said she was bored, so I said something about how I wished it wasn't rude to knit at a party, and she told me how some baby-sitter had taught her when she was in sixth grade but she hadn't done it in ages. So then I started telling her about how there were all these amazing new knitting stores in Santa Monica and at some point we said we'd go to one the next morning together and we did and had a blast. And then you took that knitting class and got all excited about starting a club—" She stood up. Wobbled. "A little high, don't you think?"

"They're platforms," Lucy said. "They don't count."

"I'm like four inches taller."

"Which brings you into normal range," Kathleen said. "Almost." She was back, now wearing her flip-flops and carrying a box.

"You getting them?" Lucy gestured to the shoe box.

"Uh-huh. I'll wear them out with Kevin tonight. So he'll forget to be mad that I stood him up this afternoon. Not that he ever gets mad, come to think of it. Those are total fuck-me boots, Sari. I love them."

"I can't wear fuck-me boots to a kids Halloween party," Sari moaned.

"Shut up," Lucy said to Kathleen. "Now you've got her all worried. They're not fuck-me boots, Sari. They're—" She groped.

"Trick-or-treat boots?" Kathleen suggested.

"Exactly! Trick-or-treat boots. They're made for Halloween."

"More treat than trick for the older boys," Kathleen said.

"Shut *up*," Lucy said. "You're going to ruin everything."

"What are you guys trying to do to me?" Sari said. "Between these and the warrior costume—"

"You'll be the hottest therapist in town. As you should be." Lucy bent down and pushed at the toe of one of the boots. "Do they fit okay?"

"I guess. They're slightly big. Wearable. But, guys—"

"We're getting them. I'm paying."

"Kathleen, don't you think—?"

"They're adorable. You'll get a ton of wear out of them. Do you have any short skirts? I mean, other than the Xena thing? Because that's what they're made for."

"I don't wear stuff like that. You guys know that."

Kathleen looked at Lucy. "Next stop, Anthropologie."

By the time they were done with her, Sari had several new outfits in addition to the costume. Lucy paid for the boots, and, at the clothing store, Kathleen picked out two extremely short skirts, a pair of super-tight, super-low jeans, and a bunch of skimpy tank tops—all for Sari.

"This is fun," Kathleen said, as she poked through the extra-small sizes. "Like dressing a doll." She pulled out her own credit card at the cashier, and Sari protested, but Kathleen said, "If I pay for them, I know you'll feel guilty if you don't actually wear them. Sari, you can't sit around complaining about the lack of great guys in your life when you're not even making the slightest effort to get noticed. It's time to show them what you've got."

"But I can't wear this stuff to work."

"Why not?"

"I run around with kids all day long. I mean, I *literally* run around with them."

"So learn to run in a miniskirt," Kathleen said. "You'll never regret it."

They walked back up Wilshire to the car, where Lucy crossed her arms and refused to unlock the doors until Sari promised—swore on her grandmother's grave—that she would wear the warrior princess costume to the Halloween party at the clinic. "There is no backing out now," Lucy said once that was settled.

"Or wearing long underwear underneath," Kathleen said.

"Or a sweatshirt over it."

"All right, all right, I promise," Sari said. "And if I get laughed out of the clinic, I'll know who to blame."

"Blame Lucy," Kathleen said. "She's the bossy one."

5

Slip, Slip, Knit

1

It was Halloween. "Please," Sari said into the phone. "Please release me from my promise. You have to. It's worse than I remembered. It's like my boobs are being served up on a platter."

"That's very poetic," Lucy said.

"Seriously."

"You have to wear it. You promised."

"I was drunk when I promised. That doesn't count."

"You swore on your grandmother's grave. And you weren't drunk anymore."

"Please, Lucy. If I wear this tonight—"

"Stop being such a coward. If not now, when?"

After Sari hung up, she looked at herself in the mirror again. The skirt seemed much shorter with the boots on, and the tight bodice shoved her breasts up so high they looked like refugees from an Edwardian brothel. The only good news was that the kids wouldn't notice—sometimes the fact that kids with autism could be oblivious to so much came in handy.

She rubbed some hair gel between her palms—she had bought it a couple of years ago when the woman who cut her hair had insisted but usually was in too much of a rush out the door to bother with it—and raked her fingers through her hair so it fell into choppy pieces, like Kathleen had told her to. She had to admit it did suit the warrior princess look. And, having committed herself that far, she felt obliged to search through the makeup she almost never wore for a dark pencil to outline her eyes and a bronzer, which she put on her eyelids and cheeks. She looked . . . defined. Her large blue eyes had become exotic and mysterious with the kohl around them.

She flexed her arm muscles in front of the mirror. "I am Xena," she said out loud. Didn't Xena have a sound she made? Like a "ki-ki-ki-ki-ki" kind of thing? Sari said, "Ki-ki-ki-ki" and stopped, because she felt like an idiot.

"I'm not Xena," she told the mirror. "Not even close."

"Whoa, baby," Christopher said when she came walking into the clinic's reception area. He was wearing a UCLA football uniform. "Wish you'd wear *that* around here more often." He nudged Shayda, who was sitting next to him, sorting candy bars into big bowls, wearing a black pirate's hat. "Hey, Shade—look at Sari."

"No, don't look at Sari," Sari said. She hugged her arms over her chest. "Sari's hideously embarrassed. My friends made me wear this."

Shayda glanced indifferently at Sari, then turned to Christopher. "'Whoa, baby'?" she repeated. "That sounded really sexual harassment-y."

"Sari knew I was joking."

"I'm just saying you should be more careful. People get sued over stuff like that."

Christopher rolled his eyes at Sari and tore open a package of M&M's, which he poured straight into his mouth.

As they all prepared the rooms for the imminent onslaught of kids and families, Sari continued to tell anyone who commented on her costume that she had been forced to wear it and that she found it embarrassing.

When she said that to Ellen, Ellen waved her hand dismissively and said, "You look great. I don't see what the problem is."

"Don't you think it's inappropriate?" Sari said. "Come on, Ellen, you're the boss here. Don't you think you should send me home to change? Because I could be there and back in ten minutes. Please tell me to go home and change."

"Actually, I think you should dress like this more often."

"Why?" Sari said. "You planning to turn this place into a clinic-slash-whorehouse?"

"Hmm," Ellen said. "That's not a bad idea. We could use the extra money." She grinned. "Come on, Sari, lighten up. The outfit's really not that bad, you know. I mean, look at Liza—" She pointed. Liza was walking down the hallway in a body-hugging black unitard. She wore a headband with black velvet ears sticking up. "Her outfit's a lot racier than yours, and you don't hear her worrying about it."

"She's a black cat," Sari said, shaking her head in disbelief. "I can't believe she went with the obvious choice."

"The point is, relax. And worry about the *kids*, not about how you look." Ellen walked away.

Sari made a face at her retreating back. Of course Ellen would see nothing wrong with Sari's costume—Ellen herself was dressed as a belly dancer with a fringy top that revealed a large expanse of soft white belly and an even larger expanse of mountainous décolletage.

As the kids started arriving, the clinicians all took up their prearranged positions. Every office and playroom in the clinic was set up like its own little "house"—the kids would knock on the room door, the therapist would open it, and whoever was with the kid would prompt him to say, "Trick-or-Treat," and then the therapist would compliment the kid and give him candy.

Ellen stayed in the main reception area, where she could greet all the families and invite them to come back and socialize when they were done trick-or-treating.

Sari stationed herself in one of the larger playrooms with a big bowl of Snickers bars. The party officially started at six, and, by six-fifteen, she was jumping up every few seconds to open the door and hand out the candy.

Sari was always surprised to see how many families used their clinic. A lot of "graduates" showed up that night, as well as dozens of kids who were currently patients. And many of them came with siblings, friends, and cousins. All of the kids wore costumes, but none of the parents did, except for one mother who had on a long black dress—which, Sari thought, was either meant to be a witch costume or was just a really goth choice.

There were, as always, more moms than dads present, and every one of the moms who came to Sari's door told her how fabulous she looked in her warrior costume. One mother actually screamed in delight when she saw her. "Oh, my God! I didn't even recognize you, Sari! Smile!" And, before Sari knew what was happening, the mom had snapped her photo.

Sari knew any embarrassing shots would be circulating at the clinic for years, and she silently cursed Kathleen and Lucy for all the future ridicule she would have to endure. She had hoped to be remembered as the clinic's most brilliant therapist—not as its resident goofball. Or sexpot. Hard to decide which was worse. Or more likely.

The few dads who came didn't compliment her as much. But they looked. Man, did they look. Lucy and Kathleen would be pleased, Sari thought, as one dad's mouth fell open in surprise when he saw her. He shut it again quickly, but she was careful not to bend over too much when she dropped a Snickers into his kid's plastic pumpkin—the dad was on the older side, and she didn't want to give him a heart attack.

For over an hour, the corridor was alive with kids running and laughing and screaming with excitement and sugar highs, but as time passed, the flood of kids slowed to a trickle. Around seven-thirty, Sari wondered if she should head toward the main room—she could hear voices and music and general party sounds coming from there whenever she stuck her head out the hallway.

She hadn't had a kid knock on the door for over five minutes, and she was getting bored. The whole thing ended at eight anyway.

She thought she should really go join the others.

Instead, she sat back down at the big table in the middle of the room and wondered what she was waiting for.

She knew perfectly well what she was waiting for.

And, at seven-thirty-seven, he came.

When she heard the knock, she just assumed it was another kid trick-or-treating, and opened the door with a big smile on her face to find Jason Smith standing there.

"Hi," he said. And then took in her costume. "Hi," he said again, but his eyes widened and he took a step back. "What *are* you?"

"Some kind of warrior princess—at least according to the woman at the costume store."

"It's great. One of the all-time great Halloween costumes, I'd say."

They had turned off half of the hallway lights so it would feel a little more like nighttime in the clinic, and Sari hoped that the dim lighting meant Jason couldn't see her blush. "My friends made me wear it."

"I like your friends. You make a good warrior goddess, Sari."

"Warrior *princess*," she said. "Haven't you forgotten something?"

"Sorry. I'm not the costume type."

"No, not that. I meant your kid. Where's Zack?"

"Isn't he here?"

"I haven't seen him."

"Oh, shit," he said, and looked up and down the empty hallway like he expected Zack suddenly to appear. "Denise was bringing him. They were supposed to have been here a while ago."

"Maybe they're in the main office," Sari said. "Not everyone makes it down this way. The real party's back there."

"I checked," Jason said. "They're not there."

"You think you should try calling them?"

"Yeah." He pulled out a cell phone and pressed a couple of buttons, then made a face. "Battery's dead." He shook his head in self-disgust. "I forgot to recharge it. That would explain why they haven't called. Do you have a phone I can use?"

"In here."

He followed her inside the room. "Door open or closed?"

"Closed, I guess. In case some other kids want to come trick-or-treating. We like them to have to knock. So it feels more like the real thing. If we left the door open, it wouldn't feel the same, you know?" She realized she was blithering on, over-explaining because she didn't want him to think she was closing the door to be alone with him. She made herself stop talking and pointed to the desk in the corner of the room. "There's a phone over there. Dial nine to get out."

"Thanks." He went over and dialed and said, "Hi. It's Jason. Denise isn't there, is she? You're kidding. Put her on, will you?"

He waited a little while, tapping one foot impatiently on the floor. Then, "Yeah, hi. It's me. What the hell are you doing still there? I'm at the Halloween thing at the clinic. Where you were supposed to be an hour ago." He listened for a moment. "So why didn't you call? I've been—" Another moment. "Yeah, the battery's out, but you could have left a message here or something." More listening. "So who's with Zack?" Then, "Do you really trust her to watch him?" After a response: "All I know is that you were supposed to have him for two hours. Just two little hours, which were supposed to include bringing him here to trick-or-treat. And you couldn't even manage that. And you better not be expecting me to go get him over there, because I'm not about to make that trip again. Do you know what the traffic is like on Halloween night? It took me over an hour to get back to this side of the hill." He looked at his watch as he listened to something else. "Since six? He'll be up all night now." He grimaced. "Fine, then. Bring him home whenever you want. It's not like he'll be asleep before midnight, anyway." He listened for a moment. "Shit, Denise, can't you even spend half an hour in a car with him? So who *is* going to be driving him?" A pause. "Terrific. What is she, sixteen? Does she even have a license?" Then, "Yeah, I know, I know. You really went out of your way to give him a fun time tonight, didn't you? Way to help your son celebrate Halloween." He slammed the phone back down into its base.

Sari had been studying the table as if the fake wood grain fascinated her, but now she looked up. "Everything okay?"

He shook his head. "She was supposed to take him out to dinner. For once. She said she wanted to, because it was Halloween and she hadn't seen him for days. And then she was supposed to bring him here and trick-or-treat with him and then I was going to meet them and take him home. She wouldn't even have had to spend the night with him." He exhaled sharply. "I dropped him off at her office at five. They never left, haven't even had dinner. He's just been sitting there watching TV with some intern—or at least he was until he fell asleep an hour ago. She made him miss Halloween."

"Maybe it's not too late," Sari said. "I mean, it is for trick-or-treating here, but maybe they could still go to some houses—"

"There's no way—now she's claiming that there's an emergency at work she has to deal with. Which just means some actor's throwing a hissy fit or something. I'd run over and grab him, but he's all the way out in Burbank, and by the time I got there, it would be too late to take him anywhere. Anyway, I wanted him to do *this*." He waved his hand at the room. "It would have been perfect. He got scared last year when I tried to take him out for some real trick-or-treating. I wanted him to do something for Halloween that would make him see it can be fun. And this would have been—" He stopped. "Perfect," he said again. "That's all. And she ruined it."

"I'm sorry," Sari said. And realized she really was. For Zack, mostly, and a little bit for Jason. "Is there anything I can do to help? I could send some candy home."

He looked at her and his face suddenly relaxed into a smile. "I don't suppose you'd be willing to kick Denise's ass? I mean, you look like you could, with those boots and all."

Sari laughed. "I doubt it—you said she was a real athlete in college and I'm kind of out of shape."

"She's got some height on you, too. In the interest of full disclosure. But you've got that whole tough leather thing going on. And you don't look like you're out of shape." He leaned back, resting his hip against the desk. "I'm so bummed about this. Poor Zack. I should never have let her have him on a holiday."

"Do you guys have a custody arrangement worked out?"

"Not really. But it's never been a problem. We both assume

I'll have him, except for those one-in-a-billion moments when she actually feels some kind of maternal pull. Like tonight. And we both saw how well *that* worked out."

"So what happened last Halloween?" Sari said. "You said Zack got scared. Did you go around your neighborhood?"

He sat down with a thump on a chair. "We drove over to my parents' house, actually. I thought I was being so smart—I figured he'd feel safe because he goes over there all the time."

"So what happened?" Sari sat down, too, across the table from him.

"Well, he started off already a little freaked out just because it was dark out and he didn't like the jack-o'-lanterns on the front porch. But it would have probably been fine, except my father decided it would be hilarious to open the door wearing a gorilla mask." He grimaced. "It was unbelievable. I mean, I had called ahead just to warn them *not* to pull any surprises on Zack and then he goes and does that."

"Why?" Sari said. "If you specifically asked him not to?"

"I don't know. Maybe he thought it was funny. Or maybe just *because* I told him not to. He's a sick old bastard."

Sari tried to remember Jason Smith's father from high school events. She had a vague sense of someone tall with thick gray hair but she wasn't sure she was thinking of the right guy. "That's kind of harsh, isn't it?"

He shrugged and tipped his chair back. "We've never gotten along very well. I'm this huge disappointment to him. Which he manages to remind me of every chance he gets." He let the chair fall back into place with a thud. "Actually, now that I think about it, I bet he scared Zack just so he could make him scream and then use that as an example of what a bad parent I am and how I can't control my own kid."

"He knows Zack has autism, right?"

"I've told him, but he doesn't believe it."

"You're kidding."

He shook his head. "He thinks all of Zack's problems come from having a mother who's the wage-earner. It screws a kid up if his dad doesn't wear the pants in the family, you know."

"I'm sorry," she said. "If that's really the way he sees things—"

He waved his hand dismissively. "I'm used to it. I've been a disappointment to the guy since I was born. Why should that change now that I really *am* the biggest loser in town?"

"What makes you such a big loser?"

"Don't make me give you a list, Sari, please," he said. "It's bad enough having to live with myself, but if you make me tell the one person I—" He stopped. "Not that you won't figure it out soon enough."

She didn't say anything. She heard a door slam down the hall and thought, *I should get up and say good night and leave this room.* But she didn't move.

"I'm sorry," he said when a moment had gone by and she still hadn't spoken. "I probably sound like a whiny brat. My father doesn't love me and all that. I'm sorry."

"No, it's okay," she said. "I wasn't thinking that. It's just . . . I'm a little confused. You were so different in high school. You were kind of on top of the world back then."

He gave a short unpleasant laugh. "I so wasn't. Maybe it looked that way from a distance, but all I remember about those days was how my parents were always screaming at me because I had done badly on a test or the coach hadn't played me or I had forgotten to take out the garbage or something like that. I was always being grounded and threatened with military school."

"But when you were actually *at* school—" Sari said. "I mean, you owned the place."

"Hardly."

There was the sound of a child either laughing or crying coming from another part of the clinic. Sari looked toward the door and said, "I should probably go help Ellen."

"Don't go yet," Jason said. "Please."

"There's always a big mess to clean up."

"I bet. How'd you end up working here anyway?"

"I went to college here and then graduate school and it just made sense—"

"But I mean, why an autism clinic? Do you have a relative with autism or something?"

He really didn't know? "My brother," she said.

"You're kidding."

She just shook her head.

"I didn't know you had an autistic brother."

"He went to school with us," she said. "He was there the whole time you were."

"Really?" Jason said. "You'd think I'd have remembered that. What class was he in?"

"He wasn't exactly in a class. There was this special needs program—"

"Oh, wait, I remember," he said. "The Resource Room, right?"

"Yeah. Popularly referred to as the Retard Room."

"Oh, man," he said. "I remember that, too, now. God, kids can be mean. It scares me for Zack."

"He'll be okay."

"I'm sorry," he said suddenly, and Sari's stomach clenched. But then he said, "It must have been rough for your family to have to deal with the whole autism thing back then. Everything I read says it was like the Middle Ages, just a generation ago. No behavioral interventions, no real understanding, mothers being blamed . . . It couldn't have been easy."

She didn't say anything. He was one of the reasons it hadn't been easy.

"What's he like now?" Jason asked. "Your brother? Does he live at home? Does he talk? I'm so insanely curious about adults with autism. I'm desperate to know what Zack will be like when he's all grown up."

"Zack won't be anything like my brother. He's getting the right kind of help. It makes all the difference." Zack wouldn't be like Charlie because of her, she thought. It was so unfair it took her breath away.

"Is he in an institution?"

"No. He lives with my parents."

"Does he talk?"

"Yeah. Mostly demands for food and dialogue from movies."

Jason reached across the table and she was looking around to see what it was he was reaching for, when he put his hand on hers. "Sounds like it's been tough," he said.

She pulled her hand away with a movement so fast it was almost violent

"I'm sorry," he said, quickly withdrawing his hand. "Please don't take offense."

"I'm not offended." She pushed her chair back. "But I should go help clean up."

"Don't go." He scrambled to his feet as she stood up. "Please, Sari. Please don't go. That was stupid of me. I just felt bad for you. That's all. I'm not some guy making moves. You have to know that."

"I don't know *what* you are," she said and meant it.

"I wish you were willing to find out. We could go have a drink—"

"I can't. I have to go help the others now." She felt all roughed up on the inside—like someone had done to her guts what she had done to her hair earlier that evening.

"After?"

"I can't."

"Are you mad at me?"

"Of course not," she said dully. "Everything's fine. I just really have to go." She went to the door. He was closer and got there before she did. He put his hand on the doorknob, and she had to stop and wait.

"Sari," he said.

"What?"

"Thanks for talking to me."

She didn't say anything.

He drew nearer. "I'm a pretty lucky guy. Getting some one-on-one time with the cutest warrior goddess in town."

"Princess," she said. "I'm supposed to be a princess, not a goddess."

"I beg to differ," Jason Smith said, and, leaning forward, kissed her lightly on the lips before she had a chance to stop him. And then he opened the door and gestured her through.

11

James joined Lucy and David in the lab the day after Halloween to go over the results of the rat kidneys they had removed, dissected, stained, and examined that day.

After they'd finished discussing their findings, he sat back and peered at Lucy. "You okay?" he said. "You've been awfully quiet. Not like you."

"It's been a lousy day."

"What happened?"

She didn't answer, so David said, "One of the rats didn't die easily. The guillotine jammed halfway through its neck and it was squirming around, screaming, blood spraying all over the place . . . It took a while to get the blade out." He looked at Lucy, but she didn't say anything. He said, "It was a lot to clean up."

"I'll bet," James said. "You guys want to go get a beer?"

"Sounds good to me," David said.

"Lucy?"

"Yeah, all right." She stood up. "Let me go wash my hands. For the next ten minutes."

"Out, damned spot?" David said.

"Something like that."

At the bar, she ordered her usual scotch, while the guys got beer. She and James sat side by side in the booth. His leg was warm against hers, and he rested his left hand on her thigh when he wasn't using it to gesticulate. He was in an ebullient mood—he had just found out that day that an article of his had been accepted for publication.

"A byline in *Science*," David said. "Pretty impressive, James."

"There's always someone doing better," he said. "You guys know Ron Johnson, right?"

"I met him once or twice around the department," David said.

"Yeah, well, he's getting a book published—and I mean mass market, not some university press."

"What is it?"

"I can't remember what it's called, but it's some kind of simplified overview of genetics—a real science lite book, with everything dumbed down so idiots can feel like they've mastered a subject they don't actually understand at all and wouldn't be able to in a million years. He'll probably make a fortune on it. Nothing people like more than to buy books that make them think they're not as stupid as they are." He curled his lip. "Not that Ron's exactly genius material himself."

"Really?" David said. "I've mostly heard good things about him."

"He's an idiot," James said. "He's done some decent research in the past, but last year he married this woman who's a religious nut and now he goes to church all the time, sings in the choir, recites his little prayers—the whole thing."

Lucy said, "Going to church doesn't automatically make you an idiot."

"It does in my book. A scientist should know better."

"So long as he's not going around teaching creationism, I don't see what difference it makes."

"How about the Tooth Fairy?" James said. "What if he were going around saying he believes in the Tooth Fairy? Would you still call him a good scientist?"

"So long as he *was* still a good scientist, sure. There are plenty of intelligent people who believe in God, James."

"Nope," James said. "People who believe in God are de facto idiots. Unless they're just claiming to believe in God to promote themselves with the stupid people who really do. In that case, they're politicians."

David laughed. "Good one," he said, and he and James high-fived each other.

Lucy just shook her head. "Everyone who disagrees with you is an idiot. Have you noticed that?"

"Actually, I have," James said. "Sad but true."

"Isn't it possible—I realize this may blow your mind as a concept—but isn't it possible that not everything is as obvious as you think it is? That maybe there are other ways of thinking than yours, and that some of those other ways might not be entirely idiotic?"

James furrowed his brow exaggeratedly. Then he shook his head. "Nope. I'm right, they're wrong. Case closed."

"*I* don't always agree with you."

"That's okay." He patted her leg. "Everyone makes mistakes, sweetheart."

She knocked his hand off. "You're an asshole, you know that?"

"Come on, Luce, you hate religion as much as I do. Why are you defending this guy?"

"I don't know," she said. "Maybe Ron *gets* something out of his religion that we don't understand. It's possible. People's brains work differently. And if it doesn't interfere with his work, then let him have it and don't call him an idiot for it."

"Even though he *is* one?"

She thumped her scotch glass down. "What about Dickens? What about Einstein? There are lots of wildly brilliant people who've believed in God."

"They probably just pretended to so they wouldn't piss off the mass population of idiots. We all do what we have to to survive." He tilted his throat back and drank some beer. "I'm bored with this subject," he said as he set the bottle back down. "So, David, Lucy tells me you have a girlfriend. Who is she and why aren't you calling her right now and telling her to come join us?"

David shrugged. "We're just dating. It's not a girlfriend thing yet."

"She at UCLA?"

"Yeah."

"Postdoc?"

"Actually," David said, "she's an undergraduate."

James hooted at that. "You're kidding me."

"A junior."

"Come on, dude, you can't go fishing in that pond. You start with undergrads, you'll get a taste for them and you won't be able to stop. There are tons of guys like that in the department, dirty old men who like little girls. You don't want to go there."

"I wasn't planning to," David said. "This just . . . you know, happened." He poked at a drop of beer on the outside of his mug. "Anyway, like I said, it's not all that serious—we've just had dinner a couple of times."

"What does she want to do when she graduates?" James asked.

"Well, she's premed—"

"A doctor, then," James said. "And, since she's a girl, I'm guessing either a pediatrician or an OB. That's what they all want to be."

"Why do you always have to generalize about people?" Lucy said. "I was premed and I didn't want to be a pediatrician or an OB."

"What did you want to be?" James asked.

"A veterinarian."

He groaned. "The only medical career that's actually *more* girly than being a pediatrician or an OB. Why'd you have to tell me that? I just lost any respect I ever had for you."

"In case you hadn't noticed, I didn't actually become one," Lucy said. "At some point I decided it would be a lot more fun to kill animals than take care of them."

"Oh, please," James said. "Would you really rather be spending your days telling old ladies to stop overfeeding their fat little pugs? Killing rats is much more fun than that."

"I like rats," said Lucy, who was starting to feel the effect of the scotch she had downed.

"No one likes rats."

"I do. I had a pet rat once. And a dog. And two cats. And a turtle."

"That's excessive," James said.

"Not all at once."

James stood up abruptly. "I've got to hit the john. Be right back." He left. There was a moment of silence.

"I hate sac'ing rats," Lucy said.

"Me, too," said David.

"Let's set them all free," she said. "Let's go back to the lab and set them all free to live a happy carefree life eating trash and having casual rat sex."

"You know we can't," he said. "They'd die within days. And the research we're doing is worth sac'ing a few rats for."

"Yeah," she said. "I know that."

"So we're trapped," he said.

"Like rats in a cage."

III

Knitting circle was at Kathleen's place that Sunday. (At Sari's the week before, Lucy had protested. "There are no chairs in her apartment. It'll kill our backs." "Oh, stop being such a princess," Kathleen had said, and Sari said, "It's her turn, Lucy.")

When Lucy walked in the open apartment door, Kathleen called out, "Hey, Luce, come quick! Sari just told me she kissed Jason Smith!"

"No fucking way!" Lucy said, dropping her bag and running over. Kathleen and Sari were cross-legged and side by side on an airbed—the only furniture in the whole room—already knitting. Lucy kicked off her shoes and sank down on the floor in front of them.

"I didn't kiss him," Sari said. "He kissed *me* before I could stop him."

"Why would you want to stop him?" Kathleen said.

"Come on," Sari said. "You guys know why this is weird for me. And it's just getting weirder. I mean, I see him with Zack almost every day, but I can't even look at him. I feel like he's waiting for me to say something. I think he thinks I'm screwing with his mind, but I'm not, I'm really not—"

"You should be," Lucy said.

"I told him about Charlie. He said he hadn't remembered that I had a brother."

"You think he's lying?" Lucy asked.

"No—he probably *doesn't* remember him. Which only shows how little he—" Sari waved her hand in the air. "You know. That even when he was mean to Charlie, he barely noticed him. Like squashing a bug or something."

"Is he really that big a jerk?" Kathleen asked. "He seemed kind of nice."

"I don't know," Sari said. "He says all the right things. But don't forget—since high school, he's had a kid with autism. It changes people."

"So maybe he's changed," Kathleen said.

"Yeah, but does that count?"

"What do you mean?"

"You know . . ." Sari thought a moment, putting her knitting down on the floor next to her and hugging her knees to her chest. "Here's a guy who treated people badly when things were going well for him, and then this thing happened with his kid. So now he's more sensitive about other people and maybe even kinder . . . But, the truth is, if he'd been given the choice, he probably would have rather gone on having a perfect life and being a total jerk." She looked up. "Can you really give a guy credit for that? If he's only a decent human being because it was forced on him?"

"I don't think you can ever really trust someone like that," Lucy said. "I mean, if a guy goes around killing people and then his own mother gets killed, it's a little late for him to decide that murder is wrong—"

"Well, *murder*," Kathleen said. "Let's just compare him to Saddam Hussein and be done with it. Come on, Lucy—being a schoolyard bully isn't the same as being a murderer." She stabbed her needles at each other, frowning in concentration. "Anyway, you can't really judge people on who they might have been if things had been different, can you? All you can do is take them the way they are and like them or not for that."

"Right," Lucy said, "and Attila the Hun was probably a great guy when he was on vacation."

"Meaning—?"

"That if you know someone's done some shitty things, you can't just take them the way they are at any given moment. You have to use the information you've got, remember the history. Sari shouldn't forget what she knows about Jason—I bet she couldn't, even if she wanted to."

"She could give him another chance, though," Kathleen said. "I mean, I did some lousy things in high school—I was this jock and I had a lot of jock friends and we all hung out and we were kind of the cool kids, and I don't think we were all that nice to some of the other kids. I wouldn't want to be judged by all that."

"But maybe you should be," Lucy said.

"When did you get so rigid?" Kathleen said. "Haven't you ever wanted someone to give *you* the benefit of the doubt?"

"I'm not rigid," Lucy said. "I can see both sides of a lot of issues. I mean, James is rigid. Compared to him, I'm the most tolerant person in the world."

Kathleen raised her eyebrows. "First Saddam Hussein, then James. You keep going to extremes."

"Are you saying my boyfriend is like Saddam Hussein?"

"No," Kathleen said. "He's better-looking. But I want to go back to talking about Cute Asshole Guy. Sari, be honest—do you want to sleep with him?"

"Yes," Sari said with a sigh. "So much. Physically he's everything I'd want in a guy. He has the most incredible body . . ."

"So . . . ?" Kathleen said.

"You know why I can't."

"What happened to the plan?" Lucy said, looking up from her knitting.

"What plan?"

"The go-out-with-him-and-ruin-his-life plan."

"Oooo," Kathleen said. "I like that plan."

"Take it—it's yours," Sari said. "I don't want a plan."

"She can't have it," Lucy said. "I made that one especially for you. Kathleen has her own plan. The marry-him-and-take-his-money-and-then-divorce-him plan."

"I never said I was going to divorce him." Kathleen took a swig of coffee. "That would be wrong. I intend to stay married to Kevin forever. Assuming, you know, we get married in the first place."

"What was that?" Lucy said with a jump and a startled look around. "I just heard a noise in your kitchen. You don't have a cat, do you?"

"Of course not."

"Then—"

They all turned toward the kitchen door in time to see Sam

Kaplan emerge. "Oh, sorry," he said, halting at the doorway. "Didn't realize you had company."

"It's okay." Kathleen dropped her knitting and scrambled to her feet. "Sari, Lucy—my upstairs neighbor. Sam."

"The guy who owns the building?" Lucy said. "Does that mean you're allowed to come sneaking into people's apartments without knocking?"

"Actually, I did knock," Sam said. He was dressed neatly in a pair of khakis and a blue polo shirt. "I always knock, but Kathleen never hears me. She usually has that iPod thing coming out of her ears. And, believe me, she has no great respect for *my* privacy." He turned to Kathleen. "I was on my way to pick up the newspaper and get some coffee. You want anything?"

"We have coffee," Sari said. "One of those big cardboard Starbucks thingies that hold like twelve cups. Please have some. Or we'll be shaking all day."

"There are donuts, too," Kathleen said.

"I haven't eaten a donut in thirty years," he said. "So what do you girls think of what Kathleen's done to the apartment?"

"Minimalist," Lucy said and he laughed.

"This used to be a nice apartment, believe it or not." He looked back and forth among them. "I thought Kathleen was the only woman under the age of sixty who liked to knit, but I guess I was wrong."

"Shows how much you know," Kathleen said. "Tons of girls our age knit. It's very hip."

"Really?" Sam said. "Why? Sweaters are cheap these days—you can't possibly save any money knitting your own. And it takes forever, doesn't it?"

"You don't do it to save money," Lucy said. "This yarn cost me more than five sweaters at the Gap. But that's not the point. It's therapy."

Sam shook his head. "Sorry," he said. "I don't get it. It would drive me nuts to do something like that—just sitting there, playing with yarn for hours."

"It keeps our hands busy while we talk," Kathleen said. "We talk a lot."

"Then I really can't stay," Sam said. "I can only imagine what three pretty young women talk about while they knit. No, actually I can't. And don't want to. Goodbye, girls."

"I'll be up later to read the paper," Kathleen said.

"Of course you will," he said and left, cutting through the living room to the front door.

"So that's the famous Sam Kaplan," Lucy said once the door had closed behind him.

"Is he famous?" Kathleen resumed her place on the airbed. "I had no idea."

"You know what I mean. Strange guy."

"No shit."

"So you two just run in and out of each other's apartments, huh?"

"Sometimes."

Lucy looked at Sari. "That's sort of an unusual arrangement, don't you think? Do you run in and out of *your* neighbors' apartments, Sari?"

"Hardly. Sometimes we run into each other at the trash chute."

"I've never even met my neighbors," Lucy said. "Kathleen, what's going on here?"

"Nothing," Kathleen said. "Absolutely nothing."

"I don't believe you."

"Why not?" Kathleen said. "When have you ever known me to be coy about my love life?"

"She makes an excellent point," Sari said.

"Well, good," Lucy said. "He looks old enough to be your father."

"So?" Kathleen said. "I've gone out with guys that much older than me before."

"I'm sure you have," Lucy said. "Is there any age you haven't covered?"

"I try to stay away from the under-five crowd. They have this whole breast fixation thing I find very disturbing."

"Plus they never pick up a check," Lucy said.

Sari laughed. "Speaking of babies—" She held up the blanket. "I'm just about done with this. Where do you guys stand on fringe? For or against?"

"It would be pretty," Kathleen said, but Lucy shook her head. "You can't put fringe on a baby blanket. They could choke on it."

"No, they couldn't," Kathleen said. "That's impossible."

"How would you know?"

"How would *you*?"

"Let's face it," Sari said. "None of us knows anything about babies. But I'll skip the fringe, just to be safe. Do you—" She was interrupted by a loud ring tone of the first few bars of Gwen Stefani's "Rich Girl." Kathleen shifted over and peered down at her cell phone, which was lying face-up on the floor.

"One of my sisters," she said, settling back. "I'll let it go to voice mail."

"What's going on with them, anyway?" Sari said. "Are they still mad at you for moving out?"

"Not really," Kathleen said. "I mean, how mad can you be that someone has stopped freeloading on you?"

"They didn't seem to want you to go, though."

"I know. And they want me to come back. Especially my mom—Christa and Kelly don't get along when I'm not around."

"Why not?"

"I don't know. It's a triplet thing."

"You have the weirdest family dynamic of anyone I know," Lucy said.

Sari raised her right hand. "Uh . . . excuse me?" she said. "I'm at least in the running on that one."

"Actually," Lucy said, "you're in a league of your own."

IV

When Kevin arrived at Kathleen's apartment to pick her up for dinner that night, he told her that he had run into Sam Kaplan in the lobby, and they had agreed it would be fun to all have dinner together. Kathleen wasn't sure who the "all" referred to but soon discovered that it meant that Sam's ex-wife, Patricia, was with him.

It had never occurred to Kathleen before how much of the time she'd previously spent with Sam Kaplan had been one-on-one, just the two of them alone in his apartment. Tonight they were with other people, and she almost didn't recognize her sharp-tongued and occasionally brutal upstairs neighbor in the sociable and relaxed guy who sat across the table from her, his arm casually resting across the back of his ex-wife's chair. If it hadn't been for the way he rubbed all his flatware clean with his napkin and occasionally rolled his eyes at things she said, she might have suspected that he, like her sisters, had an identical twin.

The wine was good, and the waiter and Sam and Kevin all kept refilling Kathleen's glass as soon as it was half empty, so she had probably had a lot more than she even realized by the time the conversation turned to Jackson Porter.

"It was wonderful seeing him and your mother at the benefit," Sam said to Kevin. "It's been a while."

"They just don't go out as much as they used to," Kevin said. "Much as I hate to admit it, they're getting older and starting to slow down."

"They may not go out *together* as much," Kathleen said, "but your father certainly manages to get around."

"Excuse me?" Kevin said.

"Oh, you know," she said with a slightly inebriated wink. "Those daily lunches with attractive young women in private hotel rooms."

"Ah," he said. "You've been listening to gossip." He turned to Sam and Patricia with a smile. "Every once in a while, the office rumor mill comes up with an exciting double life for my father. I guess it's one of the ways people keep themselves entertained during a long day at work."

"Offices can get boring," Sam said. His eyes moved quickly back and forth between Kevin and Kathleen, assessing the situation without giving any of his own thoughts away. "And everyone enjoys a good scandal, even a fictional one."

"But in this case it's true," Kathleen said. She didn't really care that Jackson cheated on his wife, but she found it incredibly annoying that Kevin was making it sound like she was some kind of gullible stooge. "Half the office could tell you which hotel he uses. Which *room*."

Kevin looked at her, his brows drawn together. He drew his breath in.

"Kevin," Patricia said suddenly, "do your parents still have that house on the beach in Santa Barbara? Or was it Montecito? We went out there once and it was just lovely."

Kevin answered in the affirmative, and the talk shifted to beach houses and whether the Southern California real estate bubble was likely to burst anytime in the near future.

They all walked back to the apartment building together. Kevin stuck with Sam, talking shop with him, while the two women strolled ahead. He hadn't really looked at Kathleen since she had said that stuff about his father, and now she wondered if he was furious with her. The thought intrigued her. She had never seen him angry.

Patricia said, "It's a beautiful night, isn't it? I love the fall. I loved it more on the East Coast, but even here there's something special about a cool autumn night."

"Are you from the East Coast originally?" Kathleen asked. They were walking in rhythm together, their high heels clicking in sync on the paved sidewalk.

Patricia nodded. "I grew up on Long Island and met Sam in college. I never thought I'd end up a Californian, but we came here after we were married and never left. And as long as Joanna's at UCLA, I suppose I'll stay. But if she settles down somewhere else, I'll probably move. Even after all these years, it still doesn't feel like *home* to me."

Kathleen nodded but she wasn't really listening. "Do you mind if I ask you a personal question?"

"What's that?"

"I've never seen a divorced couple spend so much time together before. I thought once people divorced, they usually stayed away from each other."

In the light of a street lamp, she could see Patricia smile. "That's not a question."

"Sorry," Kathleen said. "I guess my question would be: why?"

"That *is* a question," Patricia said, "but it's a vague one. Why what?"

"Why get divorced in the first place if you like being together?"

"Now that's a real question," Patricia said. "But I'll have to think about the answer." They walked in silence for a moment, the men's voices suddenly audible behind them. Kevin was talking about a development he was overseeing that Sam seemed to have some concerns about—the land, he was saying, was known to have geological problems and several previous companies had tried building there and given up.

Then Patricia spoke again. "Sam is a wonderful man and I love him dearly," she said. "But I find him absolutely intolerable in many ways. I wake up every morning delighted I don't have to live with him anymore."

"Is it—" Kathleen searched for a delicate way to say it. "Do you consider yourselves still a couple?"

"Oh, we stopped being a *couple* when we got divorced," Patricia said. "We have dinner together once in a while and that's enough for both of us. We always enjoy it but we're ready to say goodbye at the end of the evening. At least, I know *I* am."

"Sam seemed happy tonight," Kathleen said.

Patricia shrugged. "As I said, we enjoy each other's company."

"It's unusual."

"So you've already pointed out." They had reached their destination. They stopped and waited for the men.

"What now?" Kathleen said to Kevin as he joined her.

"Let's go up to your place."

She nodded, but wondered—without any real preference—if he wanted to come up to yell at her or to have sex. Or both. There was no way he could not be pissed off at her, not after what she'd said about Jackson.

He surprised her. As soon as they were inside her apartment, he went running for a soccer ball and dribbled it over to her. "Whoever makes the first goal has to do whatever the other says," he said, smiling. "And I do mean whatever. Nothing off limits."

"You're on," Kathleen said, dropping her purse and kicking off her shoes.

She was a good athlete, but he was determined, and she wanted to give him the win. She suspected (and was proved right) that he had something in mind they'd both enjoy.

The air mattress wasn't comfortable for two, so, after all the games had been played, Kevin went back to his house to sleep.

The next morning, Kathleen put on her sweats and ran across Wilshire and then wove her way around the back streets until she'd run for a solid hour, finishing in Westwood Village, where she picked up some coffee. A cup in each hand, she walked back to her building, then took the elevator straight up to the penthouse. She kicked at the door and Sam answered it dressed for work.

"You have time for a cup of coffee?" she asked.

"A quick one." He took one of the cups from her. "Come into the kitchen. Last time I let you drink coffee in here, you spilled some on the rug."

"How'd you know that?" she said. He hadn't been in the room when it happened.

"I saw you wiping at it later, when you thought I wasn't looking. It left a stain."

"Jeez," she said. "You can't get away with anything around here."

"No," he said. "You can't." A point further proven when they were sitting down at the kitchen table and he said, "That was a lovely choice you made—to publicly rub Kevin's nose in the fact his father's cheating on his mother. What son wouldn't enjoy that?"

"Shut up," Kathleen said. She had insisted on keeping her coffee in its takeout cup for no reason other than because Sam preferred her to put it in a mug. She played now with the cardboard sleeve, pushing it up and down the bottom half of the cup. "I wouldn't be so obnoxious about it if he would just for once admit what everyone knows."

"Jackson's been cheating on Caro since the day they got married," Sam said. "Literally. He invited his girlfriend at the time to the wedding. So he wouldn't get bored if dinner went on too long, I assume."

"You're kidding."

"The person who told me that is usually reliable, and I don't see any reason *not* to believe it, all things considered." He shrugged. "That's just the way it is with Jackson. He's a short ugly man with a lot of money and power who still can't believe that attractive women are willing to sleep with him. Caro must have made her peace with it years ago."

"Or is just so stoned she doesn't care anymore."

"I first met Caro twenty years ago," Sam said. "She was the most beautiful woman I'd ever seen."

"Prettier than Patricia?"

"Yes, Kathleen, prettier than Patricia. And there aren't many women I'd say that about." He took a careful sip from his pristine white coffee mug. "But she made her deal with the devil. She knew what she was getting herself into."

"Then maybe she should let her sons in on the secret."

He studied her from under his dark eyebrows. "You really think Kevin doesn't know?"

"No," she said. "I totally think he knows. That's why it drives me so crazy that he won't admit it."

"How angry was he last night?" Sam asked.

"He wasn't mad at all," Kathleen said, jerking her chin up. "He didn't say a single word about it."

"Well, that must have been frustrating for you," Sam said. "Working so hard to get a reaction out of him and then not getting it."

"I didn't want to make him *angry*," she said. "I just wanted him to admit the truth for once. For his own mental health."

"Oh, come on," Sam said. "You don't point out to a guy that one of his parents is unfaithful and a liar unless your goal is to infuriate him."

She opened her mouth to argue but had to close it again. He was right, of course. She had known that what she was saying to Kevin would make anyone furious—anyone except, apparently, *Kevin*. The truth was she had found his lack of a reaction anticlimactic. "Well, why *won't* he just admit it?" she said. "If I know it and he knows it and the whole world knows it. Why not just admit it's true?"

"If the Porters started acknowledging everything that's sick or wrong with their lives . . ." Sam didn't bother to finish the sentence. "They've found some kind of status quo in just ignoring everything. That's what works for them, I guess. And if you're going to marry into that family, Kathleen, you're going to have to learn to be as blind as the rest of them."

"I don't think I could," she said. "I mean, to sit around all the time pretending you don't know things you know—"

"It probably just takes a little practice, that's all."

"I guess." She twisted her mouth sideways, thinking. "So what else do you know about them?"

"Who? The Porters?"

"You said there's lots of dirt there."

"There is," he said. "But you're not going to hear it from me. Ask your husband-to-be."

"He won't tell me anything."

"No," Sam said. "He probably won't."

V

During the weeks following Halloween, Sari felt like she had a devil sitting on one shoulder and an angel on the other. The devil looked and sounded a lot like Lucy, and it said, "Keep things going with the guy, have some fun, make him fall in love with you, and then shatter his heart and his life into a million pieces." And the angel, who looked a little like Ellen, but was dressed for some reason in Kathleen's responsible clothes, said, "Don't do it, Sari. For your own sake."

She knew the angel was right, but it was the devil who intrigued her. Sometimes, when she said goodbye to Jason at the end of a session, she'd meet his eyes and see the pleading there and wonder what it would be like to give in to it and go out with him and follow the whole tangle through to the end—and then crush him. And sometimes she'd wonder what it would be like to follow it through to the end and *not* crush him. And that's when she would give herself a good mental shake and listen to the angel and keep herself well out of it.

There was one day when Jason was wearing a blue shirt that lightened the color of his eyes until you just wanted to stare at them forever. At the end of the session, he asked Sari if she had time to have a drink with him, and she had to struggle to say no.

That night, she ran home and got down her high school yearbook and made herself study it.

The page devoted to the Resource Room, a page on which Charlie appeared three times—once with a chef's hat on and a big smile, because they had been making cookies in class that day and Charlie loved cookies more than anything else in the world—left her throat and eyes aching with tears that wouldn't come all the way out.

After that, the pictures—page after page after page—of Jason Smith on every sports team, a smirk of athletic superiority and social dominance always on his face, successfully rekindled her anger and her determination not to be swayed by a pair of blue eyes.

Back at the clinic, it was once again easy to tell him no when he asked her out and it stayed easy—no, she didn't want to have coffee, no, she wasn't interested in seeing a movie, no, she was rushing off after this session, no, she was busy, no, she had work to do, no, she had other plans . . .

At some point, he'd have to give up, she figured. But she also knew that the one blue-eyed day she had hesitated before saying no had given Jason Smith reason to think that maybe there was hope. He took her reluctance as a challenge, and, instead of giving up, he tried harder.

She couldn't have strung him along any better if she'd been trying.

She could guess what he thought—that it was their professional relationship that made her pull back, that she was worried she was breaking some kind of unwritten (or maybe even written) clinic law. He probably assumed things would have been different if they'd met at a party instead of as client and professional. He probably told himself stories of people who overcame an awkward business situation to find love and romance together. The thrill of the chase probably made it all the more interesting to him. He was that kind of guy.

And meanwhile there was Zack, who was improving almost daily; Zack with the crooked grin who would one day stare at Sari uncomprehendingly when she tried to teach him to say, "I want a cookie," and who would two days later come walking up to her and point to the cookie jar and say, "Want cookie," as if he had always said it, as if it were the most natural thing in the world for him to utter a two-word sentence; Zack, who now crawled into her lap the second she picked out a book to show him, who grabbed her hand when she arrived at his house and pulled her outside where he would say, "Ball?" and then walk her over to the basketball court; Zack, who was calm almost all the time now, who hardly ever screamed anymore, who learned by leaps and bounds and with whom she found herself more in love every day.

With *him*, at least, her relationship was uncomplicated and satisfying.

6

Casting Off

1

The next week, Jason asked Sari if she could stay after Zack's session that coming Friday and have dinner at their house. "Denise wants to meet you, and she's free that evening."

The problem with being as confused as Sari was about everything having to do with the Smith family was that she didn't even know anymore what her normal response would be to something like that. If any other father had said to her that she should stay for dinner to meet the child's mother whom she had never met before and who really should be given a chance to consult with her . . . would she feel obliged to say yes? Or would she have every right to say no?

When feelings of anger and desire and revenge and attraction *didn't* get in the way of a decision like that, then what would the decision be?

It was paralyzing, this confusion.

Jason misinterpreted her hesitation. Or, quite possibly, he interpreted it correctly. "You don't have to worry about being alone with me," he said with a tight smile. "Denise and Maria and Zack will all be there. You won't even have to talk to me if you don't want to."

"It's not that," she said. "I was just trying to remember if I had plans that night."

"Do you?"

"I don't think so." She made up her mind. "I'll stay."

His face lit up, but all he said was, "Denise will be pleased."

Denise was late. They waited for her from five-thirty until almost seven. She called four times to say she was just about out the door. After the fourth call, Jason offered Sari a drink. Sari declined—as she had the previous two times he'd offered—but he continued to have better luck with himself and filled his own glass for the third time.

So he was definitely a little drunk by the time Denise finally made her appearance at the house with a bang of the front door and an entrance into the living room that included a cheery, "Hello! Here I am!"

Sari rose to her feet, but Jason didn't get up, just raised his glass in a brief salute and said, "Welcome."

"I'm so sorry I kept you guys waiting," Denise said.

"No, it was good," he said. "Gave me time to work on my show pitch. Want to hear it?"

She was still smiling brightly. "Jason—"

"No, no, it's great. Listen. An attractive young therapist moves in with an autistic kid and his family, and hilarity ensues. I mean it just *ensues*."

"Ha," Denise said. "I'll suggest it to the network." She strode forward to greet Sari. "Sari Hill. I can't tell you how excited I am to finally meet you. Zack has *blossomed* since you started working with him. It's beyond incredible." She took Sari's hand and squeezed it warmly. "I can't ever thank you enough. There *are* no words."

She had long blond hair, a perfectly toned body, and cheekbones you could trip over. She was dressed in a sleeveless silk top and a pair of carefully tailored black pants that showed off her tight ass and toned legs.

"So," she said as she released Sari's hand and looked around. "Where is my little Zacky, anyway?"

"That's a kind of chicken," Jason said. He hadn't gotten up from the chair he'd been sitting on when she arrived—had, in fact, slumped even deeper into it.

"Excuse me?" she said.

"Zacky Farms. They make chickens. He's with Maria having dinner in the kitchen."

"Oh, okay. I'll go say hi in a sec. Do I get a glass of wine, too?"

"The bottle's over there," he said, indicating the wet bar.

"Lovely," she said. Sari couldn't tell if she were being sarcastic or not. "Sari, would you join me in a glass of wine?"

"No, thanks."

"What about dinner?" Denise walked over to the wet bar, slid a glass out of the hanging rack, and poured wine with the ease of someone who knew where everything was. "I'm starving. What's the plan?"

"Ah," Jason said. "Here's the thing about dinner. We were waiting for you to order. You were late. Therefore, we have not yet ordered."

"Have you at least offered our guest something to eat while she's been waiting?"

"No, because you kept saying you'd be here any minute."

"Oh, you poor thing," Denise said, swiveling back to Sari. "You must be starved. I am so sorry. I had just assumed you'd go ahead and start eating without me. If I had known—"

"I'm fine," Sari said. "Really. I was sharing Zack's M&M's with him all afternoon and almost made myself sick on them. Job hazard, you know."

"'Job hazard'?" Denise repeated, raising the wineglass to her lips.

"She uses candy as a reward," Jason said. "Which you would know if you had ever come to see her work with him."

"It's not that I'm always shoving candy at him," Sari said to Denise. "I don't want you to think that he's like a dog, getting a treat with every trick or anything like that. Most things he does, the reinforcement comes naturally, like if he wants to go outside and he says, 'out,' and then I take him outside. But the M&M's come in handy for a lot of games and working on color names and stuff like that. Everyone likes candy!" She was talking too much, the way she always did when she got nervous.

"I see," Denise said politely.

Sari felt like an idiot.

"Here, Denise," Jason said. "Let me put it in terms you'll understand. Say your assistant does a really good job of lying for you when you don't want to talk to someone on the phone. You don't scream at him for five whole minutes and he gets the idea that he's been a good boy and should do lots more lying in the future. That's called positive reinforcement."

"Jason's going to give you the wrong impression of me," Denise said to Sari with a good-natured laugh. "I'm actually a pretty decent boss."

"Oh, of course," Sari said. Then: "I'm really so glad we're getting a chance to meet and talk about Zack's progress."

"Are you kidding?" Denise said. "I wouldn't have missed this for the world. I've been dying to learn more about how you do what you do."

"Sure, you have," Jason said. "That explains your constant presence at Zack's sessions."

Denise pivoted on her heel so she was facing him. "I *work* in the afternoons." She smiled at him. "So you don't have to, I might add."

"You might and you did," he said. "So what should we order for dinner? I seem to be already eating shit, but I'm open to a change of menu."

Denise turned back to Sari and took her arm. She lowered her voice. "I'm sure you realize that Jason's just trying to be funny. Sometimes drinking affects his judgment a little bit, and he's not always aware of how he sounds." Then, in her normal voice: "I just want you to know that we couldn't be more dedicated to pulling together as a team to make things right for Zack. That's priority number one for both of us."

"Oh, of course," Sari said. "And I want—" She was interrupted by a few bars of "Fur Elise."

"Excuse me one moment," Denise said, dropping Sari's arm so she could slip a tiny cell phone out of the slim Prada handbag she had left on the bar. She put it to her ear as she took another sip of wine. "Denise Cotton," she said.

Sari drifted a few steps back.

From the depths of his chair, Jason said, "She went back to her maiden name. For a few glorious years she was actually Denise Smith."

Sari didn't say anything to that.

"Oh, *damn*," Denise said. She flipped her phone shut and slid it back into her purse. "You won't believe this. I drove all the way here just to get to spend a few minutes with you, Sari, and I told everyone who works for me that I couldn't be bothered for anything short of an emergency. So of course one came up. There's been a total breakdown on one of the sets—it's a complete mess and they need me there to straighten it out." She took a sip of wine and set the glass back on the counter. "I can't believe how frustrating this is! To finally get to meet you and then not have time to talk about Zack."

"It's nice to put a face to the name at least," Sari said.

Denise shone a brilliant smile in her direction. "*Exactly* what

I was thinking. And I know we'll get together again soon." She slung her purse on her shoulder. "I hope you don't mind, but I feel like I have to hug you. You're just so wonderful." She put her arms around Sari and kissed her lightly on each cheek. "Thank you," she said. "Thank you, thank you, thank you. And we're going to reschedule this ASAP."

"Great," Sari said, and Denise squeezed her hard again before releasing her.

"Goodbye, Jason," she said and turned to go.

"Hold on." He rose to his feet for the first time since her arrival. "You're going to at least say hi to Zack before you leave, aren't you?"

She glanced at her watch and then said, "Better not. I don't want to upset him by saying hi and then having to leave right away."

"You haven't seen him in days."

"And I miss him," she said. "More than you can possibly imagine."

"It's hard to imagine you miss him at all when you won't bother walking into the next room to see him."

"You're not getting it," she said. "It's hard for both of us if I see him and then have to immediately walk out on him again."

"So don't walk out."

"I wish it were that simple. Do you think it's easy for me to have to drop in on my own child? But I've got to support him—and all this—" She gestured at the house around them. "Believe me, I would love the luxury of being able to sit around the house all day with my kid—"

"You would hate it," Jason said. "You never wanted that."

"I've wanted it," she said. "But I'm not the type to sit around whining for something that's not going to happen."

"What type *are* you?" he said.

"The type who understands that we need a lot of money to

help Zack." She gestured in Sari's direction. "How long do you think we could hire people like Sari—wonderful, talented people like Sari—if I stopped working? How about Maria and all the freedom she gives you? You ready to give that up, Jason?"

"I'm not asking you to quit your fucking job," Jason said. He stood there in the middle of the room, his body tense but still. "I just thought you might want to say hi to your son."

"If I had more time, there's nothing in the world I'd rather do." She turned to go.

"You never have more time," he said from behind her back.

She twisted to look at him over her shoulder. "I do what I do because I know it's the best way for me to help Zack."

"Come on," he said. "When were you ever going to make any other choice?"

"I've never had the chance to find out," she said. "I've always had to support this family since you never could."

"Ah," said Jason. "Back to that one."

Denise turned to Sari. "I'm sorry," she said. "We're still working things out."

"It's okay," Sari said. "I know how hard it can be—"

"I'm sure you do," Denise said. "Please excuse me now, Sari. I'll be looking forward to the next time we get together." She left the room, and, a second later, the front door slammed.

There was a moment of silence, and then Jason forced a little painful laugh. "There she goes," he said. "The former Mrs. Jason Smith."

"It's tough on a marriage." Sari was well aware how lame she sounded. "Having a kid with special needs."

"Oh, we were doomed long before Zack came along," Jason said. "I've been almost as much of a disappointment to Denise as I've been to my father. They've had some fine conversations about what a failure I am." Sari didn't know what to say to this. After another moment, Jason said, "Of course, she's right about most of it. She does have to support us. And therapy doesn't come cheap."

"She still should have said hi to Zack," Sari said.

Jason's head snapped up. "Really?" he said eagerly.

"Of course." She searched for the right way to put it. "I mean, even if it was frustrating for both of them to say hi and bye quickly—even so, she should have *wanted* to so badly she couldn't help herself. I think—" She stopped, realizing she was getting into territory that was none of her business.

"I watch *you* with him sometimes," Jason said when she didn't go on. "When you're in the backyard, I'll look out the window, see you with him, and it's hard to *stop* watching. You're always so in the moment with him. Laughing and playing, like there's nowhere else you'd rather be than with my kid. I was always waiting for Denise to look like that when she was with him. I never saw it. I thought maybe it was because of who Zack is, because he never responded to her the way she wanted him to, but I think it's because of who *she* is. I'm not convinced it would have been any different if he'd been normal."

There was a pause. "So you've been spying on me," Sari said.

He smiled. "Observing you for purely clinical reasons," he said. "Nothing stalkerish about it. I swear."

"So I should hold off on the restraining order?"

"At least let me do something to earn it."

Another pause, and then Sari said, "I should go."

"No," he said. "Don't. You were planning on staying for dinner. Stay and have dinner with me."

She knew she shouldn't. But he stood there, begging her, a handsome guy who had just been beaten up inside. And they both knew she had the evening free.

* * *

He was smart enough—or was it calculating enough? She couldn't decide—to tread carefully at dinner, to keep the conversation on things Sari could talk about freely, to sense that she had glimpsed enough of his personal unhappiness to feel sympathetic to him, but that any more would scare her off. So, over sushi and sake—they had decided they would get food faster if they went out than if they ordered in—he asked her about the work she did and about autism in general. His interest pleased her and between the warmth of his regard and the warmth of the sake, she felt herself expand and relax.

"I can see that what you're doing works," he said after they'd been talking for a while. "I'm a total believer. But what I don't get is *why*? I mean, if it's really a question of neurological damage, then why do kids get better just from playing games and talking? It seems like they should need operations or a pill or something that would actually *fix* the damage. Not just, you know . . . M&M's and encouragement."

"Neural plasticity," Sari said, speaking the syllables very carefully. She had had quite a few cups of sake. They were small and it wasn't that strong a drink, but she had lost track of the number and suspected they were starting to add up. She should stop, she thought, as she lifted the tiny cup to her lips.

"Neural plasticity," Jason repeated. And then, "I have no idea what that means."

"I like using the term, because it sounds so scientific, but it basically just means that the brain's flexible." She put her cup down. "People get brain damage from things like strokes and car accidents and since the brain can't heal, you'd think that whatever function they lose would stay lost, right? But a lot of the time, they get it back. Like if they can't talk right after a stroke, but they do a lot of speech therapy, they'll usually be able to learn to talk again."

"True for my grandmother. She had a stroke and couldn't talk and then talked again. Happy ending. Until she had another stroke and died."

"I'm sorry," Sari said.

"Actually, she was an awful grandmother," he said. "Really mean. She scared the hell out of me when I was little—every time I saw her, she would tell me I should be ashamed of myself, but she would never tell me *why*. Maybe she just figured adolescent boys always had something to be ashamed of." He made a comical face. "Not that she was wrong about that."

"Well, anyway, she's a perfect example—her brain didn't *heal* exactly, it's just that other parts of her brain stepped in and took over for the injured part."

"I believe the term you're looking for is neural plasticity," he said.

"You catch on fast. So we think—it's still just a theory, but I believe it—that it works the same way for kids with autism. They start off with some real neurological damage, but with enough therapy their brains lay down new pathways, and the undamaged part takes over at least some of what the damaged part was supposed to do."

"Now that's just cool."

"I know," Sari said. "It really is. Here's to the human brain." They both raised their sake cups and drank.

"Makes you wonder whether it could work for the rest of us," Jason said as he placed his cup back on the table. "I mean, maybe if I can find a therapist to just keep telling my dad that I'm not the loser he thinks I am, he'd lay down some new pathways and start seeing me in a whole new way. What do you think?"

"I think you'll need forty hours a week to start," she said. "It won't be cheap."

"Too bad I really *am* the loser he thinks I am," Jason said. "Or I'd be able to afford it."

"But then you wouldn't need it."

"I know. It's all so confusing."

The waitress came and asked if they wanted more sake. They had finished their food a while ago. "I guess we're done," Jason said. "Unless you want some coffee?" He looked at Sari hopefully.

She hesitated. Then she said, "It's getting late."

She had left her car at the house, so Jason drove them both back.

"Want to come in?" Jason asked as they got out of the car. "Zack's probably in bed, but you could see how cute he looks when he's asleep." When she didn't answer right away, he said, "He's like world-class adorable."

She closed the car door. "I believe you. But I should go."

"Do you have to?"

She just nodded and headed down the driveway to the street where her car was parked. He followed close behind.

At her car, she said, "Good night. Thanks for—"

He cut her off with an abrupt hand gesture. "So, I'm wondering . . . how are you going to be when I see you tomorrow? Like this? Friendly and maybe a little interested? Or are you going to be the other Sari? The one who looks at me like I'm some kind of scary nut for just smiling at her?"

"I've never looked at you like that," she said.

"Yeah, you have." He reached for her hand and she let him take it. He held it lightly, his thumb brushing against the back of her fingers. "I'm not usually the kind of guy who slams his head against a wall over and over again," he said. "But I was married for a while and I haven't dated anyone in all that time, so maybe the rules are different now. I like you, Sari. A lot. And sometimes it seems like you like me back. But sometimes—"

"I do like you," she said, trying to sound calm. She didn't feel calm. He was standing too close for her to feel calm, and the way his fingers were playing with hers wasn't helping. "But I think it should stop here."

"Is there a clinic rule I don't know about? Is this kind of thing frowned on?"

"It's not that," she said.

"What is it, then?"

"Charlie," she said.

He dropped her hand. "Who the hell is Charlie? Your boyfriend?"

Sari opened her mouth and heard a strange choking sound that she realized was a laugh. Her laugh. But it seemed wrong to be laughing when Jason was being serious, so she tried to stop, and the effort to suppress it made her shake. She put her hand to her mouth to try to push the laughter back in.

And she realized it wasn't amusement. It was hysteria.

"What's so funny?" he said.

She shook her head, gasping a little. "Nothing."

"Who's Charlie?" he asked again. Impatient now. Getting annoyed. "Is he your boyfriend?"

"No," she said, and dropped her hand from her mouth, the hysteria gone as suddenly as it had come. "I don't have a boyfriend."

"Husband?"

"No."

"Lesbian lover?"

She shook her head.

"Now we're getting somewhere," Jason said and drew closer.

"No rules, no other man, no other woman . . . Is there any good reason I shouldn't do what I want to do? What I've been dreaming about doing for weeks?"

The little Lucy devil on her shoulder said, "Lead him on and break him apart." The responsibly dressed Ellen angel said, "Get out of there while you're still okay, Sari." And the girl in between them just wanted to feel Jason's mouth on hers and his hands on her body, so she didn't say or do anything, just waited in the cool dark of the night, her face turned up to him.

She had answered his question with her silence and her willingness. He smiled and his arms came around her.

His mouth tasted a little like alcohol, but it didn't change how good it felt. She closed her eyes and let him pull her close, like she had always wanted him to.

His whole body pressed into hers. Sari pressed back, shivering. He was Jason Smith and she had wanted him since she was fifteen years old. She could get lost in him—*was* getting lost in him—in his strong chest and broad shoulders, in the feel of his hands on her back, pinning her against him so she could feel the length of his body and how he was already hard for her. She was going to get lost in it, she wanted to get lost in it, she was ready to get lost in it . . .

If this had all happened in a dark, private room, that probably would have been that, and she would have fallen into bed with him and postponed all regrets and confusion to the next day's tab. But they were outside, and the sudden headlights of a car driving by made them both start and pull back and look around, their pupils dilated from more than just the dark.

"Come inside," he said, tugging on her arm.

But she shook her head. She had been given a chance to stop and think about what she was doing. She would be an idiot not to take it. "I'd better not. It's better to take this slowly."

"You sure about that?" Jason said, his voice not sounding like itself.

"Yeah."

"I don't want to scare you off. But—" He took a deep breath, then said, " 'Slowly' isn't another way of saying you're going to pretend you've never seen me before when I walk into the clinic tomorrow, is it?"

She shook her head again. "I'm not that good an actress."

"Good," he said. "So you meant all that?"

"Yeah," she whispered, not quite able to look at him. "But I still have to go."

His fingers stroked her arm. "Really? You have to?"

She found she was leaning in toward him again. She righted herself with an effort. "I just think it's a good idea."

"I can think of better ideas," he said. "I've been thinking of better ideas for you and me for a long time, Sari."

"You *do* have stalker potential."

"No," he said. "All things considered, I think I've been pretty restrained."

"You deserve a medal."

"A medal isn't what I want."

Her mouth curved in a smile and they were kissing again—she was pretty certain she started it this time, although it was hard to tell. It went on for a while.

But still somehow, eventually, she managed to stop touching him and get herself into her car. She shut the door, but then he tapped on the window, and she rolled it down. "What?" she said.

"You never told me who Charlie was."

Euphoria fled. "My brother," she said flatly, and, as she drove away, she wondered if Jason had any idea what a huge mistake it had been for him to bring up Charlie when, for once, she hadn't already been thinking about him.

Driving home in the dark, Sari suddenly remembered something she hadn't thought of in years—some graffiti in a girls' bathroom stall in high school. It had stayed up there for months, maybe even years, and the image had eventually seared itself into her brain, to come back now in an abrupt flash.

First someone had written in dark purple marker, "I want to be raped by Jason Smith."

Underneath that, someone else had written in orange, "Rape is an act of violence not sex you fucking idiot."

And underneath that, in pink letters: "Even an act of violence by Jason Smith would be sexy." The *i* in "violence" was dotted with a heart.

Even back then, Sari had known that there was no use trying to be politically correct at her school, no use trying to save the other girls from their sick wet dreams and perverted sense of romance. You can't save people who don't want to be saved.

But where did that leave her?

She didn't sleep much that night. The bed was empty and cold without him, and as she tossed and shivered, unable to sleep, tortured by confusion and lust, she wondered if he ever felt the same way, like the bed was too big for him without Sari curled up at his side.

Not Jason, of course.

Charlie.

11

Kathleen and Kevin spent Saturday night at the San Ysidro ranch in Santa Barbara and didn't want to rush back, so the girls moved their Sunday knitting circle to the evening, which meant that Sari could serve wine and guacamole instead of bagels and coffee.

As she poured herself a second glass of wine, Kathleen pointed out that it was almost Thanksgiving.

"You doing the whole family thing?" Sari asked her.

"I'm splitting it down the middle," Kathleen said. She settled back in her seat. "Kevin invited me to come home with him—"

"Whoa," Sari said. "That's a big deal." She was flipping through a new knitting magazine. She had finished the baby blanket and was ready for her next project but was having trouble deciding what to do. Since Friday night, she hadn't been able to focus on much of anything.

"You don't bring a girl home for Thanksgiving dinner unless you're pretty serious about her," Lucy said, looking up from her knitting.

Kathleen grimaced. "Put a little pressure on me, why don't you? Anyway, I said yes, but then Mom started leaving me messages telling me that I'm always too busy for them these days, and it's the holiday season, and don't I care about my family, and so on and so on. So I've got to at least swing by there at some point. Maybe even with Kevin, if he'll come."

"Has he met the twins yet?" Sari asked.

"Once. We had dinner at the McMansion a couple of weeks ago."

"What'd he think of them?"

"He said they seemed nice. And that I'm prettier than they are."

"Has he had his eyesight checked recently?" Lucy asked.

"Shut up."

"Mom, Kathleen's telling me to shut up again," Lucy said. "Punish her."

"Does that make me 'Mom'?" Sari looked up, her finger stuck in a page. "Because I don't think I'm emotionally ready to parent two grown women."

"I knew you'd reject us one day," Kathleen said. She dipped her finger in the wine and ran it along the edge of the wineglass. "So what are you guys doing for Thanksgiving? You going home, Luce?"

Lucy shook her head. "Too far."

"What do you mean too far?" Kathleen wiped her finger on her shirt and picked up her knitting. "You grew up right around here."

"Yes, and my parents moved to Arizona three years ago—which I've told you a million times."

"You'll probably have to tell me again. I've already forgotten it. It's the way you drone on about things—I'm so bored I can't stay focused."

"Mom," Lucy said. "Kathleen's being a jerk."

"If you two don't stop fighting, I'm sending you both to your rooms," Sari said. She turned another page of her magazine. "There, are you satisfied?"

"Not really," Kathleen said. "She started it."

"I don't care who started it. Let Mommy get shit-faced in peace." Sari took a sip of wine. "What about James, Luce? What's he doing?"

"Going to his uncle's in Long Beach. He offered to bring me, but it doesn't sound like much fun—too many old relatives."

Sari said, "Any way I could talk you into coming with me to my parents' house?"

"I actually don't mind being alone," Lucy said. "I figured I'd go see a couple of movies, let myself eat as much popcorn as I want for once—"

"Sounds kind of wonderful," Sari said. "Believe me, I'm not asking you for your sake. I'm asking you for mine. The last time I went home, it was a pretty bad scene. I had to leave after like ten minutes. But my mom's always liked you, and if you're there, she'll be on her best behavior and maybe we won't get into our usual fight."

Kathleen said, "You're not exactly selling it, Sari."

"Okay, wait—let me try this again," Sari said. She plastered on a fake smile. "It'll be lots of fun! And don't forget about the delicious home-cooked meal!"

"Your mom once made me a bologna and mayonnaise sandwich," Lucy said. "I almost threw up."

"Yeah, okay, she's a shitty cook," Sari said. "But please, Lucy, I'm begging you. For real. I don't want to go home alone. Please. Please please please please please."

"Oh, fine," Lucy said. "But this is depressing. I finally get out of having to go to *my* home for Thanksgiving, and I'm stuck going to yours. You owe me big for this one, Sari."

"Name it," Sari said. "It's yours. You want my firstborn son?"

"Kids are too messy," Lucy said. "I'd take a puppy, though."

"Yeah, because, dogs aren't messy," Kathleen said. She swiped a chip through the guacamole. "They *never* shit on the floor." She stuck the entire chip in her mouth.

Sari tossed the magazine onto the table with a sigh. "Maybe I had too much wine," she said. "Everything looks ugly and wrong in there. It all seems like too much work for no good reason."

"Wine usually makes things look better," Kathleen said. "You sound more depressed than drunk."

"Yeah," Lucy said. "You okay, Sari?"

Sari just shrugged. The other two exchanged a look.

"What ever happened with Cute Asshole Guy?" Kathleen asked casually. "Last we heard, you were kissing him."

"I don't know," Sari said. Then, in a rush: "Things just keep getting weirder and weirder. I'm actually thinking maybe I should stop working with his kid."

"Really?"

"I just can't deal with the situation anymore."

"Well, maybe it's for the best then," Lucy said.

"It's not for the best," Sari said with sudden vehemence. "I like Zack a lot. And he's doing great. So it's *not* for the best, Lucy—it's all fucked up."

"Then keep working with him," Lucy said.

"I can't," Sari said. "It's not a healthy situation. Not with his dad trying to—" She stopped.

"Just tell him to back off so you can keep seeing his kid," Kathleen said.

"That won't work," Sari said. "Because of *me.*" She put her hands up in the air and then let them drop. "I can't seem to just ignore him. It's like . . . seeing him made my life that much more interesting." She stared miserably at the rug. "I don't know whether I like him or hate him, but not knowing kept things from being boring—and I like everything about him except that I hate him."

"You need a *real* boyfriend," Lucy said. "Someone decent who keeps your life interesting because he's kind and attentive and not because he used to shove poor old Charlie around."

"Brilliant," Sari said. "Know anyone like that?"

"Thousands," Lucy said. "I'm just holding out on you."

III

On Monday morning, Sari walked into Ellen's office and asked to have someone else take over Zachary Smith's program.

Ellen wanted to know why.

"I love the kid," Sari said. "He's great. But I can't keep seeing him. For personal reasons."

"You're going to have to give me more than that," Ellen said.

"No, I don't."

Ellen waited, but Sari just tightened her mouth and looked at the floor. After a moment, Ellen sighed and—for once—surrendered. "Is there anything I need to know about the family before I assign someone else? Anything you're not telling me?"

"No."

"Because if there's something wrong—if the guy's a letch, or anything like that—you'd better tell me now. I'm not about to put one of my clinicians into an ugly situation."

"He's not a letch," Sari said. "I promise you, it'll be fine for anyone who's not me."

"You're not getting out of the hours," Ellen said. "If I put the Smith kid with someone else, you'll have to take on some new kids."

"I know. That's fine."

"All right." Ellen pulled a pad of paper toward her and picked up a pen. "Let me figure this out."

"Thanks." Sari moved toward the door.

Ellen looked up again. "Tell me, should I be pissed at you, Sari? Or worried about you?"

"Neither," Sari said. "I'm a big girl."

"Not if I'm cleaning up your mess, you're not."

Sari blushed with sudden shame.

Ellen was already reaching for the phone to cancel that day's appointment for the Smiths when Sari left her office.

Sari checked her e-mail that afternoon. She had three messages from Jason Smith. She looked at the subject lines.

The first was, "About this weekend."

The second was, "Dinner tonight?"

And the third was, "What the hell is going on?"

She deleted them all immediately.

IV

The first hint something was up came on Monday evening, when Lucy and David were walking out of the lab together and he asked her if she would be in her apartment the following morning.

"What kind of question is that?" she said.

"A yes-or-no one."

"I may go to the gym," she said. "Why?"

"Don't go to the gym," he said. "Stay home."

"And again, I say, Why?"

"No reason whatsoever." And he walked off.

That made her curious. David had never come by her apartment before except to drop off work stuff.

She woke up at seven and was in a really bad mood by nine—

she still hadn't heard from him and she could have gone to the gym and been back three times by then.

Then, a little after nine, she heard the buzzer. "It's me," David's voice said, distorted by the intercom system.

"This better be good," she said and buzzed him in.

She waited by the apartment door, her arms crossed, ready to be furious with him. He came up the stairs, holding something—a big white cardboard box with handles—and flashing an enormous self-satisfied grin. "Lucy," he said, "meet your new best friend." He put the box on the hallway floor, knelt down next to it and opened up the top, then reached inside and pulled out an extremely small gray ball of fluff. It had two big eyes and a pointy chin. At the sight of Lucy, it opened its miniature mouth, revealing several tiny uneven white teeth, and gave a squeaky little meow.

"Ow," David said. "It keeps digging its claws into me." He held the animal out to her. "So what do you think?"

Lucy squatted down next to him and carefully took the kitten. "Oh," she said. It was incredibly light, like it was made out of fur and not much more. It fit on the palm of her hand, and she could feel its heart beating against her palm. "Let's go in," she said and stood up slowly, cradling the kitten safe and tight against her body, then led the way back into the apartment.

David carried the box in and shut the door behind them.

"Where did you get it?" Lucy asked. She rubbed the top of the kitten's head. There was hard bone right under the fluff.

"He's cute, isn't he? I got him at the pound. You wouldn't believe what you have to go through to get a kitten there. They found him a couple of weeks ago, but wouldn't release him until this morning and by the time they opened, there was already a crowd of people all wanting him. Someone had actually been waiting there since five. So they held a live auction, with people bidding and screaming at each other and everything. It was pretty intense."

"But you won?"

"Yeah," David said. "I was determined."

She lifted the kitten up high and peered at it from underneath. "It's a boy."

"I could have told you that if you'd just asked. Or do you get off on looking at little animal penises?"

"I take what I can get," she said with a laugh. She snuggled the kitten in both hands and put him against her cheek. "He's so soft."

"Isn't he?" He was watching her, leaning back against the door, looking very pleased with himself.

"Are you just showing him to me?" she said. "Or actually giving him to me? Because—" Because she wanted him more than she'd ever wanted anything before. Why hadn't she ever thought of getting a cat before? She had thought about a dog, but never a cat. A cat made *sense.*

"He's all yours," David said. "Although I'd like to retain some visiting rights."

"Why?" Lucy looked at him, the kitten still caught against her cheek. He had started purring—it was like a tiny motor in her left ear.

"I got attached to him on the ride over."

"No, I mean, why did you get him for me?"

"I don't know," he said. Then: "I guess, ever since that night at the bar . . . you seemed so sad about having to kill animals for work and not having any as pets. I wanted to get you something. A dog seemed way too time-consuming and a fish just isn't all that much fun. Plus, I figured you could really relate to a cat, what with you both being rat-killers and all."

"And cute," Lucy said. "Cute little rat-killers, both of us."

"Exactly. But if you don't want him, I could—"

"I want him," she said. "He's perfect."

"That's what I thought when I saw him. I thought about telling you, but I wanted it to be a surprise, and I didn't know for sure if I'd end up getting him or not."

"Was it very expensive? I mean, if it was an auction—"

"It was a *pound*, Lucy," he said. "People get animals at pounds because they can't afford pet stores. Don't worry about it."

"That's not why people go to pounds," she said. "It's for moral reasons."

"Whatever. I could afford it."

"I'd like to pay you back," she said. "Tell me how much."

For the first time since he'd arrived that morning, his grin faded. "Jesus, Lucy, just say thank you, will you? It's a gift."

"Thank you," she said. "Oh, David, thank you."

There was a short awkward pause. She thought she should probably hug him or something, but she was holding the kitten in her hands and couldn't really. She looked around and said, "I'll have to figure out where he can sleep and eat and everything. And kitten-proof the apartment."

"Yeah, you might want to cover any live wires," David said. "And no more inviting coyotes over for a cup of tea. Do you know if you're allowed to have pets in this building?"

"No," she said. "It was never an issue, so I never bothered to ask."

"If it's a problem—"

"I'll move," Lucy said.

"I was going to say I could take him in, but that works, too." He leaned forward and touched the kitten's nose. "I knew you'd like him. Oh, and I have some stuff in the car. I'll go get it. Some food and medicine for his eyes. They're a little gunky."

She raised the kitten to eye level and peered at him. "Oh, yeah. I hadn't even noticed."

"They said most of the kittens come in that way, but it clears right up with the drops. I also stopped at the drugstore for some other things—the pet store wasn't open yet. Let me go get it all." He left the apartment and Lucy could hear him clatter down the stairs.

She sat down with the kitten on her lap. "Hello," she said and rubbed the top of its bony-fluffy little head with her index finger knuckle. "I'm your new roommate." The kitten pushed its forehead hard against her hand, then started to climb up her stomach, its long thin claws slipping through the knit of her sweater so she could feel their points prick against her skin. It was a delicious feeling.

She had thought the kitten was all gray, but now, as she studied it more closely, she saw that it had two little black lines between its eyes and two tiny black dots on the top of its nose.

She was still sitting there just looking at the cat when David reappeared at her open front door.

"Hey," he said, dropping a couple of bags on the floor. "I got some kitten chow, too. By the way, they said to never give him milk or cream, because it could upset his stomach. Who knew?"

"I did," Lucy said. "Because I had cats when I was a kid. But they weren't ever kittens."

"Actually," he said, "I'm fairly certain they must have been at some point. See, the mommy cat and the daddy cat love each other a lot, and he puts a seed in her—"

"You know what I mean. I only ever knew them as adults. I've never owned a kitten before."

David sat down next to her. "Nothing cuter than a kitten." He extended his index finger, and the kitten sniffed at it, then put his own paw on top. "He's shaking hands," David said. "The world's most brilliant cat."

The kitten put his mouth on the end of David's finger and tried to suck at it.

"He thinks you're a nipple," Lucy said.

"I'm rethinking that whole brilliant thing." They both watched the kitten mouth David's finger. "What are you going to name him?"

"I hadn't even thought about it yet. You sprang this on me pretty suddenly."

"How about calling him David?"

"You want me to name my cat after you?" She raised her eyebrows. "That's asking a lot, don't you think?"

"Maybe," he said. "But think of how much fun we could have with this. You could say things like, 'David slept all curled up against me last night,' in front of other people and make them wonder what's going on between us."

"You'd take way too much pleasure in that."

"Come on," he said. "Throw me a bone. It's the only way I'm ever going to get into your bed. Besides, David is a great name. He defeated Goliath, you know."

"Fine," Lucy said and raised the kitten into the air. "I dub you David the cat. And if you're anything like the guy you're named after, you'll be an enormous pain in the butt."

"You like him, don't you?" David poked her with his elbow.

"How many times do I have to tell you?" She put the cat on the sofa next to her so she could give David a hug. "Thank you," she said. "This may be the best present anyone's ever given me."

"You're very welcome." They released each other and he sat back. "Did I mention that I got up at six-thirty in the morning just for you?"

"You want a cup of coffee?"

"I thought you'd never ask."

Lucy went into the kitchen and busied herself pouring the water and measuring the coffee. The whole time, her heart sang with joy. She was in love with a pound of gray fur. And his name was David.

V

Sari walked into Lucy's apartment the next Sunday, greeted her, dropped a bag of bagels on the table, pulled a brand-new skein of yarn, a needle, and her knitting magazine out of her workbag, sat down at the table—and sneezed. And sneezed again. And three more times.

"Man," she said, blowing her nose in a paper napkin. "Something's really bothering my allergies. Did James give you flowers or something?"

"Are you kidding?" Lucy pulled out some bagels and arranged them on a pretty dark blue plate. "He hates the whole custom of giving flowers—he thinks it's a waste of money and bad for the environment and celebrates death and blah, blah, blah—he'll go on and on about it if the subject comes up."

"Really? So how does he feel about diamonds?"

"Now that's never come up," Lucy said.

Sari sneezed again. "*Something's* bothering me."

Lucy looked up with a sigh. "You're allergic to cats, aren't you?"

"Yeah, of course. You know that. But—" Sari got to her feet and looked around. "Oh, no. Don't tell me—"

Lucy just pointed to the corner of the room, where David was curled up in a brand-new pet bed.

"Oh, shit, Luce," Sari said. "Why'd you do this to me?"

"I totally forgot you had allergies. I'm sorry."

Sneezing again, Sari reached for her purse. "Please let me have a Claritin in here." She rummaged around inside. "We won't be able to do knitting circle here anymore—not unless you want to put me in the hospital."

"You have to admit he's cute, though," Lucy said.

"I guess. I've never been much of a cat person. Given the fact that they make me totally miserable."

"Oh, but come on." Lucy went over and scooped up David. "Look at him."

"Not too close," said Sari. "Oh, good, I have one." She went into the kitchen and took the Claritin with a glass of water.

"Don't you worry," Lucy said to David, kissing him on the side of his furry little mouth. "She just has allergies. Otherwise, she'd think you were absolutely adorable."

Sari came back in. "Let's hope that works quickly," she said and immediately sneezed. She reached for another napkin. "Won't be fast enough for me. So when did you decide to get a cat?"

Lucy lightly touched her index finger to the tip of the kitten's right ear and made it twitch. "You remember my lab partner, David?"

"Why do you always say it like that?" Sari said. She sat back down at the table, pulling the magazine toward her. "Why do you always feel you have to explain who David is? I had lunch with him at the autism walk just a few weeks ago." She flipped through the magazine.

"Yeah, I know. Anyway, he got the cat for me."

Sari instantly looked up again. "What do you mean?"

"I mean he went to the pound and picked out the kitten—actually, it was a lot more complicated than that—I guess there was this whole auction thing—but the short story is that he got the kitten and gave him to me as a gift."

"Why'd he do that? Did you tell him you wanted one?"

"Not really," Lucy said. "But one night we were talking about all the rats we'd sac'd—killed—and I was kind of depressed about it and said how I had wanted to be a veterinarian when I was younger—"

"Oh, yeah, I remember. You used to make poor old Daisy lie down and let you examine her. Then you'd make pills out of rolled-up pieces of cheese and shove them down her throat."

"—and I guess he took that to mean that I'd like a pet. And dogs are too much work and you can't cuddle a fish, so . . ."

"That's an awfully romantic gesture," Sari said. "Giving someone a pet."

"Romantic?" Lucy repeated. "No, it's not. It's nice, but it's not *romantic*. Parents give kids pets all the time. Why would you even *say* that?"

"Lucy, he surprised you with a baby kitten—"

"Kittens are always babies. That's like saying a baby baby."

"Come on. Didn't you always use to say he had a crush on you?"

"Yeah, a million years ago. Before he started telling me I had a stick up my ass on a regular basis. Anyway, that's not what this was about. He just knew that I'm sick of killing rats, that's all."

"So he got you a pet that kills rats."

"It made sense to *me*."

"What'd you name it?" Sari asked

"I'm not sure yet." Lucy wasn't about to tell Sari the kitten's name was David, after everything Sari had just said. She knew Sari would try to read something into it.

"Well, congratulations," Sari said. "What does James think of it?"

"I haven't told him yet," Lucy said. She put David back into his little bed on the floor. "He hates pets even more than cut flowers."

There was a quick rap on the door, and Kathleen walked in, hand in hand with Kevin Porter. "Hey!" she said. "Kevin wanted to come up and say hi to you guys. He's dropping me off."

"Hi, Kevin," Sari said with a wave. "Want a bagel?"

"No, thanks," he said. "We just went out to breakfast. I'm stuffed." He stayed by the door and surveyed the room. "So this is the famous Sunday morning knitting circle, huh? Kathleen's always rushing out on me to get here on time."

"That's funny," Lucy said. "She's never actually on time."

"It moves around from place to place," Sari said. "But we've been doing it for a while—a couple of years now."

"I think that's great," he said. "Wish I knew how to knit. It looks like fun."

"You could learn," Lucy said.

Kevin laughed. "I don't think so."

"Why not?" Kathleen didn't seem to be as full as he was; she had gone right to the bagels and was tearing into one with her teeth. "Why wouldn't you learn?"

"You know," he said. "It would be weird. A guy knitting."

"Lots of guys knit," Lucy said.

"Straight guys?"

"Sure."

"Not that there's anything wrong with not being straight," he said. He put his hand on the doorknob. "Well, maybe one day you guys can teach me. But right now I've got a date to play golf with my father. Kathleen, are you okay for a ride home?"

Kathleen looked at Sari.

"You're covered," Sari said and sneezed.

"All right, then," Kevin said. "Bye." He slipped out, closing the door behind him.

"He couldn't leave fast enough, could he?" Lucy said.

"It's the knitting," Kathleen said. "Guys like Kevin get freaked when things get too girly. Like it might be contagious."

" 'Guys like Kevin'?" Sari repeated. "What kind of a guy is he exactly?"

"Just your average American male."

"You're madly in love with him, aren't you?" Lucy said. "Who wants coffee?"

"Do you need to ask?" Kathleen said. "And what the hell is that furry thing moving around over there? You bring one of your rats home?"

While Lucy was introducing her to David, the phone rang, and when Lucy answered it, it was James saying he'd left a book he needed at her place and could he come by now and grab it?

Lucy hung up and said, "It's bring-your-boyfriend-to-work day here at the knitting circle. James is stopping by."

"Oh, good," Sari said. "Maybe we can scare him off the way we scared Kevin off. And then we can scare off *my* boyfriend—oh, wait, I don't have one." She rubbed her eyes savagely. "God, they're so itchy I could scream."

Kathleen pointed to her magazine. "Did you find something to knit?"

"Yeah. This." She showed her the picture. It was a red, yellow, and black striped sweater.

"I like that it's cropped," Kathleen said. "Very chic."

"It won't look cropped on me," Sari said. "Not unless I make it like five inches long."

"You're lucky you're so small—you can knit a sweater for yourself in a couple of minutes. Takes me forever."

"What are you working on now?"

Kathleen had finished the tube top at their last get-together. She grinned at Sari, and pulled out her own knitting magazine. "This." She opened it to the marked page and pointed.

Lucy came over to look with Sari and groaned when she saw it was a bikini. A very skimpy hand-knit bikini.

Sari said, "Well, the good news is it can't take much yarn."

"Knitting a bathing suit in November," Lucy said. "Someone thinks she's going somewhere tropical this holiday season."

"Nothing's definite," Kathleen said, "but Kevin's parents own a house in Hawaii."

"Of course they do," Lucy said.

"You'll look great in this, Kath," Sari said. "I could never pull it off, but you totally can." She handed her back the magazine. "What color are you going to do it in?"

Kathleen pulled a skein out of her bag and showed them.

Lucy groaned again at the sight of the hot pink yarn. "Don't you ever get tired of being obvious?"

"Hasn't hurt me so far," Kathleen said.

There was a knock on the door and then James came in. "You didn't tell me you had visitors! Hi, Sari. Hi, Kathleen." He gave each of them a quick kiss on the cheek, finishing with Lucy. "Hi, babe. Did you know the door is propped open downstairs?"

"Yeah. I did that," Lucy said.

"Oh. Guess I should have left it then."

"Doesn't matter. We're all here now."

Kathleen said, "You're a guy, James. What would you think of this"—she showed him the photo of the bikini—"in hot pink?"

He tilted his head and studied the picture. "Depends on who's wearing it."

"Me."

"Then I'm all for it."

"See?" Kathleen said to Lucy. "He likes it in hot pink."

"Right," Lucy said. "A guy likes the idea of a gorgeous girl wearing a skimpy bathing suit—I'm sure it's all about the color."

"No, it's—" James stopped. "Hold on." His head turned. "What's that?"

"What?" Lucy looked in the same direction. David was sitting on the floor a few feet away, one leg in the air, his neck curved gracefully downward as he carefully licked his balls—or where his balls would have been if he hadn't been neutered. "Oh, that."

As they all turned to look at him, David froze in that position. His eyes darted back and forth among all the humans. He slowly lowered his leg.

James said, "Kathleen? Sari? Will one of you please tell me that cat is yours?"

"Sorry," Kathleen said with a cheerful shrug, and Sari said, "I can't even stand being in the same room with it. Allergies."

"That would make it—" He looked at Lucy. "Yours."

"Yeah," she said. "I got a cat. Surprise!"

"You've got to be kidding me."

"Why? You know I like animals."

"And you know I think it's idiotic to spend money and time

on something that doesn't contribute anything useful to the world."

"He's soft," Lucy said.

"Softer than you, James," Kathleen said. "I mean, I'm just guessing . . ."

He didn't even smile. "I'm serious, Lucy. Pets have to be the biggest waste— Do you know that there are children starving in this country? In this *city*? And you're going to spend money on food for this thing?"

"I'm not taking food out of their mouths," Lucy said. "I mean, I'm not *not* giving money to charity because I have a cat. It doesn't work that way."

"Yeah, Lucy wouldn't care about starving kids even if she didn't have a cat," Kathleen said.

"Stop helping her," Sari said. "Stop talking." She patted the chair next to hers firmly and Kathleen carried her knitting stuff and magazine over, sat down, and joined her in casting on stitches. But they were both listening to every word.

"I just can't believe you would go and get a cat when you know I hate the whole idea of pets," James said. "Unless that's the point."

"I realize this may come as a total shock," Lucy said. "But not everything's about you."

"You want something cute and cuddly? How about I buy you a stuffed animal? And I give this guy to a friend of mine who uses kittens for his research?"

"You're joking, right?" Lucy said.

"I'm deadly serious."

"You're sick."

"Oh, please," he said. "I thought you were smarter than that."

"I guess I'm not," she said. "I guess I'm an idiot like all those other idiots in the world who don't think exactly like James Shields."

"The world would be a much better place if people thought like me," he said. "And you know it."

"Can't you for once put yourself in someone else's shoes? Can't you see that someone might like to have a pet and still not be an idiot?"

"Nope," he said. His mouth was a flat line. There was a pause.

Lucy shifted abruptly and said, "The book you wanted—where'd you leave it?"

"In the bedroom, I think."

"Let me check."

While she was gone, Sari said, "There are bagels, James, if you're hungry."

"No, thank you," he said.

Lucy came back into the room. "This it?"

He nodded and she handed it to him. Their fingers didn't touch. "Thanks. Goodbye, everyone. Lucy, I'll call you later." He turned and left, closing the door hard behind him—not quite a slam, but almost.

There was a moment of silence. Then: "No one wants to stay with us today," Kathleen said. "I think it's all your fault, Sari. Offering a man a bagel. What's wrong with you?"

"I'm just a social klutz, I guess." Sari glanced up at Lucy. "You okay, sweetie?"

"Yeah." She sank down into a chair. "Slightly pissed, but okay. He's not right, is he? About the cat?"

"Definitely not," Kathleen said. "It's your apartment and your life. Who the hell gave him the right to say you shouldn't have a pet?"

"I don't like cats," Sari said, "but I'll defend to my death your right to have one."

Lucy stared at the knitting needle that was picking up stitches from the yarn wrapped around Sari's thumb and forefinger, like she was mesmerized by it. Then she said, "I don't know what's going on with me and James. Sometimes he just—" She stopped.

After a moment, Kathleen said, "I still think he's one good-looking dude."

"And smart and obviously good at what he does," Sari said.

"Yeah," Lucy said. "But he can be kind of a dick."

And by the way her friends didn't say anything, just suddenly got very involved in their knitting, she knew they didn't disagree.

VI

Sari checked her e-mail when she got home from the knitting circle. And there it was—her daily e-mail from Zacksdad@smithysmith.com.

The subject line was, "Worried about Zack." She went to delete it the way she normally did, but accidentally hit "read" instead.

She was fairly certain it was an accident.

She read the first line.

"I'm beginning to realize you don't actually give a shit about Zack," it began.

She closed it down immediately and this time had no trouble finding the delete button. She sat at her desk, her head in her hands, for a long time.

VII

By the time James stopped by the lab on Wednesday afternoon to check in on that week's progress, he and Lucy hadn't spoken for three days—not since Sunday morning. They were cordial, though, and kissed each other quickly on the lips in front of David, who politely busied himself changing the rats' water.

"You look tired, Lucy," James said, and she said, "I *am* tired. David wouldn't stop jumping on me in bed last night." The human David looked up with a laugh.

"So," James said when the joke was explained to him, "you're to blame for this kitten."

David went over to the sink. "I guess so." He turned on the water.

"You disappoint me, Lee," James said. "I thought better of you."

"Yeah, well, I disappoint a lot of people," David said cheerfully. "You're in good company." He washed his hands, dried them, and tossed the towel in the trash. "Shall we knock off now, Lucy? I know it's early, but I have to pack. I'm driving to my folks' later tonight." He headed to his desk.

"Sure," Lucy said. "Happy Thanksgiving, David."

David slipped his laptop into its case. "Happy Thanksgiving, Luce. Later, James."

James raised his hand silently and David left. There was a long pause. Then Lucy said, "Oh, I edited that grant proposal."

"Great."

"It's in good shape. I'll e-mail it to you tonight."

"Fine." There was a pause. Lucy sat down at her desk and shut down her computer.

Then James said, "You want to have dinner?"

She closed the laptop lid. "I'm meeting Sari."

"Oh," he said.

"You're welcome to join us."

"No, thanks." He stuck his hands in his pockets, rattled his change. "You want to come over to my place afterward? Maybe spend the night?"

"I should go home," she said. "David will have been alone all day."

"That would be David the cat."

"Obviously."

"You know," he said with a half smile, "women who choose cats over men end up crazy old ladies who live alone with a hundred cats in a smelly old house."

"I'll risk it," Lucy said. "You could come over to my place though. We could rent a movie."

"I'd hate to come between you and the kitten."

"Then don't come," Lucy said. "I don't care."

"Lovely," he said. "Thanks for that." He moved toward the door. "Does this mean we're done?"

"Done with this conversation?" she asked, standing up, holding on to the edge of her desk. "Or done for good?"

"Why don't you tell me which you'd prefer?"

She looked down at her curled-up fingers and said again, "I don't care."

"There's an answer, right there." He shook his head. "All because of that stupid cat . . ."

"No," she said. "Not really."

He shrugged and his mouth twisted suddenly. She was

touched to see that he was hurt. She let go of the desk and moved toward him but then he shifted abruptly and said, "You're pathetic, you know that? It's easy to love a kitten—all you have to do is stroke it and it'll purr. Forget about being challenged. Forget about being a good person. Just go pet something soft and let the rest of the world go to hell."

She drew back instantly. "Just because you don't get it—"

"Oh, I get it," he said. "We live in a world where mediocrity and stupidity are the norm. You're just joining the crowd."

"God, you're full of yourself," she said. "And wrong, too."

"I'm not wrong, and that's what you can't stand." He reached for the doorknob.

Lucy said suddenly, "I found out who was vandalizing your car, you know. And sending you all those e-mails and everything."

He wheeled around. "Are you serious? Who?"

"I've known for weeks," she said, "but I wasn't going to tell you."

"Why the fuck not?"

"Because," Lucy said, "I couldn't trust you to do the right thing."

He took a step toward her. "You wouldn't know what the right thing was if it jumped up and bit you in the ass."

"Maybe not," she said. "I make a lot of mistakes. But at least I can admit it."

"Congratulations," he said. "You're a successful loser. How proud you must be."

"Sure," she said. "Whatever you say, James."

He took a deep breath. "You know what? We're not going to do this. We still have to work together. And I respect you as a scientist. I always have and I always will."

"Me too you," she said.

"All right, then. Let's keep things on that level from now on." A pause. "Will you tell me who it was?"

"No."

He turned back to the door. "Goodbye, Lucy. Have a nice Thanksgiving."

"Thank you. You, too."

He left. Lucy leaned against her desk, feeling shaky and angry and like she wanted to cry. But she fought it and finished getting ready to go out. She was meeting Sari in half an hour at their favorite Thai restaurant. Sari would make her feel better. She always did.

They had to wait for a table, and by the time they were seated, she had already told Sari the whole story.

"I'm so sorry, honey," Sari said. "Breaking up is always rough."

"But it was the right thing to do, right?"

"If it felt right to you—"

"Come on, Sari, don't give me that shit. Tell me the truth. You never really liked him, did you?"

"He was a little hard to take sometimes," Sari said. "But he had a lot going for him. I could totally see the appeal."

"On paper, he was perfect," Lucy said. "He was everything I wanted."

"Are you heartbroken?"

Lucy thought for a moment. "No."

"Really not?"

"I only have eyes for David."

Sari's eyebrows soared. "For *David*?"

"The kitten, not the guy," Lucy said.

"The kitten? You named your kitten David?"

"Yeah. It was David's idea." She had forgotten she wasn't going to tell Sari.

"That's cute," Sari said. Her eyebrows still hadn't come back down. "Really. You named the cat after the guy who gave it to you. That's really adorable."

"Shut up," Lucy said.

"I'm sure it's not meaningful at all."

"Shut up. It's not. He made me do it."

"After giving you the gift of this pet you're crazy about and sleep with every night and broke up with your boyfriend over."

"Shut up," Lucy said.

The waitress came over and they ordered—pad thai for Sari, a shrimp salad for Lucy, with the dressing on the side.

"Anyone else on the horizon?" Sari asked after the waitress had left. "Like, for example, someone named David who's not a cat?"

"It's not like that with him," Lucy said. "For one thing, he has a girlfriend. And, even if he didn't, I'm not attracted to him."

"I think he's kind of cute."

"He's a nerd," Lucy said. "I dated enough nerds in college to last me a lifetime. I want to look across the pillow in the morning and be turned on."

"I want to look across the pillow in the morning and not be alone," Sari said. Then, "Oh, man, Luce, I'm sorry. I hate when people do that—make everything about themselves."

"Nah, it was your turn anyway," Lucy said. "You were looking a little sad when you got here. Everything okay?"

"I just got this e-mail from Jason Smith. He's pissed off that I stopped seeing Zack. And I feel guilty enough about it—" She made a face.

"You're too softhearted," Lucy said. "That's your problem. You don't owe him anything, Sari."

"I know. It's just—" She stopped. "Nothing. It's just nothing."

The waitress came up then with their food. Both girls stared at their plates without eating for a moment. Sari slowly brought her water glass to her lips.

"Oh, shit," Lucy said suddenly and savagely. "Oh, fuck, Sari!"

"What?" Sari said, so startled she almost dropped her glass. "What's wrong?"

"I just remembered—"

"What?"

"That fucking sweater," she said. "I've been working on that fucking sweater forever and now I don't have a boyfriend to give it to anymore. Kathleen was right. I can't believe it, but she was right. Knitting a sweater for a guy curses the relationship."

Sari laughed. "You scared me. I thought it was something a lot worse than that."

"Do you know how many hours I've spent on that sweater?"

"Well, find a new boyfriend who's the same size," Sari said. "Or . . . would it fit your father?"

"My father weighs three hundred pounds," Lucy said. She poked at a piece of cucumber. "Hey, Sari?"

"What?"

"I think I really want to rip it all apart. Tear it to shreds." She made fists out of her hands. "And then stomp on the last little bits of it. Come back with me and watch?"

"Throw in a glass of wine and I'm there."

"I am never knitting anything for anyone ever again," Lucy said. She cut a shrimp in half with one quick slash of her knife. "But don't tell Kathleen I said she was right."

7

Unraveling

1

Kathleen woke up at seven a.m. on Thanksgiving morning and decided she'd been working in an office for too long—not since high school had her body been so trained to wake up early that she couldn't sleep in late, even on a holiday. But the end of all that early rising was in sight. One way or another, she figured her days at Porter and Wachtell were numbered. Maybe even in the single digits.

She hadn't decided yet if she would be leaving the company at some point soon because she was going to marry the owner's son or because she *wasn't*. The only thing she knew for sure about her future was that it wouldn't involve any more coffee pouring or errand running. Those activities had lost their fascination, as had the water cooler gossip.

It was possible, she thought now, stretching and yawning on her airbed, that her loss of interest in the job proved that she hadn't changed and that she was still the same old Kathleen, easily bored and in search of the next new thrill. But she preferred to look at it as yet another sign of her budding maturity, that she could now assess a situation and accept calmly and rationally that what had once suited her no longer did.

Which was definitely true about her job.

The real question was whether it was also true about her love life.

Did being mature mean you continued to work at a relationship that had lost its interest and its excitement, because you knew that ultimately the rewards of constancy far outweighed its disappointments?

Or did a fully realized human being cut her losses and move on when the glow had faded?

Kathleen hadn't been pursuing this goal of maturity long enough to know the answer. She was hoping that Thanksgiving at the Porter household would give her some clues—if not about what she *should* do, then at least about what she *wanted* to do.

She lingered as long as she could in bed, but when she finally got up, it was still only eight-fifteen. She wasn't due at Kevin's parents until three that afternoon. Kevin was already there—his parents liked their children and grandchildren to spend the nights before Thanksgiving and Christmas at their more or less ancestral home. Spouses and children were included in the overnight slumber party. Girlfriends—even those invited to the holiday dinner—were not.

With nothing else to do, Kathleen decided to go for a long run. By the time she got back, she was dizzy from exercising without having eaten anything. She searched her kitchen but could only find an ice-frosted pint of ice cream and some cheese that had turned green.

She figured she'd have better luck upstairs.

Sam was still in his bathrobe and pajama bottoms. He greeted her with a scowl. "You don't have to beat the crap out of the door. I can hear you even if you knock like a civilized human being."

"I'm hungry," Kathleen said.

"Good of you to come by to tell me."

"Come on," she said. "Get dressed. Let's go get something to eat." She had showered and was now wearing torn jeans and a hooded sweatshirt. She'd change into something nice before dinner.

Sam shook his head. "It's Thanksgiving morning, Kathleen. Nothing's open."

"I passed a McDonald's on my run and it was open."

"I'm not going to McDonald's on Thanksgiving morning."

"Why not?" she said. "Against your religion or something?"

"Just come in." He stepped back with a sigh of resignation. "I'll make eggs."

"Good. I'll go see if the Macy's Day Parade has started." She headed toward the hallway.

"It's the Macy's Thanksgiving Day Parade," he said. "There's no such thing as Macy's Day."

"Whatever."

"How you can waste your time watching that—"

She turned. "Oh, come on. It's an American tradition. Did you know my sisters were on a float one year?"

"Wow," he said. "You must have been so proud."

"I'll be in the den," she said. "Can you make my eggs sunny-side up? With the yolk runny?"

"You're not eating runny yolks on my sofa," he said. "I'll make them, but you have to come back in here to eat them."

She rolled her eyes. "You spill something once and it's like some natural disaster."

"You spill every time you're here," Sam said. "That's not an accident, it's a pattern."

"Yeah, yeah, yeah." She went and stretched out on the sofa and watched the parade until Sam called that the eggs were ready. She ran back into the kitchen and was sitting down, reaching for her fork, before he'd even put her plate on the table.

"So why are you alone on Thanksgiving?" she asked him through a mouthful of eggs. She was crazy hungry.

"Put the napkin in your lap," he said, glaring at her from under his thick dark eyebrows. "And remember to use it."

"You didn't answer my question."

"And stop talking with your mouth full. I'm not alone on Thanksgiving, Kathleen. I'm having breakfast with you, and, in just a few hours, I'll be having Thanksgiving dinner with my ex-wife and daughter and former in-laws. Any other questions?"

"Your former in-laws?"

"Yes." When she just stared at him blankly, he said, "Patricia's parents."

"I'm confused."

"Do you need me to draw you a chart?"

"No," she said and stuck another forkful of egg in her mouth. She swallowed. "I get *who* you're seeing. I just don't get *why*. Do you like seeing them?"

He laughed out loud. He, of course, had carefully spread his napkin over his lap. He was still in his bathrobe, but his manners were as impeccable as always. "No, actually, I don't. You ask the right questions, Kathleen, I'll give you that."

She wiggled in her seat like a child given a compliment. "So why go?"

"Because I want to be with Joanna, and that's where she'll be."

"Why not ask her to come and have Thanksgiving alone with you?"

"Because she likes being with the whole family. And I don't want to take something she likes away from her."

"Huh," Kathleen said. "Can I have some more eggs?"

"Did you finish those already? Jesus, you're a pig. That was three whole eggs. Extra-large."

"I've been up since eight and I went running. And I think I forgot to eat dinner last night."

He sat back and regarded her. "Does it ever occur to you to stock the refrigerator with food and actually cook for yourself? You have a fully functional gourmet kitchen down there, you know."

She shrugged. "I don't know how to cook."

"It's not hard. You just follow directions. People teach themselves to cook all the time. All it requires is a tiny bit of effort and forethought—although it is possible you're not capable of either."

"I'm capable of enough forethought to ask you for more eggs before I've eaten all my toast." She tilted her head with a smile that showed all her teeth, top and bottom.

"Someone must have told you you were cute when you were little," Sam said, "and we're all paying the price now."

"No one ever told me I was cute when I was little," Kathleen said. "That's what people said to the twins. I was the responsible one."

"You've got to be kidding."

"No, really, I was. Somewhere along the way, I got less responsible, I guess. But the twins are still cute. I don't know what that leaves me."

"You have the biggest appetite of any girl I've ever seen," Sam said. "That's something."

"Does that mean I get more eggs?"

He stood up. "Come on. I'll show you how to make them, so next time you'll do it yourself and let me eat in peace."

"I don't want to learn how," she said. "I want you to make them for me."

"You're going to learn." He grabbed her arm and hauled her to her feet.

By the time she left his apartment, she could cook eggs three different ways. Sam said he'd teach her to do an omelet next, but added that he wasn't convinced it was within her capabilities.

II

"Wow," Lucy said as Sari's mother kissed her on the cheek. "You look great, Mrs. Hill."

Lucy sounded sincere, so Sari squinted at her mother, trying to see her through someone else's eyes.

Eloise Hill was a small, pretty, well-groomed woman of fifty-nine. Her thick hair was dyed a streaky blond and cut in a neat bob, and had been for as long as Sari could remember. For Thanksgiving, she was dressed in precisely tailored khaki pants, a striped blue sweater, and a pair of dark brown loafers, all very neat and nautical. She looked, as she often did, as if she had wandered out of a Ralph Lauren family photo.

For a moment, Sari let herself believe her mother was as lovely and normal as she appeared and hugged her with real warmth. "I was so delighted when Sari called to tell us she'd be bringing you!" her mother said to Lucy over her shoulder. "It feels just like old times." She released her daughter and stepped back. "I hope you two don't mind that I didn't cook the meal myself—I picked the whole meal up from Gelson's, right down to the stuffing and cranberries. It's a terrible cheat, I know."

"Are you kidding?" Sari said. "We're both delighted you didn't cook."

"Oh, you," her mother said and pushed her arm affectionately.

Look at us, Sari thought. We're adorable. Maybe this time everything will be fine.

"Your father's watching football in the bedroom," her mother said. "Actually, I think he fell asleep, or I know he would have come out to greet you. I'll go tell him you're here."

"Where's Charlie?"

"In the family room, watching one of his movies." She turned to Lucy. "He'll be so happy to see you." She smiled and the edges of her lips made neat little corners in her cheeks.

Sari and Kathleen went on into the family room, which hadn't changed in twenty years. Charlie sat on the faded brown leather sofa, watching TV. He was fatter than he'd been the last time Sari had seen him, fatter than he'd ever been, and he'd been pretty fat before. He didn't seem to notice when they entered the room.

"Shit," Sari said, grabbing Lucy's arm. "Look at that." She pointed to a pile of Balance Bars on the coffee table in front of him. There were a bunch of torn empty wrappers lying next to them. "We're about to eat Thanksgiving dinner and she goes and gives him a stack of Balance Bars. Just so he won't bother her."

Lucy didn't say anything.

Sari sat down on the sofa next to her brother and took his hand. "Charlie?"

He glanced up. "Hi, Sari," he said casually, as if it hadn't been over six months since they'd last seen each other.

She took his hand and squeezed it hard. He squeezed back. He didn't like to be hugged, so Sari always greeted him that way, and he always responded in kind. She was never sure whether it was an affectionate gesture on his part or just a learned response, but it *felt* affectionate to her.

"How've you been, mister?" she said.

"Good," he said, still watching the TV. *Star Wars* was playing—the original one, with Mark Hamill.

Sari said, "Charlie. This is my friend Lucy. Do you remember her from high school?"

He shook his head.

"Please say hi to her, Charlie."

"Hi," he said, watching the TV.

"Hi," Lucy said. "Nice to see you again."

"Look at her, please," Sari said. "Charlie, look at Lucy and shake her hand."

Lucy extended her hand, and Charlie obligingly stuck out his own hand toward the TV set.

"No," Sari said. "Not like that. Look at Lucy. Look at her, or I'll turn the TV off."

"Oh, leave him alone!" her mother said from the doorway, behind Lucy's back. Startled, Lucy dropped her hand as Eloise Hill came forward. "You know how I feel about this, Sari." She turned to Lucy. "Sari likes to get Charlie all worked up."

"He should know how to greet people," Sari said.

"Stop it," her mother said. "I want you to stop it *now*. It's not going to be like this, not this time. It's Thanksgiving. We are not going to ruin it by fighting."

"Who's fighting?" Sari said. "I'm just trying to help him."

"You're not trying to help him, you're trying to change him. Let him be himself. He is what he is. Why can't you accept that?"

"Because he could be better than this," Sari said. "I've seen so many kids turn around, Mom. Adults, too. What Ellen does is amazing—"

Her mother made a noise of disgust. "Here we go again, with the amazing Ellen."

"Please let me take him to see her. Please. I'm begging you."

"He doesn't like to leave the house. It makes him nervous."

"That's a reason to get him out *more.* Take him to do fun things, so he—"

"There was a time," her mother said, "when you begged me to keep him at home all day long. When you said he shouldn't have to go to school, that he was better off at home, that *you* were better off with him at home. Or don't you remember?"

"I remember," Sari said. "I was just a kid."

"You said the other students were mean to him at school, even violent sometimes, and he needed to be somewhere safe. You begged me to send him to private school—remember? And when I said we couldn't afford it, you said, 'Can't we just keep him at home then?' "

"I didn't know anything," Sari said. "I know more now."

"We had to send him to school then," her mother said. "It was the law. But in a way you were right. He's always been happiest at home. I mean, look at him now. He's completely in the moment, just happy to be here."

"That's because he doesn't know any better. You haven't let him see what else is out there, what he might be capable of. He could have friends, a job, interests outside of sitting on his ass watching movies—"

"Watch your language," Sari's mother said, crossing her arms tightly over her chest. "This is who Charlie is. And if you can't accept him the way he is, if all you can do is judge him without sympathy or kindness, then you have no right to sit there and hold his hand and claim that you love him."

"Oh, for God's sake!" Sari flung her hand out. "Loving someone doesn't mean you leave him alone—loving someone means you want to make things better for him. It means you don't just leave him with a stack of Balance Bars and the TV turned on all day long because that's what's easy for you."

"Oh, so now I'm a neglectful mother?" Sari's mother said. Her voice had gotten very high. "You come waltzing in here a couple times a year and accuse me of being some sort of ogre, but you know nothing about our lives. Just because you think Charlie's not a good enough brother for you—"

"Do you really think that's what I'm saying?"

"Let me tell you something: your brother is a kinder, gentler, far more *spiritual* being than you'll ever be—"

"He watches movies and game shows all day long. How is that spiritual?"

"I'm through discussing this with you," her mother said with a little stamp of her well-shod foot. "I'll simply say this: if you want to stay a minute longer in this house, then you'll treat its occupants with respect. If you can't do that, then—much as it pains me—I'm going to have to ask you to leave. I will not let you ruin another family holiday." She turned to Lucy. "Lucy, you, of course, are welcome in my house, now and at any time. I hope you'll stay, no matter *what*."

"Thanks," Lucy said with a panicked look at Sari.

"It's okay," Sari said. "I'll behave. There's no point to any of this, anyway."

"And we'll have a nice, civilized dinner together?" her mother said.

"You go on in and set up, Mrs. Hill," Lucy said. "We'll be right there."

"But no more fighting," Sari's mother said. "It's just too hard on us all."

"Of course not," Lucy said. "Don't you worry."

Eloise Hill left the room. For a minute or two, the three adults in the room silently watched planets exploding on the television screen. Then Sari looked at Lucy. "You see?" she said.

Lucy sat down and put both her arms around Sari's shoulders. “We’ll just get through dinner and then go.” She glanced at Charlie. His lips were moving in sync to the movie’s dialogue. She said quietly, “Poor guy.”

“Yeah,” Sari said. “I used to fantasize about grabbing him and making a run for the door. Not really doable, though.”

“Probably not, given your relative sizes,” Lucy said. “She doesn’t really just let him watch TV all day, does she?”

“I don’t know,” Sari said. “I honestly don’t know. But every time I come to visit, this is where I find him. He used to notice me more, used to actually seem glad I was here. Now it barely registers. And the worst part—I mean it’s all the worst part—but the worst part is someday she’ll die and then what? It’ll be too late. He won’t have any skills to deal with the world, even if he wants to.” Her voice dropped to almost nothing. “She won’t die soon enough for me to help him.”

There was a pause. Then, “I could kill her now, if it would help,” Lucy said.

Sari leaned against her. “That’s why I love you—you always know the right thing to say.” She rested her head on Lucy’s shoulder, and they sat like that until Sari’s mother called them all in for dinner.

III

Kathleen wore the necklace Kevin had given her, and his father spotted it immediately. “Tiffany’s?” he said, gesturing to her neck, after giving her a paternal kiss on the cheek.

She nodded. “From your son.”

“Tell him to get you diamonds next time,” he said with a wink.

"A pretty girl like you should wear diamonds. Kevin should know that already, but he's always been a slow learner."

Kathleen looked at Kevin, who smiled at her as if his father had just said something nice.

They sat down to eat soon after she arrived. First they had pumpkin soup, fragrant with cinnamon and cloves, then roast turkey with three different kinds of stuffing steaming in separate crystal bowls, mashed potatoes golden with butter and garlic, warm rolls and cranberry sauce and green beans, all of which was followed by the traditional desserts—pecan pie, pumpkin pie, and chocolate cake—and hot fresh coffee. The food was brought to the table by servants wearing black and white and cooked by the Porters' aging resident chef, a French woman named Marguerite who came out at the end of the meal to receive their thanks and congratulations. Caro blew her a kiss. Jackson thumped her on the back. Marguerite staggered back to the kitchen, looking exhausted but triumphant.

Obscene amounts of food were left over, both because there had been way too much to begin with, and also because the women of the family—the sisters-in-law and Caro—had barely eaten anything. None of them had touched *any* of the stuffing, let alone all three kinds. Kathleen, who had eaten six eggs for breakfast, still managed to put away ten times as much food as any of the other women.

After dessert had been cleared, Jackson uttered a quiet "Ahem." Every face immediately turned to him. "If the women will excuse us, I do have a couple of small business matters to go over with the men." He held up his hand as if to forestall objections, even though there weren't any. "I know, I know, it's a holiday. But it's not often I get a chance to sit down with all three of my boys, and I'd like to take advantage of this time together to address a few important items that have come up recently." Kathleen wondered if anyone was going to point out that he saw all three of his sons at the office every day. But:

"Of *course,*" one of the sisters-in-law said immediately.

"You should!" the other said—the one who had kids, a boy and a girl, who had eaten a few bites of food at the table, then started hitting each other before one of the women in black and white had whisked them out of the room.

As they all rose to their feet and moved away from the table, Kathleen said to Kevin, "We'd better get going—I told my mom we'd be there at six."

"I can't go right now," Kevin said. "My dad—"

"It's already past six-thirty."

"Can you call her and tell her we'll be late?"

She lowered her voice. "Can't you just skip your father's meeting?"

"That's not a good idea," he said, his eyes flickering over to check where his father and brothers were. They hadn't left the room yet.

"Why not? You'll see him on Monday."

"This stuff is important, Kathleen. I can't not be there. It wouldn't be right. Can't you just wait until we're done?"

"How long will it take?"

"Half an hour?" he said with no conviction. "Maybe less, maybe more. I honestly don't know."

"In that case, do you mind if I head on over to the McMansion by myself?"

He looked relieved. "Not at all. You should. I'll call you as soon as I'm done and join up with you there."

He kissed her lightly on the lips and then scurried to catch up with his brothers and father, who were leaving the room in a tight knot. Kathleen doubted she would see him at her sisters' later.

IV

Oh, Lord," Eloise Hill said, "we thank you for your bounty and for bringing us all together on this special day and for providing us with food for our table and shelter for our bodies and . . ."

She went on for a while longer like that.

Sari rolled her eyes at Lucy, who kicked her in the shin under the table.

"Can we eat now?" Sari asked as soon as her mother had finally said "Amen" and lifted up her head. "Or do we have to thank God for giving us the 405 freeway, too? Because, you know, we couldn't have actually gotten here without it."

"Here, Lucy," Sari's mother said, picking up a pretty painted bowl. "Please try the potatoes. I may not have made them myself, but I tasted them in the kitchen and I must say they're delicious. A tiny bit on the salty side . . ."

"Yum," said Lucy, who hadn't touched a potato in any form in over five years. She took the bowl and made a show of putting a spoonful on her plate.

"Who's having wine?" asked Sari's father. It was the first thing he had said all afternoon, other than a brief, vague greeting.

"I'd definitely like a glass of wine," Sari said, and Lucy pushed her own glass toward Gerald Hill and said, "Me, too, please."

Everyone had a glass of wine, except for Charlie, who drank white milk and ate only the mashed potatoes. After he had finished his plateful of potatoes, he got up from the table without another word and clomped his way back into the family room.

"If you're not going to make him sit through dinner, you could at least teach him to excuse himself," Sari said to her mother.

"Charlie knows he's excused. We don't stand on formalities here." Her mother extended her empty wineglass into the air in front of her. Her husband leaned forward and refilled it. They didn't look at each other. Eloise took a sip of wine and turned to Lucy. "Did you see the expression on his face when I said grace? It was—what's the word? Gerald, what's the word?"

"The word for what?"

"You know. When someone feels God's grace on them."

He shrugged. "I don't know. Happy?"

"No, not happy," she said. "It begins with a b."

"Balmy?" Sari suggested.

"Beatific!" Her mother captured the word with delight. "That's the word. Beatific. Charlie looked positively beatific." She hitched her chair closer to Lucy. "They say people like Charlie are closer to God than the rest of us," she said in a low, confiding voice. "And I believe it. He sees things we don't." She paused, and Lucy made a polite little "Huh" kind of noise.

Sari's mother took that as encouragement. She took several sips of wine and then continued, gesturing with the glass. "When I see someone—a stranger—with a child who you can tell right away is *special*—not like the other kids—I go right on up to her, no matter where we are, even in the supermarket, and I say, 'We're the lucky ones. We're *blessed.* God sends us these special children because He trusts us to take good care of them for Him.'" She put down her glass and touched Lucy's arm lightly with her damp fingertips. "I can't tell you how many women have hugged me after I've said that. Just burst into tears and hugged me. It's a wonderful thing to make a connection like that. I fly home after one of those encounters. I *literally* fly home."

"How nice," Lucy said. "Really. That's really nice. Do you—"

"We really are the lucky ones, you know," Eloise said. "Those of us with special children. God chooses us because He knows we're exceptionally strong."

"You're just all God's little teacher's pets, aren't you?" Sari said. "You get to clap erasers *and* raise the autistic kids. Hey, maybe if you're really good, he'll give you some boils on your ass."

"More wine?" her father said and took the opportunity to refill his glass as well as hers. He peered at the bottle. "Better open another. This one's almost gone." He got up and walked heavily out of the room.

"God has a plan for Charlie," Sari's mother told Lucy, pinning her in place with that hand on her arm. "He has a plan for every child. People like that Ellen woman think that they're making a difference with their mumbo-jumbo, but the path any child takes is already determined by God. He decides what will be."

"Que será, será," Lucy said with a wild and desperate gaiety.

"What we do at the clinic works," Sari said. "I could show you studies—"

Her mother finally acknowledged her, but only by making a *phhhtt* noise and waving her hand dismissively. "Studies. Oh, please. You can't tell from those. Take any child and look at him again a few years later. Who's to say what he would have been as opposed to what he is? Only the Supreme Being. Not us. Certainly not some scientist collecting *data*." She spat out the last word as if it were repulsive to her.

"You've got it all backward," Sari said. "Science is the one thing that *does* tell us anything. It shows us that when kids are worked with the right way, they improve."

"No," Eloise said. "You can fuss and bother and drive the children crazy with all your therapy jibber-jabber, but in the end, it's all up to Him."

"I wish to hell he'd open up a clinic then," Sari said. "We have a waiting list at ours. The least he could do is take up some of the slack."

"More wine?" said her father, appearing in the doorway with a freshly opened bottle.

V

Kathleen's mind wandered on the drive over to her sisters' house, and she found herself thinking not about the people and the meal she had just left, but about cooking with Sam Kaplan that morning. He had taken it all so seriously that of course she had to rebel and fool around every way possible. He wouldn't let her off the hook, not even when she dropped an egg on the floor and it broke into a huge mess—just insisted that she clean it up, and then forced her to crack the other eggs correctly, his hand guiding hers, his arm against hers, his body close behind hers.

If he had been any other guy between the age of fifteen and sixty, Kathleen would have suspected him of using the cooking as an excuse to get physically close to her. But Sam seemed genuinely determined to teach her to cook and his expression was one of grim determination rather than flirtation. And yet . . .

She left the thought dangling. She didn't know why.

She had arrived at her sisters'. She rolled down her window and punched in the security code for the gate. The man who installed it had suggested they program in a new number every six months. They had never changed it from his original example. It was 1111 and would, Kathleen suspected, remain 1111 until someone else lived there.

Her mother was already opening the front door by the time Kathleen had parked her car and walked up the steps. "Where have you been?" Her mother threw her arms around her. "You're late."

"Sorry," Kathleen said. It felt good to be hugged by her mother, even if their height differences made it a little silly. Caro hadn't hugged Kevin, had just given him and Kathleen equally distant air kisses. "Kevin's father—"

Her mother was already pulling her toward the dining room. "We started without you. We're almost done."

"Good. I already ate. I told you we'd go to Kevin's first."

"Where *is* Kevin?" Her mother looked back over Kathleen's shoulder as if he might appear.

"He got tied up at his folks', so I came without him."

"Well, the good news is that that leaves us with an even number."

"Why is that good?"

"It just *is*," her mother said and steered her into the dining room. "Kathleen's here, everybody!"

Eyes turned toward her, and Kathleen's heart sank as she realized that in addition to the expected and welcome faces of her sisters and their publicist, Junie Peterson, and her boyfriend, Peter Munoz (whom the twins had dubbed Munchie—Kathleen had never known why), were the unexpected and unwelcome ones of Lloyd Winters and his pal Jordan Fisher.

Close upon that realization was a worse one: even as he bestowed upon her a cold smile that suggested nothing had been forgotten or forgiven, Jordan was lazily stroking the slender bare arm of her sister Christa, and he was doing it with the flagrancy of someone who has staked a claim.

* * *

They were already finishing up their turkey and sides, so, as soon as Kathleen had greeted everyone, she proposed that she and Kelly clear the table while the others wait for dessert in the living room. "We'll take care of cleaning up," she said to her mother. "You relax and enjoy yourself."

Her mother seemed to like the idea. She had cooked the meal herself, and it was one of only three meals she cooked a year. There was the Thanksgiving turkey, a ham on Christmas, and leg of lamb for Easter. The rest of the time, she and the girls ordered in or just ate some yogurt. She wasn't a natural or comfortable cook, so by the time any of those holiday meals were actually eaten, she was exhausted.

She led the others from the dining room into the living room, arm in arm with Junie. Peter—a nice guy who deserved better—was being subjected to a hard sell about Lloyd's current get-rich-quick scheme (something about access to water rights and how L.A. was really a desert, you know). Behind them all strolled Jordan Fisher and Christa. He had slung his arm around her narrow shoulders and he shot the other two girls a look of triumph as they left the room.

"In the kitchen," Kathleen said to Kelly. "Now."

The second the door had swung shut behind them, Kathleen hissed, "What the fuck is going on? Why is Lloyd here? And why is Jordan Fisher feeling up Christa in front of everybody?"

"Oh, God, Kathleen, it's such a mess, you can't believe it," Kelly said. She pulled a long hank of her strawberry blond hair across her throat like she was trying to choke herself with it. "Lloyd came over one day with that Jordan guy, who kept going on and on about representing us—as if we'd leave CAA for *him*. And I thought he was, you know, totally sleazy—"

"He's disgusting," Kathleen said. "I met him before. I mean, that greasy hair—"

"I know!" Kelly squealed. "I can hardly even bear to *look* at him. And he was like trying to *flirt* with us and then afterward Christa said she thought he was *cute* and I said the truth, which was that he totally made me want to throw up, and she got really mad and wouldn't talk to me, and it's basically been like that ever since."

"He was all over her at the table," Kathleen said. "Are they actually going out?"

Kelly opened her wide blue eyes even wider. "Are you kidding me? For like *weeks* now. That's why he and Lloyd are here. Christa invited Jordan without even asking and then she said we had to invite Lloyd, too, or he'd be hurt."

"Since when is hurting Lloyd's feelings a problem?" Kathleen said.

"Well, we do have to be careful. Junie said people would think we were really horrible if we weren't nice to him since we're rich and he isn't. And he is our *father*."

"Who ran out on us when we were babies."

"Yeah, he's a jerk," Kelly said. "Don't you think it's weird how much you look like him?" She put her hand on her hip. She was wearing a skimpy tank top and jeans that were cut so low you could see every inch of her hip bone, but she was so thin there was nothing either curvaceous or sexy about the revealed flesh. "Believe me, I wouldn't have invited him, but Christa's all like, 'whatever Jordan thinks.' She's even saying she's going to let him represent her. He says we'll do better with two different agents—that it'll give us twice the clout. Like he has any clout at *all*." She rolled her eyes.

"What do Junie and Mom think?"

"Junie said no way should we switch agents, and she and Christa got in a big fight about it. And then Mom and Christa had a fight because Mom told her she should listen to Junie, and then Christa and *I* had a fight because I was like 'I can't believe you don't see what a sleazeball this guy is and everybody else does' and by the way, *you* weren't around to back me up—"

"I know," Kathleen said. "Sorry about that. I've been kind of busy, but I should have come over more."

"It's not really your fault." Kelly flipped the hair back over her shoulder. "If she can't see how disgusting he is, there's kind of nothing anyone can do, anyway. I mean, I'm her identical twin and I can't get her to see it, you know? And now she said they might even move in together. Can you believe it?"

"No," Kathleen said. "I can't. But—and believe me, no one thinks the guy's more repulsive than I do—but I guess she does have a right to her own life. Everyone does."

"Not us," Kelly said. "Not Christa and me. We can't live our own lives. Not like other people." She sighed so deeply you could see the exposed part of her stomach rise up and then relax back down. "People only want to see us together. If we separate—" She didn't bother to finish the sentence, just shrugged and waved her hand. Her fingernails were painted dark orange. "You know," she said, "you're the lucky one. You only have to deal with *you*, know what I mean?"

"Yeah," Kathleen said. "There's only ever been me."

VI

Eloise wouldn't let Sari have any more time alone with Charlie for the rest of the evening. Sari went back into the family room after dinner, but her mother followed her in there and started a conversation about some distant cousins. At one point, during a commercial, Sari said, "Hey, Charlie, let's play a game or go for a walk or something," and her mother immediately said, "If you're not really watching TV, then you can help me with the dishes," and led Sari into the kitchen. Lucy followed close behind.

The phone rang while they were still washing up, and Sari's father called to them from the bedroom to say it was Cassie. Sari's mother lit up. "I knew she'd call! She wouldn't let Thanksgiving come and go without calling. Not *Thanksgiving.*"

She pounced on the phone and said, "Cassie darling!" And then, "We're just fine! Wonderful! Sari came with her old chum Lucy and it's been just the loveliest time."

"Just the loveliest," Sari said to Lucy, who smothered a laugh.

Eloise held the phone out to Sari. "She wants to say hi to you."

Sari put it to her ear. "Hi," she said warily.

"I can't believe you're there," Cassie said. "You're even crazier than *they* are. Which I wouldn't have thought was possible."

Sari couldn't really argue with any of that. "How's your Thanksgiving going?"

"Fine. Cold."

"Where are you?"

"Vermont," Cassie said. "Bet you're losing your mind there, huh?"

"You're not wrong," Sari said.

"Still desperate to have children of your own?"

"I never said I was. I just said I couldn't promise *not* to."

"Yeah, whatever. Tell Mom I had to go. I can't talk to her again. I don't even know why I called in the first place. There was some ad on TV that got to me and I felt guilty for a second. I'm already regretting it. Don't have kids, Sari. Just don't."

"I'm not planning to at this moment."

"You're such a fucking coward. Happy Thanksgiving."

"You, too," Sari said, but Cassie had already hung up.

Eloise held out her hand expectantly.

"She's gone," Sari said, turning the phone off.

Her mother pouted. "I hardly got to talk to her. Why did you hang up so fast?"

"I didn't," Sari said. "She did."

"Oh." Eloise took the phone from her hand and popped it back into its base. "Well, she's probably busy. You know Cassie."

"Not really," Sari said. "Do you?"

"Don't be silly." Her mother left the room to get a few more things off the dining room table.

Lucy and Sari looked at each other. "Car?" Lucy said. "Now? Please?"

"Yeah, all right," Sari said. "I don't know what I'm waiting for, anyway. Let's just go."

"Sweetest words I've ever heard." They dried their hands on a dish towel and went to say goodbye.

In the family room, Sari knelt in front of Charlie, getting between him and the TV, so he had to look at her. He smiled and leaned sideways so he could see around her. "Goodbye, Sari," he said.

"I love you," she said.

"I love you," he repeated.

"You see?" Sari's mother said. She had followed Sari in there. "You see? He loves like a child, pure and simple and with his whole heart. If everyone were like Charlie, there would be no wars, no cruelty, no fighting."

"Just a whole lot of TV watching," Sari said, rising back to her feet.

* * *

In the car, Lucy said, "When did she get so religious? I don't remember her going on and on about God when we were in high school."

"It's been building up over the years," Sari said. "It's not like she ever went to church when we were kids. Actually, I don't even think she goes to church now. She worships at the House of Denial."

"She *lives* in the House of Denial," Lucy said. "What's up with all that 'God made him the way he is so we can't even try to help him' shit?"

"I've been trying to figure that one out for years," Sari said. "All I can guess is that if she let herself think for a second that Charlie could have been different, could have been *better*—maybe even have had a decent life—if she'd just done things differently, then she'd have to think that she messed up somehow."

"But it was different back then, right?" Lucy said. "No one would blame her for not having known what to do when he was little. No one knew. But now I don't get why she doesn't let you—*you,* of all people, her own daughter who's an expert in the field—why she doesn't just let you help him."

Sari stared out the windshield. "Believe me, I've asked myself the same question at least fourteen billion times. I've even asked her. All she ever says is that same shit about Charlie being what God made him. It's like she got her mind set into this place and she can't change it, because it's protected her too long from . . . I don't know. Guilt, I guess. Or maybe just reality."

"Can't you *make* her do something? For Charlie's sake? I mean there's got to be some way to protect a kid from a mother like that."

"She's not abusing him," Sari said. "She's just not expanding his world. I asked Ellen once if there were any legal steps I could take as his sister, and she said that if my mother's healthy and Charlie isn't asking for help, then I was stuck. My mom's his legal guardian, not me."

"What about your dad? Have you asked him about it?"

"All he does is shrug and say, 'That's your mother's arena.'" She let her head fall back onto the headrest.

"There's got to be something we can do."

"I wish." Sari rolled her head to look at Lucy, whose brow was wrinkled in concentration. It made Sari love her friend—that she wanted to find a solution.

After a moment, Lucy said, "What if you offered to take Charlie out—just for a little while—like once a week? And we quickly did some work with him? Help him learn enough to know he wants to learn more?"

"She won't let us," Sari said. "You don't understand."

"She might."

"She won't. She won't even let me be in the room alone with him for more than a minute."

"We could say we're just taking him out for dinner or—"

"Lucy," Sari said and sat up straight in her seat. "Believe me when I say I've tried and believe me when I say that she won't let me help him. I've spent my entire life wanting to make things better for Charlie, and she *won't let me.*"

"That," Lucy said, "sucks."

"Beyond belief," Sari said and slumped back down again.

VII

Kevin ended up staying so late at his parents' that he went straight home to sleep, but he called Kathleen before she went to bed, and they agreed to meet at ten the next morning at a diner they both liked on Pico.

Kathleen got there first and nabbed a table, and when Kevin

walked in the door, her first thought was, "Oh, good, I can order now, I'm starved." Kevin spotted her, came over, kissed her briefly on the lips, and, as she flashed a smile at him, she wondered if this was what marriage felt like—nothing hot or exciting, just a mild relief that the waiting was over.

Kevin thumped heavily into the seat opposite her. "Hi." He pulled a menu toward him. "I can't believe it's time to eat again—I'm still full from last night. We ate a huge meal of leftovers before bed. It was good, but I'm feeling it this morning." He threw the menu down. "I think I'll just have coffee and a cinnamon roll. You?"

"Pancakes."

"Ah." He nodded, like she had said something interesting.

Kathleen yawned.

"How was your family's Thanksgiving?" Kevin asked.

"Fine." She didn't have the energy to describe the Jordan situation. She figured she'd save it to make into a funny story when she felt the need to be entertaining. "What did your dad want?"

"He actually had some really exciting news." Kevin looked around and lowered his voice. "He's got a bid in on a huge parcel of land in Bel Air. It's up in the hills, very private, with amazing views all the way to the ocean. He's thinking we could build a family complex up there—you know, a main house for him and Mom, and then a separate smaller one for each of the kids. So we could all live near each other, but we'd have our own private homes. Isn't that a great idea?"

Kathleen stared at him. "You're kidding, right?"

"What do you mean?"

"It sounds like a nightmare. All of you on top of each other, no privacy, no freedom—"

"I told you, it's very private."

"Not if your whole family's there."

Kevin laughed. "Kathleen, I *like* my family. And my parents aren't getting any younger. I like the idea of being able to keep an eye on them." The waitress approached their table, and they ordered.

Once she was gone, Kathleen leaned forward. "Kevin, seriously. Think about this. You already work for the family business. You spend all of your holidays and most of your vacations with your family. Do you really want to live with them, too?"

"Honestly? I think it sounds fantastic." The waitress brought their coffees over and he shook a sugar bag before ripping it open and pouring it in. "I mean, I could see my parents and brothers whenever I felt like seeing them, but still escape to my own house whenever I wanted to be alone. Or, you know . . . with my wife." There was a slight pause. "Whoever she might be."

Kathleen shifted back in her chair, poured some cream in her coffee, took a sip and said, "She'd have to really like spending time with your family."

"I guess so," he said. "Or at least be willing to learn to." There was another pause. Then: "Did I tell you Dad wants to build an enormous pond? It's the coolest part of this whole plan—it would touch on everyone's separate property, so you could actually *swim* from one yard to the other. Or kayak. How much would kids love that? Tons of cousins all growing up together, kayaking around, visiting each other, like a family of otters or something. Doesn't that sound great?"

"Yeah," she said.

"And you're such a good swimmer . . ."

She didn't say anything.

"Kathleen," Kevin said, and she raised her head to look at him. His temples were shiny with sweat. "Kathleen, all this talk last night about building homes and families and all that—it made me realize how much I want to start building my own family."

"Building?"

"You know what I mean. I'm thirty-four years old. I'm ready to be a dad. It's all I've been thinking about lately. How much I want kids and a family."

"You'd be a nice dad," she said.

"I'm glad you think so. Because I don't think I'd be feeling that way if I hadn't found someone who I want to have those kids with."

She took a deep breath. "Me."

"You." He reached over and took her hand in his. "I should have a ring to give you," he said. "I wish I did. But we could go right now and buy one together. Have our breakfast and then go straight to Tiffany's. What do you say?"

She stared at him, wondering if she had heard him right, knowing she had. Kevin Porter—man of millions—was asking her to marry him. This was what she had wanted all along. Wasn't it? Shouldn't she be feeling excited and triumphant? All she really felt was suddenly and overwhelmingly exhausted—too tired to know how to react. "Wow," she said.

"Will you marry me, Kathleen?"

She opened her mouth to answer but realized she didn't have an answer. So she closed it again. Then she realized she had to say something, so she said, "I think I need a minute. I'm sorry. I just . . . It's a big surprise."

"I know," he said. "I know it's sudden."

"It's amazing," she said. "And sweet. But—" She stopped.

"Sudden."

"Yeah." She detached her hand from his. "I just need to think. Give me a second, will you? I'll be right back." She took her purse off the back of her chair and crossed through the restaurant to the ladies' room. She glanced back as she closed the door. Kevin was staring at his coffee mug. She locked the door behind her and fished her cell phone out of her purse. She paced around the small, cold room as she dialed.

"Hello?"

"Oh, good, there you are," Kathleen said. "Kevin proposed to me. Just now, over breakfast. One second we were talking about real estate and the next he was asking me to marry him."

"Whoa!" Sari said. "You're kidding!"

"I'm really not."

"So did you say yes?"

"Why?" Kathleen said. "Do you think I should?"

"Don't ask *me*! Haven't you answered him yet?"

"I said I needed a minute to think about it." Kathleen leaned against the locked door. "You have to tell me what to do, Sari. Should I say yes or no? Or maybe? I think I could put him off for a while without completely discouraging him—"

"God, Kathleen, I don't know! I can't decide for you. Do you love him? Do you *want* to marry him?"

"I don't know. How do people know something like that for sure?"

"Why are you asking me?" Sari said. "Me, of all people? I've never been proposed to. I don't even have a boyfriend. Ask someone who's married."

"You're the only person I trust. Come on, Sari, help me out."

"If you really want my advice, I think you should ask him to wait. Tell him you love him but you're not sure yet whether you're ready to settle down. Buy yourself some time."

"Okay," Kathleen said. "That's a good idea. Thanks. How was dinner at your parents'?"

"It was horrible."

"What happened?"

Sari laughed. "Kathleen, somewhere not far from you there's a man waiting to hear whether the girl of his dreams is going to marry him or not. Do you really want to hear about my miserable Thanksgiving?"

"Yes. I really do."

"Then call me later. I feel for Kevin, even if you don't."

When she came back to the table, Kevin was half turned in his chair, watching for her. The waitress had brought their food, but he hadn't taken a bite.

"So?" he said, trying to keep his voice casual. "Any decisions?"

"Not yet." She slid into her chair and took a deep breath. "Here's the thing . . . I think I probably do want to marry you. But I'm not ready to say it for sure. Not yet."

He reached around the plates for her hand and squeezed it. "I know. I sprang this on you pretty suddenly. I mean, I was up all night thinking about it, but for you, it's been all of five minutes."

"I probably just have to get used to the idea. I've been single all my life, you know."

"Glad to hear it," he said. There was a pause. Then, "Want to go to Hawaii with me?"

She laughed. "You're full of offers today. When were you thinking?"

"Now. This afternoon. My parents' house is right on the beach and the walls on the ocean side are all glass so it's just you and the ocean and the waves. We'd be all alone there—no families, no work, nothing but each other and the most beautiful beach in the world. It's a good place to think about things. And make decisions." He pressed the back of her hand to his lips. "What do you say, Kath? Will you come with me?"

"How could I say no to that?"

"You can't." He kissed her hand one more time before releasing it. "And do you know what the waiting period is for a marriage license in Hawaii?"

"No. What?"

He grinned. "There isn't one."

VIII

Lucy and Sari met at Sari's apartment on Sunday, because Sari refused to go to Lucy's now that she had a cat.

"I can't believe it," Lucy said, once they were settled with their coffee and knitting. "I just can't believe it. That she's in Hawaii right now with one of the richest bachelors in the country, trying to decide whether or not to marry him."

"I know," Sari said. "Only Kathleen."

"And meanwhile I'm stuck here, trying to figure out what to do with my remaining six skeins of green yarn."

"That's not enough to make much of anything other than a scarf," Sari said. "Couldn't you salvage any of the yarn you ripped out?"

"It got all curly and stretched out," Lucy said.

"I think there's a way to fix that."

"Plus I threw it down the trash chute."

"That's a bigger problem." Sari knit another row while Lucy leafed through a knitting book she had brought with her.

"It's hard to start something else," Lucy said after looking at a bunch of patterns. "I was so excited about knitting a sweater for James and now look what happened. It was all a big fat waste of time. It's ruined knitting for me forever— Ooo, that's cute!" She showed Sari a knit hat that had bands of different colors and a narrow brim, and they both exclaimed over it.

"Why don't you make that?" Sari said. "It wouldn't take long. You could do it just in that green—no stripes."

"But I don't wear hats," Lucy said.

"Maybe you should start. It seems like a good time to try something new."

"The way things are going, if I try to knit a hat, my head will get cut off."

"You're fun to be with today," Sari said.

"I can't help it." Lucy flung the book aside. "We're stuck here and meanwhile Kathleen's lying on a beach somewhere in Hawaii, drinking piña coladas and probably having her butt massaged or something decadent like that. Why does she always get to be the lucky one?"

"Bet she's engaged by now," Sari said.

"No way. She would have called us."

"No, because it's three hours earlier there, right? They probably went out for a late dinner last night, and then Kevin asked her to go for a walk on the beach and then he told her she owed him an answer and maybe even got down on his knees and pulled out a ring and—"

"I still think she'd call."

"But it would have been like one in the morning there when it all happened," Sari said. "Four a.m. here. And besides, once she said yes, they had to go back and immediately have sex, right? You've got to figure engagement sex is amazing."

"You seem sure she said yes."

"Of course she said yes. You don't say no when someone proposes to you on a moonlit beach in Hawaii, Lucy. Anyway, the point is they probably had sex and fell asleep." She gestured at the wall clock. "It's still only eight in the morning there. She wouldn't even be waking up until around now. But as soon as she wakes up—"

The phone rang. The girls looked at each other and cracked up. "You can't be that right," Lucy said. "No one is *that* right."

"We'll see," Sari said. She dropped her knitting and ran for the phone. "Hello?" Then: "Oh, wow. I didn't expect it to be *you*. Hi. What's going on there?"

"Who?" Lucy said. She had crept up to Sari's side and was desperately trying to hear what was being said. "Who is it? Who? Is it Kathleen?"

Sari held her off with the palm of her hand. "Wow, that's great!" she said. "I'm so excited for you! Congratulations!"

"What? What's great? What's exciting?" Lucy said.

"When? You're kidding. But—" A long period of time while the other person talked and then Sari said, "Yeah, it would be amazing. I totally want to. It's just . . . Well, hold on—let me ask Lucy." She punched the hold button and looked at Lucy. "You won't believe this."

Lucy groaned. "Will you just tell me?"

"It's *Kevin*. He proposed and Kathleen accepted, just like we thought. But she doesn't know he's calling us—he snuck off to call because he wants to fly us to Hawaii first thing tomorrow as a surprise for her. Because they're going to get married there in two days! Can you believe it?"

Lucy sank into a chair. "Holy shit."

"He said if he flew her family out, his family might feel hurt, and he doesn't want to get into any of that, but he knows she'd want us to be there with her. There's a nine a.m. flight tomorrow, gets us in at noon, and the wedding would be the next day. We could take the red-eye back that night and only miss two days of work."

"This is unreal," Lucy said.

"I know! So what do you say, Luce? Should we do it?" She shook the phone at her. "I have to give him an answer. He's waiting."

"What are you talking about?" Lucy said. "Of course we're going. We have to go."

"What about work?"

"Fuck work," Lucy said.

"Yeah," Sari said. "Fuck work." She punched the hold button again. "Kevin?" she said. "We're in."

After she'd hung up, she looked at Lucy. "Fuck knitting, too," she said. "Don't we need new clothes for Hawaii?"

"We do," Lucy said. "We do we do we do."

IX

When Lucy walked into her apartment several hours later, something felt wrong. It took her a moment to figure out what it was: David hadn't come warily prowling in to greet her, like he always did when she came home these days. She called for him and he still didn't come. She dropped everything she was carrying and went from room to room, calling him.

No David.

Lucy searched through the apartment again. This time, she got down on her hands and knees to look under sofas and tables. She even threw in a few high-pitched "Here kitty-kitty-kitties" just for the hell of it.

No David.

She felt suddenly really worried. The kitten had recently become curious about the bigger world outside and, several times over the past few days, he had gone darting out the door when she opened it, scooting between her legs and around her feet. She always chased him down and brought him back, but it was possible he'd snuck out that morning when she'd left, without her even noticing. Which would mean he'd been out of the apartment—maybe even out of the building—wandering alone for over three hours.

"Shit," she said out loud and ran into the apartment corridor and then down the stairs and out into the street, calling and running, searching desperately for a tiny kitten who had gone missing in a very big, very dangerous world.

"I can't find David," she said into the phone half an hour later.

"The cat or the lab partner?" Sari asked.

"This isn't funny. I got back from knitting and he was gone. Sari, I'm worried he got out of the building and is lost somewhere."

"Did you look outside?"

"I went around the whole block. I can't find him anywhere."

"I'm sorry, honey," Sari said. "But cats usually find their way home, don't they?"

"Big cats do," Lucy said. "Big grown-up cats who've lived for a long time in one place and who have sharp claws and can defend themselves against any danger—they find their way home. But little tiny kittens who haven't even been in the world very long—"

"Don't start imagining the worst."

"Too late."

"Well, then, *stop* imagining the worst. I'm sure he'll come back."

"Are you really sure or are you just trying to get me off the phone?"

"A little of both, actually," Sari said. "I'm sorry, Lucy, but I'm overwhelmed with everything I have to do if I want to be able to leave tomorrow. I can't just disappear—I need to find replacements for all the kids I see. So I'm sort of losing my mind right now. But I honestly think David the kitten—being the most amazingly wonderful and brilliant kitten in the world—will find his way back to your side safe and sound before the end of the day."

"Yeah, whatever," Lucy said. "Go do your stuff. I'll see you in the morning." She hung up the phone and stared at it miserably for a minute. Then she got up off the bed and went through the apartment and opened the front door and called for David again. Then she went back into the apartment and called for him some more. Then she went out of the apartment and down the stairs to the street and called for him some more. Then she went back into the apartment and checked inside the stove and all the cabinets in the kitchen. Then she got out a suitcase and opened her underwear drawer and stared at its contents without seeing them for a minute or two. Then she got up and opened the front door and called for David.

"This is insane," she said out loud. She picked up the phone again.

There was no answer at David's apartment, but she waited, knowing it would ring through to his cell. "Hey," he said once it had, "what's up?"

"The kitten's missing," she said. "I can't find him anywhere.

I think maybe he got out this morning, which means he's been gone for hours."

"Oh, shit," he said. Then, "Well, at least it's not dark. The coyotes shouldn't be out yet."

"Thanks," she said. "Thanks for bringing up coyotes. Where are you?"

"Having coffee."

"With someone?"

"Yeah."

"Oh," she said. "I was hoping—I mean, I was thinking—that maybe you could come help me look—but you're busy, so—"

"I'll be there in ten," he said and hung up.

It was closer to twenty, but Lucy didn't complain.

"I looked around the block," David said as she let him in. "No surprise reappearance here, I assume?"

Lucy shook her head. She suddenly didn't trust herself to speak. At the sight of David's familiar, slightly homely face, she was overwhelmed with the desire to burst into tears. She fought it desperately. But it must have shown, because he said, "Don't worry, Lucy. He'll turn up. Cats have a way of being okay. This is where that whole nine lives thing really comes into play."

Lucy nodded but couldn't manage a smile. "He's so little," she said. "He's so little and I was responsible for him."

"Come on." He put his arms around her and she rested her head against his shoulder. "You're being silly. He's a cat. Cats always escape. And they always come back."

"Unless a coyote gets them. Or a car hits them. Or—"

"Someone sells them to evil scientists to experiment on?"

She pushed him away. "That's not funny."

"It's a little bit funny."

"I'm not in the mood for jokes."

"I'm sorry," he said. "No more jokes. Let's focus. Is your phone number on his ID tag?"

"He doesn't have one. I kept forgetting. I was at Petco a million times, but I just kept forgetting, but if I'd only just gotten him one . . . I'm such a fucking *idiot*!" And with that, she finally burst into the tears that had been threatening to break through for the last half hour.

"Come here." David steered her to the sofa and pushed her down on it. Then he sat next to her and took her hand. "Take a deep breath, Lucy, and calm down. The guy's only been missing a few hours. Cats often vanish for days and then reappear. He's going to come back. But we might as well do what we can to help. Do you have any photos of him? We could put them up somewhere."

"I didn't have any batteries in my camera," Lucy said, extricating her hand so she could use her knuckle to wipe away the tears under her eyes. "I tried to take his picture—I wanted to—but I didn't have any batteries and I kept forgetting to get new ones."

"You need some help running your life," David said.

"I know," she said with a sob.

"Whoa there," David said. "I was joking. And this isn't even close to calming down."

"I can't help it."

"Come here," he said, and pulled her so her face was against his chest. He wrapped his arms around her and she shoved her forehead hard into his shoulder and let herself go.

Interestingly, once she gave in to her tears, they didn't last all that long. She trembled and hiccupped and sniffed for a few minutes, while David rubbed her back and made soothing sounds. Even when the tears had stopped, she didn't move for a while, just stayed where she was, her cheek pressed against his shirt.

After a little while like that, she said, "I can hear your heart beat."

"Interesting," he said. "Would you say it's got a hip reggae kind of a beat?"

"It just sounds normal to me. Tha-boomp, tha-boomp." A pause. Then: "I need a tissue."

"You've been doing pretty well with my shirt up till now."

"Sorry." She righted herself, embarrassed. "Hold on. Let me go wash my face."

In the bathroom, she splashed cold water on her face and toweled off. There was a bottle of suntan lotion on the vanity, and it occurred to her she shouldn't even go to Hawaii if David stayed missing—she'd need to stay and keep looking for him. And even if she *did* find him, she'd have to get someone to take care of him while she was gone. She hadn't even thought about that before. She was a bad, bad pet owner.

When she came back out, David was sitting at her computer. "I found a Web site about missing pets. They say the first thing you should do is check with all your neighbors."

"I don't know my neighbors," Lucy said. "I've never even *met* them. Oh, except for the time I yelled at the people downstairs for making too much noise."

"How long have you lived here?"

"Four years."

David shook his head with a laugh. "You might want to work on your people skills, Lucy."

"Do you think we should go talk to them?"

"It can't hurt."

She liked that he didn't question her use of "we," just stood up and joined her at the door.

* * *

"I know this may sound selfish at a time like this, but I'm really hungry," David said when they returned to the apartment a while later, having checked in with all the neighbors who were home—no one had seen the cat—and searched around the block one more time. "How about we order in a pizza while we make some flyers? I can post them when I leave."

"Yeah, okay," Lucy said. She felt disoriented and dazed. The sun was setting and she still hadn't found the cat and the thought of eventually trying to go to sleep for the night knowing he was out there alone somewhere—or dead somewhere—was so awful she couldn't even think about it.

"What kind do you like?" David asked.

"Kind?"

"Of pizza."

"Oh. I don't care."

"Is there something else you'd rather eat?"

She shook her head. "I'm not really hungry. I kind of feel like I'm going to throw up." She did, too. She felt shaky and queasy, even though she hadn't eaten since she'd left Sari's apartment hours and hours ago.

"Maybe you'll change your mind once it's here," David said and picked up the phone to place the order.

They designed the flyer while they waited for the pizza to be delivered. Since they didn't have a photo of the cat, Lucy wrote a brief description, biting her lip to keep the tears back as she typed "very small, with two black dots on his nose."

"I think you should offer a reward," David said from behind her.

She paused, her fingers poised on the keyboard. "How much?"

"Enough so that people will bother to return him, but not enough to attract a con artist."

"And in dollars, that would be—?"

"A hundred maybe?"

"Ouch," she said, typing it in. "But okay. Anything for David."

"I'll split it with you," he said. "Fifty-fifty. Which would be fifty-fifty."

"No," Lucy said. "You paid for David in the first place and it's my fault he got lost, so I should pay the whole amount."

"We're in this together," David said. "And he's my cat, too—remember the visiting rights?"

"You can't visit what isn't here," Lucy said. Her voice broke on the last word.

He put his hand on her shoulder. "He'll be back."

Lucy did think the pizza smelled kind of good when it arrived, but as soon as she looked at it, her stomach tightened and she felt sick again, all shivery with a sudden chill, so she put it back down and excused herself for a moment. She went into the bedroom. She had left her window open and it was freezing in there. She closed the window, then went to her closet to get a sweater. When she opened the closet door, she let out a scream.

David came running. "What's wrong?"

She was squatting down, her back to him, but now she stood up and turned to him, gray fur clutched to her chest. "Nothing. Nothing. Everything's right."

"The little guy!" He stroked the cat's head. "How the fuck—? Is he okay?"

"I opened the closet and he was just there."

David wrinkled his nose and peered into the closet. "Smells like he left you a present in there."

"It's not his fault—he must have been in there for hours." Lucy cuddled the kitten tightly against her chest. "Oh, David, you scared the shit out of me. Don't ever go missing like that again."

"He didn't go missing," David said. "You must have shut him in there."

"I have no idea when or how I did that. And I swear I checked in there when I was looking all over for him. I know I did."

"Maybe he was sleeping then."

"We should feed him," Lucy said. "And give him some water."

"And take him to the litter box," David said. "There may still be something left in him, although, to judge by the bottom of your closet, I doubt it."

He took care of the kitten while Lucy cleaned up the mess then David the human went back to eating his pizza while David the kitten crouched on the floor and lapped eagerly at some water. Lucy sank into a chair and took a deep breath. Everything was okay. She had her kitten back.

"Sure you don't want any?" David said, as he took another piece of pizza from the box.

She realized with a sudden ache in her stomach that she was starving. Relief had brought back her appetite with a vengeance. "Yeah, actually, I do," she said. She reached over and snagged the biggest slice that was left and devoured it.

She couldn't remember the last time she had eaten a slice of pizza like that—the whole thing from the top of the triangle to the bottom, without bothering to blot the grease with a napkin or pick the cheese off or leave the crust or play any of her usual calorie-cutting games.

"I can't decide who looks more blissed out, you or the cat," David said as she swallowed the last bite. "Of course, the cat has a slight advantage in being able to lick himself clean."

"Does that mean I have pizza sauce on my face?" Lucy said.

She didn't even care. Nothing bothered her. David was back, safe and sound.

"Just a little. On your chin."

She swiped at it with a napkin. "Did I get it?"

"Not yet." He leaned forward. "Right there." He touched his fingertip lightly to the right side of her chin.

She wiped at the spot. "That better?"

"Yeah." He was still leaning forward.

"Thanks," she said.

He let his arm fall. "Want another slice?"

"God, no. It was good, though."

He closed the pizza box and stood up. "I should probably head off."

"Oh, right." Her contentment suddenly dropped away. "You left someone waiting. I'm sorry I wasted your whole day. And for nothing."

"It's okay," he said. "I'm glad it turned out to be for nothing. Here he is, safe as can be. No one's going to be experimenting on *this* little kitten tonight."

"Or ever." She stood up as he moved toward the door. "Hold on," she said.

He turned back, questioningly.

"I'm sorry," she said. "I was a total idiot about everything. Panicking about the cat when he was fine the whole time."

"You're not an idiot," he said.

"I totally overreacted. I was a hysterical girl."

"It's okay to react to things," he said. "Not everything has to be a thought-out position in life with a defensible argument, Lucy. Sometimes it's okay to just react."

"Even if it makes you look like an idiot?"

"Especially."

They were both quiet for a moment. Then, "Thank you,"

Lucy said, moving forward. "For coming today and caring about David."

"You don't have to thank me for either."

"Thank you, anyway," she said, and hugged him. He hugged her back. They stood like that a moment, their bodies pressed together in friendship.

And then Lucy felt something move against her leg. For one ridiculous moment, she thought of the cat. And then she realized it wasn't an animal.

David had a hard-on.

So maybe it wasn't just friendship.

The polite thing to do was to ignore it, she thought.

And then she deliberately pressed her hip against him.

"Excuse me?" he said startled and taking a step back.

"I didn't say anything." She moved up against him again and pushed her thigh right where his dick was jutting up inside the light fabric of the scrub pants he was wearing.

There was a pause. Then: "Yeah, about that," he said, twisting away from her. His face had turned red, and he wouldn't look at her. "I'm sorry. I can't always—you know—control it—and we were kind of . . . shoved up together there. And all men are pigs. Did I mention that before? That all men are pigs? Because that pretty much sums it up. And these scrubs don't hold you back at all. Or the boxers, either. Anyway . . . I should probably go. I already stayed too long."

"No," Lucy said. "Don't go." And, pressing the length of her body against his—making sure her hip was right up against his erection—she lifted up her face and offered him her mouth. Which he accepted, at first uncertainly and then with growing enthusiasm.

The kiss didn't do anything to subdue or calm the hot dick against her leg. It bobbed about even more enthusiastically than before.

When they finally came up for air, Lucy hid her head in his shoulder and said, "I can't believe we're doing this."

"We can stop now," David said. He cleared his throat. "I could still go."

"You sure you can walk?"

"I could probably limp out of here." He took a deep breath. "Seriously, Lucy, if you want me to go, I'm gone. We still have to work together. I'm not saying I haven't dreamed about this—okay, fantasized about this—from day one, because I have. But you made it clear a long time ago that it was never going to happen and I've accepted that."

"Have you?" Lucy said, looking down at the tent in his pants.

"Yeah," he said. "Intellectually I have. Maybe not so much physically. But I can still walk out of here and never say another word about any of it."

"Really?" she said, gently bouncing her leg right where his dick was straining hard against the thin fabric. "Just walk right out of here?"

He closed his eyes with a little moan and said, "I think I can."

"You sound like the little engine."

"Are you just torturing me or is there a point to what you're doing?"

She answered his question by taking him by the hand and leading him into her bedroom.

There was a pause after she rolled off of him. They lay side by side on their backs, eyes closed, breathing hard. And then he said, "I thought I could, I thought I could," and they both cracked up. "Uh-oh," David said suddenly. "We're not alone."

Lucy opened her eyes. David the kitten was crouched on the end of the bed watching them. "Here, David," Lucy cooed.

"Here, kitty. Don't be afraid." He came walking toward her, picking his way carefully among the folds and lumps of the quilt. Lucy held her hand out to him and he came closer and cautiously sniffed at her fingers. "Now that he's seen some very grown-up things, I think we'd better explain the facts of life to him, don't you?"

"Definitely. Let me." He scritched behind the kitten's ear and said, "Kid, stay away from girls. They'll only break your heart."

"Hey!" Lucy propped herself up on her elbow. "That's so not true."

"Been true in my experience."

"I'd say you were the one with some explaining to do. Didn't you leave some cute little undergrad back at Starbucks, sobbing into her extra-foamy decaf latte?"

"I have to assume she's gone home by *now*."

"Seriously," Lucy said.

"I can't help it if I like you better. And I didn't actually leave her there, you know. I dropped her off at her place."

"You like me better?" she said.

"Always have," he said. "But you were never available or interested."

"I'm both now," she said.

"I can't believe it," he said. "I should have given you a cat a long time ago."

She reached down for the quilt and pulled it up over both of them. "You want to stay the night?"

"You really want me to?"

"Yeah. That way, in the morning— Oh, my God! The morning!" She sat up. "I'm going to Hawaii in the morning!"

"You're kidding."

She shook her head.

"Jesus, Luce, when were you going to tell me? You can't just take off on a vacation—we have a ton of work this week."

"I'm sorry," she said. "I swear I was going to call you as soon as I got home, and then the whole thing with David happened and I totally forgot." She told him about Kevin's call.

"All right," he said. "I guess you kind of have to go if your friend's getting married. But you can't stay any longer than that, no matter how beautiful it is there."

"I won't. I promise."

"Wish I could go with you."

"Well, you can't," she said. "Which is a good thing."

"Thanks a lot."

"No, I mean, it would be nice to have you there—but if you're here, you can take care of David for me."

"Yeah, okay," he said. He scooped David up in his hand. "Looks like it's going to be just me and you for the next few days, buddy. Let's have some fun. Let's go find us some *pussy*."

"I knew that sooner or later you were going to make that joke," Lucy said. "You are so predictable."

"*He* thinks I'm funny." He held up the kitten. "I mean, he's trying to keep a straight face, but you can tell that on the inside he is totally losing his shit."

"You're a nut," Lucy said. She flung back the quilt and swung her legs off of the bed. "I'm going to pack as quickly as I can, and then I'm coming back to bed, and you both better still be here. Understand?"

"Understood," David said. "Do we have to be awake?"

"Nah," she said with a grin. "I think I can figure out a way to wake you up."

He wasn't asleep when she came back, but he pretended he was.

8

Knit Two Together

I

You know," Lucy said, craning her neck to get a better view, "I don't think we need to bother trying to go see a volcano. The most impressive rock formation in Hawaii is right here in front of us."

"It's not bad, is it?" Kathleen said, moving her hand so the diamond caught the light and released its hidden rainbow of hues. "A little heavy on the finger—"

"Are you complaining?" Lucy said. "Because if it's too heavy for you, darling, I could be persuaded to carry it around a while."

"Just don't expect to ever get it back, Kath," Sari said. She tilted her face up to the sunlight. "Man, this is the life, isn't it?" They were sitting on beach chairs on the sand, the ocean booming and crashing just feet from their toes, the sun warm, the breeze soft, and the sky an intense turquoise blue. They wore bikinis and sarongs and were covered with sunscreen, floppy hats, and sunglasses.

Lucy sighed with pleasure and dug her toes into the sun-hot sand. "Kathleen, you are no idiot."

"That's the nicest thing you've ever said to me."

"I can't believe Kevin actually owns this place," Lucy said. "It's beautiful. It's beyond beautiful. It's what Eden would have been like if it hadn't been a garden, and I'll take the ocean over some dumb flowers anyday. If you don't marry Kevin, I will."

"I never knew you were so materialistic," Kathleen said.

"I don't think it's materialistic to want *this*," Lucy said. "The beach and all. I'm just appreciating nature."

"A minute ago, you were appreciating her diamond," Sari said. "Any more appreciation from you, and Kathleen better start looking over her shoulder. Especially now that you're back on the market."

"I'm off the market again," Lucy said. She lifted up her chin to let the breeze cool off her neck.

"You and James make up?" Kathleen said.

"No," Lucy said.

Sari said, "She even destroyed the sweater."

"She destroyed the sweater?" Kathleen said. "No one told me that."

"I had to," Lucy said. "It was a symbolic gesture."

"I told you," Kathleen said. "I told you not to knit a sweater for a boyfriend."

"And I told *you* not to knit a bikini in hot pink."

"Hey," Kathleen said, flinging out her arms and posing like a catalogue model. "I think it looks pretty fucking fabulous on me."

"I dare you to go in the water with it."

"No way. As you just pointed out, I'm no idiot." Kathleen relaxed back on the chair. "Anyway, the point is that I was right about the sweater."

"Fine," Lucy said. "You were right."

"Which means you were wrong."

"Whatever."

"Say it. Say you were wrong. I just want to hear the words

come out of your mouth. Have you ever admitted you were wrong? In your life?"

"Shut up." Lucy kicked some sand in Kathleen's direction. "Don't you even want to know why I'm off the market again?"

"Of course," Kathleen said. "What's going on?"

"I slept with David Lee last night," Lucy said.

"With David Lee?" Kathleen repeated.

"My lab partner," Lucy said. "The half-Jewish, half-Chinese guy you met at the walk."

"I know who David Lee is," Kathleen said. "That's why I'm confused."

"Fuck you," Lucy said. "I happen to like the way he looks."

"Whoa, whoa," Kathleen said. "I think he's adorable. I'm just having trouble processing it. Remember when you first started working together? You said he had a crush on you and you had to shut him down completely."

"Things change," Lucy said. "I changed."

"*I* wasn't surprised," Sari said. "I knew when he gave you that friggin' cat that there was something going on between you two."

"There wasn't, though," Lucy said. "I was still with James then."

"Maybe," Sari said. "But the kitten definitely started something."

"Yeah, I guess. It's weird, though."

"What?" Kathleen said. She extended her right foot so she could admire her bright red toenail polish. She had gone out to get a manicure and pedicure that morning in preparation for the wedding and when she walked back in the house afterward, Lucy and Sari were there waiting for her. She was so surprised, she had screamed. Then they all screamed and hugged one another while Kevin beamed. "What's weird?"

"That someone can be right there and you don't think of him in any special way. And then suddenly you do think of him that way and it makes sense. Has that ever happened to either of you?"

"Does sixth grade count?" Sari asked. "Because I remember suddenly noticing Fidel Mateo in sixth grade, and we'd been in school together since kindergarten."

"Before my time," Lucy said. "So what happened with Fidel?"

"Coco Kronenberg was a big fat slut who stuffed her bra. That's what happened."

"His loss," Lucy said.

Kathleen said suddenly, "Let's go to a hotel bar and get royally drunk. It's the night before my wedding, girls. I need to get wrecked."

"What about Kevin?" Sari said.

Kathleen stood up. "He can stay home." She picked up her beach chair and folded it. "Starting tomorrow, I'll be stuck with him every night for the rest of my life."

"That's so romantic," Lucy said. "I may cry."

Three hours and nine daiquiris later, they had achieved in triplicate Kathleen's goal of getting wrecked.

They had found the perfect hotel bar, one that was completely open to the beach so they could watch the sun set while they drank their first round of freezing-cold strawberry daiquiris. Then there were greasy appetizers and more strawberry daiquiris—tonight even Lucy was eating and drinking—while they watched the hotel staff blow conch shells and race around lighting gas torches all over the property in some ancient Polynesian torch-lighting ritual. Then there were hula dancers and more daiquiris.

They laughed and talked for hours, all three of them with their hair rough and wavy from the salty ocean wind, their faces glowing from the sun they'd soaked in that afternoon and from the torchlight that fell on them now. They were dressed similarly in sleeveless cotton summer dresses and their bare legs were smooth above flat jeweled sandals. It was no wonder various guys all night long tried sending them drinks and stopping by their table. They took the drinks, sent back the men, and every one of them knew that this was one of those nights you remember forever, when the drinks are as cold and sweet as a childhood Popsicle but leave you reeling from a bitter punch that makes you glad you're an adult.

"So tell us about Kevin," Sari said to Kathleen when the night sky was dark everywhere except where the torches fought back. "Tell us what you love about him, why you want to marry him. So if we ever meet the right guy, we'll know it's him."

"I may have met him already," Lucy said.

"All the more reason for you to shut up and listen."

Kathleen took the tiny umbrella out of her drink and held it open above her head. "Look, it's raining," she said, which seemed to strike her as incredibly funny.

"Come on," Sari said, with the determination of the seriously drunk. "I want to know. Why do you love Kevin?"

"I don't," Kathleen said. Then she said, "I'm kidding, I'm kidding. Of course I do. He's nice, don't you think? Have you ever met anyone nicer? Look how he flew you guys here just to surprise me. How nice was that?"

"He even paid for our tickets," Lucy said. She let her head flop back against her chair. "He's a prince."

"He's *the* prince," Kathleen said. "Prince Charming."

"Was he mad you wanted to go out alone with us tonight?" Lucy said.

"Of course not," Kathleen said. She twirled the toothpick part of the umbrella between the palms of her hand, and the brightly colored paper spun until the colors all merged. "He doesn't get mad. Kevin doesn't get mad, he doesn't get upset, he doesn't get excited, he doesn't get *anything*."

"Except laid, I hope," Sari said.

"Not if he doesn't get aroused," said Lucy and they all laughed wildly at that—so wildly that a couple talking at a nearby table gave them annoyed looks.

"But you love him, right?" Sari said.

"Of course," Kathleen said. "I love my Prince Charming. Would it matter, though, if I didn't? People get married all the time without being in love. Don't they?"

"I wouldn't want to," Sari said.

"Doesn't matter," Kathleen said. "Because we do. Love each other. He really really loves me. And I kind of really love him." There was a beat. Then, "Did I tell you he wants to start a family?"

"Like right away?" Sari said.

"He says he can't wait to have kids."

"Did you tell him you hate kids?" Lucy asked, raising her head.

"Of course not."

"So you lied to him? Way to start a marriage, Kathleen."

"It wasn't a lie." She opened and shut the little umbrella rapidly. "Maybe I don't hate kids as much as I think I do. I could probably learn to like my own, don't you think?"

Before either girl could answer, a guy came up to their table. He was slightly younger than they were and a little on the plump side, but not bad-looking. He was wearing a brightly colored Hawaiian shirt over jeans. "Hey, guys," he said with a nervous laugh. "My friends and I have been sitting over there—" He pointed to another table and three guys there raised their hands in greeting. The girls waved back. "—and we were wondering what you girls might be up to for the rest of the evening and whether you'd like some company."

"That's so sweet," Kathleen said. "Do you have a car with you?"

"Sure do."

"Terrific!" she said. "Our house is a little ways down the beach. You want to take us home?"

"Are you kidding?" he said. "That's like so . . . Wait—just let me go tell the guys. Don't go anywhere." He dashed off.

"What are you *doing*, Kath?" Sari said. "Inviting four men back to Kevin's house? The night before your wedding? Are you insane?"

"It's easier than calling a cab," Kathleen said.

"No, it's not. All a cab driver expects is money."

"Well, these guys won't get even that."

"So we're going back to the house now?" Lucy said, confused. "To sleep?"

"No." Kathleen tossed the umbrella on the table and gathered up her purse as the men eagerly approached them. "To knit and talk."

They all packed into the guys' small Volkswagen convertible—three of them in front, four in the back. The girls were sitting on top of their hosts, who didn't seem to mind it at all. "Excuse me," Lucy told one of them. "My ass seems to be inserting itself into your hand. One of us should probably be doing something to fix that situation." The guy turned red and adjusted his hands accordingly.

When the driver—the guy who had come up to them at the restaurant and whose name, they had since learned, was Sanjesh—

pulled up to the house, he gave a low whistle of appreciation. "This is yours? Sweet!"

"Well, not ours exactly," Lucy said. She opened the door and basically fell out of the car, then stumbled into an upright position. Kathleen and Sari also slipped out quickly. "It belongs to Kathleen's fiancé."

"Who's Kathleen?"

"She is," Sari said, pointing.

"Oh, man," said Sanjesh. He had turned the car off, and he and his friends were all getting out. "You didn't tell us you were engaged."

"Sorry," Kathleen said. "I guess I forgot. Thanks for the ride, boys. Don't feel you need to walk us to the door. We can find our way." She and the other girls moved forward.

Sanjesh froze. "Aren't you going to invite us in?"

Kathleen considered briefly. Then she shook her head. "Nope."

She, Sari, and Lucy scurried up to the door and threw themselves inside, slamming the door shut behind them. They burst into incontrollable giggles.

"Hey!" A door opened on the floor above and they all tilted their heads to see up the stairway to the landing, where Kevin appeared in a pair of boxers and a T-shirt. "There you are," he said. "Welcome back. Do you need me to take care of the cab driver?" He came down the rest of the stairs.

"No cab," Kathleen said. "Some nice young men gave us a lift."

He raised his eyebrows. "I'm not sure how I feel about that."

"I'm guessing you're not angry," she said and collapsed into fresh giggles.

"You guys got a little drunk, huh?" he said.

"What makes you say that?" Lucy asked, with a snort of laughter.

"Just a lucky guess. How 'bout we all go to bed now? Get a good night's sleep, wake up all bright and cheerful for our wedding day? Our wedding day." He shook his head. "It still sounds unreal."

"You go to bed," Kathleen said. "I want to stay up with the girls. We're going to knit."

"You want to knit right now?" he said. "It's past one."

"That's what all brides do on their wedding nights," Sari said. "They knit. It's kind of an old tradition."

"Only the men aren't supposed to know about it," Lucy said. "That's why you've probably never heard about it before."

"Really," said Kevin, with a broad grin that meant he knew he was being made fun of and was prepared to be a good sport about it. "Well, don't let me stand in your way. Just do me a favor and don't drink any more tonight, will you? You're all starting to scare me."

"He says we're scaring him," Kathleen said to the girls. "And yet he doesn't *seem* scared, does he? Or nervous, or anything? That's my guy!"

"I have no idea what you're talking about," Kevin said. "Which must mean it's past my bedtime. Good night, girls." He started back up the stairs.

"Oops," said Kathleen. "My knitting's in the bedroom. Let me just grab it and I'll meet you guys back in your room." She joined him on the stairs.

Sari and Lucy stumbled their way across the house to the room they were sharing. It was a huge guest bedroom suite, with a king-size bed, a marble-floored bathroom, and a lanai that, because the house was built on a cliff, had a stunning view of the ocean.

Sari closed the door behind them and turned to Lucy. "We have to stop this wedding," she said.

"You're drunk," Lucy said. "Me, too." She collapsed down on the bed.

"I know," Sari said. "But I mean it. She doesn't love him."

"Big deal." Lucy rolled onto her back and closed her eyes.

"She can't get married—it would be a huge mistake."

"Maybe yes, maybe no," Lucy said sleepily.

"Will you please take this seriously?"

"Fine." Lucy sat up and leaned back against the headboard. Sari sat down on an upholstered chair facing her. "Even if it is a mistake," Lucy said, "what difference does it make in the long run? They'll just get divorced. No big deal. Maybe she'll even get some money out of it."

"It's depressing to get divorced," Sari said. "I see divorced people all the time, and it's like this emotional tattoo you can't ever get rid of. And if she takes his money, then she becomes the kind of girl who marries rich guys and takes their money and I don't want Kathleen to become that."

"Why don't you think she loves him? She said she did. And he's a nice guy."

"He's nice enough. But there's no spark. He's . . ." She groped. "He's spark-less. Kathleen sparkles and he's spark-less. That's a huge difference."

"Just one *s*," Lucy said.

"Please, Lucy, help me. We have to try at least, or we'll never forgive ourselves."

"We can't," Lucy said.

"Sure, we can. I mean, she listens to us—"

"No, I mean, we could maybe change Kathleen's mind, but it would be wrong. The guy bought us plane tickets to Hawaii, Sari. He put us up at his house. We'd be repaying him by ruining his life. That's fucked up. As am I, by the way."

"No, wait—I have an argument to that."

"What?"

"Shit, I forgot it." Sari banged her hand on the side of the chair. "Oh, no, there it is again. I knew I had one. Kevin's better off losing Kathleen now, before he's committed his whole heart and bank account to a marriage that won't work. We're doing him a favor."

"It doesn't feel like we're doing him a favor."

"Well, we are. And we'll know it even if he doesn't." There were footsteps outside their door. "Quick," Sari said. "Get your knitting out!" They both pounced on their knitting bags, pulled out their work, dived into chairs, and propped fake smiles on their faces.

Kathleen opened the door. "Hey," she said. "Room for one more?"

"Pull up a bed," Sari said.

Kathleen kicked off her shoes and climbed onto the bed, where she hiked her dress up above her thighs so she could sit cross-legged. She pulled out her knitting. "Kevin wanted to have sex," she said, as she detangled the yarns and straightened out the work she'd done.

"Did you?" Lucy asked.

"How fast do you think I can do it? No, I told him I'd rather hang out with you guys. We have years of matrimonial screwing ahead of us, right?"

"Right," Sari said with a meaningful glance at Lucy. "Years and years with the same guy every night. Just the one guy forever more."

"No one else," Lucy said. "*Ever.*"

"I hope it's the best sex of your life, with Kevin," Sari said. "Because it's him and only him from now on."

"What are you trying to do?" Kathleen said with a little laugh. "Scare me shitless?"

"We just want to make sure you know what you're getting into," Sari said. "That you're going into this with your eyes open."

"I know what I'm doing."

"So you think the sex is better with him than it could ever be with anyone else?"

There was a pause. Then Kathleen said, "That's a stupid question, Sari. It's un—unanswerable." She stumbled over the last word, but got it out.

"Think about this then," Sari said. "Is there any guy out there right now—*anyone*—who, if Kevin were out of the picture, you'd want to sleep with?"

"Is there any guy out there she *doesn't* want to sleep with?" Lucy said and dissolved into high-pitched giggles that rapidly turned into snorts and then hiccups.

"How much did she have to drink?" Kathleen asked Sari.

"Same as us."

"Man, then we must be totally wasted."

"You haven't answered my question," Sari said.

Kathleen knitted in silence for a moment. Then, looking up, she said slowly, "If the question is, is there another guy out there who—" She stopped.

"Who what?" said Sari, when several seconds had gone by and Kathleen still hadn't finished her sentence.

"Oh, what difference does it make?" Kathleen said. She went back to knitting, stabbing the needles at each other with a sudden wild energy. "It's all just what maybe could be or might be but isn't and I have Kevin now and he loves me and he gave me this ring and this is the most beautiful place I've ever been in and even the twins don't own a beach house in Hawaii and why are you doing this to me, Sari? Why won't you let me enjoy it? Are you jealous? Is that what this is about?"

"Yeah," said Sari. "I'm jealous. That's what this is about."

Kathleen looked up then and their eyes met. "I'm sorry," Kathleen said. "That was a stupid thing to say. But why are you making this so hard on me? The decision's been made, Sari. I'm wearing the guy's engagement ring, in case you hadn't noticed."

"It's a surprise wedding," Sari said. "No one else knows you're even engaged. So why not wait? If you and Kevin really love each other, you can get married a year from now and—"

"If I don't marry Kevin tomorrow, we won't last another week," Kathleen said.

There was a pause. Then Lucy said, "Well, then, why—"

"Because of me," Kathleen said. She let her knitting drop from her fingers and curled herself up into a ball. "Because of the way I am. I'm always getting bored with guys—you two know that better than anyone. And I'm sick of it. I'm sick of not having someone steady and I'm sick of not having anything I really like to do and I'm sick of not knowing what I want my life to be."

There was another pause. Then Lucy said, "You like to knit."

"Yeah," Kathleen said with a sigh. "I like to knit. Maybe that'll keep me busy when I'm old and all alone."

"You won't be alone when you're old," Sari said. "You'll have us."

"You guys will have husbands and kids. And cute little grandchildren."

"Our husbands will die and our kids will ignore us," Sari said. "We'll need you as much as you'll need us."

"I don't think so."

"Still," Sari said, "you shouldn't marry a guy because you're scared."

"Fuck you," Kathleen said. "Why the fuck do you have to be so fucking right all the time?" No one said anything for a moment. Then she flung her hand out. "Fine, Sari, you win. No wedding. But you guys have to be with me when I tell him."

"Does this mean you have to give the ring back?" Lucy said.

They slept together in the king-size bed that night, all three of them. They left the doors to the lanai open and ocean breezes sent them all spinning into a strange, dreamy doze, until the alcohol wore off in the middle of the night and they woke up in turns, wildly thirsty and needing to pee.

At one of her more-awake-than-asleep moments, Kathleen stumbled into the bathroom and slurped water greedily straight from the faucet. When she came back, Sari whispered hoarsely, "You okay?"

"Yeah." She crawled into bed next to Sari. "Except I feel like whatever I do tomorrow, I'm going to be making a big mistake."

"That means that whatever you do, you're saving yourself from a big mistake," Sari said. "Look at it that way."

"That helps," Kathleen said. She snuggled close and eventually they fell back to sleep.

The girls were subdued in the morning, not talking much as they showered and got dressed—not in sarongs and bikinis this time, but in their regular jeans and tank tops.

"Oh, shit," Lucy said, picking up the knitting she'd left on the chair the night before. "Oh, *shit*!" She held it up for the others to see. A bunch of stitches had fallen off the circular needles and one stitch had pulled out in a run that went halfway down the whole thing. "I can't believe it," she said. "I'm going to have to start all over again."

Sari exclaimed in sympathy, but when she went to pick up

her own knitting, she realized she had her own problems. "Oh, man, look at this. I forgot to switch colors. Now the red part's twice as wide as it's supposed to be. I'm going to have to rip out everything I did last night."

"And mine's all tangled," Kathleen said, shoving it into her knitting bag. "I'll deal with it later. But clearly it's a mistake to knit when you're drunk."

"They should warn people about this," Sari said. "Maybe even make it a law—don't drink and knit." She looked at Kathleen. "How are you doing this morning?"

"A little hungover."

"Any change of heart?"

Kathleen shook her head. "No. You're right. I shouldn't get married."

"Is there someone else?"

"Not really. Maybe. But it's not that. It's—" She fingered a shell on the desk; Lucy had brought it back from the beach the day before. It was bone-white and smooth. "I like Kevin. But I don't really want to spend the rest of my life with him. I get bored whenever we're alone together for more than an hour or two." She looked up. "I was drunk when I said yes. And I thought if I pretty much stayed drunk from then until the wedding, I'd get through it and then it would just be done and once it was done, I'd just, you know . . . kind of *go* with it."

"Someday you'll meet a guy you won't have to get drunk to marry," Lucy said.

"Or not," Kathleen said.

"Or not," Sari said. "Either way, you're right not to do this."

They all went into the kitchen together. Kevin was already sitting at the table, drinking coffee and leafing through a newspaper. He looked up with a pleasant smile. "There you are! I figured you all fell asleep in a great big heap last night, like a litter of puppies."

"Yeah, basically," Sari said with a quick sideways glance at Kathleen, who was hesitating, biting her lip. It was strange to see Kathleen look so unsure of herself.

Kevin didn't seem to notice, though. "I made coffee, if anyone wants some. From Kona beans—the best there is. Help yourselves."

"Thanks," said Lucy and went to pour herself a cup.

Sari stayed right at Kathleen's elbow.

Kevin turned the page, smoothed the paper out in front of him and said to Kathleen, "So, ready to go get married?"

"No," Kathleen said.

"I know." He was still smiling. "I'm nervous, too."

"It's not that," she said. She reached for Sari's hand and squeezed it painfully tight as she went on. "I'm not ready to get married, Kevin. I'm sorry. We talked a lot last night and I realized I'm just not ready for this."

"Oh," he said. He looked disappointed. "I know I was kind of rushing things. It just seemed so perfect doing it here." He brightened. "But maybe it does make more sense to wait a little while."

Kathleen was silent.

"Right?" he said. "We can go back home, enjoy being engaged, make some long-term plans . . . Actually, I was a little worried about my family's reaction—you know, not being included and all. Maybe it's better this way. We can do the whole big wedding thing in the spring and make my mother happy."

Kathleen let go of Sari's hand and tugged the engagement ring off her finger. "That's not what I meant." She stepped toward him and held the ring out. "I want you to take this back."

"What are you talking about?" He stared at the ring like he didn't know what it was or what he was supposed to do with it.

"You're a nice guy," Kathleen said. "The nicest. And this is a record for me. I don't last long with guys. You can ask the girls—" She gestured at Lucy and Sari with her free hand. "This has been one of the longest relationships I've ever had."

"It has," Lucy said, over the rim of her coffee cup. "Really."

"See?" Kathleen said. "So that proves, you know, that you're special. And wonderful. But it's still . . . I mean . . . I can't—" She took a deep breath. "Time's up, I guess. That's all."

"Ah," he said. "Time's up." He still hadn't moved.

Sari nudged Lucy on the arm and gestured with her head toward the door. "Excuse us," she said and pulled Lucy out of the kitchen, leaving the other two frozen in position behind them, Kathleen holding the ring toward Kevin and Kevin sitting there, not taking it.

"She said she wanted us to stay with her," Lucy said when they were out of earshot. She set her mug down on a side table they were passing. "Why are we leaving?"

"Because Kevin deserves some privacy right now. He doesn't need us rubbernecking while his hopes are being crushed."

"Oh, sure," Lucy said. "Now you're all concerned about him. But last night, when I was the one defending him—"

"We did the right thing. But that doesn't mean we get to watch. Come on—" Sari led her toward the back of the house. "Let's go say goodbye to the beach."

"If you hadn't talked her out of marrying him, all this could have been ours," Lucy said as they stepped out onto the deck and looked around. It was a perfectly glorious morning. But then it was probably always a perfectly glorious morning there.

"You're assuming we'd have been invited."

"Well, for sure we won't *now*," Lucy said. "How much do you think he hates us?"

"Kevin?" Sari said. "I don't think he's the hating type."

"I was right all along. I said he was too nice for Kathleen."

"That's sort of true. But nice isn't everything, Luce. I mean, you don't want a guy to be mean, but you do want him to be—"

"What?"

"Something more than just nice," Sari said and turned her back on the ocean.

They made a pretty sober group on the flight back. For once, no one felt much like talking. Sari had brought her laptop, so she worked. Lucy watched the movie and knit—her circular needles were plastic, so the airline allowed them onboard. Sari and Kathleen had brought metal needles, which they'd had to check.

Kathleen put her seat back as far as it would go and closed her eyes—either she was asleep or just thinking, and, either way, the others felt they should leave her in peace.

Lucy was the only one with a car at the airport, so she drove the other two home. They dropped off Kathleen first. Kathleen pulled her suitcase out of the trunk and turned to face her friends, who had gotten out of the car to say goodbye.

"You okay?" Lucy said.

"I'm fine."

"You want us to come in for a while?" Sari asked.

"Nah," Kathleen said. "I'm really okay. And—no offense, guys—but we've had a lot of togetherness lately."

"She's breaking up with *us* now," Lucy said to Sari. "We've created a monster." They all hugged and said goodbye and then Lucy drove Sari home.

II

The next day, Sari was back at work, where the usual craziness made her feel within minutes like she'd never been away, never sat on a beach or relaxed in her life.

Late in the morning, she walked a mother and son to the front door of the clinic and said goodbye to them. As she walked back into the building, she heard shrieking coming from the hallway. New kids always screamed a lot until they got the idea that there were better ways of communicating, and everyone who worked at the clinic learned to tune out the noise. But the kid let out a particularly loud scream, impossible to ignore, so Sari grinned at Shayda, who was working at the front desk. "Wow. Good lungs on that one."

Shayda looked up from the textbook she was highlighting. "You should know. It's Zachary Smith."

"You're kidding." Sari could feel the smile freeze on her face. "That's weird—he had pretty much stopped tantruming weeks ago."

"Maybe with *you* . . . But Christopher said the kid's had a tough time accepting the switch in therapists."

"Oh," Sari said.

Shayda snapped the cap back on her highlighter. "Christopher's thinking maybe they should start taking him in another entrance or do something else to break the routine, so he'll stop expecting to find you here when he comes. But I don't know—

I think maybe it's good for Zack to learn to accept change. He'll come around."

"Yeah," Sari said, but now that she knew it was Zack and he was crying for *her*, the shrieks she had barely noticed a minute ago tore at her heart.

Or maybe it was the guilt.

She wanted to run back to see Zack, to give him a hug and let him know that she still loved him. But she knew she couldn't do that—it would only make him think that screaming for her worked, and next time he would scream even louder and longer and be even more crushed if she didn't come. And Christopher would kill her.

She couldn't go back there, but it hurt not to.

She sighed and looked down at the file she was holding, for the family she had just seen. She had work to do. She plucked a pen off of the desk and sat down in one of the chairs in the waiting area to jot down some notes on the session. The screams got louder and sounded more like sobbing. She gritted her teeth and tried to concentrate on the papers in front of her.

She heard someone enter the room. Shayda said, "Rough in there?"

"He was clinging to me, and Christopher thought it would be better if I left." Jason Smith's voice. Sari looked up at the sound, and he spotted her. "Well," he said. "So you do still work here."

"Hi." She managed a casual smile. "How's Zack doing?"

"Can't you hear for yourself?"

"Yeah," she said. "Sounds like he's having a bad day. It happens with all the kids from time to time."

He came over to where she was sitting. Shayda was watching them from the desk, her eyes round with curiosity—she probably knew that Sari had asked to be taken off the family, had probably already speculated with the others about why.

"He never had a problem before." Jason was standing right over Sari now, looking down at her. "Or have you already forgotten what he's like? He's crying because you're not there, Sari. He's done it every session since you dropped him. He goes into the room and he looks around for you and he even says your name sometimes—did you know he could say your name? Because I didn't—and then he starts screaming for you."

She stared down at the file in front of her, not seeing it. "Kids get used to certain routines—"

"That's bullshit," Jason said. "It's bullshit and you know it. He thought you were his friend and then one day you just disappeared and you never even said goodbye to him."

Sari darted a look at Shayda, whose mouth had fallen wide open. "I know it happened fast, but I just thought—"

"I don't care what you thought. And right now I don't even care that you jerked me around and dropped me flat and made me feel like an idiot for ever—" He waved his hand with an angry noise of dismissal. "But to stop working with Zack, with no reason or explanation—man, that was *cold*. You're supposed to want to help kids, not break their hearts. What the hell is wrong with you?"

"You don't understand," she said. "I couldn't do it. Not anymore."

"Why not?"

She just shrugged and wouldn't look at him.

He squatted down so his face, his eyes, were at her level. "Was it because of me? I *asked* you if it was okay—everything I did, every time I—" He banged his fist against the side of the sofa—not near her, but it made her jump anyway. "Do you think I would have done anything that might end up hurting Zack? Or you, for that matter? What do you think I am?"

"It wasn't because of that." Sari wished Shayda wasn't watching. They were speaking in low voices, but Shayda could probably still hear a lot. "You don't understand—"

"I know I don't understand!" he said, his voice rising. "That's my whole point. *I don't understand.* Why would someone like you want to hurt a kid?"

"I don't know!" Sari said with a rush of anger that was a relief, since it blew away the guilt. "You tell me! Why did *you* want to?"

"Excuse me?" he said.

"No," she said. "I won't."

He rocked back onto his ankles. "What are you talking about?"

She leaned forward. "Why did you torture my brother on a daily basis? Why did you and your friends make fun of him and shove him around and make him scared to go to his own school? Why did you have to make me ashamed of him—of my own brother, who never did *anything* to hurt me—until I couldn't even stand the sight of him?" Her voice broke on the last word, so she stopped, but she fought the tears and glared at him.

"Your brother?" he repeated.

"My brother. Charlie. I've told you about him. He has autism, just like Zack. And just like Zack, he could have had a shot at a better life, only unlike Zack he didn't get it. Instead, he got to be treated like shit, called a retard, have his lunch stolen and his pants pulled down in public. All thanks to you and your friends."

"Me? What are you talking about? I never did anything like that."

"Oh, please!" She curled her hands into fists on her knees, almost giddy with the relief of being the one on the attack now. She didn't even care if Shayda heard them. "I remember you, Jason. *You,* strutting around in your team uniforms, laughing with your friends, acting like you were hot shit because you could knock something out of the hands of a kid who couldn't even defend himself. And then I saw you again here, and I was supposed to help your kid. And I actually tried to. I tried to help your kid because he deserved it even if you didn't, but I couldn't take it anymore. Charlie's got *nothing* in his life and your kid will be fine, and it's not fair. It's just not fair."

"You're wrong," Jason said. His face had softened, lost its anger—exchanged it for bewilderment. "You're wrong, Sari. I'm sorry if kids were mean to your brother, but it wasn't me. I saw stuff like that happening sometimes, but I wasn't the one doing it."

"Right," Sari said. Her fingernails were digging into her palms, but the pain felt good. "It was always someone else. That's how people do things like that—they do it in a group and then no one takes the blame for it. There was always a bunch of you around whenever anything bad happened. I always got there too late to see who'd done it, too late to stop it—but you were there laughing at him. I *saw* you. I saw you there laughing at him. I can still see you laughing at him."

He shook his head, but not in denial. More like he was trying to clear it. "Maybe I laughed. I don't know. If I did, God knows it wasn't because I actually thought anything like that was funny. But I was—" He shook his head again. "It was *high school,* Sari. It was scary and miserable and mean and you did what everyone else was doing because if you didn't they'd turn on you next. It was all about saving yourself."

"You think that excuses it? I went to the same school, you know, and *I* didn't torture anyone."

"Well, good for you." He rose abruptly to his feet. "Good for you, Sari. You weren't mean at all to anyone back in high school." He shoved his hands in his pockets and looked down at her.

"No, you just waited another ten years or so before you decided to ruin an autistic kid's life."

"I've spent the last six years of my life helping these kids," she said.

"Five minutes ago, my kid was screaming because they wouldn't let him see you," Jason said. "I may have been a jerk in high school, but I know I never made your brother—or anyone else—scream like that." And he turned on his heel, crossed the room, kicked open the front door to the clinic, and was gone.

There was silence.

After a moment, Shayda came over to where Sari sat, unmoving, on the sofa. "Do you need me to get Ellen or anything?" she asked.

Sari stared at her blankly. "Ellen?"

"Yeah. Is everything okay? I mean, what just happened here?"

"I'm not sure," Sari said.

The last thing she wanted was to see Ellen or anyone else for that matter, but she still had several clients to see before the end of the day, so she couldn't just vanish. She was able to swear Shayda to secrecy, though, by telling her she'd been stupid enough to get a little bit involved with Zack's dad before realizing she needed to call it off and that he was kind of upset about the breakup. She made a big show of how she was too embarrassed to have anyone else at the clinic know how dumb she'd been.

"He's really good-looking," Shayda said, clearly thrilled by the whiff of scandal. "I don't blame you."

Sari didn't trust herself to reply to that, so she just reminded Shayda not to tell anyone and then excused herself.

III

Hey," Kathleen said, early that evening, poking her head into the office in the back of Sam's apartment. "Can I talk to you?"

Sam was sitting at his desk. He jumped at the sound of her voice and turned. "Jesus. Don't sneak up on me like that."

"I knocked at the kitchen for a while and you didn't answer, so I just came in."

"I've got to remember to keep that door locked."

"You want me to go?"

He got up from his desk with a sigh. "No, now that you're here, I might as well take a break." He rubbed his eyes. "I'm supposed to stop every half hour, according to my ophthalmologist—if I stare at the computer too long, I get headaches. One of these days, she's going to admit that we're dealing with a malignant brain tumor." He moved past her. "I could use a cup of tea. You?"

"Sure," she said and followed him back into the kitchen.

He picked up the teakettle and carried it over to the sink. "Where have you been lately?" he said, as he ran the filtered water into it. "I haven't seen you around."

"Hawaii. Why don't you use the insta-hot? It's faster."

"Water that's actually boiling makes better tea." He turned the faucet off. "What were you doing in Hawaii?"

She hesitated for a moment then said, "Breaking up with Kevin Porter."

He set the kettle on the stove. "You picked a nice place to do it." He turned on the burner, then moved to the cupboard and got out two cups and two saucers. He arranged them on the counter so the handles on the cups were facing in the exact same direction. "Darjeeling or Earl Grey?"

Kathleen waved her hand impatiently. "Do you really think I know the difference?"

He smiled and shook his head and plucked out two teabags from a jar on the counter.

"So," Kathleen said, after another moment of silence, "it's ended. Me and Kevin Porter."

"So you already said. And more grammatically. How did he take it?"

"He's fine, I think." She hoped no one—especially not Sam—would ever find out that she had agreed to marry Kevin right before breaking up with him. Sari and Lucy knew, but they didn't count.

Sam gave her a hard look. "Are you saying that because you really think so, Kathleen, or because you don't want to feel guilty?"

She smiled sheepishly. "Both."

The kettle whistled. Sam took a blue-and-white pot holder out of a drawer and carefully wrapped it around the teakettle's handle, then poured the water into the cups. Steam rose up in puffs around his hand. He had boiled exactly the right amount of water for two cups. "I've got to admit I'm surprised." He put the kettle back on the stove and the pot holder back in its drawer before turning to her again. "Just a few weeks ago, you told me you were going to marry Kevin and live off his fortune for the rest of your life."

"I never said I was definitely going to do that—I just said it was an interesting possibility."

"One that you seemed very invested in pursuing. What happened?"

"Nothing happened." She shifted, pressing the flat of her back against the counter. "I guess I just got bored."

"What happened to the young woman with plans and forethought? The one who wasn't going to be like her mother and throw her life away on some loser? The budding philanthropist?"

"They got bored, too."

"I see." He dunked the two teabags, then got a clean mug out of the cupboard and deposited the used teabags inside. He put that mug in the sink. "Do you want milk or sugar?"

"Sugar. A lot."

"Are you sure you wouldn't just prefer a tea-flavored cup of sugar?"

"Are you offering?"

"Sit down, Kathleen." She sat while he doctored the tea and then he joined her at the table and slid a cup and saucer across to her.

She picked up the cup and put it to her lips. "Fuck," she said, dropping it down onto the saucer with a clatter. "It's really hot." She put her fingers to her burned lip.

"Brilliant," Sam said. "You watched me boil and pour the water with your own eyes, but you had to burn yourself to realize it was hot?"

"Whatever."

"Try thinking before you do things, Kathleen. You'll get hurt a lot less."

"But will I have as much fun?" And suddenly—crazily—she thought of leaning forward and kissing him. And immediately rejected the idea. Kiss Sam? Who was stern and disapproving and usually annoyed with her? The thought was both untenable and exciting—tempting the way the idea of setting off the fire alarm on a school corridor is tempting and not something you'd ever actually do.

Distracted by the thought, she took another sip of tea and immediately scorched her lips again, but this time suppressed the curse that rose to her tongue, so Sam wouldn't know she had been stupid not once but twice.

Sam was stirring his tea slowly with a spoon. "You said you wanted to talk to me about something. Was it just to tell me about Kevin?"

She brought herself back to the conversation. "Sort of. It's connected. I wanted to let you know that I'm quitting my job. Since you helped me get it. It's not that I hate it or anything, but it's kind of not that exciting and—"

"And you've already used up and discarded the boss's son, so what's the point?"

"Shut up."

He didn't. "Jackson has two more sons, you know. There's no reason to quit yet. They're married, of course, but I think you and I both know that marriages aren't necessarily permanent. You could even argue that the extra obstacle will make it a more exciting challenge, couldn't you?" She didn't answer, just glared at him, so he shrugged and went on, still stirring his tea. "Actually, I think you made a mistake going after Kevin in the first place, Kathleen. His brothers are bigger players than he'll ever be."

"I didn't go after him. It wasn't like that."

He stopped stirring and looked across the table at her, his eyes flat and unreadable. "Oh, please. You can tell anyone else that. But not me."

She couldn't meet his look. "All right," she said after a moment. "Maybe it *was* like that." She poked, defeated, at the handle on her teacup.

He resumed his mocking tone. "So are you hoping I'll find you another job? Because I'll have to put some thought into it." He placed the spoon carefully on the saucer, to the side of his teacup. "Do you care how handsome the son of the boss is at your next office? Or is it enough for him just to be roughly the right age? I can't promise Kevin-quality looks and broad shoulders every time, you know. Come to think of it, does it even have to be a son? Or could it be, say, a nephew? Or a daughter?"

"Sorry not to laugh," Kathleen said, "but you're not actually being funny. I just thought you should know I was quitting, that's all. Since you got me the job. Which I *am* grateful for, whether you care or not."

"You never took that job seriously."

"Come on, Sam. I was pouring coffee and stapling papers most of the time. How seriously could anyone take that?"

"That's all you're qualified to do." He took a careful sip of his tea and lowered the cup. "So what's the next job going to be?"

"I haven't decided yet. But I'm not going to rush into anything this time. I'm going to sit down and really think about what's right for me, how it's going to work out in the long run. Not just grab at the first thing that comes along."

"You've really matured since I met you, Kathleen, you know that?"

"Shut up," she said. She pushed her cup away. "I'm going to go watch TV."

"Mine, I assume."

"Well, *I* don't have one."

"Can't you find somewhere else to watch?"

"Not without putting on shoes. I'll be quiet, I promise."

"All right," he said. "But don't bother me. I have a lot of work to do."

"I won't." She stood and picked up her cup of tea.

"That doesn't leave this room."

"I know. I was going to put it in the sink."

"Bullshit," he said. "You've never once cleaned up a dish around here."

"You see?" she said. "I *have* grown. So there." And she put her cup and saucer in the sink.

But she was lying. She had picked it up to take into the other room.

IV

When Sari was almost done at work, she called Kathleen.

"I need a drink," she said as soon as Kathleen answered. "I need to talk to you and have a very large drink and you need to tell me I'm not a horrible human being."

"I can tell you right now that if *you're* a horrible human being, the rest of us are in deep shit," Kathleen said. "You're the most decent person I know. But I like the drink idea."

"Should I call Luce?"

"Of course."

The bar was in Brentwood Village. Sari got there first and had their drinks already set up at a table by the time Kathleen walked in wearing a torn sweatshirt and no makeup, with her hair pulled back in a sloppy ponytail. "Is Lucy coming?" she asked as she slid into a chair and picked up her drink—vodka and cranberry juice, same as Sari's—with a nod of thanks.

Sari shook her head. "She's working late and then she's going to meet some friend of David's."

"How dare she have a wonderful time with a wonderful guy instead of being miserable with us? Doesn't she know I just broke up with my fiancé? What kind of friend is she?"

"It is kind of a betrayal," Sari said. "And what's up with her going straight from one great guy to another when I haven't even had a date in months? She's definitely getting more than her share."

"Wouldn't it be nice if friends could always be in sync?" Kathleen said. "Like you could all be happily in love at the same time and then have your hearts broken at the same time? Then there wouldn't ever be availability issues or resentment or anything."

"That never happens," Sari said. "One person's always running around thinking that love totally rocks while the others are curled up in a fetal position listening to Alanis Morissette and sobbing." She took a sip of her drink. Then another. "But when you think about it, maybe it's for the best. If everyone got depressed at exactly the same time, who'd be around to cheer you up and pull you out of it? You'd just sink deeper and deeper. It could get ugly."

"That's so not how it works," Kathleen said. "Misery loves company. The only way to cheer up is to feel like other people are even more miserable than you are—especially your closest friends."

"Aw," said Sari. "That's so sweet and generous of you. Remind me to avoid you whenever I'm happy."

"I was joking."

"Doesn't matter," Sari said. "I'll never be happy again anyway."

"You *are* in a funk," Kathleen said. "Tell me about your day."

And Sari did.

"First of all," Kathleen said when Sari had finished, "you are so *not* the bad guy in this. You couldn't be cruel to a kid even if you tried, and Cute Asshole Guy is way out of line trying to lay a guilt trip on you. You know that, right?"

Sari stared morosely at her drink, which was already depressingly close to empty. "I don't know. He has a point. I shouldn't have cut things off with the kid just because— I mean, I knew who Jason was from the beginning. If I had a problem with it, I shouldn't have started working with Zack in the first place."

"You didn't know the guy would come on to you," Kathleen said. "That changes everything. Anyway, even if the kid misses you and cries a little now and then, you haven't actually hurt him, have you? I'm sure you're the best therapist there and all, but I've got to assume there are other decent ones at the clinic—"

"Of course."

"So there you go. The kid's totally fine. Jason Smith was just trying to make you feel bad. And I'm guessing he succeeded." She tilted her forehead questioningly toward Sari, who smiled weakly. "Well, don't let him win. You're the best girl around, and who should know better than me?"

"No one," Sari said. "I wish you'd been there to defend me. Or that I'd at least defended myself a little. I could have said—" She stopped. "I don't know what I could have said, but *something*. Instead, I just sat there like an idiot while he told me how mean I was to Zack and then let him leave thinking he'd won. I'll be up all night torturing myself about it, thinking about all the things I should have said. It'll keep me up for *weeks*."

"Yeah, but if you *had* said something, you'd probably be up all night wishing you'd said something completely different or even that you'd just kept quiet. These things never go the way you want them to."

"Life doesn't go the way you want it to," Sari said.

"And on that cheerful note, we drink," said Kathleen. They clinked glasses.

V

With Zack coming to the clinic four days a week, it was inevitable that Sari would run into the Smiths again and she knew it. She thought a lot about what she might say if Jason accused her again of having been cruel to Zack but didn't like anything she came up with.

The truth was that she actually felt pretty guilty about abandoning Zack, which made it hard to come up with a good argument defending her right to have done so.

Every day at work, she worried about running into Jason and reopening all the old wounds, and every night she went to bed relieved it hadn't happened.

Mostly relieved. There was a tiny bit of disappointment mixed in there—whether she liked to admit it or not, there had been a thrill to seeing Jason and, with that gone, the days just felt like work again, tedious and monotonous and extremely unsexy.

And a sense of unfinished business hovered over her. She wanted to see Jason again—she *needed* to see him again, to set everything straight so they could be done with each other.

She wanted to see Jason again.

She turned a lot whenever she heard a man's voice at the clinic.

Her heart would start knocking hard against her chest for a second or two, and then she would realize that it wasn't Jason, was just some other guy who had no right to be standing there talking and not being Jason. And the disappointment and relief were just about equal.

* * *

One Thursday, a couple of weeks later, Ellen was out at a school IEP meeting, and Sari had gone into her office to try to find a client's folder that Ellen had sworn she'd left on the credenza in there. Sari's back was to the open door when she suddenly felt something hit her from behind—and there was Zack, throwing his arms around her leg and clutching it to his small chest as if he were drowning and her leg was the only flotation device he could find.

With a rush of delight, Sari bent over him, sniffing at the good sweet little boy smell of his hair and neck.

"Sari," he said. "Hi, Sari."

"It's good to see you," she said and squeezed his shoulders hard. When she lifted her head, she saw Jason watching from just outside the open office door, his face tight and expressionless.

Still holding on to her leg, Zack looked back at his father. "Sari," he said.

"Yeah," his father said. "I remember." He held out his hand to Zack. "Come on, pal. We have to go."

Zack shook his head. "Sari."

"She's busy," his father said. "Too busy for us. Come on."

"I've missed you, Zack," Sari said. "How are you?"

"How are you?" he replied politely.

"No, say, 'Good,' Zack."

"Even if he's *not* good?" Jason took a step forward, into the office. "That's the great thing about autistic kids, isn't it? They'll say what you tell them to, even if it's not true. Why don't you teach him to say, 'I don't miss you at all, Sari'?"

Sari stared at him. "You don't need to make me feel guilty, you know. Zack *is* fine. He's doing great."

"How do *you* know that?"

"The way he's talking to me. I can tell he's making progress."

"Sure," Jason said. "Whatever gets you through the night."

"Stop it," Sari said. "Stop it. You're not being fair." She swallowed hard, then plunged in. "I didn't quit to be mean to Zack. I quit because it was all too hard. And he's okay. He's going to be fine. He's got Christopher, who's a really good therapist, and he's got you to take care of him. And Maria, too, who means well even if she's—" She stopped, shook her head, got herself back on track. "Anyway, the point is he's going to be fine, you know he is, whether he sees me or not. Because you're doing the right things for him. So it's not fair to make me feel bad about it. I love the little guy." She rubbed Zack's back. "I think he's great. And I would have kept working with him, only it was too hard."

"Why do you keep saying that?" Jason asked. "That it was too hard? What was so fucking hard about it?"

"You know," she said. "High school and—"

"You recognized me the first day we came in," Jason said. "And you started working with Zack anyway. And kept working with him for a while. So that's not it. That's not what made it so hard."

"It was part of it," Sari said. She brushed her fingers through Zack's curls, looking down so she wouldn't have to meet Jason's eyes. "And then you and I started—I don't know what we started doing. But I didn't feel right about it. I kept trying to stop—"

"Yeah, I noticed."

"But I couldn't." No matter how hard she swallowed, the swelling in her throat wouldn't go down. She was grateful at least that they were alone in Ellen's office, not in one of the public areas. "It was all too much. Thinking about Charlie and seeing you all the time and knowing that Zack needed my help—I just couldn't take it anymore."

"I'm sorry," Jason said after a moment. "I probably shouldn't have been so hard on you the other day. But I hate it when Zack cries like that. I can't stand it. And then seeing you sitting there, not caring, filling out your little forms like it had nothing to do with you at all—" His voice, Sari noticed, was as shaky as hers. "I told you, I used to watch you two together and I thought he meant something to you. And that meant something to me."

"He did," Sari said. "He *does*. I miss being with him. But it's all been so complicated that it just seemed better for everyone if I stayed away."

"That's exactly what Denise said that night you came to dinner. And you said she was wrong."

"I'm not Zack's mother," she said. "I'm Charlie's sister. And that makes all of this . . . impossible." There was a silence and then she sighed and said, "Okay. That's it." She gently removed Zack's hands from her leg. "Time to go, sweetheart."

"Hold on," Jason said. "Just hold on a second. It's my turn to say something."

"I think it's been—"

"I said hold on."

Zack suddenly let go of her leg and slid down onto the floor as if he had become too bored with standing to do it any longer. He flopped onto his back and looked up at the ceiling.

Jason said, "I've been thinking. Since we last talked. And if I was ever mean to your brother back in high school—and maybe I was—God knows it's possible, even if I don't remember it—if I was, I'm sorry. Deeply and horribly and painfully sorry. If I could go back now and help him out, I would."

"I know," she said. "I know you would. But only because of him." She gestured down at Zack.

"What do you mean?" Jason said.

"If Zack hadn't been born—if you'd had the perfect golden

child you thought you'd have—you'd probably still be walking around, acting like an asshole, thinking you were better than everyone else—maybe even still being mean to anyone who was different, maybe even teaching Zack to be mean to the other kids at school—"

"Whoa," he said. "I would never have taught my kid to be mean . . . But say it's true that if things had been different, I'd have been different—doesn't the same go for you? If Charlie hadn't been born, do you really think you'd have been such a saint your whole life?"

"I never said I was a saint."

"Pretty much—all that talk about how you were never mean to anyone in high school . . ." He ran his hand through his hair. Some of it stayed sticking up, and Sari had to fight the urge to reach up and smooth it down. "Of course having Zack changed me. I don't think I was ever really as bad as you seem to think I was, but either way, I'm a more decent human being now and I'll freely admit it. Does it matter why? You had a brother a couple of decades before I had Zack, so maybe you had an advantage there. But you and I ended up in the same place. And for the same reason."

"I would never have been mean to a kid with special needs. Even if Charlie hadn't been my brother."

"How can you be sure of that?"

"I just know."

"Whoever you think I was—whatever you think I was—back in high school, I'm not that guy now," Jason said. "I'm not sure I ever was him, but I'm definitely not him now."

"It doesn't matter," she said. "You can't just say 'I'm good now' and have everything suddenly be forgotten."

"Why not?" Jason rubbed his temple savagely. "Why are you fighting this so hard, Sari? Why do I have to be evil through and through? Why can't I have changed? Why do you *want* to think badly of me?"

"I don't." She sagged back against the wall, suddenly exhausted. "At least . . . I don't think I do."

"Then why can't you give me a break?"

It was so hard to explain. "I've hated everyone from high school for so long. I've gone to sleep thinking about how much I hated you all for years now. I don't think I could even go to sleep without thinking about all that." She gave a little painful smile. "It's like my security blanket."

"You need to give it up."

"Charlie's been so screwed over," Sari said. "In every way. He never had a chance, Jason. You don't know what it's like. Zack will be fine. Charlie won't."

"You can't blame the kids from high school for that."

"If they'd been kinder to him—"

"It would have been better," he said. "But it wouldn't have cured his autism. There has to be more to the story than that."

"Maybe," she said. "I mean, of course. But—"

"But what? Why do you have to keep hating me?"

"Because it's easier than—" Than what? She turned away from him, pressing herself against the wall, trying to think, trying to find something coherent to say.

It was all such a mess, everything to do with Charlie. First there was her mother's craziness and her father's indifference, and then the cruelty of the kids at school . . . and then when all that was behind her, she had thought *I'll learn how to make everything better for him*, but nothing she learned had ever made any difference—and the truth was she hadn't helped him at all.

She hadn't helped him at all.

God, it hurt to think that. She had spent the last six years of her life studying how to help Charlie, but he was still stuck at home watching TV and eating too much, isolated from the real world. For all her schooling and good intentions, she hadn't done a thing for Charlie. Her mother always got in her way when she tried to change things, and eventually she had given up even trying.

It was too awful to think about—all that failure, all that giving up. It was so much easier to blame everyone else—her mother for not getting it, her father for not caring, her sister for running away, everyone at school for laughing at him—

But what had she ever done to make Charlie's life better? Who had hurt him more in the end—some strangers who made fun of him or the sister he loved who used to hit him and scream at him because he couldn't change? What good had any of her promises or hopes or anger actually done him?

"Oh, shit," Sari said. She hid her face in her hands, her body crouched against the wall. "I can't do this."

"Do what?"

Through her fingers, she said, "I can't just suddenly change the way I've been thinking about things."

"Why not?" Jason was suddenly standing very close to her. "Didn't you tell me the brain is very good at reshaping itself? Ever hear of a little thing called neural plasticity?"

Sari let her hands drop to her sides. "If you tell me to lay down some new neural pathways, I swear I'll—"

"You'll what?" Jason said.

"I don't know," she said and wouldn't look at him. "It's just not that easy."

"We could schedule some interventions for you, if it would help," Jason said. "I know some excellent therapists." He took her hand. She looked at their fingers and saw how quickly hers twined around his. "I know how hard it is to change the way you think about things," he said. "Do you know how long I've clung to the idea that I'm going to make it in Hollywood? That I'm some undiscovered genius? And meanwhile I'm just a part-time kids basketball coach whose wife—soon to be ex-wife—has to support him. I need to lay down some new pathways of my own." He rubbed his thumb softly against the rounded part of her palm. "You could help me, Sari. You're good with all this brain-retraining stuff. It's what you do."

"Why would you *want* me to help you?" Sari said. "I was mean to you and Zack. You said so yourself."

"Yeah, you were," he said. "And back in high school, I used to laugh when someone tripped a retard."

"So what are you saying? That we're even?"

"Not that. More like . . . people can act badly and not be bad people."

"How do you tell the difference? Between a bad person and one who just acts badly? Because I've been trying so hard to figure that one out and I can't. I can't."

"You just know," he said. "One pretty good indication is when the person devotes her life to helping other people. Truly bad people don't usually do that. Not unless it pays well."

"It doesn't pay well," Sari said. She couldn't look at him, just kept focusing on their hands—on how her fingers were clutching on to his. She felt choked with hope and dread and uncertainty.

"Also," he said, "when someone kisses you and it's all you can think about for weeks and weeks, you just can't believe that person is bad."

"Bad people can be good kissers."

"I'm sorry." Jason pulled on her hand, gently reeling her in toward him. "I just can't think of you as evil. God knows I've tried, Sari. For the past few days, all I've done is try. I've been so pissed off at you . . . But I keep seeing you throw your arms around Zack because he said 'more' one day, and everything else gets lost."

"I know," she said and extricated her hand from his, but only so she could slide it up his arm, feel the muscle there and the warmth of his skin. "I've been trying even harder to hate you. To keep hating you, I mean." She was whispering now, not to be quiet, but because it was so hard to find the breath to speak out loud. "But you keep making it almost impossible."

"Sari," he said, and it was a question, only she didn't try to answer it, just pushed herself against him, and maybe that was answer enough. She could feel his whole body sigh with relief. She buried her face in his chest. She only came up to his shoulders, and it felt good to just collapse onto him, to let someone else hold her up for a change. "Sari," he said again. His fingers went to her hair and he stroked it gently for a moment, but then he caught some of the short strands in his fingers and tugged it back—not painfully, but firmly enough to force her head back and make her look at him. His face—his so-handsome-it-hurt-to-look-at-him face—was taut and anxious, and his voice was hoarse when he said, "If this is another one of those times when you're playing with me—if you're going to turn on me again like you did last time—"

"And the time before," she said, ashamed, remembering how every time she started to like him and let him see that she liked him, she'd force herself to be cold and angry with him again, with no explanation or apology. "I won't. I swear I won't. And I wasn't playing with you before—I was fighting with myself."

"That's not what it felt like from where I was standing."

"I was pretty awful, wasn't I?"

"Just a little cruel."

"Here I was thinking you were the bad guy," Sari said. "And it was me all along."

"Yeah." He kept the firm hold on her hair, kept her head pulled back, his eyes studying her face. "But I forgive you." He bent over her. There was enough anger left in him that his kiss was hard and violent.

She was instantly aroused, instantly drawn under. She had been waiting a long time for this, she realized, and her body was already tightening with the lust she'd been trying to ignore for all that time. This time, there was no holding back, no wondering whether she was making a mistake. All she wanted was to be this close to him forever, always feeling his mouth and body demanding hers and hers demanding his.

And then someone cleared her throat just a few feet away.

They sprang apart.

"Hi," Ellen said, standing in the doorway, holding her briefcase across her chest like a shield. "Am I interrupting? Or am I allowed to come into my own office?"

"Oh, God," Sari said. She felt her hot face flush even hotter. "I'm so sorry, Ellen. Oh, God."

Ellen came into the room. "Hey, cutie," she said, holding her free hand out to Zack, who was still lying on his back on the floor. "How about standing up now? It's time to go home. *Past* time, I'd say," she added with a sharp look at Sari as she hauled Zack to his feet and extended his hand to his father.

"Come over later?" Jason whispered to Sari as he slipped by her on the way to taking Zack's hand.

Sari nodded. She wasn't capable of speaking at the moment.

"Really?" he said.

She nodded again, and he led Zack to the door. "Sorry," he said to Ellen. "We never meant to—"

"Just please take your child and go," Ellen said. Jason hesitated, looking at Sari, who gestured with her head toward the door, and he nodded and left. Ellen dropped her briefcase on the floor and turned to Sari. "Tell me why I shouldn't strangle you."

Sari forced a smile. "You'd be short a clinician?"

"That's the only reason I'm not. But if you ever do anything like this again—"

"I'm so sorry, Ellen," Sari said. "I—" It was hard for her to get words out, but she cleared her throat and tried again. "I wouldn't. Ever. I never have before, I swear."

"Well, that's a relief. I'd hate to think you're in here making out with men whenever my back is turned."

"This was the first time—"

"First, last, and only. You understand?"

"Of course. Of course."

"The kid was right there," Ellen said. "God knows I'm no prude, Sari, but the poor kid was lying on the floor and his parents aren't even divorced yet. What were you thinking?"

"I wasn't really thinking," Sari said.

"That's obvious." Ellen studied her carefully. "I assume this was connected to the whole 'I can't work with Zack but I swear his father's not a letch' thing?"

"Kind of. I mean—"

"Do we want to revisit the question of whether his father's a letch or not? Because it seems to me—"

"Please," Sari said. She put her hand to her forehead. "It's not like that, Ellen."

"Really? So tell me what it's like."

"I don't know," she said. "Can I get back to you on that?"

"Whatever it is or isn't, keep it out of the office," Ellen said.

"I promise."

"And if you ever ask to be taken off a child's case again for personal reasons—"

"I won't."

"You better not. Or you'll be out of here. You understand?"

"Yes."

"All right then."

Sari went to the door.

"One last thing—" Ellen said.

"What?" She turned.

Ellen scooped up her briefcase off the floor and dropped it onto her desk. "Don't forget to go over there later. Might as well finish what you started. Only this time in the appropriate environment."

Sari managed a nod and stumbled out of the office.

Jason was putting Zack to bed when Sari arrived. She volunteered to read Zack a bedtime story, and Jason sat on the bed and watched her intently through the whole book. It made it hard to read.

Once she was done, she put the book back in the bookcase while Jason tucked the blanket around Zack's little body. Over his shoulder he said to her, "I have to lie down with him until he falls asleep or he'll scream for an hour."

"You should let him scream," she said. "Eventually he'll learn to—"

"No," he said. "Not tonight. I want him to go to sleep quickly tonight."

"Yeah," she said. "Me, too."

"Wait for me in the family room?"

"Okay."

She was alone in the family room for almost half an hour. Which gave her plenty of time to wander around looking at photos she would rather not have looked at and then to torture herself by studying them minutely—photos of Jason and Denise getting married (she wore a satin slip dress cut on the bias and was gorgeously slim and elegant), photos of a weary but triumphant Denise cuddling a newborn Zack, photos of the whole family on vacation near a beach, Zack just a toddler in his father's arms—photos, over and over again, of the perfect family, perfectly happy together.

Jason walked in while she was still studying one of the older photos—Denise and Jason in their college graduation gowns, kissing, each of them holding a diploma up to the camera, but otherwise apparently oblivious to its presence.

"Hi," he said, coming to stand next to her.

"Is he asleep?"

He nodded then gestured at the photos surrounding them. "So what do you think?"

"There are a lot of them," she said, carefully placing the one she was holding back among the rest.

"I know. I'd like to get rid of some of them. Or even all of them. There's something sad and creepy about having to look at them all the time, like nothing's changed. But I don't know how Zack would feel about it if they all just disappeared."

"Yeah, that might be hard on him."

"It might." They were both silent for a moment.

Then Sari said, "She's really beautiful."

"I guess." He nudged her shoulder with his. "I like the way *you* look."

"You didn't back in high school."

"I barely knew you. If I had ever stopped and really talked to you—"

"It wouldn't have made a difference," she said. "We weren't in the same place back then."

There was another pause. Then: "How mad was Ellen?"

"Pretty mad. I don't blame her. We were acting like—" She stopped.

"Like what?"

"I don't know. Teenagers, I guess. Getting carried away by our hormones."

"That's not such a bad thing," he said, and he grinned suddenly. "Want to do that again?"

"Yeah," she said. "I do." But when he reached for her, she suddenly ducked away. "I'm sorry," she said, twisting her hands together. "It's just a little scary."

"What?"

She gestured toward a photo of Denise sitting by a pool and laughing. "Well, *she* is, for one thing. The way she looks . . . it just makes me wonder how many other beautiful women you've been with."

"Not that many," he said. "You'd be surprised."

"Oh, come on," she said. "In high school alone, they must have numbered in the dozens. All those cheerleaders."

He shook his head and reached for her hand. Just the touch of his fingers on hers made her want to jump out of her skin in a good way. "You're nuts. I had two girlfriends in all of high school, and they both ended up dumping me."

"You were always with some girl or another," Sari said. "Always. You were like this movie star on the campus. All those girls, all over you—they were always giving you massages on that wall behind the cafeteria and—"

"*You* gave me a back rub not that long ago," he said. "That I remember."

"A back rub?"

"With a hot towel."

"Oh, right," she said. "Did you like that?"

"Are you kidding? It was maybe the most erotic two minutes of my life."

"Don't say that. I was there to work with Zack, not to turn you on."

"Sorry," he said. "I did my best to hide it."

"Anyway, what are you talking about, two minutes? It was a lot longer than that."

"It was not. You were in and out. Got me all excited and then walked away—telling me to go take Advil. You're a cold, cold woman, Sari Hill."

"Turn around," she said and he obeyed her. She pulled up his shirt, put her hands against his warm back.

He shivered. "You really *are* cold. Your hands are like ice."

"They'll warm up," she said. She slid her hands all the way up under his shirt, to the muscles of his shoulders and let herself really feel how warm and strong he was, then she slipped them down and around his waist to his flat stomach and up again to explore the broad planes of his chest.

"Ah," he said.

They stood like that for a moment, her hands pinning him against her, front to back. She rested her cheek against the swell of his right shoulder. And then he turned around, so her hands were caught for a moment in his shirt and by the time she had worked them free, his arms were pulling her tight against him, and then his mouth came down on hers and for once—for *once*—they were alone somewhere private, with no cars or people to stop them from doing what they both wanted to do so badly, and no anger left in Sari to make her pull back and reject something that she wanted with all of her body and all of her heart.

9

Yarn Over

As the old year gave way to the new one, Kathleen found herself with a lot of free time on her hands.

For one thing, she no longer had a job. After Hawaii, she had never even bothered returning to the office. "You can kiss any references goodbye," Sam said when he found out she hadn't given two weeks' notice. It didn't matter: her sisters had asked her to come back to work for them and she had said she would, after a few more weeks of vacation.

So her days weren't busy, but neither were her nights. Although both Lucy and Sari continued to show up faithfully at the Sunday morning knitting circle, once the evening rolled around, they almost always had plans with their new boyfriends. They often invited her to join them, but Kathleen had never much liked being the odd man out, despite—or because of—all her childhood experience in that role.

Getting a boyfriend of her own would have solved that problem, but since the whole Kevin thing Kathleen hadn't felt much like going out to bars and meeting new guys. Sometimes at night she remembered that she might have been married at this moment—*would* have been, if her friends hadn't interceded—and her heart would start pounding with fear. It wasn't the thought of marriage itself that was so scary—just the realization that, left on her own, she was capable of making such a hugely bad decision. How could she have come that close to marrying Kevin, when now she didn't even *miss* him? She felt that, for the moment at least, she should avoid putting herself in the position of making more mistakes.

So she spent her days sleeping late, running until she was worn out, napping, grabbing something to eat, then knitting for hours in front of Sam's TV set, whether he was home or not. Her choice of project echoed her newfound sobriety: she was knitting a fisherman-style throw made out of an expensive brown cashmere mix.

She hadn't intended to make something so uncharacteristic, had, in fact, gone to the yarn store with the intention of knitting herself a little glittery evening bag with lots of fluffy fringe on top, but she had seen the yarn piled up in a barrel and the sight and touch of it had called to her in some weird way and she had leafed through all of the yarn books and magazines at the store until she found a pattern that seemed right for it. It had cost a fortune, but she wasn't spending money on going out, so she figured she could spring for it.

The growing afghan felt warm and soft as it piled up on her lap. She frequently admired how well the color went with Sam's den and thought that maybe she would just leave it there when she was finished—for her own use, of course. She spent a lot of time there.

The afghan was one more element to add to the general comfort and coziness of Sam's den, and Kathleen almost always found herself lingering there on long dark winter evenings, watching TV—turning the volume down or off when Sam was around, since he would only join her there if he could work—and on equally long Sunday afternoons, when she'd lie on the sofa lazily skimming the Style and Art sections of the newspaper while Sam read all the business articles sitting upright in the leather armchair. At some point they would realize they were hungry, and Sam would go into the kitchen, where a half an hour later the smell of garlic or roasting chicken would reach out and pull Kathleen in there with him to chop up vegetables or set the table or do something equally unchallenging and basic that he would still accuse her of somehow botching up and insist on redoing himself.

One late afternoon, early in February, Kathleen let herself into Sam's apartment. He wasn't back from work yet. She foraged through his cabinets, found a bag of pistachios and a bottle of iced tea, took her provisions into the den, and turned on the TV. There wasn't anything good on, but she had nothing else to do, so she stayed where she was, cracking pistachios and dropping their shells on the shiny dark wood coffee table, while she flipped aimlessly through the channels.

She intended to clean up the mess she'd made, but the drone of the changing channels made her sleepy, and she snuggled down into the length of the sofa, thinking she'd just rest a few minutes before getting a towel.

She woke up when Sam came into the den. "I thought I heard the TV," he said. He flicked on the lights. It had grown dark while she slept.

"Hi," she said hoarsely, blinking and pushing herself into a sitting position. "What time is it?"

"Seven-thirty." He looked down at her. "Were you asleep?"

"I'm not sure. But it was five-thirty just a few seconds ago, so maybe." She yawned.

His eyes fell on the coffee table. "Oh, for Christ's sake, Kathleen," he said. "There are shells everywhere."

"I'll clean it up." She arched her back in a big stretch that ended with a grunt of pleasure. "I'm hungry. What are we having for dinner?"

"You're on your own tonight," he said. "I'm heading out in a few minutes. You can stay if you want to, but you'll have to cook for yourself. I think there's some pasta left from last night."

"Where are you going?"

"A Thai restaurant in Santa Monica."

"Can I come with you?"

"Sorry," he said. "I'm meeting people."

"Who?"

"Patricia and a couple of her friends."

Kathleen made a face. "Oh, come on."

"Come on what?"

"Don't go out with her." She was sort of joking, but sort of not. She really didn't want him to go. She wanted him to stay there with her like he usually did. His going out felt like a betrayal.

"I can't cook you dinner every night, Kathleen," he said. He adjusted his right sleeve cuff minutely. "Much as I'd like to spend all my free time waiting on you hand and foot, I do occasionally like to broaden my horizons."

"I don't care about the *food*." She stood up. "I'm just saying you shouldn't keep going out with Patricia."

"Why not? I enjoy her company. And it gets me out."

She took a step toward him. "But don't you think it's time you moved on?"

"'Moved on'?"

"To still be clinging to your ex-wife . . ." She shook her head. "Come on, Sam. I've never seen you with anyone else. But you're not that old."

"Thank you."

"You know what I mean." Her hair had fallen into her eyes, and she shoved a couple of strands behind her ears with fingers that twitched with a sudden nervousness. "You're still in the game. Or could be if you tried. It's time you found someone new, put some excitement into your life."

"I like that you're giving me advice about my love life," Sam said, unsmiling. "You sure you're an expert on how to do it right?"

"I never said I was an expert, but at least I know how to move on."

"You *only* know how to move on," he said. "From what I've seen."

Their eyes met directly for the first time, and Kathleen said, "Don't knock it until you've tried it."

"It's time for you to go." She had never heard his voice unsteady before. "I have to finish getting ready."

"No, you don't," she said. "Stay with me tonight, Sam." She came closer, a little scared of him, but confident in her youth and her beauty and the strength of her long arms and legs. They'd never failed her before.

He didn't retreat, but he didn't welcome her, either, just held his ground. "Go away, Kathleen. Before you ruin everything."

She laughed a little. "I'm not going to ruin anything. This is a good idea. It'll be fun."

"Go away," he said again and when she kept advancing on him he turned away from her.

She caught at his arm. She was almost his height and when she made him face her, their eyes were at a level. "What are you afraid of?"

There was a pause. Then: "Losing *this*," he said quietly. "Not having you here to mess up my place and watch TV."

Her heart suddenly thumped. "That's important to you?"

"Maybe," he said in a voice so low she could barely hear him.

She drew closer, close enough that she could feel the heat of his body near her skin. She was only wearing shorts and a tank top, and she was cold, but he would be warm against her, she knew. "You won't lose anything," she said. "This will be even better. I promise." She caught him around the neck and put her mouth against his. It felt wrong—like she was breaking the rules.

She liked that feeling.

He responded the way she knew he would, his mouth first closed and uncertain against hers and then finally giving in to her insistence. She opened her eyes just in time to see him close his, and triumph flashed through her. She pressed herself against him.

But then he was pulling back, away from her. He pushed her to arm's distance. "I just can't help wondering," he said, "whether I left a bank statement lying open around here recently."

"What?"

"I'm talking about you figuring out that I'm as rich as Kevin Porter."

She thought he was joking. She laughed a little. "Nothing wrong with that," she said and reached for him again.

This time, there was real anger in the shove he gave her. "Jesus Christ, Kathleen, what kind of an idiot do you think I am?"

She stumbled but caught herself against the back of a chair. "What are you talking about?"

"You really expect me to believe that a beautiful girl twenty years my junior with no income who's already told me she's on the make—" He stopped and shook his head hard, like he was getting rid of something buzzing around it. "You really expect me to believe that she—that *you*—have anything but money on your mind?"

"It's not like that," she said. Horrified. "*I'm* not like that."

"The hell you're not," he said. "You lay on that sofa, right there—what was it, three months ago, four months ago?—and you told me you were *exactly* that way. Did you think I'd forget? Or were you just thinking that I'm so old and pathetic I wouldn't care? That I'd just be grateful for whatever I got from you? Even if I had to pay for it?"

"Stop it," she said. "You know I wasn't thinking anything like that."

"I can't promise you Tiffany necklaces," he said. "Or whatever else it is you might be hoping for."

"I don't care about that stuff—"

"I've always been reluctant to buy myself a girlfriend. There are better investments."

"You *are* an idiot," Kathleen said, struggling to find her voice and her balance and something to say that would throw it all back at him. "But not the way you think. You're an idiot because you don't even see that this is for real, that I mean it—"

"*I'm* the idiot?" he said. "You're the one who had to ruin everything, even after I warned you not to."

"*You've* ruined everything, not me."

"We can at least agree that we're done here," he said. "Say goodbye, Kathleen. And get the hell out of my apartment."

"With pleasure," she said and fled.

Back downstairs, her only thought was that she had to get out, had to move, had to do something—anything—to stop thinking about what had just happened. She threw on a jacket and running shoes and left the apartment.

When the elevator door opened, Sam was inside, wearing an overcoat. So he had just calmly continued to get ready to go out, even after all that. It made her hate him.

Their eyes met and Kathleen took a step back, but the elevator man was waiting and gestured her in impatiently. So she lifted her chin and walked in without a word, turning her back on Sam and staring blindly at the display of floor numbers.

They descended to the lobby in silence. Even the elevator man didn't bother announcing their arrival as he sometimes did, just pulled the doors open and signaled her out. Sam stayed on for the parking level.

As she stepped out of the elevator, she heard Sam say, "Kathleen."

"What?" She turned slightly toward him but kept her head averted.

"It's already dark out. Are you going running?"

"Yeah."

"Where?"

"I don't know."

"Keep to well-lit places, will you?"

She didn't bother to respond to that, just walked out.

But it made her furious that he would pretend he cared about her safety—after having made her feel like a piece of shit just a few minutes earlier—and that fury kept her pounding along the pavement for several miles, miles during which blocks and buildings passed in a blur and she didn't even think she had a destination, didn't know where she was or where she was going, until she looked up and realized she was on Sari's block and had been heading there all that time, her feet apparently knowing what it took her brain a few minutes longer to process—that she needed a friend to comfort her.

Fortunately Sari was home from work, getting ready to go over to Jason's house. She immediately called him to cancel their plans. Three hours, a bottle of wine, and a few tears later, Kathleen was able to fall asleep on the floor of Sari's apartment. But the hurt waited patiently all night for her to wake up and was there to greet her in the morning.

11

One day at the end of February, Sari stopped by her parents' house to ask her mother if she could throw a small brunch for her friends there on the following Sunday. "My apartment's too small to have more than one or two people over," she said. "And I've been wanting to do this for a while. I'll do all the work and clean up afterward. All you'll have to do is sit and eat."

"I'm not sure if all that commotion will be good for your brother," Eloise said.

"There won't be that many of us," Sari said. "And he can always go into the other room to watch TV if he feels overwhelmed."

"It'll be fun," said Jason, who had come with her.

"Will you be there?" Eloise said.

"Of course," he said. "I go wherever Sari goes. Plus it's always a pleasure coming to see you. And I make a mean mimosa, Eloise. Just wait till you try it."

Eloise smiled and gave in.

The second they were in the car, Sari said to Jason, "You should be ashamed of yourself. 'It's such a pleasure seeing you and I make a mean mimosa.' You manipulative little—"

"You love that I can get your mother to do whatever I want."

"I'm counting on it," she said with a grin, and he leaned over and kissed the grin right off her face and made it go down deep where it meant something.

So a week later there they were at Sari's house—the three knitting friends and David Lee and Jason and Zack. Sari had brought all the food—fruit, bagels and muffins, and, of course, champagne and orange juice to make mimosas—and they all lingered at the table for a while, lazily chatting, except for Sari's dad, who had disappeared into the bedroom as soon as he was done eating, and Charlie, who ate a couple of bagels and then went to watch TV.

"How are your sisters doing, Kathleen?" Eloise asked. "The twins?" She was on her best behavior, playing the gracious hostess.

"They're okay," Kathleen said. "They had kind of a big fight recently, but they're doing better now. For a while, they weren't even talking to each other. They're back to talking now, which is a good thing since they're in preproduction on a new movie, but they're not the friends they used to be."

"So they're going to keep working together?" Lucy asked.

"They don't have a choice," Kathleen said. "They're a gimmick. Which means they're stuck together, no matter how much they might come to hate each other."

"That's the most depressing thing I've ever heard," David said.

"Tell me about it," Kathleen said. "In the end, I may be the lucky one of us three—I mean, I may not be famous, but at least I'm my own person."

"Says the girl who's going back to work for her sisters," Lucy said.

"Yeah, I know," Kathleen said with a sigh. "I ran out of options. And money."

"What kind of work will you be doing for them?" David asked.

"Same as I used to," Kathleen said. "Sort of in-house assistant to their PR person. You know, planning parties and making phone calls and stuff. It was actually kind of fun. Best job I ever had."

"You've only ever had two jobs," Lucy said.

"Yeah, and this one was the better one."

"Are you all moved out of your apartment yet?" Sari asked, looking up. She was holding Zack on her lap, trying to get him to taste a slice of melon.

"Sort of. I'm basically living at the McMansion these days, but I still have some stuff over at the apartment."

"You should go get it," Sari said. "Time to just be done with that place and everything that goes with it."

"I know. I just can't seem to get myself over there." Their eyes met. "I'll do it," Kathleen said. "Soon." She balled up her napkin and dropped it on the table. "Excuse me." She rose from the table and left the room.

Jason said, "May I pour you another mimosa, Eloise?"

"Thank you, darling." She held her glass out to him. "You were right, by the way. These are absolutely delicious."

There was a giggle from the other side of the table and they all turned. Sari was playing a game with Zack—she'd offer him a grape, and then, when he'd open his mouth to eat it, she'd pull it away and pretend to put it in her own mouth. Zack found it all hysterically funny. It was hard to watch them and not smile. So they all smiled and then Lucy said, "Oh, hey, did I tell you guys we're looking at houses?"

"Wow." Sari stopped playing for a moment, her hand paused in midair. "You can afford a house?"

"Not to buy—just to rent. We want a yard so we can get dogs."

"Dogs?" Jason repeated. "Plural?"

"Two of them. Preferably siblings from the same litter. So they'll have company even if we have to work late."

"Don't you have three cats already?" Sari said. "Every time I talk to you, it's like, 'Got another one.' I'm going to start sneezing just at the sight of you pretty soon." Zack tugged at her hand and pulled it toward him, pretending he was going to eat the grape, then shoved the hand back in the direction of Sari's mouth. She laughed and said, "Good playing, Zack."

Her mother said, "Sari's always had bad allergies."

"Well, allergies aside, as far as I'm concerned you can't have too many pets," Lucy said.

"Yeah, you can," Sari said.

"Not if you're rescuing them from a shelter."

"They still poop, even if they're from a shelter."

"Excuse me," her mother said. "Not at the dinner table."

"Is poop a bad word?" Sari said. "I thought I was being *polite*."

"What about becoming a vet?" Jason asked Lucy. "Didn't you say you were thinking about that?"

"Yeah, I was—for about two seconds. I'd really rather do research. I like what I do. So I'm just going to keep rescuing pets one at a time and get all my animal ya-yas out that way. Will you all excuse me a moment?"

"Of course," Eloise said, and Lucy got up and left the room.

"Hey, Mom," Sari said quickly. "I told you that Jen's pregnant, right?"

"Jen who?" asked Eloise, watching as Jason topped off her glass again.

"My friend from college. Kind of frizzy-haired and short?"

"Look who's calling somebody short," Jason said. He was over a foot taller than Sari.

"Oh, yes," Eloise said. "She came with you once to visit. She brought laundry."

"No, actually, *I* brought laundry but I told you it was hers so you wouldn't get mad at me. Anyway, she just found out she's having a boy."

"Life's greatest adventure," Jason said.

"I wouldn't mind being a grandmother," Eloise said. "I always thought I would be by my age. But God had a different plan in mind." She sipped delicately but effectively at her drink.

As soon she put her glass back down on the table, Jason refilled it. "My mother hasn't taken to the grandparent thing all that happily," he said as he poured. "The day she found out Denise was pregnant, she scheduled a facelift."

"Think of how great she'd look if you'd had more kids," David said.

"As it is, there's not a wrinkle on her."

"Zack's getting a little restless," Sari said, standing up with him in her arms. "I'm going to take him on back so he can watch some TV with Charlie. Excuse us."

Her mother turned toward Sari as if she were about to say something, but just then David said, "So, Eloise, Lucy told me this is the house that Sari grew up in. How long have you lived here exactly?"

Eloise swiveled back to him, and Sari and Zack slipped out of the room.

"Let's see," Eloise said, pursing her lips. "Sari's what? Twenty-eight? But we haven't been here her whole life—for the first few years, we rented a little bungalow in Westwood. But once the kids were a little older and we had some money saved up, we found this house and fell in love with it. That must have been about twenty-three years ago. We had to stretch to buy it back then, but I really think it was the best investment we could have made."

"Absolutely," David said. "Even just looking at houses to rent, I can't believe how expensive real estate has gotten in Southern California." There was a noise in the hallway. He raised his voice slightly. "This mimosa is really good. I don't even know what's in it. How do you make a mimosa, anyway, Jason?"

"You just mix champagne and orange juice," Jason said, more loudly than was necessary given that David was sitting right across from him. "The trick is to get the proportions right. Not everyone agrees what those are."

"Interesting," said David.

"You don't want too much orange juice," Jason said. "But then you don't want too much champagne. May I fill your glass, Eloise?" She nodded, and while he was filling it, Jason said, "Hey, David, I've never quite understood the kind of research you and Lucy are involved with. Could you explain it in detail to me?" David proceeded to do his best. Neither man seemed to notice that none of the women had come back into the room.

But Sari's mother did. It took a while, but she did. She looked around the table and interrupted David's rather lengthy discussion of the adrenal gland in *Rattus norvegicus* to say suddenly, "What's going on? Where is everyone?"

"What? We're not enough for you?" David said jovially, indicating himself and Jason. "Guess I've been a little boring, going on about all my experiments and everything—"

"No, no, not at all," Eloise said absently. "But where are the girls? Why aren't they at the table anymore?"

"Oh," Jason said, "you know the way those three are. They probably started talking about something and forgot to come back in."

"Or else they're knitting," David said. "Those girls and their knitting—it's not a hobby, it's an obsession."

"Ha," said Eloise. She patted her hair carefully, even though there wasn't a strand out of place. "You're probably right."

* * *

Actually, for once the girls *weren't* knitting, and the men knew it. But their job was to keep Eloise distracted. It was all part of THE PLAN, which had been hatched several weeks earlier at a Sunday knitting circle when Sari mentioned that she had taken Jason to meet her family, and her mother had fallen all over him.

"I've never seen her like that before," Sari said. "She was civil all night long. The second she'd start going off into one of her insane rants, Jason would smile at her and change the subject, and she'd just let him. It's a little weird—I mean, she was practically *flirting* with him—but I'm going with it. Makes it much easier to be around her."

Lucy bent over her work, her brow creased. She had finished the hat a while ago and was now knitting a mouse toy for David the kitten. She knit for another minute in thoughtful silence, and then she looked up. "Hey, Sari?" she said. "I have an idea."

And that's when they decided to kidnap Charlie.

Toward that end, the girls had quietly slipped away from the table one by one—or two, in Sari's case, since she was carrying Zack in her arms—and reconvened in the family room.

Sari sat down next to Charlie, with Zack perched on her knee. "Hey, Charlie?" she said. "I'm going to take you out, just for a little while. I want you to meet a friend of mine."

"I don't want to go," Charlie said, staring at the TV.

"There'll be ice cream," she said.

That got his interest. Charlie liked ice cream. "What place?"

"Ben & Jerry's."

He absorbed that. "Can I have hot fudge?"

"Absolutely."

"I want to eat it here."

"No," Sari said. "We have to go out to get it."

"You go."

"You have to come with me."

Again, he thought for a moment. "I don't want mint ice cream," he said. "That's spicy."

"No mint," Sari said. She squeezed Zack. "How about you, kiddo? You want ice cream?"

"You want ice cream," said Zack, who was prone to be echolalic these days.

"I'll take that as a yes." Sari handed Zack to Kathleen, flicked the TV off with the remote, and held her hand out to Charlie. He took it and she hoisted him—with some difficulty—to his feet. "Let's go," she said.

"Hey, look," Kathleen said to Lucy as they moved toward the door. "I'm holding a baby. Do I look like a total mom?"

"Just don't drop him," Lucy said. "And he's not a baby. He's a kid."

"Oh, what's the difference?" Kathleen said. They followed Sari and Charlie out of the family room, then crept quietly through the house to the front door. They could hear the men desperately chatting away to Eloise in the dining room.

"Listen to them," Lucy whispered to Kathleen. "Aren't they good guys?"

"Sure, rub it in." Kathleen shifted Zack over to her other hip. "You and Sari have the best boyfriends ever and I have no one in my life. Are you happy?"

"Deliriously," Lucy said. "Thanks for asking."

Charlie hesitated at the front door. "Just ice cream, right?" he said suspiciously. "No doctor?"

"No doctor," Sari said. "Why? Do they bribe you with ice cream when they take you to the doctor?"

"I don't know," he said.

"No doctor, no mint ice cream," Sari said. "Just lots of hot fudge and a friend."

"Okay," he said and held her hand as they walked out of the house.

As planned, Ellen was waiting for them at Ben & Jerry's, sitting at a table near the front window.

She rose to greet them as they all came inside.

"This is my friend Ellen," Sari told Charlie. "Say hi to her and shake her hand."

"Hi," he said and shook her hand.

Everyone else was introduced and then Ellen asked Charlie what kind of ice cream he wanted.

"Not mint," he said.

"All right," she said. "They have lots of flavors that aren't mint. Come with me so you can order for yourself." They walked over to the counter together. The others could see her prompting Charlie to speak directly to the ice cream scooper.

"So that's Ellen," Lucy said. "Nice to finally meet her. She's not exactly what I pictured."

"I thought she'd have short gray hair and wear a tweed suit," Kathleen said. "But she's kind of a babe. For an old lady."

"She's not that old." Sari gave Zack's hand a squeeze. "Hey, guys, do you think in a parallel universe Ellen's my mother?"

"Yeah, and you're my sister," Kathleen said. "In the perfect parallel universe."

"What about me?" Lucy said. "Am I your sister, too?"

"Yeah," Kathleen said. "You're the annoying much older one who's always telling us to get out of her room."

"That's because you always mess up my stuff."

"Come on, Zack," Sari said. "Let's go get you some ice cream."

"Just stay away from the mint," Lucy said. "That stuff will kill you."

Sari took Zack to the counter, while the other two pulled up some extra chairs to a table, and then they all sat down with the ice cream.

"Zack looks pretty comfortable on your lap," Lucy said to Sari.

"He spends a lot of time here."

"We all thought it was Jason you were in love with."

"Nope. It was always this guy." Sari cuddled him close. He had an ice cream cone, which he was steadily licking in the same spot, over and over again.

"So, Charlie," Ellen said, "Sari tells me you like movies a lot. Especially science fiction movies."

"Yeah." He dug into his ice cream. There was, as promised, hot fudge on top.

"I want to see how much you know about movies," Ellen said. "I'm going to ask you some questions, okay?"

"Okay." He didn't look up from his ice cream.

Ellen said, "Who was Luke Skywalker's father?"

"Darth Vader," he said. "Of course."

"Good job. Who was his sister?"

Another spoonful of ice cream went into his mouth. "Princess Leia."

"With the bun-bun hair," Kathleen said.

"Shush," said Sari, watching Charlie. He was methodically eating his ice cream, but he was definitely also listening pretty carefully to Ellen.

"What was the name of the elf in the *Lord of the Rings* movies?" Ellen said.

"Legolas," he said. "And Gimli is the dwarf and Gandalf is the wizard and the hobbits are Frodo, Pippin, Merry, and Sam. Frodo has the ring."

"Good," she said. "Do you know this much about a lot of movies?"

"I know a lot more than that," Charlie said. He wiped his mouth with the back of his hand. "Those were easy questions. They were kind of stupid."

"Charlie!" Sari said.

"No, he's right," Ellen said. "I don't know enough about these movies to ask really good questions, Charlie. I'm sorry. But I'm impressed with how much you know. And there's a reason I was asking you these questions. I have a friend who owns a video store. Do you know what that is?"

"You get movies there," Charlie said.

"That's right," Ellen said. "You rent movies there. And my friend told me he needs someone to help him out, someone who knows a lot about movies."

"Help him out?" Charlie repeated. "What do you mean?"

"I mean, answer people's questions about movies. Like, if someone came in and said, 'What's that movie with Will Smith where aliens come and try to take over the earth?' then he needs someone who could say . . ." She waited.

"*Independence Day*," Charlie said.

"Exactly," Ellen said, beaming. "And he also needs someone to help put movies back in the right places on the shelves and to restock things like candy and popcorn."

"Restock?" Charlie repeated. Sari had never seen him question a word before—he usually ignored things that he didn't understand, but he was following this conversation eagerly. He had even stopped eating the ice cream, though he stayed hunched over it protectively.

"'Restock' means to put more out on the shelves. So my friend asked me if I knew anyone who could help him, and Sari told me she thought you would be really good at a job like that."

"It's a job?" Charlie said.

"Yes," Ellen said. "It's a job and you'd get paid for doing it."

Charlie looked at Sari. She said, "I think you'd really like working there, Charlie. And you could buy all sorts of things for yourself with the money you made. It would be *your* money."

"I don't know," he said. "Does my mom say okay?"

"She will," Sari said, and her eyes met Ellen's.

"Yes, she will," Ellen said with a determined nod and Sari thought, *Maybe this could actually happen.* Ellen turned back to Charlie. "Now, Charlie, if you really want to have an adult job, you have to be responsible about your appearance and your behavior. You'll have to take a shower and shave every day."

"My mother shaves me," Charlie said.

"It's time you learned to shave yourself."

"She says it's dangerous."

"Not if you do it right. I can teach you. And you'll have to dress appropriately. Do you know what that means?"

"Sort of."

She gestured toward the baggy sweatpants and the too-tight T-shirt he wore over his bulging stomach. "You'll need real pants. Some plain khaki ones would be nice and neat. And you need to wear shirts with buttons. Sari can take you shopping and help you get the right clothes. You'll want to look nice for your job interview."

"Okay," he said.

"And when you're at work, you have to be polite to everyone and not get upset about anything. That's very important."

"Okay."

Ellen smiled at him. "I like your attitude," she said. "I think you're going to make a wonderful employee."

"Yes," he said. He went back to spooning up his ice cream. Some collected at the corners of his mouth, but he didn't seem to notice.

"Sari?" Lucy said. "I don't want to interfere, and I know you're the child expert here, but I'm fairly certain that if you don't do something soon, Zack's ice cream is going to drip all over both of you."

"Oops," Sari said, and caught up Zack's wrist, swiftly bringing his cone up to her mouth. She licked the edge in one long circular motion.

"Wow," Kathleen said. "Nice tongue moves. That Jason is one lucky guy."

"My boss is sitting next to you!" Sari said, but Ellen was laughing.

They couldn't stay much longer—if Eloise found out they were gone, there was no way of knowing how she'd react, and no one wanted the guys to have to deal with the fallout.

While Charlie and Zack finished their ice cream, Sari walked Ellen to the door.

"Thank you," she said. "Oh, Ellen, thank you."

"Don't be silly," Ellen said. "Like this is anything but a pleasure for me. Sari, if we can make things better for your brother—"

"I know," said Sari. "I know." And found she was crying. Ellen hugged her tightly before saying goodbye. Sari watched her walk away. Even through her tears, she could see that Ellen had a huge run down the back of her black tights and that her slip showed below the hem of her dress.

She was the most beautiful, perfect woman Sari had ever seen.

* * *

Eloise realized they were all gone about fifteen minutes before they got back. The men tried to keep her in the dining room, but eventually she insisted on getting up to clear the table, and then started calling to the girls to come help her . . . and finally went looking for them and realized that they weren't anywhere in the house. And that Charlie was gone, too.

"They're all missing!" she said, with some alarm.

Jason hit himself in the forehead. "Oh, that's right—I totally forgot—Sari said she was thinking of taking Zack and Charlie out for ice cream. They must have done that. I'm sure they'll be back any minute. Want me to call her on the cell?"

"Sari should have asked me," Eloise said. Her brows had come together. "I don't like Charlie to go out without me. He gets very nervous."

"I'll tell her that when she gets back," Jason said. He took her arm. "But don't worry about it—I'm sure they're fine. Let's go sit in the living room and wait for them."

The men did what they could to entertain Eloise with their conversation, but she was less distractible now, and her eyes stayed fixed on the front door.

When the girls and Charlie finally walked in, Eloise jumped to her feet. "There you are!" she said. "You didn't tell me you were going out."

"Sorry." Sari put Zack down and he ran to his father, who picked him up and gave him a hug. "We went out for ice cream. It was fun, wasn't it, Charlie?"

"Yeah," he said. "I'm going to watch some movies now. I have to get ready for my job." And he went into the TV room.

"What did he say?" Eloise whipped her head around. "A job? Sari, what have you been saying to the poor boy?"

"Nothing," Sari said. "It's just . . . we ran into Ellen, my boss—"

"Oh, no," Eloise said, clutching at her heart. She took a staggering step backward. "You wouldn't."

"We had ice cream," Lucy said, coming forward. "That was it, Mrs. Hill. And Charlie talked about movies a lot. He really loves movies."

Eloise stared at her. "I know he likes movies," she said. "But—"

"He was really happy," Kathleen said, also stepping up. "Honestly, if you had seen how happy Charlie was, eating his ice cream and talking about movies, you wouldn't have worried at all."

"We just want him to have fun," Sari said. "And to be part of something. The job would be at a video store, which you have to admit he'd love. He's so excited at the idea of it—"

"He doesn't know what could happen out there," her mother said. "I know. I know how cruel the world can be, how vicious people are. And I thought you did, too."

Jason put a gentle hand on her arm. "Give this a chance," he said. "Sari just wants what's best for Charlie."

"I'm his mother," Eloise said. "I *know* what's best."

"And I'm his sister," Sari said. "I love him as much as you do."

"I can't let him go out in the world unprotected. I can't. It would be like sending a lamb out to be eaten by wolves."

"I think it's a good idea," said a voice from behind them all. Everyone turned around. Sari's father was standing in the hallway that led to the back bedroom. "He should try getting a job like other men his age. Why not?"

"You don't know anything about this," Eloise said.

"I know that grown men get jobs," her husband said. "I'd

like to see my thirty-year-old son get up off the sofa and give it a try."

Eloise opened her mouth to say something, but there were too many people circled around her, too many eyes watching her, too many faces waiting. She held up her hands, more like she was warding something off than in surrender. "If he gets hurt, it'll be your fault, Sari."

"He won't get hurt," Sari said. "Not this time."

"We'll be looking out for him," Jason said, guiding Eloise into a chair and down into a seated position. "I promise."

She clutched at his arm. "You, at least, I trust," she said. "You understand me."

"Of course I do." He knelt at her side. "We both know what it is to love a child with special needs and to want to do right by him."

She burst into drunken tears and he stayed there, patting her shoulder, while the others busied themselves cleaning up and getting ready to go.

"And you call *me* a miracle worker," Sari said to Jason a little while later, after they had said their goodbyes and left. They were all standing together in front of the house. "You were amazing with her."

"Yeah, that was pretty impressive," Lucy said. "Let's hope you only ever use your skills for good and not evil."

"It wasn't bullshit," Jason said. "I really do know how she feels. I mean, not the religious stuff, but the part about just wanting to keep Charlie safe at home. I get that."

"So what now?" David said. "Want to go to the pound and make out with the dogs, Luce?"

"Sorry," she said. "Can't." She indicated the other two girls. "It's knitting time."

"No, it's not," he said. "It's the afternoon."

"That's because we had to come here first," she said. "We switched it around."

Jason looked at Sari. She smiled apologetically. "Sorry," she said. "Just for a couple of hours, okay? I'll be back in time for dinner."

Jason picked up Zack and said, "Looks like we're on our own for a while."

"Do you mind driving David home?" Lucy asked him. "So I can take the girls in my car?"

"No problem."

The men watched the girls pile into Lucy's car.

"Ever feel extraneous?" David said. "I mean, if Lucy didn't need someone to feed the cat when she's out of town—"

"Can't get in the way of their knitting circle," Jason said. He hoisted Zack up onto his shoulders. "I've learned not to try. Anyway, girls like these are worth waiting around for, right?"

"Yeah," David said, but not completely happily.

They lifted their hands to wave in unison as the car drove by them.

The girls didn't even notice. They were too busy talking and laughing.

III

"I still can't believe you're knitting an afghan," Sari said to Kathleen, reaching across the table to touch the yarn. "It's so unlike you to be knitting something warm."

"And *brown*," Lucy added.

Since it was already late afternoon, they had decided to flout custom altogether and take their knitting out to a bar. They had scored a small table, which held their drinks and some of their knitting paraphernalia, and their knitting bags were on the floor at their feet, the skeins of wool coiling up along their legs to the needles they held. The guys who were crowded in front of the TV watching football and drinking beer had given them some strange looks when they first got settled, but they didn't care.

"Isn't it nice?" Kathleen said, lifting the needles up high so they could see the afghan in all its glory.

"Who's it for?" Lucy asked.

"Me, of course. I don't knit for anyone else. You know that."

"But it's so unsexy," Lucy said. "Unless . . . You're planning on lying under it naked and surprising someone, aren't you?"

"I doubt it," Kathleen said. "There's no one worth being naked for these days."

"Speak for yourself."

"I *am.*" Kathleen put down her needles and took a sip of her drink. "Believe me, I'm well aware that of the three of us, I'm the only one going home to an empty bed tonight. It's like the world has turned upside down—everyone's having sex but me."

"I'm sorry, Kathleen," Sari said. "It's not fair."

"Yeah, it is." She wrapped a strand of yarn around her index finger. "It's totally fair. This whole thing with Sam . . . It's my fault and I know it. I said some really stupid things about wanting to marry Kevin for his money." She tugged the yarn off her finger and slumped down in her seat. "You guys are supposed to be my friends. Why didn't you stop me from going around saying stupid shit like that?"

"We stopped you from getting married to someone you didn't love," Sari said. "Don't we get credit for that?"

"Keeping you from ever doing anything stupid would be a full-time job," Lucy said. "And you're old enough to know that you can't go around telling people you're going after guys for their money and not expect it to bite you in the ass sooner or later."

"But people shouldn't have to pay forever for stupid things they said and did in the past," Sari said. "Look at Jason—he did far worse things than Kathleen—at least, I think he did—and here I am kind of madly in love with him. People deserve second chances."

"You gave Jason a second chance *because* you were madly in love with him," Lucy said. "The madly in love part came first."

"So what are you saying?" Kathleen said. "That Sam just didn't like me enough to give me a second chance?"

"That's not what I meant."

"Yes, it is. You're saying that if Sam had been madly in love with me, he would have forgiven me."

"I don't know the guy," Lucy said. "I don't know how his mind works."

"I do," Kathleen said. "He's not the kind of guy who gives people second chances. I actually think he *was* sort of in love with me, in his own way. I can tell when a guy's not interested—and that's not the problem. He just doesn't trust me."

"It's his loss," Sari said. "You'll find someone better. You could snap your fingers and have any guy in this room right now."

Kathleen looked around. "Yeah," she said. "I probably could." There was a pause and then she wearily gathered the needles back up in her hands and resumed her knitting while Lucy and Sari exchanged worried looks above her bent head.

IV

When they were saying good night, Sari reminded Kathleen that she had to clean out her apartment. "You can't just leave your stuff there forever."

"I won't."

"It'll just get harder and harder to go back."

"I know," Kathleen said.

"Make the break," Sari said. "I want to see you happy again, Kath. And I don't think you will be until you're completely out of there."

"You're right." Kathleen fished her car keys out of her purse. "Maybe I'll just run by there tonight. Just throw everything in the car and then find a way to let Sam know I've moved out."

Sari checked her watch. "Want me to come with you?"

"Nah. Jason and Zack are waiting for you."

"I can call them—"

"No, don't. I'm fine. I'm just going to run in there, get my stuff, and leave. A clean break, like you say."

"Good," Sari said. "And then you'll be able to move on. You'll have a new job, a new place to live—"

"My old job, my old place to live . . ."

"It's still a new beginning in its own way."

Kathleen shrugged.

Sari hugged and released her. "I'm sorry things suck right now."

"My own fault." She trudged toward her car, her head down.

"Hey," Sari called. "You really okay?"

Kathleen turned to look at her. "Totally. Nothing gets me down for long. I'm tough." She squared her shoulders. "I'm more than tough. I'm Xena, the warrior princess. And I don't need no fucking costume to prove it." She threw her head back and gave a passable Xena cry. People in the parking lot turned to look at her. "See?" she said. "See how tough I am?"

"You're a nut," Sari said and got into her own car.

Kathleen watched Sari drive away. Even the car looked like it couldn't wait to get where it was going.

Kathleen herself was in no such rush. She took her time on the drive over to the apartment building, uncharacteristically gliding to a stop at every yellow light and staying well within the speed limit. She dreaded walking back into the apartment she had fled from, but Sari was right—it was time to clean it out and move on.

The doorman and elevator man greeted her with uncharacteristic warmth. "Haven't seen you around here much lately," the first said. The elevator man actually smiled at her. "Good to see you again," he said, before closing the door and taking her up to her floor.

Once she was inside the apartment, Kathleen looked around it with disgust. What *was* this place that she had lived in for several months? It could have been nice—it was big and pretty and well built—and instead it was a graveyard for balls and goals and dirty clothing and half-filled air mattresses. She hadn't even *tried* to make it livable. What was wrong with her? Why did everything good evade her touch, leaving her with nothing to call her own? Why did other people's lives fall into place and never hers?

She threw herself down on the air mattress in the living room and stared up at the ceiling. She never wanted to move again, just wanted to lie there forever in the peaceful quiet of the empty room, wallowing in self-loathing and misery.

Unfortunately for that plan, a loud banging started up somewhere in the building. She was getting more and more annoyed about it, when she realized it was coming from her own kitchen.

For someone who was never going to move again, she jumped up quickly enough. She ran, even, into the kitchen and flung the door open.

Sam was there, in gray pants and a white button-down shirt. No tie or jacket tonight. "Hello, Kathleen," he said. "Do you have a moment?"

She stared at him. He seemed very calm, but then she noticed that one of his hands was opening and closing spasmodically at his side. The last time they'd spoken was when she had gotten off the elevator after their fight. "Yeah, I guess," she said and took a step back.

"Thank you." He entered and she let the door close behind him with a click.

"What do you want?" she said.

"I heard you come in."

She waited.

"You haven't been here for a while. I was thinking maybe I should be worried."

"I'm fine. As you can see."

"I'm glad," he said. Then, "I was hoping you'd come back. I thought maybe we should talk."

"Really?" she said. "Because I feel like we wrapped things up pretty well last time I saw you. You pretty much answered any remaining questions I might have had with that get-the-hell-out-of-my-apartment shit."

"I was angry," he said. "But I've been waiting for you to come back, hoping maybe we could—"

"I'm only here to grab my stuff. In two hours, this apartment will be all yours again."

"You don't have to move out."

"I don't?" she said. "Weren't you planning on throwing me out anyway? Or is that the problem—I'm ruining all of your fun?"

"Kathleen—"

"Huh," she said, leaning back against the counter. "Are you still here?"

He let out a deep breath. "I know you're not the world's greatest listener, but could you maybe just try for once?"

She looked at her fingernails. "It's not that I can't listen so much as it is that I'm not interested."

"Pretend I'm talking about shoes."

"Shoes?" she repeated. "How fucking shallow do you think I am?" She turned and walked out of the kitchen.

He followed her. "I'm sorry," he said. "I didn't mean it that way. I was just trying to—" He stopped. "I'm sorry," he said again. "But will you please just listen to me for a second?"

"Okay, fine," she said. "What?"

He pushed his hand through his hair. His fingers were shaking. "I'm still trying to figure things out," he said. "I didn't want to get hurt. I still don't." She stayed silent. Then he said, "But I miss you when you're not around. It's been way too quiet around here, way too lonely. Unbearable even. You're like—" He opened his hands. "You're like a *pet*—company when I want company, so long as I don't mind a few stains on the rug and couch."

"Jesus," she said. "I'm not a fucking cat, Sam."

"No," he said. "I was thinking more a dog. Cats are very clean."

She turned her back on him, took a step away, then whirled back around. "You know what? We're both idiots."

"Okay," he said.

"We're both idiots," she repeated. "We've just been taking turns at it. Sometimes I talk too much and say things I don't mean. And when I said that I wanted to marry Kevin and be rich forever, I didn't mean it. Because—" There was no way to say it and make herself look good. So she didn't even try. "Because I've never known what to do with myself. I have nothing I want to do and nothing I'm good at. So sometimes I just try things out to see if they fit. And I thought maybe going after money was a sign of—I don't know, maturity or something. So I tried it out. Tried to be—what's the word? When all you care about is money?"

"Mercenary?"

She nodded. "Yeah, that's it. I tried being mercenary. And it didn't fit. I'm a flake and I put my foot in it all the time and I can be a pig when I eat—"

"I've noticed."

"I'm a pig and all those other things, but I'm not mercenary, Sam. If I were, I'd have married Kevin in Hawaii like I was supposed to."

"You were supposed to get married?" he said.

"But I *didn't.*"

He smiled weakly. "I wouldn't call that one of your strongest selling points at the moment—that you were engaged to be married to someone else a couple of months ago."

"It is, though," Kathleen said. "I didn't marry Kevin, not because I *couldn't* but because I didn't *want* to. Doesn't that prove I don't just care about money?"

"It doesn't change the fact that I'm rich. And I can't quite see what other charms I'm likely to hold for someone like you." He gave a twisted smile. "I'm well aware you could have any man you wanted."

She took a step toward him. "Sam—"

He held his hands up, holding her off. "I don't want to be anyone's sugar daddy, Kathleen." He looked at the floor and then back up at her again. "You have no idea how scared I am of becoming something like that."

"If it makes you feel better," she said, "you're not the sugar daddy type. I mean, if I wanted someone to take care of me and buy me things, I'd find someone who's actually *nice* to me. Isn't that kind of the point of a sugar daddy?"

"The money's the point."

"I don't want your money, Sam. I don't even need it—I've started working for my sisters again."

"That can't pay very well."

"Well enough," she said. "Well enough that if it would help you learn to trust me, I could pay my half of anything."

He gestured around them. "This apartment costs two point five million dollars."

"Well, not *that*, obviously. Anyway, I'm living with my sisters again. I just meant I can pay for my meals. And movies and stuff like that."

"You think that will solve the problem?"

"Fuck it, Sam," she said, flinging her right hand out. "Either you believe that I'm not just after your money or you don't. What else can I say?"

He studied her for a moment. "You're right," he said finally. "And I do believe you. Maybe it's a mistake, but I do. So where does that leave us?"

She was silent for a moment. Then she said, "I don't know." She took another step toward him. "But if I *were* a dog, I'd be a stray. I have nowhere to go, no place to call my own—just be nice to me and I'll probably follow you home."

"But what if this is something else you're just trying out? Going after—" He shook his head. "Christ, I don't even know how to define what this might be. But what if you realize this—whatever it is—doesn't fit, either? What if you follow someone else home one day?"

"It's a risk," she said.

"I don't know if it's one I want to take."

Her mouth curved up in something that wasn't a smile. "Then get a golden retriever. He'll be yours for life."

"They shed." He took another deep breath. "Look, Kathleen, I don't expect anything permanent. And I don't want any promises. I've already been through that whole until-death-do-us-part thing and the fact that I'm here with you right now proves how meaningless those promises are. But I've been protecting myself for a while. To put myself out there again—with someone with your kind of track record—knowing how badly I could get hurt—" He stopped and said again, "I don't want any promises. But I need some sense of the risk/gain ratio. How much time am I likely to have?"

"Do you have to sound like such a businessman?"

"I'm using the terms I know."

"Do you really expect me to have an answer for you?" she said. "Because I don't have any idea how much time we'll have. All I know is that there's nowhere else I want to go right now except upstairs with you. And not just because your sofas are comfortable."

"I'll have to Scotchgard them," he said. "I mean, whether it's you or the golden retriever . . . either way." They regarded each other in silence a moment. Then Sam held his hand out and she took it. "I am going to get so hurt," he said before pulling her fiercely against him.

"It'll be worth it," she whispered.

"I hope to hell you're right," he said. And then they were done talking.

The airbed had lost some of its pressure, but by the time they had fallen down on top of it, neither of them noticed or cared.

Afterward, they lay there quietly, each listening to the sound of the other's breathing.

Kathleen broke the silence. "I'm knitting something for you," she said. "That brown afghan thing I've been working on all month. It's for you—for your den."

"Really?" he said. "I didn't know that."

"Neither did I," she said. "But I'm pretty sure it is."

His leg found hers under the blanket. "No one's ever knit anything for me before."

"That makes us even," she said. "I've never knit anything for anyone before."

About the Author

Claire LaZebnik: I was born in Newton, Massachusetts, the youngest of five children. My father once claimed my umbilical cord was never completely cut, which may explain why I went to a college (Harvard) only twenty minutes away from home. I was sixteen when I entered college and couldn't even drive; I left when I was twenty and still couldn't drive. I moved to New York (so I wouldn't have to drive) and puttered around there for a while before ending up in Los Angeles, where you *have* to drive. I failed my first driver's license test—so badly the DMV guy made me get out of the car and drove the last block by himself—but passed the second time, bought myself a car, and became a true, if reluctant, Angeleno.

In L.A. I wrote for magazines, including *GQ*, *Vogue*, and *Cosmopolitan*, and met my husband, a TV sitcom writer. We got married in 1989 and from 1991 to 2000, I pretty much kept myself barefoot and pregnant. I gave birth to three sons and one daughter, and when the youngest was six months old, I decided I was done producing kids and gave birth to a novel instead. *Same as It Never Was* (St. Martin's, 2003) was also published in England and Australia, translated into French, and made into a movie called "*Hello Sister, Goodbye Life*" for the ABC Family cable channel.

My oldest son was diagnosed with autism at the age of two and a half, which led to my meeting Dr. Lynn Kern Koegel, who runs the Koegel Autism Clinic at the University of California, Santa Barbara, with her husband, Dr. Robert Koegel. One day Lynn asked me to write a book with her, and a year or so later we published *Overcoming Autism: Finding the Answers, Strategies, and Hope That Can Transform a Child's Life* (Viking/Penguin 2004). I also have a son who has celiac disease and a daughter who has Addison's disease, but I have yet to write a book on either subject.

I taught myself to knit from a book back when I was in high school and happily knit my way through many a boring college seminar. I didn't like to measure or block and the sleeves always came out too long or too short. Which was fine with me: I've always believed that with knitting it's the journey and not the destination that matters.

Cats, dogs, and children put a crimp in my knitting habit—I'd leave half a sweater sleeve and come back to find a big old tangled knot—but now that the kids and pets are older and knitting is actually considered *hip*, I've returned to my old love.

Claire

This novel is a cautionary tale: if you drink and knit, there *will* be consequences. Of course, if you're anything like our heroines, you're willing to risk it. So invite some friends over, pull out your knitting, and mix one (or more) of the five following drinks inspired by Kathleen's, Lucy's, and Sari's knitting projects.

Pink String Bikini

Light and tropical—and likely to make you reveal a little more than you intended.

2 oz rum
1 oz Triple Sec
3 oz ginger ale
pomegranate juice
grenadine
maraschino cherries

Combine the rum and Triple Sec in a cocktail shaker filled with ice. Strain into a highball glass filled with ice cubes and pour in the ginger ale. Add a splash of pomegranate juice and a splash of grenadine. Spear several maraschino cherries on a toothpick and lay across the top of the glass. (Girls like to eat cherries and guys like to watch them eat them.)

The Glittery Scarf

Indulge yourself. Elegantly. You deserve it.

1 oz blue Curaçao
champagne
star fruit

Pour the blue Curaçao into the bottom of a tall champagne flute. Fill the glass with champagne and garnish with a single slice of star fruit, dropped sideways into the glass so the star shape is visible.

Striped Cropped Sweater

Youthful and a little kooky. (I'm not entirely sure if you should shoot these or eat them with a spoon, but I suspect you'll have fun figuring out which way works best.)

1 (3-oz) package each berry blue, strawberry, and lemon gelatin
4½ cups boiling water
1 cup vodka
½ cup Citron vodka

Mix berry blue gelatin with 1½ cups of boiling water and stir until completely dissolved. Add ½ cup of vodka. Fill 20 2-oz clear shot glasses ⅓ full with mixture and refrigerate until solid. Meanwhile, mix strawberry gelatin with 1½ cups boiling water and stir until dissolved. Add the remaining ½ cup of vodka and stir.

When the blue layer is solid, pour the strawberry gelatin on top, filling up another ⅓ of each glass. Put glasses back in the refrigerator to harden.

Mix the lemon gelatin with 1½ cups boiling water, stir to dissolve, and then add the ½ cup of Citron vodka and stir.

When the strawberry layer is solid, fill the glasses to the top with the lemon mixture. Put back in the refrigerator and chill at least one more hour before serving.

The Cozy Brown Afghan

This one's my favorite. It's alcoholic comfort food.

1 oz coffee liqueur
½ oz chocolate liqueur
½ oz Irish Cream liqueur
chocolate-covered cinnamon reception stick

Mix coffee and chocolate liqueurs in a small cordial glass. Pour Irish Cream liqueur over the back of a spoon so it floats on top. Garnish with reception stick. Bliss.

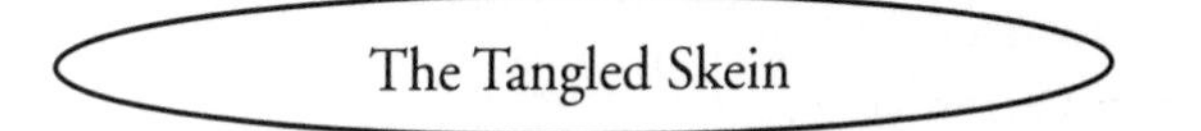

The Tangled Skein

Drink too many of these and you're likely to end up in a complicated situation that's difficult to untangle.

1½ oz tequila
1½ oz Lemoncello
2 oz orange juice
maraschino liqueur
lemon zest

Shake the tequila and Lemoncello with ice in a cocktail shaker. Strain into a martini glass and add the orange juice and a dash of maraschino liqueur. Using a lemon zester, make long narrow strips of lemon zest and toss them into the bottom of the glass—you can tie them into knots first, if you still have that kind of motor control.